TH

Terror Beneath the Waves

By

JEREMIAH SHERMAN

"Mastering the ghastly and possessing a brilliance for instinctive tension, this author's ink bleeds fear onto the page, suspending even the bravest reader in a dance of terror."-—*Sidney St. James*

Table of Contents

BEEBOP PUBLISHING GROUP
Publisher Since 1972
BeeBop Publishing Company does not participate in, endorse, or have any
authority or responsibility concerning private business arrangements between
our authors and the public.

Library of Congress Cataloging-in-Publication Data
Child actors – Fiction 2. Granddaughters – Fiction 3. Motion Picture Actors
and Actresses – Fiction 4. Grandmothers – Fiction 5. City and Town Life –
Fiction
10 9 8 7 6 5 4 3 2 1 0
Book Cover Design by Sidney St. James
Foreword by Sidney St. James

Available in eBook and Paperback Editions
Audio Coming Soon
Certain content is not suitable for anyone under 18 years of age.

Dedication

To my brother, Sidney St. James, who inspired me to continue my writing to the finish!

FOREWORD
IN MEMORY OF DARRELL ALVIN STRUSS
1945-2023
AKA JEREMIAH SHERMAN

In the quiet embrace of sorrow and memory, I face the task of introducing a labor of love that has taken on a life of its own. A novel, a creation woven from the threads of dreams and imagination, poised on the precipice of release. As I begin writing this Foreword, I'm reminded of the heartache that has marked the journey leading to this moment.

Jeremiah Sherman, known to many as Darrell Struss, my beloved brother, left this world a mere few weeks ago. In 2011, he embarked on a remarkable storytelling voyage, crafting the pages of a science fiction tale that spoke of mysteries lurking beneath the surface of the deep - a tale of a colossal shark. His vision was as vast as the ocean itself, and I, a fellow storyteller with a catalog of over 60 novels, willingly took on the role of support, not the helm. Yet, fate took us on an extraordinary, unexpected voyage, a journey of collaboration that stretched over twelve years. Edit after edit, we refined and sculpted his vision, inching closer to the culmination of his passion.

Almost on the cusp of unveiling his literary offspring to the world, life took a poignant turn. The very air seemed to hold a whisper of change as we stood on the brink of taking his debut novel, "*Throwback – Terror Beneath the Waves,*" to the world. At the Methodist Hospital in the heart of Houston, my brother breathed his last, a poignant goodbye to a life dedicated to storytelling. As family members and friends mourned the loss of Jeremiah, a twist of fate intertwined our destinies further. While at the hospital bidding farewell to my brother, I learned that another pillar of our family, my brother John, had passed away in Lexington Park, Maryland, a mere few hours before.

Amidst the echoes of grief and the turmoil of managing the estate of my dear brother John, the promise I made to Jeremiah beckoned me. His unwavering dedication to his craft had to be honored. I felt the weight of his hopes and dreams press upon my shoulders, urging me forward. In Lexington Park, Maryland, where the memories of another cherished brother mingled with the occasion's solemnity, I embarked on the final chapter of my journey with Jeremiah's literary legacy.

Sitting at my keyboard, I reflect upon the brotherhood bond transcending this earthly realm's boundaries. "Throwback," a testament to Jeremiah's passion and creativity, emerges from the depths of his imagination to the surface of reality. It is a story of intrigue and wonder, shaped by countless hours of dedication, passion, and collaboration. I invite you, dear reader, to immerse yourself in these pages that hold a piece of my brother's heart.

And to Jeremiah, my dear brother above, I know you're watching over us with that familiar twinkle in your eyes. As the final words are set, the last edits made, and your story is set to take flight, I imagine your laughter resonating among the stars. We did it, big brother... we did it!

——*Your brother, Sidney St. James*

Preface
A New Day Dawns

The morning unfolded with the customary rhythm of the Southern Pacific Basin, an immense stretch of ocean spanning thousands of miles from civilization's reach. This obscure maritime realm was a realm of intrigue, its depths shrouded in enigmatic mysteries that had eluded human comprehension. Little did humanity realize that nestled within this remote expanse lay a concealed treasure trove of secrets, untouched and unexplored across the epochs of time.

At the heart of this sequestered realm lay an ancient atoll, a geological marvel hidden beneath the waves, its circular ramparts rising tantalizingly close to the water's surface. The atoll's origin had remained an enigma through the annals of human history, a testament to nature's capacity for secrecy. Yet, this submerged citadel held more than just geological wonder. Plunging nearly a mile into the abyss, a thermal anomaly manifested, maintaining the water at a temperature akin to the balmy climates found thousands of miles away on tropical shores.

Below the surface, a clandestine network of small caves had formed, shaped over time by the ceaseless dance of currents and tempests. Within this subterranean labyrinth, life thrived in astounding diversity. Evolution here seemed to have paused as creatures of antiquity persevered in this sanctuary, harkening back to epochs long past, ensconced within the warmth of their aquatic prison.

But on this particular day, the forces of nature primed an exceptional convergence, linking the distant echoes of the past with the pulse of the modern era. The ocean floor quivered, initially sending forth subtle tremors that soon escalated into violent convulsions, causing the atoll's encircling walls to sway like a mere plaything in a dog's jaws.

In a breathtaking spectacle, a monumental fissure fractured the conical seabed, unleashing torrents of molten lava that infused the surrounding waters with an oppressive and intolerable heat for the marine denizens. Simultaneously, a network of rifts tore open the ocean floor, stretching thousands of miles across the seabed. These upheavals disturbed the east-west oval current that had for ages coursed tirelessly between the Southern Pacific islands and the southern tip of South America.

In an epic crescendo, a colossal five-mile stretch of the atoll's eastern ramparts crumbled away, revealing the once-protected waters to the vast and capricious ocean beyond. Fueled by escalating temperatures, the inhabitants of this hidden realm surged through the newfound passage, fleeing into the frigid and unfamiliar embrace of the Pacific's outer reaches.

Yet, as abruptly as this mass exodus had begun, it inexplicably halted. A strange, unsettling calm descended, casting the creatures into an eerie limbo of uncertainty. Then, an ominous presence emerged from the depths—an elongated, gray silhouette navigated with caution through the breach, its trajectory aimed northward, steering resolutely toward the warming currents that guided the way to the western coast of South America.

An enthralling saga commenced in this remote Southern Pacific enclave, weaving together the tapestry of ancient marvels and contemporary upheaval. The

collision of epochs and life forms was ready to permanently change nature's delicate equilibrium in its intricate choreography, etching an unfolding drama across the ocean's canvas.

CHAPTER 1
Major Currents in South Pacific

A my Barnett sat perched at her small, weathered desk, nestled within the hallowed chambers of the Scripps Institute of Oceanography. The dance of morning sunlight painted a mosaic of warmth upon her auburn hair, rendering it a tapestry of fiery hues that seemed to crackle with energy. She had strewn a constellation of charts and satellite images before her, each forming a piece of an intricate puzzle waiting to be solved. With each sip of her third cup of morning coffee, the invigorating caffeine mingled with her contemplative musings, fueling her determination to dive into the mysteries that beckoned.

Amy was a conductor of oceanic currents and the balletic rhythms of sea life patterns in the sanctum of her workspace. This pursuit was etched into her soul as she neared the culmination of her academic odyssey. Yet, amid the scholarly sanctuary, an unseen tempest churned. News arrived like a secret breeze, whispering of seismic upheavals at the heart of the South Pacific's central southern currents. Concurrently, tales emerged of creatures undergoing bewildering transformations in their migration and feeding rituals. The tendrils of this revelation wound around Amy's resolve, tugging at the very core of her purpose. "This could reshape the very foundation of my research," she murmured, her voice a delicate thread in the symphony of her thoughts.

The portrait of Amy emerged with vivid strokes. She stood at the crossroads of her late thirties, embodying elegance and vitality. The blend of French and English heritage bestowed upon her a bronzed complexion that seemed to defy the passage of time. Each sunbeam transformed her auburn tresses into a cascade of flames, a living embodiment of her spirit's fervor. An intricate duality of purpose and spontaneity converged within her – a mind anchored in academia yet prone to bursts of unbridled exuberance.

As her fingers danced gracefully across notes and papers, a sense of urgency fueled her motions. Amy orchestrated a symphony of organization, a prelude to her imminent voyage. This expedition, she knew, would unfurl the enigma of the unknown, and every artifact before her held the tantalizing promise of revelation.

Amidst the tapestry of her preparations, one name took root – Jake Crandle, a captain of the seas, a guardian of secrets on an uncharted isle. Amy's voice traversed the ethereal distance, bridging the miles that separated them. Negotiations unfolded like an intricate minuet, an accord struck between two souls. And thus, her destiny was etched onto the map of an island haven.

Across the room, a sprite-like figure materialized – Jenny, the freckled muse whose vibrant energy electrified the air. "Everything's secure!" Jenny chimed her voice, a melody of assurance that resonated through the room. "Flights confirmed, even that 'no-name' seaplane jockey who'll ferry us to the edge of nowhere, where we'll rendezvous with the enigmatic Mister Crandle at his island sanctuary!" With laughter as her cadence, she twirled away like a whirlwind of anticipation.

Jenny's footsteps echoed the rhythm of their impending journey, a dance set into motion during an unexpected encounter in the Caribbean. Amy's gaze lingered on her, gratitude unfurling like a blossoming flower.

"Jenny, did you ensure the tanks and photographic equipment were packed securely?" Amy's voice echoed like a clarion call, her words serving as the heartbeat of their preparations.

A wink and a nod later, Jenny's response flowed like a playful melody. "Absolutely, Captain! Everything's locked down tighter than a clam's shell."

A chapter of Amy's narrative found its place in the memory of a Barbados bar, a night vivid as a painted tableau. "You didn't kill him, did you?" Amy's sheepish inquiry lingered in the air, the aftermath of a chivalrous intervention.

"Nah, just a refreshing dip to beat the heat," Jenny's words danced like notes on the breeze, accompanied by a playful grin. Their laughter intertwined like ivy, weaving the threads of camaraderie.

Curiosity ignited like a newborn star, prompting Amy's inquiry. "Why did you step in for me? You barely knew me."

Jenny's laughter bubbled forth like a hidden spring. "Been there, done that. Figured a little adventure wouldn't hurt."

The symphony of laughter forged bonds transcending time, weaving connections that spanned oceans and chance encounters. The two women, a harmonious duet, embarked upon uncharted waters, united by purpose and spirit.

As the world gradually receded, the journey unfurled. Farewells and embraces painted a tableau of transition, a canvas adorned with the spectrum of human emotions. Stepping into the embrace of a plane, they embarked on a voyage leading them from bustling cities to the remote reaches of Tierra Del Fuego, their path an unfolding saga of exploration and discovery.

Ushuaia, an outpost at the world's edge, stood before them. They crossed paths with Amos Scoggins, the steward of a push-pull charter plane that would carry them closer to 'Crandle's Keep.' Their journey, a fusion of curiosity, friendship, and the pursuit of knowledge, stretched before them like an unwritten epic.

The flight hours to reach the island stretched out, punctuated by glimpses of other islands that peppered the expanse. "So, do you know this Crandle fellow very well?" Amy queried Scoggins, her voice carrying the anticipation of their destination.

Amos glanced back, his features etched with a curious blend of wisdom and mischief. "Yep, as well as most, I guess. Jake showed up one day about two years back, claimed his piece of land with the local magistrate, and dubbed it 'Crandle's Keep.' Said he'd run a small charter fishing retreat there, but he wasn't exactly chasing customers. Got the notion he might just be trying to escape from the world, if you catch my drift." His gaze held Amy's, an unspoken message lurking within. "I sure hope you young women can handle this adventure of yours alone with just Jake on the island. Well, him and Bolo, I should say."

Amos's tone carried a playful edge, and Amy could sense that he was spinning his tales with a hint of mischief. She met his gaze, her eyes twinkling with understanding. "We'll manage just fine, Amos. Thank you for all your insights."

Jenny's apprehension grew palpable as they drew closer to the designated coordinates. The island, 'Crandle's Keep,' awaited them, its secrets shrouded in anticipation. Their journey's tapestry was still woven, a story that promised to bridge the unknown with the familiar, guided by curiosity, camaraderie, and the inexorable pursuit of truth.

The journey stretched out over several hours of flight, a traverse through the boundless sky that carried Amy and Jenny ever closer to their enigmatic destination. As they soared above the open ocean, the plane's windows revealed glimpses of other islands scattered below like scattered gems, most minuscule in comparison, their presence whispered by the ripples of waves breaking upon their shores. With a gnarled chuckle that carried a hint of mystery, Scoggins divulged that these tiny landmasses were likely uninhabited, save for the presence of other solitary souls akin to

Jake, the man they sought. His laughter, a broken symphony of amusement, resonated with secrets hidden beneath the surface.

Amidst the backdrop of azure skies and endless ocean expanse, Amy's voice broke the reverie. "So, do you know this Crandle fellow very well?" she inquired, her tone laced with curiosity.

Amos Scoggins, a figure of weathered experience, glanced back at the two women with a curt nod as though sizing them up. "Yep, as well as most, I guess," he replied, his words succinct, carrying a note of reservation. "Jake, he showed up one day about two years back. Got himself a government bill of sale registered with the local magistrate for the little island we're fixin' to land on. He dubbed it 'Crandle's Keep.' Said he was gonna run a small charter-fishing getaway out there. Told the rest of us in the area to spread the word to any lost tourists foolhardy enough to want to seek him out. But honestly, he didn't seem too keen on finding charters. Got a sense he might just be trying to lose himself in this world if you catch my drift." Scoggins' gaze shifted to Amy, his words heavy with implication. He paused, his eyes holding her gaze to emphasize his last statement. "I make the journey out here every six or eight weeks. Bring Jake a few things he might need – food, fuel, rope, soap, and whatnot. A supply boat swings by about every two months, keepin' him stocked up. But Jake, he's a solitary sort. Hope you young women are ready to take on your adventure out here with just Jake on that island. Well, I guess he's not all alone. I nearly forgot about Bolo."

Amos' words carried a weight that seemed to sink into the plane's interior, hanging in the air like an unspoken question. The atmosphere in the cabin shifted, a mixture of excitement and uncertainty weaving through the minds of its occupants. The distant horizon drew nearer, and with it, the promise of an encounter that would test the bonds of solitude and companionship.

Jenny's voice carried a tinge of intrigue as she blurted out, "Who's Bolo? Sounds like a strange name to me!"

Old Scoggins' wrinkled face contorted into a sly grin. "Well now, little lady, Bolo's a behemoth of a man, about as colossal as a mountain and as silent as the night. He works with the strength of five men, never a word of complaint. He's a shadow devoted to Jake, handles the boat like an artist, and hauls in most of the catch single-handedly. Don't let his gentle demeanor fool you; he's as tender as a kitten unless you cross him or threaten Jake. Then, he transforms into a force of nature. If he took on a killer whale, my money's on Bolo. Mark my words!"

Amos Scoggins' mischief-laden eyes met the uncertain gaze of the girls. He seemed to revel in the unease he was stirring. His tales wove an aura of mystique around their impending destination, adding layers to their excitement.

By the time their journey brought them within the vicinity of the island, Jenny's initial excitement had morphed into an anxious curiosity. In contrast, Amy had caught onto Amos' game, her eyes meeting his in a knowing conspiracy.

Amos's voice, imbued with a lifetime of experience, broke through the cockpit's hum. "We ought to be pretty close now, ladies. If you could lend me a hand in spotting it, you'll see that the island takes on a 'figure eight' shape." His words were measured, a steady rhythm echoing the ebb and flow of the waves. "The heart of it features a plateau where the main buildings sit, overseeing a calm harbor. Then, a narrow rock bridge leads to a partly freshwater lagoon, completing the other loop of the eight. Trust me, you won't miss it. However, we better spot it soon. I'm running a bit lower on fuel than I'd like, and word is the weather back home's about to turn sour tonight. Gotta refuel at Jake's and make it back before the storm hits."

Amy's eyebrows arched in surprise. "You're not planning on staying overnight?"

Amos' chuckle held a touch of mischief. "Nah, Miss. Gets a bit too lonely for my liking around here. I'll fill 'er up, check the engines, and return. Loneliness doesn't sit well with me for long. Besides, my old dog back home gets mighty impatient."

Jenny, practicality prevailing over-excitement, pointed ahead. "Look, at two o'clock! That's got to be it."

Amos followed the line of her finger, his eyes narrowing in agreement. "Sharp eyes you got there, little lady. That's indeed the place. You see the resemblance to a 'figure eight'?"

With the island drawing near, the girls nodded in unison. The form of the island resolved into view, revealing its true character as a 'number eight.' The central mass held an ensemble of buildings, their proximity to piers and docks hinting at a life interwoven with the sea. On the opposite end, a rocky formation linked to the rimmed lagoon formed the upper 'O' of the eight, somewhat smaller in scale.

As the plane descended, the island's features took on more detail. A substantial boat was moored near the harbor's edge, a testament to the island's connection to the sea. The cliffs, once mere bluffs from a distance, now loomed tall and imposing as they flanked the entrance to the harbor, their towering presence a stark contrast to the azure expanse.

The plane descended gradually, its wheels brushing the water's surface before transitioning into a gentle cruise, almost like the aircraft had become a boat. Amos guided the plane deftly, navigating the intricate passageway through the cliffs. They glided across the placid waters inside the protective embrace of the cliffs, making their way toward a wharf where an aged filling station pump awaited.

Amos silenced the engine as the dock neared, and the plane glided toward the dock's edge. Suddenly, a colossal figure materialized, seemingly out of thin air. Startled, both girls let out an involuntary yelp. This titan of a man took hold of the plane's front, guiding it expertly to the dock with gentle precision. A broad grin adorned his face as he welcomed the plane's occupants.

With a hearty laugh that resonated with everyone present, the massive man addressed Amos. "Looks like y'all came in a bit early this month! What's the hurry, showing up without my usual gift?"

Amos returned the laughter with a knowing smile. "Hold on for that, Bolo. First, help me get these ladies out of this flying contraption."

Bolo, oblivious to the girls within the aircraft, chuckled. "Oh! My apologies, ladies. As you might've heard by now, I'm Bolo!" His smile radiated warmth as he offered his massive hands to assist the women onto the dock.

"I'll take care of your belongings, ladies. Mister Jake's expectin' you up at the main building," Bolo informed them.

Amos interjected, addressing Bolo. "Now, are you planning to stay the night so we can set up an extra place for dinner?"

Bolo's tone was light as he responded, a playful twinkle in his eyes. "Well now, 'Old Man,' you know how it goes. Dinner can wait; first things first." He exchanged a grin with Amos, invoking a shared camaraderie.

Amos laughed heartily. "She'll be ready for you when you return."

"Thanks, my friend!" Amos chortled as he guided the girls up the hill from the wharf, Bolo's hearty laughter trailing behind them.

Atop the hill, a tableau of the island's layout sprawled before them. Amidst a wide clearing stood a corrugated Quonset building, weathered and proud, with a sign that read "Main Building." Adjacent was a slightly smaller square structure, its corrugated exterior hinting at a cooler interior, marked with a sign that declared it the "Stores." The presence of a stout door hinted at the refrigerated haven within. Further to the left, three cabins dotted the landscape, one grander than the others. A sign proclaiming "Jake's Rest" revealed the owner of the largest abode. On the right side of the Main Building stood three more cabins, their dimensions uniform. On their approach to the clearing, a substantial building loomed, adorned with a concrete pad in the back, encircled by chicken wire and crowned by a corrugated tin roof. The sight was completed by a smokestack that vented black smoke and emitted a steady, low growl.

Amy's curiosity spurred her to inquire, "What's housed in that building, Amos?"

Amos' courteous tone held a note of patience. "That's where the generators are, Ma'am. It also houses equipment left behind by the government when Jake acquired the island. According to Bolo, Jake hasn't explored everything they left, just what proves useful now and then. Oh, and there's a frozen food locker next to the generators."

At that moment, Scoggins gestured across the clearing. "Looks like Mister Jake's making his entrance."

Their gazes followed Scoggins' indication, alighting upon a man who defied the island's rugged setting with an air of unexpected elegance. Dark hair framed a face that seemed at ease, a commanding and comfortable figure in his own skin. This was Jake Crandle, the man of the hour.

Emerging from the Main Building, Jake's smile was warm and welcoming. With confident strides, he traversed the distance to greet his guests. "Welcome to 'Crandle's Keep,' ladies. I'm Jake Crandle, your host. I assume you've already had the pleasure of meeting Bolo?"

"I'm Amy Barnett, and this is Jenny Landis," Amy introduced, only for Jake to interrupt with a genial request.

"Please, call me Jake. We keep things informal around here."

Apologies tumbled from Amy's lips. "We're absolutely delighted to meet you, Jake. Yes, we've crossed paths with Bolo—a remarkable man, I must say."

Jake's laughter mingled with theirs. "You're right about that, Ms. Barnett."

Amy's smile held a spark of mischief. "And now, it's my turn. I'd prefer it if you called me Amy."

Jenny's enthusiasm couldn't be contained. "You can call me Jenny, Jake." An unmistakable twinkle in her eyes suggested an immediate fondness for their host.

Amy's smile held a hint of indulgence as she glanced at Jenny's unabashed excitement. Despite herself, Amy found Jake to be an attractive figure, a blend of ruggedness and allure.

Meanwhile, Bolo had made his way up the hill, a small cart in tow, ready to transport the girls' belongings. Following Jake's directive, he headed toward the cabins on the left. As Bolo's form disappeared, Jake queried Amos, "Are you planning to stay the night?"

Amos' response was tinged with regret. "Not this time, Jake. Bolo's taken care of refueling, and I need to make it back before the storm hits the tip. They're predicting a pretty fierce gale tonight."

Jake's disappointment was palpable. "That's unfortunate. Well, next time, I'll prepare your favorite crab dish. How's that sound?"

Amos seized the opportunity for a jest. "You've got yourself a deal! I might even bring over a case of your favorite island beer for the occasion."

Jake's laughter carried as he waved Amos off. The old pilot descended the hill, vanishing over its crest, en route to his plane that Bolo had thoughtfully fueled.

As Jake's gaze followed Amos, he observed the old aviator's preparations, from a pre-flight inspection to sliding into the cockpit. The engine purred to life seamlessly, and with practiced ease, Amos guided the aircraft away from the dock and into the expanse of open water. A precise maneuver directed the plane into the wind's embrace, its throttle pushed to full power. The aircraft's ascent was deliberate, tracing a rhythmic dance between the waves. Gradually, it transformed from a water-skimming vessel to a soaring machine, ascending from the blue embrace to point homeward. Jake watched, captivated, until the plane dwindled to a distant speck, signaling its return to its starting point.

With anticipation, Jake stepped inside the main building, focused on the final arrangements for the new charter that would commence the following day.

As the day ended, the girls settled into their respective cabins. Meanwhile, Bolo carried out his assigned tasks, beginning a tranquil interval on "Crandle's Keep." Little did they know, this serenity was but a fleeting reprieve as a storm of events loomed on the horizon.

CHAPTER 2
Incomprehensible Dread Draws Near

As Amos embarked from Ushuaia that morning, the girls beside him, a hundred miles west of the islands bordering Isla Hoste at the tip of South America, a hidden life-and-death drama unfolded, destined to reverberate across the tranquil island of "Crandle's Keep" to the southeast.

The day dawned gray, ominous, with the promise of an impending gale. The sea, despite its calm exterior, held an undercurrent of tension. Gentle swells, ranging two to three feet high, undulated eastward. Remarkably warmer than usual for these Pacific waters, the temperature resulted from currents originating thousands of miles away in the Southern Pacific Basin.

Unexpectedly, many sea creatures, which had recently thrived in these waters, vanished as if in response to an intangible dread. An unidentifiable and overwhelming terror rippled through the marine life, leaving behind a newfound desolation.

Amidst this eerie vacancy, a pod of gray whales pressed onward, swimming purposefully through shifting waters, guided by an inexplicable force. Their journey led them further south along the western edge of South America in pursuit of nourishing, food-enriched currents, their instincts driving them unfalteringly.

He moved through the waters in a parallel realm, driven by an insatiable hunger and ruthless determination. Having been dislodged from his ancestral home in the distant west, he had grown unchallenged by the rules of evolution. For decades, he had feasted on the abundant sea life in his secluded territory.

A seismic shift had recently forced him into unfamiliar waters, and he had embarked on a relentless eastward journey. He existed solely to feed and grow. His formidable size only matched his unending appetite. Guided by primal instincts, he honed in on the scent of potential prey, honing his predatory prowess.

As the warm currents turned south, he sensed a convergence of life nearby. His senses heightened, and his hunger intensified. He stalked his prey, his massive form propelling him forward with deadly intent.

Meanwhile, the pod of gray whales navigated shifting currents, the convergence of warm waters causing turbulence and confusion. Oblivious to the looming danger, they continued their journey, gradually falling victim to an unknown menace.

Amid the chaotic waters, he struck, ruthlessly attacking his prey. One by one, he closed in on the whales, a sequence of violence that transformed the ocean into an arena of death. The water turned crimson with blood, and the remnants of the once thriving pod floated amidst the aftermath.

The scene painted a haunting picture, a large dorsal fin – an embodiment of primeval terror – gliding southward through the oceanic carnage. As the sun dipped below the horizon, he encountered shallower waters, his massive form emerging from the depths. Rain pelted his skin, a fierce gale enveloping him as he navigated the tempest.

Drawing closer to the channel, his instincts surged. The scent of abundant prey stirred his ancient instincts, igniting a frenzied determination. As night descended, the Indian fishermen on the twin islands southwest of Isla Santa Ines sought refuge from the ferocious storm.

Recently blessed with an unexpected abundance of fish, the villagers constructed nets and makeshift storage, anticipating a future of plenty. As the gale howled and rain lashed against the island, a visceral tension hung in the air, a prelude to the impending turmoil that would engulf "Crandle's Keep."

Yet, on this tempestuous night, as the fierce gale thrashed against their homes and the fish storage crates, a group of men battled to secure the containers, shielding them from the storm's wrath. The rain lashed like stinging needles, and the wind howled like a banshee. Amidst this chaos, a few men struggled on the bridge, tossing ropes to their comrades below to anchor the boxes.

Among these men, one paused, his gaze drawn to an inconceivably colossal and gray form lurking in the dim twilight beyond the feeble light cast by the village houses. Unbelievable and elusive, the sight sent a shiver down his spine. Dismissing the vision as a trick of the weather-addled mind, he returned to his task.

Beneath the surface, he navigated the deep waters, driven by ravenous hunger and the anticipation of the feast ahead. The scent of unfamiliar prey drew him into a frenzy, his predatory instincts igniting in a blaze of excitement. This was the moment for which he had journeyed, the culmination of his relentless pursuit.

Back on the bridge, the men focused on their task, unaware of the horrors unfolding beneath. Suddenly, a tremor shattered their reality. A deafening crash split the air as the water erupted, and their comrades vanished in a vortex of water and gore. What was once a calm labor scene had transformed into a blood-soaked spectacle of violence.

His massive form breached the water's surface as he surfaced, his triumphant roars blending with the storm's fury. He had secured his sustenance, and the chaotic aftermath was the orchestra of his savage victory. Unbeknown to him, he had left death in his wake, shattering lives and homes alike.

Two men on the bridge glimpsed fragments of the carnage through rain-blurred vision, their senses overwhelmed by the brutality they barely comprehended. The monster's enormity and the vicious chaos he unleashed transfixed them as the nightmare played out before their eyes, flashes of horror illuminated in brief respites from the rain.

The bridge, an innocent bystander to the terror, met its demise as he plummeted back into the water. The impact shattered the support structure, and the bridge crumbled, vanishing into the depths. The two men, witnesses to the devastation, screamed as they plummeted into the dark waters below, their fear mirroring the fate they had just witnessed.

Desperation fueled their efforts as they swam towards the nearest shore, the rain blinding them and the raging waters fighting against their progress. Underneath the line of stilt-mounted houses, their struggle intensified. Hope flickered as they neared the shore, but terror struck anew. A gargantuan dorsal fin crested a monstrous wave, hurtling towards them, its enormity casting a chilling shadow over their fate.

As the fin loomed, the stilted houses began to splinter and crumble, descending into the abyss one after another. Panic rekindled, and the two men renewed their efforts. Yet, their escape was cut short as the shadow engulfed them, their screams lost in the relentless roar of the storm.

Returning to his feeding frenzy, he savored the bounty of his triumph, smashing through homes and lives with unrelenting force. Houses splintered like matchsticks, lives were extinguished in his voracious path. He feasted on the terrified souls and the wreckage he had wrought, a remorseless destroyer at the mercy of his insatiable appetite.

Half an hour later, silence reclaimed the village. Destruction painted a macabre tableau – a once-thriving community reduced to ruins, the air heavy with death. Every soul had been claimed, their stories forever silenced. The tranquil village had morphed into a battlefield, a haunting echo of the terror that had consumed it.

In the aftermath, he departed, leaving behind a maw of chaos and the shattered remnants of a serene existence. A single artifact stood as a testament to his presence – a tooth, a monstrous relic of unfathomable proportions, embedded in the twisted wreckage of a bridge post. A clue, a warning of the monstrous force that had descended upon them.

As the gale continued its lament, he faded into the storm, venturing towards the southern currents, seeking his next feast in the uncharted depths of the ocean.

CHAPTER 3
Jake Prepares Gourmet Dinner

As the sun began its flirtation with the horizon, a gentle knock reverberated through the sturdy wooden walls of the girls' cabins, stirring them from their slumber. Bolo's knuckles rapped against the doors in a manner that bespoke care and thoughtfulness, a melody of consideration that graced the nascent morning somewhere around the neighborhood of six-thirty. The night had been embraced by the tender symphony of wind and rain, a lullaby that had serenaded them into a peaceful slumber. The gusty gale, a tempestuous ballet of nature's own choreography, had danced its performance throughout the evening, its crescendo fading into the depths of the night. As the morning light filtered softly through the windows, they roused from their dreams, greeted by the promise of a brand-new day.

Their feet met the cool touch of the wooden floor as they emerged from their beds, a refreshing energy tingling through their bodies. The tempest of the previous night had abated, leaving in its wake a refreshed calm that belied the ferocity of the wind that had whipped around them. Shaking off the last remnants of slumber, they set out to acquaint themselves with their surroundings, their gazes drifting toward the windows that framed an awe-inspiring view. The early sunlight painted the sky with vivid strokes of pastel pinks and golden oranges, an artistic palette that signaled the dawn of an untarnished day. Not a single wisp of a cloud dared to mar the canvas of azure above, and as they dressed themselves, the thrill of adventure beckoned on the horizon.

The previous evening had been a whirlwind of activity – unpacking, organizing, and ensuring their equipment was meticulously ordered for the upcoming survey. Amid the tasks at hand, a few revelations about their host, Jake, had injected an extra dose of intrigue, adding to the exhilaration in the air.

But it was the dinner that had lit an unexpected fire in their experience. With a culinary mastery that defied expectations, Jake had prepared an opulent feast centered around the local delicacy – dolphin. When the first bite graced their lips, they were transported on a journey of flavors that caressed their taste buds like a gourmet escapade. Ravenously, they delved into their portions with the fervor of explorers famished from their expedition. With the final morsel savored and the last sip of wine relished, they raised their glasses in a toast to Jake's culinary artistry, acknowledging his expertise and cherishing the memories they were weaving.

Still aglow with wonder, Amy couldn't contain her curiosity. "How on earth did you learn to cook like that?" Her eyes widened in amazement as she searched Jake's gaze, seeking the hidden stories beneath the surface.

Jake's lips curved into an affectionate smile, his gaze momentarily shifting to Bolo, who was meticulously tidying up the remnants of their extravagant meal. "Well," he replied, mischief twinkling in his eyes, "you could say it's one of the many skills I picked up during my travels. That was before I anchored myself here and served wonderful ladies like you." His voice danced with playful sarcasm, a chuckle escaping him as he took another sip of the rich red wine.

Amusement tinged Amy's flushed cheeks as she said, "I appreciate the compliment, good sir!" Her smile illuminated the room, capturing the essence of her gratitude and the light-hearted atmosphere that enveloped them.

Jenny's laughter sounded, a clear sign of her slightly tipsy state. "Count me in too!" she interjected, her words a playful melody that hung in the air, a testament to the camaraderie flourishing among them.

With a sparkle in her eyes, Amy turned her attention back to Jake, her smile retaining its brilliance. "One day, you'll have to tell me about the origin of all your charming talents... in detail, that is." Her gaze held a blend of curiosity and allure as it locked onto his, a connection forged through their shared moments.

But practicality soon took over. "For now, Jenny, I think it's time we hit the hay," Amy proposed, her voice a gentle reminder of the late hour. "It's getting late, and an early morning is just around the corner." With that, the duo rose from the table, their intention clear as they prepared to retire for the night.

"Sleep well, you two," Jake's warm voice trailed after them, a sincere and genuine farewell. "Bolo will rouse you around six-thirty, and we'll enjoy a light breakfast before we set out!"

Their gratitude echoed through the air as they thanked Jake, making their way to their cabins without much fanfare. And now, over seven hours later, seated once again around the table, they were united in purpose. Their faces, free from the embellishments of makeup, radiated a raw, natural beauty that harmonized with the rustic charm of their surroundings.

With a gracious smile, Bolo reappeared, a plate laden with scrambled eggs, crispy bacon, and flaky biscuits balanced in his hands. Steam rose invitingly from the cups of robust black coffee he carried. As they savored the morning feast, a chorus of "Good morning, ladies!" announced Jake's arrival, his figure framed by the doorway. He sported attire that echoed the laid-back spirit of the island – faded jeans, a well-worn denim shirt, and sneakers that had certainly seen better days. Perched atop his head was a beloved "skipper's cap," a tangible connection to his affinity with the sea.

Jake's eyes swept across the table, landing on the nearly empty plates that had been relished moments before. "Are we almost ready to set sail?" he inquired, his gaze shifting between Amy and Jenny as he gauged their progress.

Amy's voice held conviction. "Absolutely, but you haven't eaten anything yet."

A warm smile curled Jake's lips as he met their concern with reassurance, a glint of humor dancing in his eyes. "Oh, don't you worry about Bolo or me? We had our fill around five o'clock to ensure we could check all systems on the boat. It's a routine we follow religiously – a precaution against any unforeseen troubles. Out here, any mishap can leave you stranded for days."

Amy's expression shifted, a tinge of worry weaving into her features. "I hadn't really considered that," she confessed, a note of apprehension tinting her voice.

Jake's grin was infectious, his amusement undeniable. "That's what you're paying me for," he replied, his words carrying a playful camaraderie. The moment of unease dissolved into laughter, unraveled by the threads of worry that had briefly tightened their hold.

With breakfast concluded and remnants cleared away, the trio was on the brink of another adventure. They made their way to the boat, each step echoing with determination and anticipation. As they stepped onto the vessel, Jake and Bolo worked in harmonious tandem to cast off, their movements a seamless choreography that mirrored the rhythm of the sea.

The boat charted a course across the harbor, navigating skillfully through the towering cliff walls that framed their passage. Beyond the sheltered confines, the boat turned northeast, guided by Jake's unwavering hand. The warm currents that held so much intrigue beckoned them onward, and the boat glided into the vast stretch of water that mirrored the hue of the endless sky.

Within the vessel's embrace, Amy and Jenny transformed into scientists amid a scientific sanctuary. With Jenny's assistance, Amy calibrated her measurement instruments, each adjustment a delicate ballet of precision. The morning evolved into the afternoon, taking temperature readings, becoming a rhythmic dance as they ventured deeper into the currents.

Then, as the sun reached its zenith, two minuscule dots emerged on the distant horizon. Consumed by her work, Amy barely glanced up as she inquired, "What's that?" Curiosity dripped from her voice as her eyes darted between her instruments and the distant figures.

Jake, ever attuned to the nuances of the environment, responded with casual expertise. "Those are two small islands – they don't have formal names, but we call them 'Bric' and 'Brack.' They're like forgotten gems adorning these waters." His words painted a vivid tableau. He continued, "In fact, we're not too far from the coastal islands of South America." Amidst the dialogue, his gaze shifted to Amy. "How are your measurements progressing?"

Amy's reply came in an enthralled exclamation. Her eyes were ablaze with fervor. "Pretty well... actually, they're incredible! You know, Jenny," she directed her excitement toward her collaborator, "this warm water core has never extended this far south before. The currents are undergoing a significant shift in this area of the Pacific. It's a phenomenon that's largely gone unnoticed, and its repercussions are immense." Her voice was a blend of astonishment and eagerness, the scientist within her animated by the uncharted territories she was navigating.

Seizing upon her observation, Jake contributed his insights. "So, we might soon witness the arrival of larger species following this modified food chain, creatures that have never ventured this far into these waters."

The exchange between Jake and Amy crackled with a fusion of surprise and fascination. Amy's gaze locked onto Jake's, an unspoken understanding forged beyond the boundaries of academic discourse. Ever attuned to the dynamics between her companions, Jenny playfully intervened, "And how do you know all this?"

Jake's confession, tinged with a touch of sheepishness, ignited an atmosphere of playful banter. "I suppose it's a remnant of what I learned back in college," he admitted, his gaze unwavering as it met Amy's. His vulnerability was a portal to his past.

Jenny's curiosity mirrored Amy's. "Where did you go to school, Jake? And what led you to delve into ecosystems and food chains?"

Jake's gaze briefly flitted to Bolo, the enigmatic presence in the room that held fragments of Jake's history. Bolo's grin, as unchanging as ever on his chiseled features, seemed to nod at Jake – the spotlight was squarely on him now.

"Don't look at me, Mister Jake. You've walked into this labyrinth, and you've got to find your way out," Bolo's voice interjected, the sagacity of a friend well-acquainted with Jake's enigmatic nature.

Jake's eyes shifted to the wooden deck beneath him, contemplation etched across his features. A quiet pause stretched before he finally met Jenny's gaze with a distant expression. "I attended Texas A&M Maritime Academy in Texas, where I studied Marine Biology. I even earned my Master's," he shared, his voice laced with nostalgia. "But I never truly pursued it afterward. Some of that knowledge has lingered, though." A chuckle escaped him, revealing his embarrassment and a glimpse of his past.

Amy's curiosity still blazed within her as she voiced her astonishment. "I can't believe it! How could someone with a Master's degree in Marine Biology not build an impressive career around it?" Her candor was followed by a flush of embarrassment as she realized the audacity of her words. "I'm sorry, Jake... I mean, I didn't mean to sound..."

Jake's head shook slightly as he gazed at the horizon, the sea breeze ruffling his hair. "No problem, Amy. Your surprise is understandable," he replied. A smile tugged at the corner of his lips, and his gaze returned to her. "In addition to my Master's, I also took a commission in the Navy. I took a different path for various reasons – I became a Navy SEAL."

Amy nodded in understanding, her empathy evident. "So, your Master's in Marine Biology ended up leading you in a different direction," she mused, the complexities of his past unfolding before her.

Jake's attention remained on the water, his voice a mere whisper. "That's right. I was young and maybe a bit impulsive at the time. I believed I could make a real impact in the world, even in its most dangerous corners. So, I chose to become a SEAL."

Jenny's laughter rang out like the tinkle of bells. "Come on, Jake. A seal is a sea lion that swims around. Were you daydreaming or what? You're kidding, right?"

Amy's expression turned stern, her head shaking vehemently. Her disapproving gaze met Jenny's, communicating her disapproval. Jenny, perplexed by the sudden change, couldn't fathom what had triggered Amy's reaction. Unaware of elite military units within the Navy, she assumed Jake's words were simply a playful jest. Amy's eyes shifted back to Jake, a spark of fiery confrontation hanging in the air.

However, Jake's response surprised them both. His gaze lifted slowly to meet Jenny's, a subtle smile playing on his lips. "No, Jenny, I'm not kidding," he responded, his tone infused with amusement. Laughter danced beneath his words. "The SEALs are a specialized branch of the Navy, trained for assignments that... well, let's just say they're far from ordinary. They're highly skilled, and at that point in my life, I was drawn to the challenges they offered. You understand?"

Jenny's skepticism faded in the face of Jake's earnest explanation. The warmth in his tone dispelled any lingering doubts. "Um, yeah, I guess so. I just... I never..." Her voice trailed off as realization dawned on her. The topic shifted, but the boat jerked violently before Jenny could fully express herself as if a massive aquatic hand had grabbed it and thrown it sideways. The trio, except for Jake, stumbled off balance, their bodies tossed around the deck like ragdolls. A collective bewilderment was etched across their faces, the event's suddenness leaving them in shock. Unlike the others, Jake remained steady, secure in his captain's chair.

Reacting swiftly, Jake sprang to his feet and rushed to the boat's edge, scanning the water for any signs of what had caused the disturbance. Swirls and small whirlpools marked the water's surface, remnants of an inexplicable force gripping the vessel. His cap flew off in the wind, and he ran a perplexed hand through his tousled hair as he turned to Amy, his brows knitted in bewilderment. "Okay, Doc, how does your PhD-oriented mind explain that? What the Hell just happened here?"

Jake's confusion mirrored the others', yet Amy's response was fueled by her pursuit of understanding. "Perhaps we crossed through a convergence zone, where different currents collided, creating a maelstrom-like effect." She grasped for an explanation as baffling as the phenomenon itself, her voice a mix of uncertainty and frustration. The awkwardness of her answer was met with incredulous stares, and she conceded, "I can't provide an explanation for something that seems inexplicable, can I?"

Jake's calming presence intervened, his hands resting lightly on Amy's shoulders as he sought to ease her distress. "Take it easy, Amy," he urged soothingly, his eyes locked with hers. "The question was more rhetorical than anything." His smile was reassuring, inviting her to share in his understanding. "None of us know what just happened, right?" He glanced at Jenny, their unity unspoken but palpable.

Jenny's voice chimed in, a confirming note amid the uncertainty. "Absolutely, Amy. None of us have a clue. Let's just chalk it up to another 'mystery of the deep.'" A forced chuckle accompanied her words, her attempt at humor tinged with lingering unease.

Amid their contemplations, Bolo's voice broke through the tension, his words carrying the wisdom of a seasoned observer of the ocean's enigmatic ways. His gaze remained fixed on the southern horizon as if seeking answers beyond their grasp. "You know, folks, I've spent most of my adult life on this ocean... seen a lot of things, some explainable, others not. I've learned that if you can't make sense of it, let it go. If you don't, it'll consume you." He turned back to them, his words steeped in the weight of experience.

Jake, emerging from his thoughts, addressed the group as he returned to the controls. "I guess we better get back on track." His question directed at Amy underscored their mission's continuity. "Amy, do you still want to continue with your measurements and plotting?"

Amy's voice conveyed a hint of lingering apprehension as she returned to her instruments. "Yes, definitely." She rearranged her scattered tools, her anxious glances occasionally flicking toward the southern horizon as if hoping for answers.

With the boat once again in motion, their journey resumed. The twin islands grew closer, their shapes solidifying as the vessel navigated toward them. Jake's intent was clear – he wanted to approach the fishermen who inhabited these isles, hoping to glean insights into the bizarre events they had encountered.

For hours, they pressed northward, the waters remaining calm after the inexplicable incident. Their voyage was accompanied by the steady thrum of the boat's engine and the gentle sway of the waves, a symphony of sea and sky. As they traversed the currents, the twin islands beckoned with intrigue, their presence inviting exploration.

Bolo's role at the bow, armed with a measuring line, was pivotal in their cautious approach. He took depth readings as the boat inched through the channel, his focus unwavering. Jake took a moment to elucidate their surroundings to the girls. "This channel usually runs deep, a couple hundred feet, but tides can play tricks, and I'd rather not run into any unexpected sandbars. We should spot the village bridge soon." A light-hearted note colored his words, "And don't worry about the villagers. They're friendly and might even offer you some fish." His laughter resonated with camaraderie.

The boat continued its advance, and soon, Bolo's voice broke the silence, drawing their attention to a floating piece of debris. Bolo extended a boat hook pole with practiced precision, snagging the fragment. It bore remnants of a wall, perhaps a window. Bolo's efforts brought the piece close enough to touch, and as he lifted it, something tumbled from the window area, landing at the feet of the others. The girls' screams echoed their shock, while Jake's expletive mirrored his disbelief.

The object that had fallen, a human arm, lay before them, an unsettling intrusion into their reality. Jake's quick actions became a balm for their jangled nerves. He directed the women to the back of the boat and offered them brandy from a hidden flask, a temporary respite from the shock.

In the subsequent stillness, Amy's voice trembled as she voiced the question on everyone's mind. "Jake, what's happening? That was a human arm, right? I'm not losing my mind, am I?"

Jake's reassuring influence prevailed as he quelled their fears. He signaled Bolo to dispose of the arm and fragment before guiding the boat forward. As the water stretched ahead, more pieces of homes came into view, each a chilling reminder of an unseen catastrophe. The boat's trajectory unveiled a scene that defied comprehension, and as the wooded section gave way, the full extent of the devastation was laid bare.

Jake turned to the girls, their shock mirrored in his own expression. He embraced them both, steering them toward the cabin below. His gentle yet resolute words guided them to safety amidst the chaos. "Both of you, head to the cabin and rest. The AC's on, and you'll be comfortable until we can make sense of what's going on." The gravity of their experience was etched into their faces as they retreated, seeking refuge from the unfathomable.

Jake led Amy through the sliding door into the central area of the boat's cabin. After closing the door behind them, he moved purposefully back to the control console. He retrieved an automatic pistol from a drawer and checked the magazine for bullets before securing the weapon in his belt. The boat's console became his command center, and today's events had elevated his caution to a level that demanded readiness.

With the pistol now at his side, Jake steered the boat toward the remnants of the fish traps and the shattered bridge entrance on the left bank. As he approached, the wreckage that lay before him was a haunting sight. Amidst the twisted debris, he could make out more than wreckage – fragments of bodies floated in the water, shards of lives obliterated.

The bridge, once a symbol of connection, had been reduced to rubble. Despite the destruction, some of its supports still stood as somber sentinels, a reminder that this place had once thrived with life. Jake and Bolo's voices echoed along the deserted bank. A desperate call met with an eerie silence. The absence of fish was unnerving. The waters that should have been teeming with life now felt devoid. Fish traps lay broken, splinters of wood bearing witness to their violent destruction. A sense of foreboding gripped Jake and Bolo, their gazes meeting across the deck, an unspoken question lingering – what unimaginable horror had unfolded here?

The weight of the situation settled upon Jake like a heavy fog. He turned his gaze toward Bolo, his words laced with incredulity. "Where have all the fish gone?" Bolo's eyes met his, the shock mirrored in their depths. In a slow, deliberate tone, Bolo voiced a fear that resonated deeply with them. "Mister Jake, this be the Devil's doin'! I've faced many challenges, but this is beyond anything I've seen. This ain't no creature I ever heard of."

Jake's fear found an echo in Bolo's words, yet he managed a reassuring nod. "You're right, Bolo. It's... it's something beyond our grasp." It was a small gesture of shared comfort in the face of the unknown.

A glimmer caught Jake's eye as they grappled with the unsettling scene before them. He pointed out an object lodged in one of the shattered bridge supports. Bolo followed Jake's line of sight and finally saw what had captured his attention. The triangular shape stood out amidst the chaos, an anomaly begging for an explanation. Bolo's curiosity was piqued, and he gestured toward it. "Could you bring us closer, Mister Jake?"

With skillful maneuvering, Jake guided the boat within reach of the mysterious object. Bolo, leaning precariously over the side, freed it from its entanglement. With the thing secured in his hand, Jake navigated the boat back into open waters, allowing them a clear view for examination.

Approaching the front deck, Jake's voice held a hint of intrigue. "What do you make of this, Bolo?" His steps took him to where Bolo stood, both gaze locked onto the enigmatic object. Jake's hand found Bolo's shoulder, his touch gentle yet firm, drawing his attention. Bolo started slightly at the contact, a jolt of surprise running through him. Turning toward Jake, his voice trembled as he offered the enigmatic artifact. "Mister Jake, this ain't like nothin' I've seen before. I told ya, this ain't natural. It's somethin' darker, somethin' not of this world."

Accepting the object, Jake's pulse quickened as he examined it closely. A sense of cold dread swept over him as he realized what it was – a tooth. But not just any tooth – a triangular tooth with serrated edges. The resemblance to the front feeding teeth of a Great White shark was unmistakable, yet this one was significantly larger. Its proportions defied belief, indicating a creature that should not exist. Carefully placing the tooth inside the same drawer as his flask, Jake preserved it for further study.

Jake's attention returned to Bolo, and his voice took on a sense of urgency. "Bolo, I need you to promise me you won't mention this to the girls until we're back at the Keep. We can't burden them with this despite everything we've faced today."

Bolo nodded solemnly, understanding the gravity of the situation. He retreated to his tasks, preparing sandwiches and coffee in an attempt to bring a semblance of normalcy to a world that had been upended.

The boat's journey back to the Keep was marked by Jake's cautious navigation, ensuring the safety of his companions. Amy emerged from below decks, but seeing Jake's demeanor, she thought better than to disturb him. The sun dipped below the horizon, casting an eerie calm over the waters that had been tumultuous earlier.

Finally, the harbor lights of the Keep appeared on the horizon, a beacon of refuge. As the boat glided into the sanctuary, darkness shrouded the scene. Exhausted and shaken, they quickly disembarked, collecting their equipment and ascending the hill to their cabins.

Jake ensured the boat was securely anchored before joining them, a small duffel bag slung over his shoulder. Inside his cabin, he settled down at the radio transmitter and receiver. The old equipment stood as a lifeline to the outside world, a means of reaching out when needed.

Jake's fingers moved deftly, establishing a connection with Amos Scoggins' Charter Service on the mainland. His voice held a sense of urgency, demanding attention. After a series of attempts, the grizzled voice of Amos finally crackled through, curiosity evident in his tone. Jake's words conveyed the situation's urgency, compelling him to request Amos' presence.

The conversation shifted, and Amy's unexpected entrance gave her insight into Jake's intentions. Amy's eyes, devoid of emotion, locked onto Jake's as he revealed his intention to send a package to Lamar Toombs. The atmosphere grew tense, emotions raw. Amy's voice quavered with accusation. "You ask me, 'Why do you ask?'" The tension escalated, Amy's anger boiling over, her words sharp and punctuated.

Jake felt his world constrict as he comprehended the depth of his mistake. He rushed to explain, his voice heavy with remorse. Amy's resolve wavered as Jake's sincerity became apparent, his vulnerability laid bare. Amy's emotions shifted from anger to confusion, her eyes seeking truth in his words.

The moment of truth arrived as Jake retrieved the tooth from the drawer. Wrapped in soft fabric, the artifact emanated an eerie energy. Jake's voice conveyed both dread and an urgent need for answers. "Amy, please understand. I wanted to shield you from this, but I can't keep it to myself any longer." The tooth represented a mystery that defied understanding, a reality that threatened to shatter their comprehension of the world.

"Amy," Jake's voice was measured, carrying a solemn weight. "Before I show you something, I need your promise that you won't mention it to Jenny until we can confirm with an expert. Can you agree to that?"

Amy strained to discern the object in Jake's hand, the fabric concealing its form. Her concern was palpable as she responded, her voice tinged with apprehension. "Jake, you're starting to worry me. Why are you keeping this from Jenny? She deserves to know, doesn't she?"

Jake's interruption was firm, his urgency evident. "Agreed?" He pressed, his tone brooking no resistance.

Amy's patience was wearing thin, the day's events taking their toll. Her voice trembled slightly as she reluctantly acceded. "Alright, agreed." She was on edge, her nerves frayed by stress and fear.

With the agreement established, Jake slowly unwrapped the bundle before them. Amy's eyes widened in astonishment as the mysterious object came into view. Her reaction, a mixture of shock and terror, was palpable. For a moment, Jake feared she might scream, but instead, her mouth opened soundlessly, her trembling hands covering her lips. The unfolding scene left her speechless, her body shaking as she sank back into her chair. Overwhelmed, she struggled to find her voice.

Her words emerged as a whisper, disbelief tinging each syllable. "This is a sick joke, Jake." Tears welled in her eyes as she gazed at him, the weight of the day's events taking its toll. "A really sick, twisted joke, and I think I hate you right now." Her voice broke as her emotions surged forth, tears tracing silent paths down her cheeks.

Jake's response was resolute, his tone devoid of amusement. "Amy, this is no joke. This is deadly serious." He met her gaze steadily, underlining the gravity of the situation. Amy's tears and distress began to give way to a mix of curiosity and professionalism.

Her demeanor shifted as she reached out to take the tooth, examining it closely. The scientist within her overcame the fear, replaced by a thirst for knowledge about the unknown. She studied it carefully, her fingers tracing the serrated edges. While she concentrated on the tooth, Jake pointed out specific details. "Notice the tissue fragments from the jaw socket; this couldn't be more than a few days old. And the size of this thing... my God, Amy, if..."

Interrupting his words, Amy gently placed a hand over his mouth, her eyes beseeching him for restraint. "Jake, please. Let's not jump to conclusions." She met his gaze, her voice calmer now as she attempted to restore some sense of rationality. "I agree that sending this to Toombs is the right move. As for Jenny, keeping her out of this, for now, is the right choice. This situation is too chaotic to involve her in."

With the tooth back in Jake's possession, Amy turned toward the door, her emotions still raw but now more composed. "I'm heading to bed," she announced, her voice tired yet carrying a hint of a smile. "I've had my fill for today. See you in the morning, Jake."

As Amy left, Jake watched her retreat across the porch. Bolo's presence caught his attention as the big man rounded the corner of the storage shed, fatigue etched onto his face. He stopped by the porch, addressing Jake with an air of resignation.

Bolo's words were heavy with acknowledgment. "Mister Jake, this sure is the devil's day." He wiped his forehead; his weariness was evident. His gaze shifted toward the northern horizon, gesturing toward the village.

Jake's response was thoughtful, his expression pensive. "Tomorrow, I'll contact the mainland's Provost and arrange a boat to investigate the islands. But after that..." Jake looked at Bolo intently, his resolve unwavering. "We'll take the researchers back to their work as if nothing happened."

Despite the grim circumstances, Bolo's grin was a testament to his respect for Jake's unwavering resolve. "You're quite a character, Mister Jake. One of a kind."

With Bolo retiring to his cabin, Jake was left alone on the porch, leaning against the doorframe. The night was silent, save for the distant sounds of the ocean. The weight of the tooth, the enigma it represented, pressed on Jake's mind. His gaze lingered on the starlit horizon, lost in thought, uncertainty lingering in the darkness around him.

CHAPTER 4
The Morning Meal Awaits

The gentle morning light painted the tranquil waters with a soft, golden glow as the new day unfolded. Emerging from their cabins, Jenny and Amy, the two girls, faced the fresh challenges of the day almost in synchrony. Jenny's chuckle carried a touch of amusement as she observed Amy's tired appearance. "Looks like you're feeling as worn out as I am," she commented, her muscles protesting the toll of the previous day's events.

Amy cautiously stretched, attempting to work out the knots that seemed to have occupied her body. It felt as if she had been through a train wreck. "I could say the same about you," she responded, a mix of exhaustion and amusement tinging her voice. "Shall we see what the chef has cooked for us this morning? Today, I might actually eat something and keep it down." A faint chuckle escaped her lips as she considered the simple joy of a meal without the threat of seasickness.

Jenny nodded in agreement, and together, they headed toward the main house, drawn by the tantalizing scent of sizzling bacon and eggs that hung in the air, promising a delicious feast ahead.

Upon entering, they nearly collided with Bolo, who appeared to have finished his breakfast. Jenny playfully quirked an eyebrow at him. "Where's the rush, Bolo?"

"Mornin', young misses," Bolo greeted them with a weary but genial smile. "I'm off to service the boat and get shipshape for our day's trip. You ladies take your time with breakfast, and when you're ready, we'll have everything set for our return to the currents." With a brisk nod, he strode purposefully toward the docks, his enormous figure moving with determination.

Amused by Bolo's brisk departure, the girls exchanged a knowing smile. "Looks like we're in good hands," Jenny remarked.

"Absolutely," Amy agreed, a glint of amusement dancing in her eyes. "Now, let's see what culinary delights await us." Their footsteps led them to the table, where a tempting spread of freshly cooked eggs, platters of Canadian bacon, and crispy bacon awaited.

Jake, looking remarkably refreshed and untouched by yesterday's events, emerged from the kitchen carrying a coffee pot and a platter of hot biscuits. "Good morning, ladies. Breakfast is served, and it seems like a perfect day to continue your studies." He placed the coffee pot and biscuits on the table, motioning for them to take a seat.

As they settled into their chairs, they couldn't help but regard Jake with a mix of surprise and disbelief. Amy was the first to voice her thoughts. "Jake, I understand you want to honor your charter commitments, but considering what happened yesterday, I think—"

Jake interjected, his tone animated as he cut through her concerns. "Nonsense, Amy. Both of you must continue your research. I believe in your work, and today is a golden opportunity for you to resume your measurements." His demeanor was cheery, his words carrying an air of encouragement.

Amy sensed Jake's efforts to maintain a cheerful facade, even as he concealed his underlying apprehensions. She had witnessed his early morning radio call to the mainland, reporting the tragic events at the village and providing a statement to the authorities. The line of questioning had clearly made Jake uncomfortable, a fact he couldn't mask with his strained expressions. Yet, he pushed forward, resolute in his determination to keep the girls focused on their work.

After breakfast, the girls returned to their cabins to prepare for the day while Jake efficiently cleared and stored the breakfast dishes. A schedule needed to be maintained; Amos was expected to arrive around two o'clock, and Jake needed to ensure their timely return. Amos was familiar with the Keep and would make himself home until Jake came.

When the girls joined Jake at the boat, they found him deep in conversation with Bolo. Jake made his final point, and Bolo responded with a shrug before moving to the front of the boat to prepare for departure.

Jake outlined the plan for the day once they were settled onboard. "Today, we'll head just beyond the island to where the warm core begins. While Amy takes temperature and velocity readings, I thought Jenny and I could take a dive to collect samples of species carried by the new currents into this area. What do you both think?"

Amy's initial response held a hint of skepticism, but she swiftly recognized the potential benefits. Despite her reservations about putting Jenny at risk again, she acknowledged the opportunity to enhance their study. "Alright, that sounds like a plan, Jake. Jenny, are you up for a dive to gather specimens and strengthen the credibility of our research?" She turned to Jenny, her gaze a mix of curiosity and challenge.

Jenny glanced between Amy and Jake, searching their expressions for reassurance. After contemplating, she nodded and headed below deck to check the tanks and other equipment.

The boat once again departed from the tranquil harbor, its course set for a point several miles north of the Keep. As they sailed, the girls enjoyed drinks and sandwiches, easing into a state of relaxation. The journey would take about an hour and a half, granting them ample time to bask in the warm sunshine and the boat's gentle rocking.

Meanwhile, Captain Lozario Bonilla of the Provical Provost Martial was driven by a sense of duty into action in the early morning hours. Rallying a squad of police on his twenty-eight-foot patrol boat, he navigated the vessel toward the twin islands Jake had reported. As the sun climbed higher in the sky, they reached the island's channel around noon, following the same route Jake had taken just days before. Upon arriving at the grim scene, a heavy silence descended upon the squad. Catholic tradition guided their actions as they crossed themselves, each offering silent prayers in the face of the heart-wrenching spectacle.

Among the officers, Sergeant Cardon approached his Captain, his expression a mixture of astonishment and dread, voicing the question that weighed heavily on everyone's mind. "Dios, Capitan! What could have possibly caused this?"

Captain Bonilla's gaze remained fixed on the scene, his features displaying a blend of apprehension and an understanding that transcended human comprehension. He shrugged slightly, his voice carrying a note of resignation. "I don't know, Sergeant. But whatever it is, I don't intend to be here when it returns." His gaze swept across the wreckage, his thoughts turning inward as he privately acknowledged the presence of a force beyond their control.

Issuing orders to the helmsman for a turnaround, Bonilla's intentions became clear. Panic flickered in the eyes of the men, replaced by confused glances exchanged among them. All eyes shifted to Sergeant Cardon, who stood at the Captain's side, embodying their collective bewilderment. He hesitated for a moment, gathering his thoughts before addressing his superior. "Sir, I thought we were here to investigate what happened. Are we abandoning our mission without even stepping on the island?"

Bonilla understood the necessity of maintaining his facade of authority, even as his fears gnawed at him. He regarded Cardon with a mixture of condescension and firmness. "We won't find anything substantial amidst this wreckage. Our priority is to question Crandle on the other island and uncover the truth. Now, do you understand, Sergeant?" His tone conveyed unwavering authority, an attempt to mask his inner unease.

Sergeant Cardon snapped to attention, his acknowledgment accompanied by a hint of nervousness. "Of course, Captain. Your decision is perfectly logical, Sir." With a crisp salute, he turned and set about rallying the rest of the squad, guiding them through their tasks in preparation for their journey to the Keep.

Meanwhile, back on the island, Jake steered the boat around the end of the "figure eight" formation. Familiar with this route, he knew precisely where to direct them. He gestured eagerly toward the horizon. "Look over there! Those little specks in the distance?" Excitement brimmed in his voice as he slowed the boat. "Those are the rocky islets. Jenny, use the binoculars; you should spot some large sea lions basking in the sun."

Jenny accepted the binoculars, raising them to her eyes to capture the distant scene. Through the lenses, she spotted the rocks and the sun-drenched sea lions, a group swimming about a hundred yards north. "Yes, I see them," she exclaimed. "This is incredible! Amy, take a look." She handed the binoculars to Amy.

Amy took her turn with the binoculars, focusing on the scene as Jake and Bolo engaged in a quiet conversation about the island's channels. While she observed the sea lions resting on the rocks, Jenny described them, her attention shifted northward, anticipating the sight of the swimming sea lions. To her astonishment, however, there was only water. "Jen, I can only see the ones on the rocks," she reported, baffled by the absence of the swimmers.

Returning the binoculars, Jenny intended to demonstrate the view she had witnessed earlier. However, her perspective showed no sea lions in the water. "That's strange," she mused, sharing a perplexed look with Amy. "I could swear I saw them swimming around earlier."

Deciding that seal-watching could wait for now, Amy gracefully approached Jake, extending his binoculars. "Thanks for the detour, Jake. This diversion was a nice break, but Jenny and I were exhausted. We'd like to head back to the house, organize our equipment, and maybe catch a bit of rest. We're still recuperating from yesterday." She stretched mildly, finding a comfortable spot in the shade to sit alongside Jenny.

Meanwhile, beneath the waves, the colossal creature moved with deliberate purpose. Hunger propelled its massive form through the water as it scoured the depths for sustenance. Its appetite was unrelenting, an insatiable drive pushing it forward. As it traversed the waters, it sensed vibrations and sounds from above, hinting at potential prey.

Its focus honed on the activity above, instincts recognizing a potential feast. Slowly, it ascended, its enormous body narrowing the gap between itself and its quarry. A powerful cross-current jolted its path as it drew nearer, compelling it to rise abruptly. Its dorsal fin grazed the boat's underside, causing it to dive swiftly to regain control and prepare for its assault.

On the boat, the sudden jolt sent shockwaves through its occupants. Startled awake, the helmsman swiftly cut the power, bringing the vessel to a halt. Bewildered and disoriented, the men scanned their surroundings, seeking signs of impact. Yet, nothing met their eyes, and the water's surface appeared undisturbed.

Captain Bonilla, shaken and unnerved, struggled to regain his composure. Anxiety clawed at him as he grappled with comprehending the chaos around them. A sense of unease gnawed at his determination, recognizing that whatever had caused this upheaval might return.

His anxiety escalated as the unimaginable occurred. The water's surface quivered again, but it wasn't just a jolt this time—the boat itself was torn. The cacophony of splintering wood and bending metal was deafening as the vessel shattered. Bonilla clung to the remnants of the wheelhouse, thrown into a confined space amid the wreckage.

Beneath the waves, the massive creature ascended, positioning itself beneath the disintegrating boat. With swift precision, it surged upwards, its gaping jaws swallowing officers two or three at a time. Each gulp drew them deeper into its cavernous maw, leaving a horrifying spectacle of splashing water and men vanishing. The colossal form of the creature plunged back beneath the water's surface, executing its deadly ritual with exacting accuracy.

Sergeant Cardon's panicked splashes caught the creature's attention amid the chaos. As the sergeant flailed in terror, the immense head emerged from the depths, launching him skyward in a grotesque display of power. Cardon's fate was sealed as the creature's jaws snapped shut, claiming him instantly.

Huddled within the wreckage, Captain Bonilla bore witness to the macabre spectacle. His mind teetered on the precipice of madness as the horror played out before him. The beast's chilling exhibition of violence had shattered his sanity, and he muttered to himself, consumed by rage born from terror.

Meanwhile, Amos's charter plane neared the island, catching Jake's attention as it approached the harbor entrance. With calculated finesse, the seasoned pilot executed daring maneuvers, his plane offering a salute before gently descending onto the water's surface. The roar of the engines ceased as Amos skillfully guided the aircraft to a berth near the fuel pumps.

Jake, Jenny, and Amy observed the landing with gratitude, watching as Amos disembarked from the plane. Simultaneously, the boat glided to its own berth, and they prepared to greet Amos, thankful for his punctual arrival.

Unbeknown to them all, beneath the waves, the colossal creature had concluded its gruesome feast and ventured southward, propelled by its ceaseless hunger. The cycle of survival and destruction persisted, a silent force of nature lurking beneath the surface, forever altering the lives it encountered.

The girls greeted the incoming pilot with cheerful waves as the sun cast its warm, gentle glow. Amos returned the gesture, his smile radiating camaraderie. Meanwhile, Jake and Bolo were immersed in organizing equipment and refilling diving tanks for the upcoming day's expedition. Amos made his way toward them, his strides exuding familiarity and cheer.

"Hey, Jake!" Amos called out with a playful grin, his voice laced with a touch of humor. "Hey to you too, you old retread!" Jake chuckled heartily, extending his hand for a firm handshake. Jake genuinely cared for the seasoned pilot, his concern for Amos's well-being evident. He worried Amos might be stretching his limits with long flights over open waters.

"Glad to see you made it, Amos. Were you able to set up the delivery?" Jake's tone was tinged with eagerness, a testament to his growing apprehension from the tooth he had uncovered.

Amos nodded, his eyes gleaming with a spark of mischief. "Yep, got it sorted out. It wasn't exactly smooth sailing, though. One of them brothers tried to slow me down and lighten my pockets for the favor." Amos spat a stream of snuff into the water, his eyes dancing with mischief.

Jake smirked at the tale, recognizing Amos's knack for storytelling. "I'm glad you managed to work things out. Come to the main house with me; I'll fill you in on the details." Jake set off briskly up the incline, expecting Amos to keep up.

Amos followed suit, playfully waving his hand. "Hold on, Jake! You're not even curious about the cost of this venture?" He quickened his pace, breezing past the girls who watched in amusement. He zoomed past them with a tip of his hat, hurrying to catch up with Jake. Amy and Jenny exchanged a laugh before returning to their cabins on the hilltop.

From his vantage point, Bolo had completed the equipment transfer and was now tending to Amos's plane. He meticulously serviced and refueled the aircraft. Checking the fuel levels, he noted the consumption for future reference. The tanks were roughly three-quarters full due to their last servicing three weeks earlier.

As Jake and Amos descended the hill, their animated conversation caught Bolo's ear. Drawing near, Bolo overheard Amos's disgruntled tone and chuckled under his breath. "Darn it, Jake! You're always spoiling me with your cooking, and now you're withholding? Besides, it's getting late, and I'll fly back in the dark. You wouldn't want me to crash due to an empty stomach, would you?"

Jake halted a few feet from the plane, meeting Amos's demeanor with a blend of seriousness and humor. "Listen, Amos, I promise I'll make it up to you when you return next week. I'll cook every single one of your favorite meals. And you know you're an exceptional pilot; there's no need for dramatic guilt trips. I've stressed the importance of safely delivering this package to the courier, especially considering recent events. Now, get on that plane, and here's a bag of sandwiches to hold you over." Jake handed over the bag, observing how Amos's irritation seemed to abate somewhat.

"Fine, fine, I'm going." Amos playfully shook his head, then turned to Bolo with a hearty handshake. "Thanks for checking on the plane, big guy. See you next time." The two men exchanged a knowing smile, their camaraderie evident. Amos climbed into the pilot's seat, closing the door behind him. With the roar of the engines, the plane started moving away from the dock. Amos saluted Jake and Bolo with a smile before accelerating, heading towards the open water where he would prepare for takeoff.

The plane ascended into the sky, its silhouette shrinking until it vanished from sight. Jake lingered for a moment, lost in thought, before gazing at Bolo. "Bolo, I hope we don't hear the news we've feared ever since the village incident." His gaze carried a serious note as he met Bolo's intense gaze.

"Mister Jake," Bolo's deep voice resonated, his breath showing signs of exertion. "What creature could produce a tooth like that? I've grown up around the sea, and my elders taught me all I know about its denizens... but nothing prepared me for this." Bolo's expression conveyed both confusion and concern.

Jake placed a reassuring hand on Bolo's arm, searching for words to soothe his friend. "Bolo, let's wait for Toombs to share his insights. I don't want us to speculate and cause unnecessary worry." His voice remained steady, attempting to alleviate Bolo's unease.

Bolo nodded slowly, his gaze returning Jake's with understanding. He offered a faint smile, a mix of gratitude and resignation. With a sigh, he headed up the hill to his cabin, ready to clean up and rest before dinner. Jake followed suit, and a sense of tranquility enveloped the island for a few hours.

Dinner came and went, punctuated by subdued conversation. As Jake and Bolo tidied up the table, the girls huddled in whispered conversation about the day's events. Jake finished his tasks and was about to pour himself a cup of coffee when Amy entered the room. He extended the offer of coffee, and Amy accepted, settling at the work table. Since discovering the tooth, Jake aimed to keep the conversation light, given Amy's apparent mood.

"Did you find what you were looking for today?" Jake inquired, attempting to divert the topic from the package he had sent.

Amy's smile seemed forced, her gaze focused on her coffee cup. "I suppose I did," she replied, her tone tinged with uncertainty. She suddenly looked up at Jake, her eyes intense with mixed emotions. "Jake, can I ask you something? Can you give me an honest answer?"

Jake nodded, positioning himself across from Amy, his coffee cradled in both hands. Leaning in, he met her gaze with keen interest. He sensed the gravity of her question, his heart pounding in anticipation.

"Absolutely, Amy," he responded calmly. "Go ahead and ask."

Amy's eyes radiated determination, her words charged with urgency. "Please, no beating around the bush. Do you know what creature that tooth came from?"

Jake paused, his thoughts racing to frame an appropriate response. He finally spoke, "Yes, Amy, I'm afraid I do." He met her gaze, his demeanor revealing the weight of the truth he had shared.

A moment of silence hung in the air as Amy absorbed the revelation. Then, she pressed on with unwavering determination. "Well, so do I. It sounds crazy, I know, but let's stop pretending. No creature on this planet could have produced that tooth except... the Megalodon, right?"

Jake inwardly winced at the mention of the name but outwardly maintained his composure, his expression revealing nothing. "Amy, this is a wild thought. The Megalodon has been extinct for countless years, and—"

"Thought to be extinct," Amy interjected with conviction. "It's always been assumed to be extinct, but why? Because researchers believed the modern food chain couldn't support its species. But let me tell you about documented cases that suggest otherwise. Fishermen in Australia or New Zealand claimed they saw a shark the length of a pier tearing apart nets and devouring most of their catch in 1918. That pier was over 100 feet long! And don't forget the credible accounts of an 80-foot shark off the northeastern U.S. coast in the 1980s. These were respectable men—why would they lie? Can you explain that, Jake?"

Amy's impassioned delivery bordered on hysteria, and Jake recognized the urgency in her voice. He reached out, his hand calmingly resting on her arm. "Amy, please. Let's wait for Toombs to examine the tooth and share his insights. I understand how this sounds, but I don't want us to get carried away with theories until we have more concrete information. Can we try to relax for now?" Jake's eyes conveyed empathy and concern as he sought to alleviate Amy's distress.

Amy's breath caught, her intensity beginning to waver. She sighed, offering a reluctant nod of agreement. "Alright, Jake. I'll try to hold off until we hear from Toombs. But this entire situation... it's consuming me." She managed a weak smile, a mix of relief and trepidation flitting across her features.

They finished their coffee silently, exchanging only light banter about their backgrounds and interests. Jake collected the cups, quickly washed them, and prepared to secure the kitchen for the night. He escorted Amy to the front porch, where Bolo's storytelling had enraptured Jenny's attention. "So, another big day tomorrow, right?" he said, steering the conversation back to their upcoming plans.

Amy nodded, her thoughts momentarily shifting from the disconcerting topic. "Yes, we'll be heading to the edge of the current we explored today to gather more samples. We need to establish some boundaries. So, let's call it a night and rest up for tomorrow, Jenny."

Jenny chimed in. Her youthful enthusiasm was unabated. "Sounds like a plan! Goodnight, Bolo. We might catch you later before we leave." With that, the girls headed to their cabins, leaving Jake and Bolo to exchange knowing glances.

"Let's hope Toombs sheds some light on all of this," Jake murmured, his gaze following the girls' path.

Bolo solemnly nodded, his imposing figure reflecting the concern that gnawed at him. "Mister Jake, if it's as serious as we fear, we'll need a plan."

Jake's eyes met Bolo's, a weighty understanding passing between them. "I know, Bolo. Let's just hope it doesn't come to that." With those words, they turned in, prepared to confront the unknown that lay ahead.

CHAPTER 5
It's a High Stakes Confrontation

The sunlight streamed through the window of Amy's cabin, casting warm hues on the wooden floor. She awoke with a stretch and a yawn, gradually realizing her surroundings. Checking her watch on the bedside table, she exclaimed, "Seven thirty? Damn it, Jake, why didn't you wake me up at five-thirty like we planned?" Frustration tinged her voice as she hurriedly got out of bed and took a quick shower. There was no time for leisure today; she tied her hair back, changed into fresh shorts, and swiftly exited her cabin. Ignoring Jenny's cabin, she headed straight to the main house.

Amy arrived at the main house to find the trio engaged in light chatter at the breakfast table. Her entrance was marked by her visibly annoyed demeanor. "Jake, seriously, why didn't you wake me up? It's almost eight, and we should have been out on the water by now," she reproached, not bothering to sit until she received an explanation.

"Well, I did try, Amy," Jake responded, slightly taken aback. "I knocked on your door three times around six in the morning, but you didn't answer."

Amy stood there, shaking her head in disbelief. "No way. I would have woken up. You're just saying that to cover up the fact that you forgot," she asserted, finally sitting down with a pointed look at Jake.

Jenny interjected with a knowing smile, "Actually, he's telling the truth. I heard him knocking on your door when he woke me up."

"Oh, well... fine, Jake. I apologize. I just didn't expect to sleep in that soundly," Amy admitted, her annoyance softening as she looked at Jake, who was smirking a little.

Apology accepted. No harm done," Jake said, trying to lighten the mood. "Anyway, we're not too behind schedule. We'll still have enough time to reach the convergence zone and get our samples."

"Great," Amy replied, trying to muster enthusiasm. "Now, could I get something to eat before we head out?"

"Sure thing. Anything you want," Jake said, heading toward the kitchen. "I can whip up a quick breakfast for you."

Their exchange elicited laughter from the group, and the tension from earlier dissipated.

Once Amy had finished her breakfast and Jake had tidied up, they made their way down to the boat, which was being prepared by Bolo and the girls. The vessel was ready well ahead of schedule, which brought a satisfied smile to Jake's face. He was relieved the girls were trying to return to their usual routine after the recent stressful events.

"Alright, everyone," Jake declared as he leaped onto the boat. "It looks like we're all set. Let's cast off Bolo and get this show on the road. Ready to go, right?" His peppy tone brought smiles and chuckles from the group.

Jenny had taken Jake's binoculars and scanned the surrounding waters as they made their way to the dive area. She spotted dolphins and humpback whales, making casual observations. While looking toward the east, the sun's glare played tricks on her eyes, making it challenging to distinguish objects. Focusing on a large dorsal fin in the distance, she wrongly identified it as a killer whale and moved on.

Amy, preoccupied with her notes, inquired about Jenny's earlier statement. "Hey, Jenny, what did you see out there?"

"Oh, nothing much," Jenny replied, trying to dismiss her earlier comment.

"Come on, spill the beans," Amy urged, genuinely curious.

"Okay, well, I saw something floating in the water, far off toward the horizon," Jenny confessed, still peering through the binoculars.

Jake took the binoculars from Jenny and focused on the area she indicated, spotting wreckage. "Bolo, head that way, please," he instructed, eager to investigate.

As they neared the debris, Jake recognized the remains of a boat's wheelhouse. Bolo deftly maneuvered the boat next to the wreckage, and Jake secured it to the railing. Jake leaped onto the debris with Jenny and Amy watching, collecting charts and papers strewn around. A faint noise caught his attention from beneath a tarp, and he lifted it to reveal a man in a provincial provost marshal uniform, appearing close to collapse.

Realizing something serious unfolded, Bolo queried, "Mister Jake, what's going on? Something happened down there?"

Jake looked up at Bolo, his face devoid of color, and began to recount the encounter with the supposed Mako shark. Bolo listened in disbelief as Jake told the story, tension thickening in the air.

Standing up slowly, Bolo prepared to set sail. Meanwhile, Jenny had taken the binoculars and scanned the waters, spotting something on the horizon. Her shout pierced the air, drawing everyone's attention to her.

"What is it, Jenny? Do you see something out there?" Jake hurried over to join her, fearing another dangerous creature was approaching.

"Something's floating out there, in the water," Jenny urgently said.

Jake took the binoculars and focused on the spot Jenny indicated. Realizing they needed to investigate, he instructed Bolo to change their course.

After thirty minutes, they reached the floating wreckage and secured it to the boat. Jake recognized the remnants of a boat's wheelhouse and collected scattered charts and papers. As he sifted through the debris, he heard a faint noise and found a man in a provincial provost marshal uniform in critical condition.

Bolo's concern deepened as he witnessed the unfolding events. He could sense the gravity of the situation and focused on his role as the boat's captain, ready to assist as needed.

"Bolo, I could use your help here," Jake requested urgently. "We've got a live one, but he won't last long unless we get him back to the main house. I need saline and glucose. He's in shock." Bolo immediately jumped to action, rushing to the floating wheelhouse to assist Jake in returning the injured man to the boat. The man emitted soft groans of distress as they carefully transported him onboard. With the stranger secured in a bunk below deck, Jake changed the boat's course and sped toward home, hoping that this man might hold some answers about the unsettling events unfolding.

The journey back to the Keep was tense for all on board, the weight of their recent experiences evident in their demeanor. As they reached their familiar docking slip, the boat's arrival triggered a burst of panic in the two girls, who dashed for their cabins before Bolo had even finished securing the lines. Recognizing the urgency of their actions, Jake made a mental note to check on each girl after he ensured the injured man's comfort in the main house.

With the boat safely moored and the engine silenced, Jake turned to Bolo. "Bolo, lend me a hand here. Let's get him inside and ensure he's covered until he stabilizes enough for us to administer fluids."

Bolo followed Jake below deck, and together, they gently lifted the injured man onto the deck. They adjusted their grip and carefully carried him to the main house. Once inside, they settled him into a spare bed, ensuring he was adequately covered.

"He's not looking good, Mister Jake," Bolo remarked worriedly. "We need to get some soup or broth into him soon, or he might not make it." His somber words were punctuated by a slow shake of his head, underlining his concern.

As Jake inserted a saline glucose drip into the unconscious man's arm, he confirmed Bolo's assessment. The man appeared pale, dehydrated, and in shock—an ominous combination. Leaving Bolo to watch over the unconscious man, Jake headed to his office to contact the mainland and arrange for old Amos to fly out at first light to transport the injured man to a hospital.

However, upon reaching his desk, Jake was met with a flashing recorder light, indicating an incoming message. Settling in, he switched on the external speakers and keyed the recorder for playback. A voice with a New England accent crackled through, identifying itself as Lamar Toombs. Toombs expressed his desire for Jake to call him back, mentioning that he had received the tooth package and wanted to discuss it further. Jake quickly jotted down the phone number and noted the urgency in Toombs's tone.

With the sun setting, Jake returned Toombs's call before tracking down old Amos at the bar. Setting up the radio, he contacted the radio telephone operator on the mainland and provided the number in Sao Paulo. After a series of clicks and hisses, the line connected, and Toombs's voice came through.

"Good afternoon; Toombs here," came the somewhat weary voice on the other end.

"Dr. Toombs, this is Jake Crandle," Jake introduced himself, eager to address the matter. "I'm the one who sent   " Toombs's eager interruption cut him off.

"Ah, the famous, or should I say, the infamous source of the tooth that has captured my attention. Tell me, Mister Crandle, from what dig did you procure this specimen? Was it somewhere in the U.S. or perhaps Indonesia? Why did you bring it to me? Did you anticipate a financial reward? What's the actual story behind all this?" Toombs's tone grew more caustic and skeptical with each question.

Feeling the frustration bubbling within him, Jake seized his chance to respond. "If you're done with your wild speculations, I'll tell you precisely why I sent this to you. I didn't get this tooth from a dig or buy it from a drunk paleontologist. My mate and I found it embedded in a broken section of bridge support in a recently destroyed village. Also, if you examine the tissue along the tooth's base, you'll see it's still malleable. It's recent. Do you begin to understand why I sent this to you? I'm a marine biologist, and I can't rationalize this myself, much less explain it to others. What do you honestly think?"

Toombs seemed taken aback by Jake's fervent response. "My dear Mister Crandle, do you comprehend what you're suggesting? The notion of a living Carcharadis Megalodon is absurd. Even considering your revelation is laughable within the professional community. Megalodon has been extinct for about 150,000 years due to insufficient food."

Jake persisted, his voice charged with frustration and anxiety. "I know how it sounds, Doctor. I wouldn't have sent the tooth if there were any other explanations. Would I send it with just a request for a professional opinion if I had ulterior motives? I don't want to be considered a lunatic more than you do!"

A brief silence was on the line before Toombs replied, his conviction wavering. "I'm sorry, Mister Crandle, but suggesting that Megalodon exists today is preposterous."

"Dr. Toombs," Jake's tone softened, his urgency becoming evident, "I believe this is exactly what we're dealing with. It's following new warm water currents, which might explain the events in the village. That's why I contacted you. But it's hard to accept, I know."

Toombs's enthusiasm began to overshadow his skepticism. "Mister Crandle, would you mind if I and an associate came to your island? This is an extraordinary historical event. Doesn't it excite you even a little?"

While wary of Toombs's eagerness, Jake understood the discovery's significance. "Alright, Lamar. If you move quickly, I'll let you bring others into this. But remember, I have an injured soldier here who needs immediate attention."

Toombs agreed and began discussing his plans, but Jake couldn't help but sense the scientist's eagerness to be a part of something monumental. As their conversation continued, Toombs's demeanor shifted, and he asked Jake to call him by his first name. In return, Jake insisted Toombs call him Jake.

After the call ended, Jake felt a mix of apprehension and excitement. He had opened a new chapter in this unfolding mystery, and the prospect of uncovering the truth about Megalodon's existence was both exhilarating and terrifying.

"Will do. Until then, Jake, do take care in the waters around there. If indeed he exists, this beast is unlike anything man has encountered in recorded history. You grasp my point?" Toombs' voice had taken on a very somber air now.

"Oh yes, Lamar. That I do. Goodbye for now." Jake prepared to sever the connection.

"Bye, Jake." Toombs initiated a click as the phone was lowered into the cradle.

Jake switched the radio off, put his notebook into the desk, and turned to check on the injured man in the other room...and saw Amy and Jenny on the other side, quietly leaning against the wall. The look on their faces told Jake that they had been there for quite a bit of the conversation with Toombs. Jake initially let an angry look play across his face, but as quickly as the look came, it was gone, replaced by one of sincere concern for the girls. They both were obviously horrified, and Jake wanted to keep them from becoming hysterical. "Ladies, I can only presume that you both came in and eavesdropped on my discussion with Dr. Toombs, right?" He looked at them with an expression that said he wanted an answer.

He looked from one girl to the other until Amy, after looking at Jenny, said, "Jake, we're sorry, but we were talking, and Jenny said that she thought nothing of it at the time, but when she was scanning the horizon from the boat, this afternoon, she saw what looked to be a giant killer whale fin somewhere out toward the horizon. Since she had no reference point, she couldn't be sure how big the fin was. We were coming to tell you about this before you talked to Toombs, but when we came to the front of the house, we heard you telling Toombs about the events of the past few days, and.....well...we just felt that we had to know the truth about that tooth."

Amy looked a little sheepish now but mustered the strength to continue, watching Jake directly in the eye. "Now we know, don't we? Jake, this is a terrifying situation, for sure, but I, for one," She looked to Jenny for corroboration, and Jenny nodded in ascent. "feel that Toombs was right about this being, possibly, the most significant marine discovery in the history of man." Amy's eyes had a glint of genuine excitement mixed with the fear of the moment.

Jake frowned inwardly because he could see, in Amy and, perhaps, also in Jenny, the look of lustful excitement brought on by a dangerous challenge, like a game of "chicken" in automobiles or challenging a freight train to see who gets to a crossing first. Jake knew this was a fundamental human emotion because he had been experiencing it since they left the village. However, in this case, he felt an ominous feeling of dread. There was an unknown creature out there that neither Jake nor anyone else, for that matter, had ever encountered, and Jake wasn't sure of how he could cope with it. One thing was for sure, though; Jake wasn't about to give up and run away from the home he had built on this island, so he knew that if this thing was anywhere near the Keep, he would have to find a way to deal with it.

"Ladies, it's getting late, and may I suggest that we all climb into our beds and try to get a nice long night's sleep?" Jake suggested, coming back to the here and now from his reveries. He motioned mockingly with his hand and arm, showing the two girls the door like a butler might do.

Jake's attempt at levity accomplished its intent. Both girls broke into a slight giggle, shaking their heads from side to side, and headed out the front door, but as they reached the steps of the main house, they heard a scream from the bedroom inside. Bonilla had, apparently, come out of his coma and was crying hysterically.

Jake and Bolo, who had come running at the sound of the screaming, rushed into the room to find Bonilla, pale as a ghost, sitting on the bed and screaming the exact words repeatedly. "What's that he be sayin', Mister Jake?" Bolo asked as he tried, as gently as possible, to subdue the man's thrashing.

Jake was on the opposite side of the bed, attempting to help calm the thrashing sailor. Jake looked into Bolo's face with an expression of cold terror. "He's saying "Tiburon de Diablo!"...Devil Shark...over and over!"

The girls had slipped into the room and positioned themselves to help if needed, and Jake had asked Jenny to go into the kitchen to make some hot broth from the pantry. She ran out the door to do what Jake asked. Amy stood still behind Jake, trying not to interfere in what he and Bolo were doing. However, Amy stood close enough to hear what was being discussed by the two men, and when Jake translated the ravings of Bonilla, she gasped and ran out of the room, crying as she went out of the door.

Jake noticed Amy's exit but couldn't do anything about it now because he needed to try getting Bonilla calmed down and taking liquids if possible.

Suddenly, as quickly as his wild ravings started, Bonilla went limp in the bed. Jake felt a coldness in the pit of his stomach as he examined the man for life signs and found none. He jumped up on the bed, straddled the silent figure, and proceeded to administer CPR to try and revive Bonilla, but Jake knew deep inside that Bonilla was gone.

Bolo watched as Jake tried, in vain, to bring Bonilla back, but after a few minutes, Bolo put a gentle hand on Jake's arm, and when Jake snapped his head around to look at Bolo, the big man just sadly nodded his head from side to side as a signal that it was no use. Jake slumped over, his head resting on the dead constable's chest, sobbing openly now.

Bolo helped Jake off of the bed and offered a little explanation of what he felt had happened. "Mister Jake, you need to be calmin' yourself, now. This poor fella was dead when he saw what he saw. He just didn't know it at the time. He done been scared to death, Mister Jake, and that's God's truth...yessir...scared to death!"

Jake lifted his face out of his hands and looked at his big friend. "He just didn't seem to be hurt that bad, Bolo. I just don't understand it." Jake said with a little whimper in his husky voice.

"There are many things we don't understand, Mister Jake, but I am as sure as I am sitting here that this poor man, bless his soul to heaven, died from pure fright." As Bolo finished speaking, neither man said another word for several minutes, each lost in their own thoughts of what had just happened and what may lie ahead.

Jenny returned to the room with a bowl of steaming soup about this time, but she stopped as she surveyed the scene before her. "He's dead, right?" Jenny had seen people die before, but not like this. She started to shake a little, and Bolo recognized what was happening and jumped to her side to take the hot soup before she dropped it.

He set it on a table and helped Jenny to a chair. She was just staring ahead, her eyes blank as she looked at the floor as if she were in a state of concentration. In fact, she was blank at the time, thinking of nothing as her mind defended itself from the tragedy that assailed her senses.

Although still plainly affected by the events of the past few minutes, Jake had come to his senses and was standing now. He spoke with quiet authority. "Bolo, help me get him over to the refrigerated storage room where we can keep him until I can get Amos out to ferry the body back to his people on the mainland." The two men wrapped the body in a blanket and carried it across the clearing to the meat storage locker in the large storage and generator building on the other side. There, they ensured the body was wrapped safely and laid it on a cot in the corner, away from the meat in the locker.

When the two men emerged from the building, they found Jenny consoling Amy on the end of the porch. Jake sauntered across to the two girls while Bolo went to the storage shed to check on supplies, put his hand on Amy's shoulder, and rubbed it gently. He spoke to Amy then, but he was talking to both girls. "We've been through a lot, and I can understand how we all probably want to close ourselves in our rooms and pray that the cavalry will come charging over the hill, but that's not likely to happen. I can call the mainland and tell them everything we know about this thing, but they are not likely to truly believe us. Oh, they might accept the fact that there's a big shark out here somewhere, but even if I tell them that I think their missing boat was attacked by a creature out of the dinosaur era and that their captain just died as a result of his encounter with it, they are going to think I'm crazy or on something, or both."

Jake took a long swallow of Bolo's beer from the refrigerated shed and continued. "Hell," His voice softened as he looked down at Amy sitting before him. "I feel, at times, that there has to be a more sensible, believable answer to all that's happened than some "super shark" out of some distant past era that we can't begin to know anything about... not really."

"Jake," Amy reached up, softly clasped Jake's hand on her shoulder, and squeezed it just a little to emphasize what she was about to say. "Many tragic and unexplainable events have happened in the past couple of days, but we have all gotten through them, and we are just fine, right?" She was trying to get Jake to calm down and lighten up because she knew that Jake was their "rock," if they were to get through the days ahead safely, Jake must be emotionally sound and mentally alert.

Jake looked up at Amy for a moment, then at Jenny, before he relaxed and spoke. "Amy, you are truly wise beyond your years. You're right; we are just fine......a little the worse for wear, but just fine." He had forced a small smile before he went on. "Now, I think you both need your beauty rest," He beckoned to the steps with both arms as if to show them down with a grandiose gesture. "So, if you would be so kind as to retire for the evening, I will try to clean up a bit and hit the rack myself."

"Thanks, big guy. I always knew that chivalry was not dead...just dormant." Amy laughed at her pun and saw Jake smiling despite the dangerous situation.

"No problem, lovely lady." Jake tipped his hat and knew that Amy was blushing at the comment even though he couldn't see it in the dark. "Good night, Amy," Jake added softly.

"Night, Jake." Amy turned and strolled toward her cabin. Jake watched her until she went inside, trying to keep new emotions from creeping into his head.

Turning to go back inside to get ready for bed, he saw Bolo coming from the boat and equipment shed. "Everything secure for the night, Bolo?" Jake spoke up across the distance between them.

"Yessir, Mister Jake. All the ladies' stuff is stored in the warehouse, and the boat is tied down with three extra lines tonight." Bolo turned at Jake's voice and started across the clearing toward him. "Anything else you be needin', Mister Jake before I go clean up, grab a bite, and go to bed?"

"Nah, ol' friend. I believe that's all for the night. By the way, we won't be going out tomorrow. We need to know a little more about what might be somewhere out there and what we must do to rid ourselves of it. Understand?" Jake spoke slowly and distinctly so Bolo would understand as much as possible.

Bolo assured Jake that he did understand, and Jake offered to make Bolo something to eat, but Bolo just smiled and told Jake not to bother. Bolo chuckled a bit, and he joked with Jake. "Don't bother, Mister Jake. I got some of that great ham we brought back from our last trip to the mainland, and I cherish every bite I take from it. It's great, Jake, really." Bolo sensed that Jake felt he was being "taken for a ride."

"Bolo, I know you're feeding me a line of crap!" Jake smiled lightly and continued. "You just want to get away from me tonight because you think I'm heading to the edge, right?" Jake looked inquiringly at Bolo with his eyebrows raised.

Bolo looked down at the floor and then slowly back up at Jake, a somewhat sheepish look on his face. "Well, Mister Jake, you have been up against it these past few days, and, after that call with that Toombs fella, who could blame you for kinda pullin' in your head like a turtle and just wait and see what happens! I was just thinkin'

I'd get on outta here and leave you to your thoughts. Know what I mean?"

Jake smiled again, this time, a little bigger one. "My friend, if I seem to be on edge, it's just that I genuinely care about you and the girls, and I just think that nothing really earth-shaking will be served by going out tomorrow. Anyway, I would bet my last dollar that, from how he sounded, Toombs will be out here within a few days. I could hear the lust of discovery in his voice. Yep, he'll be here in no time." Jake was talking a little more to himself than to Bolo, but Jake's attention snapped back to Bolo as soon as it had left. "So! You feel a little more comfortable that I'm not ready to explode now?" Jake laughed sincerely now as he offered Bolo a beer.

"Yessir, I do that. Now, Turkey." Bolo sat down at the table and grinned at Jake.

"Turkey...what?" Jake asked, a bit confused.

"Well, Mister Jake, you asked if you could make me a sandwich, and I think I'll take you up on it...Turkey, please, sir." Both men laughed, and Jake fixed a giant turkey sandwich with a nice helping of potato salad for Bolo. They carried their beers and Bolo's sandwich out to the porch, sat, and talked about life and other mundane issues for a couple of hours. Neither wanted to talk about the possible danger that had haunted them since the day at the village.

Clouds built up and covered the moon, and the night became black. Jake and Bolo sat on the porch and stared into the darkness at where they both knew the mouth of the harbor was, and each silently shivered at the chill in the air. But was the chill from the approaching squall, or was it caused by the fear a man feels from the unknown things that dwell in the darkness? They finished their beers, had one more, and then Bolo bid Jake good night as he headed for his cabin and the security of his bed.

Jake watched Bolo for a moment, then turned his eyes toward the sea beyond the island, even though he couldn't see anything. He took in a deep breath, let out a long sigh, and turned to go back inside. He couldn't shake a feeling of fear that was gnawing away at his insides.

Some would have called Jake psychic because, had the skies remained clear, and the moon's light has been allowed to bathe the waters of the sea outside the harbor, he and Bolo might have witnessed the massive fin as it glided silently by the mouth of the port on its way to the sea lion habitat at the west end of the island.

He had followed the large thing's trail around the island but had lost its scent as the storm's approach had stirred up the water. *He* was famished now, and *his* senses led *him* past the refuge of the 'thing' *he* sought toward the place *he* knew, instinctually, had provided *him* an excellent meal earlier. *He* swam slowly but determinedly toward the sea lion herd, and as *he* drew nearer the end of the island, *he* picked up the scent and sound of the large mammals.

He closed in on the targets of his rising frenzy and captured three large males in *his* enormous jaws as *he* broke the wind-whipped surface from below, about two hundred yards from the rocks. *He* immediately zeroed in on another group of six animals as they raced toward the relative safety of the rocks. The rest of the herd had already clambered onto the rocks and barked loudly as their comrades lost their race with fate and disappeared into the tooth-lined jaws that enveloped them.

To some degree, he had satiated *his* endless hunger for the time being, but not wanting to pass on another meal, he slowly circled the rocks, all of *his* senses on high alert for any of the sea lions that may venture off the rocks and into the water. None did, however, and after an hour or so, *he* turned and retraced the path *he* had come from, descending to the bottom to digest *his* current feeding.

He swam aimlessly at this point, not sensing any threat or food source of note. Deep inside *his* primitive brain, however, *he* knew that *he* would take up residence in these waters for the time being because *he* had found a food source that would provide *him* with a constant food supply. Between the sea lions and the other more significant 'things' *he* had encountered, *he* had found a fertile territory...a sort of home!

CHAPTER 6
Nice to Hear from the Old Man

The following day brought a late start for everyone, including Jake. The sun had risen high in the sky when the girls stirred from their cabins. Dressed for the day, they went to the main house, anticipating a hearty breakfast fueling their steps. However, as they approached the front porch, they exchanged puzzled glances.

Jenny wrinkled her nose. "Do you smell that, Amy? Or rather, the lack of it?"

Amy's brow furrowed as she sniffed the air. "You're right. There's no aroma of eggs, bacon, or ham from the kitchen chimney. That's strange."

As they reached the porch, they spotted Bolo making his way up from the dock. His broad smile greeted them. "Good mornin', young misses! You both look like you had a fine night's rest. Have you seen Mister Jake today?" His eyes shifted from one girl to the other.

Both girls shook their heads, conveying that they hadn't seen Jake yet. "And no breakfast smells either," Jenny added, her voice laced with disappointment.

Bolo's face registered surprise, and he agreed to investigate. He entered the house with the girls trailing closely. As they entered the dining room, it was clear that no activity had occurred since the previous day. Bolo moved to the back room, and there, in his bed, lay Jake, utterly unaware of their presence, lost in a deep sleep and snoring loudly.

A bemused smile crossed Bolo's face, and he motioned for the girls to see. Amy and Jenny couldn't help but giggle as they took in the unexpected sight. Amy found herself intrigued by this rare glimpse of vulnerability in Jake. She noted how peaceful he appeared, an oasis of tranquility amid their turbulent circumstances. She felt a pang of gratitude for Jake's respite from the chaos that awaited them, an unspoken connection forming between them.

As they turned to leave the room, Jake's eyes flickered open, catching sight of their retreating figures. He mustered a half-smile, his voice a playful drawl. "I suppose you're all hunting for your breakfast, huh?"

Their laughter filled the room as Jake raised himself onto his elbows, still nestled under the covers, his hair in disarray. Bolo joined in the amusement, taking on the role of spokesperson. "Yes, indeed, Mister Jake. We're a hungry bunch, and considering you're the culinary wizard around here, we're all hoping for one of your legendary omelets!" Bolo chuckled heartily, the tension of the past days momentarily dissolving in the shared mirth.

The trio settled around the dining table as Jake quickly dressed and began brewing coffee. He deftly assembled the ingredients for a trio of omelets in a large fry pan, the sizzling sounds filling the air as intoxicating aromas enveloped the room. Hunger gnawed at them as they waited for the eggs to set.

When the food was ready, they devoured the omelets with gusto, hunger satisfied by the satisfying meal. Afterward, they sat back, sipping hot coffee and engaging in light conversation about trivial matters, enjoying the camaraderie that had united them on this isolated island.

As Jake and Bolo cleared the table, the radio suddenly crackled to life, a familiar voice piercing through the static. "Jake, come in. This is Amos! Where in tarnation are you? Come in, Jake!"

Jake grabbed the microphone, flipping a switch on the front of the radio. "Hey there, Crandle here. That you, Amos?" He released the button on the mic, waiting for a response.

"You bet your boots it's me! Who else would be bothering your hide, Jake?" The old pilot's voice resonated through the speaker, combining familiarity and exasperation.

"Good to hear your voice, Old Man," Jake retorted playfully. "What's got you calling me out of the blue?"

Amos chuckled, his gravelly voice filled with amusement. "Well, that Toombs fella you had me send the package to? He rang me up last night."

Jake's interest was piqued. "Yeah? What did he want?"

Amos spat tobacco into a cup before continuing. "He said he's coming to the island with another fella. They're itching to get here, and he told me to let you know. He said he'd be here in a day or two as soon as he can arrange the trip."

Jake's mind raced, processing the information. "Bring them over, Amos, but don't forget to make them pay you upfront. And don't cut them any deals on your rate."

Amos laughed heartily. "You got it, Jake. I know how to handle these city folk. I'll give you a holler before we head your way."

"Sounds like a plan, Amos. Talk to you when they're about to arrive." Jake's voice held a mix of anticipation and readiness.

Jake turned to the others, watching him closely as the radio connection broke. "Toombs is coming, along with another guy. They'll be here in a day or two."

Bolo's expression was contemplative. "Jake, did Toombs mention who the other man is?"

Jake shook his head. "Nope, he didn't share that detail. But it looks like we'll be meeting them soon."

The atmosphere on the porch began to relax as they discussed this new development. Their focus shifted from the sea monster that lurked beyond to the arrival of the researchers. However, Jenny's anxious energy surged back to the forefront as she stared at the water.

Suddenly, the tension was broken when Amy and Jenny bounded up the steps, their arms laden with laundry baskets filled with clothes. They were on a mission to do laundry.

"Jake, where's the washer?" Amy asked, looking around.

Jake pointed out the laundry nook's direction when he remembered the broken washer. "Ah, shoot, I'm sorry, ladies. The washer's out of commission at the moment. I haven't received the parts to fix it yet."

Their disappointment was palpable, and Jenny began to ask another question before Jake intervened. "But don't worry, we've got a solution. We use the lagoon."

Amy raised an eyebrow, intrigued. "The lagoon? How?"

Jake grinned, glad to share some island wisdom. "We'll take you down to the lagoon. It's a protected area with calm water; we can use it for laundry. It's a bit unconventional, but it gets the job done."

With the promise of a lagoon laundry adventure, their spirits lifted. The tension of the sea monster was momentarily set aside, replaced by the practicality of daily tasks. As they prepared for the lagoon excursion, the island's tranquility embraced them, reminding them that life continued with its routines despite uncertainty.

"How do you wash in salt water?" Jenny's voice piped up, curiosity evident in her tone. She continued with a touch of sarcasm, "Seems like a bad idea for clothes and skin, doesn't it?"

Jake chuckled at her remark, his weathered face breaking into a knowing grin. "You're right, Jenny. We definitely don't wash in salt water. The lagoon's water is mostly fresh, actually. Comes from a little spring in the side of that small knoll over yonder." He pointed toward the far end of the island, his finger tracing the invisible path of the water source.

He began to explain the island's unique layout. "You might've noticed from the air that the island looks like a figure-eight. The harbor out here is the base of the 'Eight,' while the top lagoon is surrounded by rocky shoals. The connecting point between the two parts of the 'Eight' is a special rock bridge over a shallow channel to the open sea, about forty or fifty feet wide. Only during rare tidal surges or storms does seawater mix with the lagoon's freshwater." Jake gestured with his hands, painting an imaginary picture in the air. "So, we've got 'mostly' fresh water for washing. Clear enough, girls?"

Amy nodded thoughtfully, recollecting their aerial approach to the island. "Actually, yes. I remember that figure-eight shape as we approached."

Jenny chimed in, her eyes distant as she recalled their initial view of the island. "I thought that water was just a part of the sea. I never imagined it was fresh water."

With the explanation in mind, Jenny's gaze shifted toward the lagoon end of the island. "Hey, Jake, isn't that where the sea lion colony is?"

Jake nodded, impressed by her memory. "You're spot on, Jenny. The colony is just off the northwest end of the lagoon, about half a mile out. Sometimes, after extended wet spells, a few sea lions enter the lagoon for a sunbath before returning to their rocky home."

Their understanding deepened, and Jake called out to Bolo, who was working on a boat by the dock. Jake addressed the girls' intention to do laundry as Bolo returned to the house.

"Jake, we can manage finding the lagoon on our own," Amy began, but Jake cut her off with a raised hand, a mischievous glint in his eye.

"No, no. Not this time, Amy. While I know you're both capable, the path gets tricky near the rock bridge and can be slippery. Plus, it's important for Bolo to feel like he's playing the gallant protector for his favorite visitors." Jake's playful grin punctuated his request.

Amy and Jenny exchanged amused glances. "Alright, fine," Amy relented, laughter in her voice. "Bring on our designated babysitter."

Jenny said, "We can't let these clothes wash themselves!"

As Amy headed to her cabin, she turned back to Jake. "Tell Bolo to meet us at the cabin. We'll grab some brushes and soap to hand wash these things, okay?"

Jake agreed with a nod and headed down to the harbor. Just as he reached the dock, he crossed paths with Bolo, making his way up the hill.

"Bolo, there you are." Jake motioned for Bolo to join him away from the cabins. He looked at his friend with a serious expression. "I need you to take Amy and Jenny to the lagoon for their washing. Make sure they don't run into any trouble, alright?"

Bolo's puzzled expression showed his confusion. "Mister Jake, what's botherin' you? The trail's clear enough, and these young ladies know how to handle themselves. Why are you concerned?"

Jake's somber demeanor matched his voice. "It's not that I doubt them. It's just... I worry that whatever's out there might come closer. I need you to make sure they stay safe."

Understanding dawned on Bolo's face. "Ah, I see what you mean. You're afraid that the creature might be lurking around. Don't worry. I'll keep an eye on them."

A sense of understanding passed between the two, and Jake gestured for Bolo to join the girls. "Exactly. Just take them to the lagoon, supervise their washing, and return them immediately. Can you do that?"

Bolo's affirmative nod was accompanied by a resolute expression. "I got it, Mister Jake. They'll be safe with me." With that, Bolo headed toward the girls' cabins while Jake watched, knowing he had entrusted their safety to a steadfast friend.

The girls emerged from their cabins, and Jake couldn't help but feel relief and concern as he saw them join Bolo on the path down to the lagoon. The task seemed simple—doing laundry in a freshwater lagoon—but despite their strange circumstances, even the most mundane activities carried an air of uncertainty.

CHAPTER 7
His Hunger Returns with a Vengeance

He had been gliding through the crystalline waters around the island's tip for what felt like an eternity, his insatiable desire for sustenance burning anew. The scent of his prey lingered in the currents, and he moved with calculated caution, keeping close to the ocean floor to avoid alerting it. His primal instincts guided him gradually through the narrow strait that separated the island's tip from the sea lion domain—a dependable food source to quench his relentless hunger.

His massive form moved in a deliberate, erratic pattern, his senses honed to detect any hint of his impending meal. The underwater terrain shifted as he curved around the island's western edge and continued south. The seabed on his left side began to rise, forcing him to alter his course and turn right, back toward deeper waters.

Having traveled a quarter mile from the shallows, his heightened senses detected the rhythmic motions and distant echoes of two surface-dwelling entities that resonated with his primitive memory as the same type of "food" he had encountered earlier.

His substantial size made swift course reversals challenging, but driven by hunger, he dove and twisted, executing a powerful, arching maneuver that realigned him with his original path in reverse.

His instincts fully engaged. He locked onto the presence of his two potential meals and gradually accelerated. His massive jaws parted slightly in anticipation of the forthcoming feast, a respite to his gnawing appetite.

Meanwhile, two imposing sea lion males—leaders of their dwindling herd—had ventured from the safety of their rocky refuge in search of sustenance. Their pack had suffered an inexplicable attack that had claimed many members, and the usual food sources had become scarce.

After hours of swimming and hunting, fatigue was setting in. A deep-seated instinct told them it was time to retreat to the rocky rim of the nearby lagoon for rest before continuing their quest for sustenance.

Approximately two hundred yards from shore, the elder sea lion sensed an abrupt disturbance in the deeper water on his seaward side. A sudden rush of fear gripped him, and he swiveled towards the coast, his powerful flippers propelling him forward as he emitted a warning roar to his younger counterpart.

However, the younger sea lion had descended in pursuit of a mackerel, oblivious to his companion's alarm. The vibrant marine life he'd been pursuing seemed to vanish instantly, and as his gaze roved the depths, he was greeted by a looming, shadowy silhouette growing more significant with every heartbeat.

Though inexperienced in open water survival, the young bull's instincts ignited a primal panic. He turned towards the safety of the rocky outcropping roughly two hundred yards away. Every muscle strained as he pushed himself to evade the approaching menace. Bursting through the surface, he saw his elder companion also racing towards the haven of rocks.

In a desperate attempt to call out, the young sea lion's world exploded into chaos. A sharp, searing pain struck his neck, and his life force dimmed as he ceased to resist. His world went dim, then dark.

Closing the distance with swiftness, the predator lunged and captured the smaller creature in its monstrous jaws. Though his hunger persisted, the small meal hardly satisfied his insatiable appetite. He consumed it almost whole, then surged onward in pursuit of the other prey before it could reach safety.

The elder bull sea lion comprehended the urgency of his predicament. With all his strength, he propelled himself forward, flippers and tail working in unison. The approaching shore loomed just yards away, and he strained to maintain his lead.

The massive sea creature surged, breaking the surface in a majestic display. His dorsal fin pierced the air, and the water pushed ahead by his snout formed a towering wave that dwarfed the usual breakers. Closing in on his quarry, he prepared to seize his meal, but something was amiss. The ocean bottom scraped against his side, and a sense of imbalance overcame him.

Struggling to correct his trajectory, the predator found himself grounded on the shallow seabed, his momentum too great to halt. Panic surged as he thrashed to dislodge himself, finally pushing his bulk back into deeper waters with his powerful tail and fins. He wasted no time fleeing the treacherous shallows, seeking refuge in the safety of the depths to resume his endless hunt for sustenance.

CHAPTER 8

A Massive Sea Lion Soars Above the Lagoon

Amy and Jenny followed Bolo along the serpentine path that meandered from the heart of the main compound, delving through the dense foliage. After a quarter mile of traversing the verdant terrain, they finally emerged at the edge of a glistening freshwater stream, which melded with the tranquil expanse of the lagoon.

Their eyes were treated to the spectacle of the rock bridge, an architectural marvel that arched over the channel connecting the lagoon to the open sea, standing about 150 yards to their left.

With a subtle gesture, Bolo directed their course along the lagoon's edge, guiding them toward the land bridge. Crossing the bridge, they were greeted by a small landing bordered by smoothed boulders—a perfect spot for their laundry endeavor.

As they approached the land bridge, a breathtaking sight halted them in their tracks. A colossal sea lion catapulted over the lagoon's rim, rolling uncontrollably before resting just a few feet from the bay's crystalline waters. The spectacle was followed by a surge of water and debris as an enormous wave crashed over the rim.

After regaining their composure, Bolo motioned for the girls to continue. Crossing the land bridge carefully, they positioned themselves on a vantage point on the rock wall that overlooked the lagoon and the ocean. They gazed at the serene ocean waters, searching for clues explaining the strange events they had just witnessed.

Despite their scrutiny, the calm ocean revealed nothing about the peculiar behavior of the sea lion or the enigmatic wave it had triggered.

The distressed sea lion caught Amy's attention as it lay near where it had stopped after tumbling. Its agitation or trauma was palpable, sparking her curiosity.

On the other hand, Jenny remained focused on the ocean, her mind racing to comprehend the mystery unfolding before them. Amy nudged her, prompting her to share her thoughts. "What do you think, Jenny?"

Jenny mulled over the question, her gaze shifting between Bolo and Amy. "Honestly, I have no idea. That sea lion might just be one lucky creature." She pointed toward the sea lion, now resting on a sun-drenched boulder.

Bolo's gaze lingered on the ocean before he turned to the two young women. "Well, it's time to get on with your washing," he said somberly. He mustered a thin smile and began leading them down the path toward the landing. "Mister Jake might start getting worried if we take too long."

As Amy and Jenny set about washing clothes, Bolo wandered along the lagoon's edge, lost in his thoughts. Despite his seemingly casual demeanor, he maintained a discreet watch over the girls, acutely aware of the potential dangers lurking beyond the rocky barrier.

Amid the rhythmic scrubbing sounds, Amy gazed into the distance, her cotton blouse twisting beneath her fingers. In an absentminded tone, she posed a question to Jenny, seemingly lost in her contemplation. "What do you make of Jake? Is he genuine, or does his ambition sometimes cloud his judgment?"

Amy's thoughts spilled out, Jenny joining in the musing. "Yeah, he's quite a puzzle. Kind and caring on one hand, but then there are moments when he seems driven by self-interest." Jenny's gaze shifted to meet Amy's. "What's your take on him?"

Caught off guard, Amy attempted to downplay her emotions. "Oh, come on! He's just a good friend, someone we can trust." Amy met Jenny's knowing smile, her inner turmoil evident.

"You've got it bad for him, don't you?" Jenny teased, her eyes dancing with mischief.

Amy chuckled, feigning annoyance. "You're incorrigible, Jenny!" She playfully swatted Jenny with a wet cloth.

Jenny retaliated with a well-aimed splash of water. Laughter erupted between them, the playful exchange continuing until they settled back into their tasks. As the moments slipped by, each woman drifted into her own reverie, their shared laughter gradually fading.

Unknown to them, Bolo had been observing their antics from a concealed vantage point, an approving smile gracing his face.

After about an hour, they completed their washing and packed the damp clothes back into the baskets for the journey back to their cabins. Now laden with wet clothing, the baskets made their trek uphill more arduous. The trio was so engrossed in their ascent that they nearly missed an imposing shape—a towering dorsal fin gliding past the land bridge on the other side of the rim.

Arriving at the landing beneath the bridge, they cast a final glance at the ocean before ascending the main path to the compound, finding nothing unusual in sight.

The main compound came into view, and they spotted Jake standing atop a hillock, his gaze sweeping across the harbor and the trail leading from the lagoon.

"Worried about us, Jake?" Amy called out, her voice carrying fatigue from the climb but punctuated by a warm smile. Bolo and Jenny joined in the laughter.

Jake responded with mock innocence. "Me? Nah, I just like the view from up here. Excellent lookout point," he quipped, fully aware that his friends were unconvinced.

As the late afternoon sun descended, casting a warm glow across the landscape, Jake and Bolo settled into chairs on the porch, savoring the tranquility. However, their relaxation was interrupted by the radio's sudden crackling to life.

"Hello! Scoggins here! You there, Jake?" Amos Scoggins' distinctive voice emerged from the static.

Jake couldn't suppress a grin, knowing Amos rarely followed proper radio protocol. He set his beer aside and went to the radio set, pressing the microphone switch to reply. "This is Jake, Amos. What's up? Over!"

Amos' response came, laced with humor. "Hell, Jake! Over where?" He chuckled before getting to the point. "Listen, Jake. Toombs called from Buenos Aires and said they're coming in tonight and want to head out at first light tomorrow. Okay?"

As Jake responded, he detected a hint of skepticism in Amos' voice. "For sure, Amos. Bring 'em on out!" Jake agreed, then seized the moment to present his own proposal. "Hey, Amos, I've got a favor to ask. Could you stay a couple of extra days? We need you to fly over these waters and search for a... um... wreck that might be uncovered by the current. Sound good?"

There was a pause before Amos replied, his voice slightly wary. "A wreck, huh?" Amos sounded intrigued yet cautious. "Well, I'm not tied up with anything right now. I plan to stay a day or two. But, Jake, you better keep my fuel in check. And I'm gonna need $300 per day, got it?"

Jake laughed, not surprised by Amos' shrewd negotiation. "Deal, you old bandit! It's highway robbery, but you've got it. Bring them here!"

Amos chuckled. "Will do, Jake. See you tomorrow! Scoggins out!"

As Jake hung up the radio, he was struck by a chilling sensation that seemed to herald the arrival of the looming unknown terror that had consumed his thoughts.

CHAPTER 9
Jake Focuses on Amy's Words

Jake shook off the unsettling feeling of foreboding that had gripped him, throwing himself into the preparations for dinner. He deftly maneuvered around the kitchen, frying chicken and boiling potatoes, the clatter of utensils and sizzling in the skillet filling the air.

As the aroma of the cooking food wafted through the air, Amy made her way into the kitchen, drawn by the enticing scents. She settled herself at the small table, propping her chin up on her clasped hands, her eyes following Jake's movements with curiosity and contentment.

Pausing in his cooking, Jake glanced up and met Amy's gaze, a playful smile tugging at the corners of his mouth. "Supervising my culinary skills, huh?" he teased with a hint of amusement in his tone.

Amy chuckled softly and shook her head. "Not really. I was just getting antsy waiting in my cabin, so I thought I'd keep you company. Hope you don't mind."

"Of course not, Amy," Jake responded warmly, his focus on her unwavering. "Where's Jenny?" he inquired, secretly hoping she wouldn't join them just yet.

He was gradually becoming more attached to Amy, their age difference fading into insignificance. She stirred something within him that he hadn't felt in years, and he relished the sensation.

"She's taking a nap before dinner," Amy informed him. "I guess the stress has hit her pretty hard."

Nodding in agreement, Jake continued to attend to the cooking. He wiped his hands on a kitchen towel before turning to face Amy, curiosity evident in his eyes. "Tell me, Amy," he began the sizzle of the frying chicken as a backdrop to their conversation. "With all that's happened, the fear of the unknown...why haven't you insisted on leaving and returning to the mainland immediately?"

Amy considered his question, her gaze distant momentarily before refocusing on Jake. "I suppose I've always had a streak of adventure in me. I want to know what's behind every closed door or beneath the surface, especially in the sea," she mused, a philosophical undertone to her words. "Do you understand?"

Jake listened intently to her words. The cooking was momentarily forgotten as he realized how much he resonated with her perspective on life. Amy's outlook mirrored his own, and he felt a deeper connection to her than he had anticipated.

Amused by Jake's absentmindedness, Amy laughed lightly and playfully snapped her fingers in front of his gaze. "Jake! Earth to Jake! Don't burn the chicken," she teased.

Startled, Jake blinked and snapped back to the present, his cheeks flushing slightly. "Oh, sorry. Guess I got lost in thought," he admitted, a sheepish smile tugging at his lips as he returned to the stove.

Chuckling, Amy couldn't help but find his embarrassment endearing. "I thought I'd have to take over dinner for a moment."

Grinning, Jake turned from the stove, his first genuine smile of the day lighting up his face. "I appreciate the offer, but I think I've got it under control. By the way, you might want to let Jenny know her favorite chicken is almost ready."

"Sure thing, Chef Jake," Amy saluted playfully as she headed towards the porch. However, her attention was caught by Jenny's approach up the path toward the main house.

"Hey, great timing, Jenny!" Amy called out. "Jake's almost done with your beloved chicken. You must be starving!"

"It's strange, but I'm actually famished," Jenny replied as she joined Amy, a hint of her usual cheerfulness returning to her expression.

"Smellin' the chicken on the table, I reckon?" Bolo's voice interrupted from the distance as he walked up the hill. "Better hurry or I might just eat it all!"

Laughter filled the air as Bolo approached, his lighthearted remark setting the tone for the upcoming dinner. The group gathered around the table, the meal proceeding smoothly as they chatted and enjoyed each other's company.

After dinner, the conversation shifted toward the impending arrival of Toombs the next day. The specter of their recent experiences and the uncertain future loomed over them, but there was also a sense of anticipation and camaraderie as they prepared to confront the unknown together.

FINALLY, AS JAKE AND Amy completed the meticulous task of washing and drying each dish, their movements synchronized like a well-practiced dance. The sound of water droplets cascading into the sink formed a delicate melody that harmonized with their quiet conversation.

With the dishes now immaculate and glistening, Bolo's deep voice resonated like distant thunder. "Jake," he began, his tone carrying a mixture of purpose and responsibility, "I'm going to head down to the fuel station. Gotta make sure it's primed and ready for Amos' plane tomorrow."

Jenny's voice, unusually spirited, broke the rhythm of their activity. "Hold up, Bolo!" she chimed in, her words carrying a newfound energy. "Mind if I tag along?"

Bolo's massive frame loomed near the screen door, and his hearty laugh rumbled through the room. "'Course, Missy," he boomed, his smile as wide as his shoulders. With a gentle sweep of his arm, he held the door open for Jenny, her figure radiant against the evening's dim light. "Ol' Bolo always likes the company," he added warmly, and the duo set off into the velvety darkness beyond.

As Bolo and Jenny vanished into the night, their camaraderie forming a beacon of connection, Amy and Jake remained, bathed in the soft glow of the kitchen's warm lights. The kitchen felt cozier than ever, a refuge from the world outside.

With a sense of accomplishment, they stowed away the final dish and condiment, Amy sinking into one of the overstuffed side chairs. The silence was broken only by the gentle clinking of the dishes and the soft rustle of fabric as Jake reached into the pantry.

Jake's voice cut through the quiet as he produced a tin, his tone soft and inviting. "Coffee?" he inquired, his eyes meeting Amy's with a warm smile.

Amy's response was accompanied by a soft smile of her own. "Please," she accepted graciously, her words punctuated by a gentle flutter of her lashes. "Oh, with cream, no sugar," she added, her preferences offered with a sweet hint of vulnerability.

As Jake prepared the coffee, Amy's eyes followed his movements, quietly observant. The minutes ticked by, their shared silence filling the space with a comforting presence. Finally, Amy ventured a question that hung like a fragile thread in the air, her tone gentle. "Jake, tell me if I'm too nosy, but what's your story?"

The atmosphere shifted, Jake's gaze distant as if traversing the corridors of memory. The coffee pot percolated in the background, a subdued rhythm to their conversation. Amy watched him with a blend of curiosity and empathy, her fingers tracing invisible patterns on the chair's armrest.

Jake's gaze met Amy's, his eyes holding a mixture of reflection and trepidation. The coffee was ready, and he set out the shortbread, cream, and sugar, creating a small tableau between them. Their mugs were filled with the fragrant brew, and he sat across from Amy, his features etched with a thoughtful solemnity.

"Well, let's see," Jake began, his words tinged with a wistful air as he leaned back in his chair, gazing past Amy as if retracing the lines of his past. "After I graduated from Texas A&M, I parlayed a degree in Marine Biology into a Masters degree before taking my commission in the Navy." He paused, the weight of memories hanging heavy in the air.

Amy's eyes remained fixed on Jake, her full attention locked onto his narrative. "And the SEALS?" she interjected gently, a glimmer of curiosity shining in her hazel eyes.

A wry smile curled on Jake's lips, his expression a blend of reminiscence and self-deprecation. "Yeah, the SEALs," he acknowledged with a nod, his eyes searching Amy's for understanding. "We were young, and peer pressure can be quite the motivator." He chuckled softly as if sharing an inside joke with himself.

With the coffee now a tangible presence between them, their conversation ebbed and flowed, punctuated by sips and shared understanding. The weight of Jake's history was palpable, his voice carrying the undertones of life experiences that had shaped him.

Amy's gaze held steadfast, her empathy like a beacon as she listened intently to Jake's tale. She nodded in understanding as he recounted the journey that had brought him to this remote island, nodding as if trying to catch the fleeting wisps of his emotions.

As Jake continued, his voice carried a somber weight, the cadence of his words woven with the threads of pain and regret.

"Many times, I laid awake at nights," he confessed, his voice softening as if speaking to himself. "I cursed God for choosing me to have the...uh...gift...of being able to kill, calmly and coolly, while mentally divorcing myself from the whole act." He chuckled, a touch of bitterness in the sound. "Actually, when you think about it, He indeed bestowed a curse on me at that time that haunts me today! What a gift, right?"

Amy's expression held a mixture of compassion and concern, her hand reaching out to rest gently on Jake's. Her touch was tender, a silent reassurance that she was here to listen, to share in his burdens.

As Jake's tale progressed, his words carrying the weight of friendship, competition, and tragedy, Amy's heart went out to him. She offered words of solace, her voice warm and sincere. "Jake, you can't blame yourself for what happened to your friends. They were adults who made their own choices."

Jake's eyes met Amy's, their connection intensifying as he absorbed her words. He paused as if caught between his past and the present, then continued his story, his voice tinged with resignation and resilience.

The room's gentle illumination played on their faces as their conversation flowed, creating a cocoon of shared understanding. Amid the poignant stories and revelations, their connection deepened, and their unspoken bond grew more assertive.

With their stories shared, Amy stood, her legs feeling slightly numb from sitting for so long. She walked around the porch to alleviate the stiffness, her mind still engrossed in Jake's narrative. Unbeknownst to them both, a gray fin glided across the harbor's entrance, a silent observer of their conversation.

Returning to Jake's side, her eyes met his with a renewed sense of connection. "Jake," she said softly, her voice holding a blend of compassion and conviction, "your journey has led you here. You're not defined by your past but by the choices you make today."

Jake's gaze met hers, and his grip on her hand tightened. He looked at her with a mix of gratitude and wonder, the weight of his history seeming to lessen, if only for a moment. "Thank you, Amy," he murmured, his voice sincere and touching. "It means more than you know."

Their eyes locked, their connection profound and unspoken. Their stories intertwined as the night stretched on, leaving behind the remnants of their past and the promise of an uncertain yet hopeful future.

"Old Joe Spangle, their long-time attorney, asked me to stop by his office a few days later." The invitation arrived in a calligraphy-embossed envelope, summoning me to the quiet chambers of Old Joe Spangle, the seasoned attorney who had known the family for decades.

Jake's expression transformed from a veneer of composure to a haunting bitterness as he delved further into his narrative. His eyes clouded, and his features contorted, revealing the pain in his heart. "I was almost at the lowest point of my life by this time," he confessed, his voice carrying the weight of his memories. The tavern air seemed to thicken with his somber confession. "I drank heavily every night and hadn't shaved or bathed since the service." His voice faltered, choked by the emotions he was reliving.

"My whole character seemed to have changed," he continued, his eyes distant as he recounted the descent. "I didn't really want to talk to, or even see, anybody." Jake's gaze met the swirling depths of his coffee cup as he took another drink. "So, I didn't leave Charlie's little house for several more days except to get more Scotch." The liquid seemed to mirror his isolation, swirling and dark.

Finally, after what felt like an eternity, a week-and-a-half after the funeral, a knock as persistent as an insistent heartbeat echoed through the silence that had settled over the cottage. "There was a persistent knock on the door," he recounted, his words weighted with anticipation, "and two of Johno's crew asked if I'd seen Johno." The memory seemed to trigger an internal jolt within Jake, snapping him back to reality. The tavern's hum felt intrusive against the gravity of his recollection.

"It was then that I realized that Johno hadn't been heard from since 'that night,'" he revealed, his voice a mix of concern and anger. The details of the disappearance became a stark revelation, a shadow creeping into the corners of his consciousness. "Sure, I guess that somewhere, in the back of my mind, I'd kind of wondered why he hadn't at least shown up for the folk's memorial services, but I had just figured that he had gone on one of his junkets and was laid up with one of his women somewhere."

His fingers drummed gently on the rim of his coffee mug, the tension in the room palpable. "However, now, I was experiencing a mixture of worry and anger," Jake admitted, the turmoil reflected in his chest's rapid rise and fall. "Johno's boat, 'The Red Spirit,' was gone from the docks and had been since that night." The mere mention of the vessel seemed to awaken a dormant unease.

Jake's fingers tightened around the mug, his knuckles whitening as he recounted the past. "This isn't unusual since Johno often took it out on some of his little trips, but he'd never been gone this long before." He paused, the silence in the room echoing his internal turmoil.

His fingers released their grip on the mug, and it clinked against the table as he took a deep breath. "I needed a moment, Amy," he confessed, his voice quivering as if standing on the precipice of a painful truth. "Just bear with me." His gaze met Amy's, searching for understanding before continuing.

The emotions that had been bottled up within him surged forth like a torrent. "The Coast Guard from Puerto Rico and St.

Thomas sent investigating teams over to the island," he recounted, "to check out the fire a couple of weeks afterward, which was routine in cases like this, where deaths result." His voice conveyed resentment toward the bureaucratic procedures that had invaded his life.

"In the meantime, I had managed to pull myself together enough to get by Joe Spangle's office," he divulged, his words revealing a mix of vulnerability and determination. "He informed me that Charlie and Maggie Mae had re-written their wills recently, and all they owned went to me." The shock of the revelation resonated in his words. "To tell you the truth, this was a major shock." His eyes flickered with a mixture of disbelief and gratitude.

The memory of that pivotal meeting lingered in his expression. "Anyway, Joe told me that the folks had come to view me as the son they'd never had," Jake recounted, his voice tinged with warmth as he spoke of the unlikely bond that had formed. "I asked him about Johno, of course, and Joe was a bit evasive." The tension in the room seemed to intensify as if the weight of the unsaid words was bearing down on them both. "He'd only tell me that they had written Johno out of the will for personal reasons they chose not to go into."

Jake's hands clenched into fists, the memory of that conversation still vivid. "When I asked if Johno knew about this, Joe only nodded yes, but his expression said that there was a lot of unpleasantness involved." The undercurrent of tension was a palpable force in the room as if the weight of secrets was straining against the veneer of civility.

He took another swallow of coffee as if the liquid could wash away the lingering bitterness. But the cup soon became a projectile, hurled across the room with violence that shattered the suffocating atmosphere. Amy's startled yelp added to the raw emotions swirling around the room.

"Oh! I'm sorry, Amy! Are you okay?" Jake's sudden shift from turmoil to concern was as disorienting as the shattered mug. He was on his feet instantly, his large hands enveloping Amy's arms in a gesture of genuine worry.

"Of course, I'm all right, Jake," Amy reassured him, her voice gentle and understanding. She offered a smile to ease the tension that had gripped the room. Her touch, a delicate pat on Jake's hand, spoke of her growing rapport with him. "Go ahead... that is if you want to, and finish, okay?" Her words were an unspoken promise of her willingness to listen and witness to his pain.

"Okay, Amy; there's not much left to tell, though." The space between them seemed to hold a newfound connection, a bridge between their emotions. Jake's movements were more deliberate as he resumed his place near the stove, pouring another cup of coffee as if the warmth could soothe his restless heart.

"The Coast Guard officer," Jake continued, his voice carrying a mix of determination and reminiscence, "didn't mean to say anything, but the Constable was an old friend of Charlie's and Maggie Mae's, and he just nodded resignedly at the officer." The complexities of the past were etched into the lines of Jake's face, shaping his expressions as he spoke. "The Constable, Fred Kenyon, I believe his name was, asked to come in and motioned for me to sit across from him in the old sitting room."

Their shared moment of vulnerability was a testament to the bond between them. "He looked down at the old rug and slowly shook his head from side to side," Jake recounted, his voice reflecting the Constable's somber demeanor. "Then he looked up at me and told me the fire was no accident." The words hung in the air like a heavy fog, thickening the silence between them.

"Amy, I just refused to believe it!" Jake's voice carried a mix of disbelief and defiance. "Not even a little weasel like Johno Tesoro would go this far!" The force of his conviction seemed to fill the room, a response to the weight of the accusations that had been hurled at his friend.

"The Constable, of course, told me that he understood my disbelief," Jake revealed, his words a reflection of the lingering shock, "but if I did hear from, or about, Johno, please let the appropriate officials know, and, as an afterthought, when leaving, he asked me to promise not to take things into my own hands!" The heaviness of the situation seemed to press down on them, a burden that Jake had carried alone for so long.

"Honestly, Amy, I was so overwhelmed with the shock and disbelief at the time," Jake admitted, his voice tinged with vulnerability, "along with all the other emotions of the past several days, that I hadn't even begun to think, seriously, about going after Johno." The admission carried a mix of regret and acceptance, as if he was coming to terms with his choices in the turmoil of that time.

"But as the days wore on," Jake continued, his voice steadier now, "I began to realize that my life had profoundly changed with all that had occurred." The journey through his memories seemed to have a cathartic effect as if recounting the past had released some of its grip on him.

"I knew that I couldn't even run the business effectively anymore," Jake revealed, his voice carrying a mix of resignation and determination. "The pain was just too great, and my heart wasn't in it." The weight of his realization seemed to hang between them, a turning point in his life that had ultimately led him to where he was now.

"I decided, then, to sell everything," Jake recounted, his voice carrying a mix of resolve and nostalgia, "everything, that is, except the 'Maggie Mae,' the folks' boat that I had re-fitted and upgraded to make it entirely seaworthy and comfortable for one person on a long voyage!" His gaze turned towards the vessel in the harbor, the connection to his past and the anchor of his present.

Amy's gaze followed his gesture, resting on the boat with a newfound understanding. "Anyway, after I had sold the business and the real estate to a buyer from Miami," Jake continued, "which, luckily, only took a few weeks, I consolidated this new money with what my previous investments had grown to, and I found that I was a pretty wealthy man." The admission was accompanied by a wistful smile, a glimpse into a life that had taken unexpected turns.

"But, ya know, I swear I'd give it all away just to have those sweet old people back again!" The sentiment hung in the air, an ache that transcended material wealth.

The room seemed to grow still as Jake's memories wove through time. "A week or so after I met with the lawyer," he resumed, his voice carrying a mix of reflection and resolution, "I was trying to understand Charlie's fishery contracts and the inventory of the old couple's holdings, when there came a knock on the door." The sound seemed to reverberate within the room, a reminder of the past that had refused to fade away.

Jake's hand reached for the coffee pot, a familiar gesture that seemed to ground him. "It was a Coast Guard officer with the local Constable," he recounted, his voice carrying a mixture of anticipation and dread. "I asked them what was on their minds, and they looked at each other before one asked me if I had heard from Johno or, possibly, knew of his whereabouts." The question seemed to hang in the air, a shadow cast over the room.

"I told them that I didn't know where to begin looking for him... and, by the way, why did they want to know," Jake recounted, his voice carrying a tone of curiosity and skepticism. The weight of the unknown seemed to press down on him, a reminder of the mysteries that had haunted his life.

"The Coast Guard officer didn't mean to say anything," he continued, "but the Constable was an old friend of Charlie's and Maggie Mae's, and he just nodded resignedly at the officer, who returned the nod, turned, and walked away." The weight of the unspoken words lingered between them, a testament to the bonds that had shaped their lives.

"The Constable, Fred Kenyon, I believe his name was, asked to come in and motioned for me to sit across from him in the old sitting room," Jake recounted, his voice carrying a mix of reverence and recollection. The intimacy of that moment seemed to linger in his words, an echo of the past that had refused to be forgotten.

"He looked down at the old rug and slowly shook his head from side to side," Jake revealed, his voice carrying the weight of the Constable's solemnity. "Then he looked up at me and told me the fire was no accident." The words sent a shiver down Jake's spine. A chill mirrored the grave revelation.

"One of the Coast Guard pathologists had lifted a latent fingerprint from a piece of broken rum bottle in the forward bilge of my boat... along with traces of gasoline on the label," Jake recounted, his voice carrying a mixture of shock and indignation. The image of the evidence seemed to linger before them, an echo of a crime that had taken place on the periphery of their understanding.

"Amy," Jake's voice trembled as he spoke, "I guess that deep down inside, I had wondered about the coincidence of Johno's disappearance following the fire, but, to tell the truth, at the time, I was more relieved that he didn't show up." The admission was accompanied by guilt and relief, a reminder of the complex emotions that swirled within him.

"It gave me personal time to face my grief... alone!" The words hung in the air, a confession of vulnerability that Jake had held within him for far too long. The room seemed to hold its breath as he bared his soul, his emotions laid bare for Amy to witness.

"Well, the old Constable seemed to measure my reaction as he went on," Jake continued, his voice carrying the weight of the past. "He told me of finding some of my hair embedded in a fish club tossed into a corner of the main deck near where I had been knocked out." The investigation details unfolded before them, each piece of evidence etching into Jake's memory.

"Also, he said that some orange threads from a garment, like one of the shirts Johno wore all the time, were found in one of the hatch jams under the wheelhouse." Jake's words were punctuated by a heavy sigh, the weight of suspicion settling heavily upon his friend.

"All-in-all, he said that, sadly, it looked as if Johno was a prime suspect in the fire and murder of the old couple." The accusation hung in the air, a shadow that had long reached their lives.

"Amy, I just refused to believe it!" Jake's voice trembled with anger and disbelief, bubbling to the surface. "Not even a little weasel like Johno Tesoro would go this far!" The vehemence of his defense seemed to resonate through the room, a testament to his loyalty to his friend.

"The Constable, of course, told me that he understood my disbelief," Jake's voice carried a combination of resignation and defiance, "but, if I did hear from, or about, Johno, please let the appropriate officials know, and, as an afterthought, when leaving, he asked me to promise not to take things into my own hands!" The heaviness of the request seemed to weigh heavily on him, a reminder of the responsibilities he had been burdened with.

"Honestly, Amy, I was so overwhelmed with the shock and disbelief at the time," Jake admitted, his voice carrying a mix of vulnerability and exhaustion, "along with all the other emotions of the past several days, that I hadn't even begun to think, seriously, about going after Johno." The weight of his admission hung between them, a confession of the limitations of his own emotional capacity.

"But as the days wore on," Jake's voice steadied, a renewed sense of determination evident, "I began to realize that my life had profoundly changed with all that had occurred." The realization seemed to lift a weight from his shoulders, a recognition of the shifting currents that had shaped his path.

"I knew that I couldn't even run the business effectively anymore," Jake revealed, his voice resonant with a mix of acceptance and resignation. "The pain was just too great, and my heart wasn't in it." The admission carried a note of sadness, reflecting the changes that had transformed his purpose.

"I decided, then, to sell everything," Jake's voice carried a mixture of contemplation and nostalgia, "everything, that is, except the 'Maggie Mae,' the folks' boat that I had re-fitted and upgraded to make it entirely seaworthy and comfortable for one person on a long voyage!" His gaze shifted towards the boat, a tangible link to his past.

"Anyway, after I had sold the business and the real estate to a buyer from Miami," Jake continued, "which, luckily, only took a few weeks, I consolidated this new money with what my previous investments had grown to, and I found that I was a pretty wealthy man." The admission was accompanied by a note of gratitude, a reflection on the twists of fate that had led him to this point.

"But, ya know, I swear I'd give it all away just to have those sweet old people back again!" The words hung in the air, heavy with the weight of his longing.

Jake paused, his gaze distant as he navigated the labyrinth of his memories. "A week or so after I met with the lawyer," he began again, his voice carrying a mix of contemplation and determination, "I was trying to understand Charlie's fishery contracts and the inventory of the old couple's holdings when there came a knock on the door." The sound seemed to echo in the room, a harbinger of the changes unfolding.

"It was a Coast Guard officer with the local Constable," Jake recounted, his voice carrying a mixture of curiosity and apprehension. "I asked them what was on their minds, and they looked at each other before one asked me if I had heard from Johno or, possibly, knew of his whereabouts." The question seemed to hang in the air, a reminder of the mysteries that had enveloped their lives.

"I told them that I didn't know where to begin looking for him... and, by the way, why did they want to know," Jake recounted, his voice carrying a mix of skepticism and concern. The weight of the unknown seemed to press upon him, a reminder of the darkness surrounding his friend's disappearance.

"The Coast Guard officer didn't mean to say anything," Jake continued, "but the Constable was an old friend of Charlie's and Maggie Mae's, and he just nodded resignedly at the officer, who returned the nod, turned, and walked away." The unspoken tension between the two officials seemed to linger in the air, echoing the complicated relationships that had shaped their world.

"The Constable, Fred Kenyon, I believe his name was, asked to come in and motioned for me to sit across from him in the old sitting room," Jake recounted, his voice carrying a mix of respect and nostalgia. The moment's intimacy seemed to come alive in his words, a snapshot of a time long past.

"He looked down at the old rug and slowly shook his head from side to side," Jake revealed, his voice carrying the weight of the Constable's grave realization. "Then he looked up at me and told me the fire was no accident." The declaration hung like a storm cloud, casting a shadow over their understanding of the events.

"One of the Coast Guard pathologists had lifted a latent fingerprint from a piece of broken rum bottle in the forward bilge of my boat... along with traces of gasoline on the label," Jake recounted, his voice carrying a mix of shock and disbelief. The evidence seemed to materialize before them, a testament to the reality of the situation.

"Amy," Jake's voice trembled, "I guess that deep down inside, I had wondered about the coincidence of Johno's disappearance following the fire, but, to tell the truth, at the time, I was more relieved that he didn't show up." The admission carried a mix of guilt and uncertainty, reflecting the complex emotions that had consumed him.

"It gave me personal time to face my grief... alone!" The words lingered in the air, heavy with the weight of his emotions. Jake's vulnerability seemed to radiate from him, an unguarded revelation of his inner turmoil.

"Well, the old Constable seemed to measure my reaction as he went on," Jake continued, his voice carrying a mix of recollection and introspection. "He told me of finding some of my hair embedded in a fish club tossed into a corner of the main deck near where I had been knocked out." The details of the investigation unfolded, each piece of evidence etching itself into Jake's memory.

"Also, he said that some orange threads from a garment, like one of the shirts Johno wore all the time, were found in one of the hatch jams under the wheelhouse." The weight of the suspicion seemed to settle heavily upon Jake, a reminder of the darkness that had crept into their lives.

"All-in-all, he said that, sadly, it looked as if Johno was a prime suspect in the fire and murder of the old couple." The accusation hung in the air, a shadow that had cast its pall over their world.

"Amy, I just refused to believe it!" Jake's voice wavered, a mixture of anger and disbelief. "Not even a little weasel like Johno Tesoro would go this far!" The force of his defense seemed to reverberate through the room, a testament to his loyalty to his friend.

"The Constable, of course, told me that he understood my disbelief," Jake revealed, his voice carrying a mixture of resignation and defiance, "but if I did hear from, or about, Johno, please let the appropriate officials know. And, as an afterthought, when leaving, he asked me to promise not to take things into my own hands!" The weight of the request seemed to bear down on him, a reminder of the responsibilities he had been given.

"Honestly, Amy, I was so overwhelmed with the shock and disbelief at the time," Jake admitted, his voice carrying a mix of vulnerability and exhaustion, "along with all the other emotions of the past several days, that I hadn't even begun to think, seriously, about going after Johno." The weight of his admission hung between them, a confession of the limitations of his own emotional capacity.

"But as the days wore on," Jake's voice steadied, a renewed sense of determination evident, "I began to realize that my life had profoundly changed with all that had occurred." The realization seemed to lift a weight from his shoulders, a recognition of the shifting currents that had shaped his path.

"I knew I couldn't even run the business effectively anymore," Jake revealed. "The pain was just too great, and my heart wasn't in it." The admission carried a note of sadness, reflecting the changes that had transformed his purpose.

"I decided, then, to sell everything," Jake's voice carried a mixture of contemplation and nostalgia, "everything, that is, except the 'Maggie Mae,' the folks' boat that I had re-fitted and upgraded to make it entirely seaworthy and comfortable for one person on a long voyage!" His gaze shifted towards the boat, a tangible link to his past.

"Anyway, after I had sold the business and the real estate to a buyer from Miami," Jake continued, "which, luckily, only took a few weeks, I consolidated this new money with what my previous investments had grown to, and I found that I was a pretty wealthy man." The admission was accompanied by a note of gratitude, a reflection on the twists of fate that had led him to this point.

"But, ya know, I swear I'd give it all away just to have those sweet old people back again!" The words hung in the air, heavy with the weight of his longing.

Jake paused, his gaze distant as he navigated the labyrinth of his memories. "A week or so after I met with the lawyer," he began again, his voice determined, "I was trying to understand Charlie's fishery contracts and the inventory of the old couple's holdings when there came a knock on the door." The sound seemed to echo in the room, a harbinger of the changes about to unfold.

"It was a Coast Guard officer with the local Constable," Jake recounted, his voice carrying a mixture of curiosity and apprehension. "I asked them what was on their minds, and they looked at each other before one asked me if I had heard from Johno or, possibly, knew of his whereabouts." The question seemed to hang in the air, a reminder of the mysteries that had enveloped their lives.

"I told them that I didn't know where to begin looking for him... and, by the way, why did they want to know," Jake recounted, his voice carrying a mix of skepticism and concern. The weight of the unknown seemed to press upon him, a reminder of the darkness surrounding his friend's disappearance.

"The Coast Guard officer didn't mean to say anything," Jake continued, "but the Constable was an old friend of Charlie's and Maggie Mae's, and he just nodded resignedly at the officer, who returned the nod, turned, and walked away." The unspoken tension between the two officials seemed to linger in the air, echoing the complicated relationships that had shaped their world.

"The Constable asked to come in and motioned for me to sit across from him in the old sitting room," Jake recounted, his voice carrying a combination of respect and nostalgia. The moment's intimacy seemed to come alive in his words, a snapshot of a time long past.

"He looked down at the old rug and slowly shook his head from side to side," Jake revealed, his voice carrying the weight of the Constable's grave realization. "Then he looked up at me and told me the fire was no accident." The declaration hung in the air like a storm cloud, casting a shadow over their understanding of the events surrounding them.

"One of the Coast Guard pathologists lifted a latent fingerprint from a piece of broken rum bottle in the forward bilge of my boat... along with traces of gasoline on the label," Jake recounted with shock and disbelief. The evidence seemed to materialize before them, a testament to the reality of the situation.

"Amy," Jake's voice trembled, "I guess that deep down inside, I had wondered about the coincidence of Johno's disappearance following the fire, but, to tell the truth, at the time, I was more relieved that he didn't show up." The admission carried a mix of guilt and uncertainty, reflecting the complex emotions that consumed him.

"It gave me personal time to face my grief... alone!" The words lingered in the air, heavy with the weight of his emotions. Jake's vulnerability seemed to radiate from him, an unguarded revelation of his inner turmoil.

"Well, the old Constable seemed to measure my reaction as he went on," Jake continued, his voice carrying a mix of recollection and introspection. "He told me of finding some of my hair embedded in a fish club tossed into a corner of the main deck near where I had been knocked out." The details of the investigation unfolded, each piece of evidence etching itself into Jake's memory.

"Also, he said that some orange threads from a garment, like one of the shirts Johno wore all the time, were found in one of the hatch jams under the wheelhouse." The weight of the suspicion seemed to settle heavily upon Jake, a reminder of the darkness that had crept into their lives.

"All-in-all, he said that, sadly, it looked as if Johno was a prime suspect in the fire and murder of the old couple." The accusation hung in the air, a shadow that had cast its pall over their world.

"Of course, there was much more that he told me," Jake's voice carried a mix of sadness and resignation, "but I'm tired now, and I'll save it for another time if you don't mind." The weight of his memories seemed to tug at his energy, a reminder of the emotional toll that recounting these events had taken on him.

"Thank you, Amy," Jake's voice softened, a note of gratitude evident, "for listening to all of this." His gaze met hers, a connection formed by sharing his past.

"You're welcome, Jake," Amy's voice was gentle, her understanding evident in her eyes. "I'm here for you, and whenever you're ready, I'm here to listen."

The room fell into a thoughtful silence, the weight of the past and the complexity of their emotions swirling around them. The sea breeze filtered through the open windows, carrying with it the salty tang of the ocean, a reminder of the life they had both known.

Jake's expression softened as the sun dipped lower on the horizon, casting long shadows across the room. "You know, Amy," he began, "I think it's time I made peace with my past and faced whatever comes next."

Amy nodded a supportive smile on her lips. "It's a brave step, Jake. And remember, you're not alone in this journey. Whatever you decide, I'll be right beside you."

With a deep breath, Jake seemed to carry the weight of his history and future possibilities as he looked out towards the 'Maggie Mae.' The boat symbolized his resilience, a vessel that could carry him forward as he navigated the uncharted waters of truth, forgiveness, and healing.

Jake let out a hearty laugh. The sound was genuine and unburdened as he reminisced about his early relationship with the old pilot. He shook his head in amusement before growing serious again, his eyes turning reflective. "Now, there's a story. When everything was signed with the Navy, Bob and I got good and shit-faced one last time together," he chuckled at the memory, "and, as he was leaving the next morning, he told me that I'd probably need a pilot from time to time and that this ornery old bush pilot he'd met, named Scoggins, would most likely be available. Bob said the old man didn't look like much... boy, what an understatement!" Both of them shared a hearty laugh, the camaraderie deepening.

"But, he could actually fly his old seaplane," Jake continued, his voice holding a mixture of admiration and fondness, "and he was as dependable as the day was long! And... I've got to tell you, Amy, a truer description was never spoken."

"Sounds like quite the character," Amy responded, her eyes twinkling with interest.

"Yeah, you could say that," Jake agreed, a smile tugging at his lips. "After Bob had left, I was alone on my boat for a couple of days, and I was virtually numb thinking about the enormous, unbelievable spontaneity of what I had done."

He leaned back, his gaze distant as he retraced his steps. "Finally, one morning, I left the café and decided that I wanted to go out to the island to try and settle in, but I realized I wouldn't have any provisions or anything to set up housekeeping with. Now, I definitely wanted to take stock of things, at least, so I thought that, at this point, this was a perfect time to look up the old pilot that Bob had told me about and see what he was like."

His expression shifted to curiosity, his eyes glinting with the memory. "I wandered down to the far end of the docks, and behind an old shack, I found an old twin-engine seaplane moored in front of the old building. I went inside and found a young native girl seated at a beat-up old desk behind the old wooden counter. She was leafing through some papers as I walked in but dropped them to give me a big smile and undivided attention as if to say, *'Damn, a real live customer!'*"

Jake's voice took on a hint of amusement as he imitated her tone, "'Welcome to Scoggins Air Service, sir! What can we do for you?' I remember what she said because her efficient use of English told me she had me pegged as an American the moment I walked into the office."

Amused by the interaction, Amy grinned. "Seems like she made quite an impression on you."

"Absolutely," Jake agreed with a chuckle. "I asked to speak to Mister Scoggins, and before she could respond, this grizzled, silver-haired old fella came out of a small side room, his hair wild and looked as if it hadn't been combed in a month. His old white sweatshirt and his old engineer's coveralls were dirty."

Jake's expression grew fond as he continued, "He stretched like he'd just gotten out of bed, and when he saw me, his eyes showed a twinkle as he grabbed my hand with both of his and told me how great it was to see another American down here. I told him who I was and what I'd just purchased, and the old guy had to sit down and catch his breath in disbelief."

They shared a moment of amusement, picturing the encounter in their minds. "We talked about the island and other things, including how he'd ended up here," Jake said, his voice echoing nostalgia and respect.

Amy leaned forward, intrigued. "How did he end up here?"

Jake's gaze turned inward, his thoughts drifting back. "It seems he had met an Indian exchange student many years before while crop dusting in Nebraska. She had come to the States from Tierra del Fuego at the invitation of a distant relative to go to school and hadn't made too many friends. The language barrier had made it difficult for her, but Amos said she was fascinated by his flying, which she first saw when riding through the country one weekend."

His voice took on a touch of amusement as he recalled the story. "She insisted that her relative take her to see the little plane land, and when they got to the landing strip, Amos noticed her and introduced himself. Apparently, she spent most of her free time, from then on, watching Amos take off and land... and he loved it."

He paused, letting the memories settle, then continued with a wistful tone. "Well, I guess they didn't realize it at that time, but they must have fallen in love, and after a short courtship, Amos wanted to marry her right there in Nebraska, but she wouldn't do it until she had a chance to introduce Amos to her mother, personally."

A hint of a smile played on Jake's lips as he recounted the story. "I suppose you can guess the rest. Amos sold his dusting service to a friendly competitor and came down with her."

As Jake's words painted a vivid picture of the past, the room seemed to come alive with the presence of the old pilot and his journey.

CHAPTER 10
A Boring Old Sea Dog

"**So!**" **Jake straightened up quickly,** giving Amy another start. "Enough about a boring old sea dog like me, Amy! Your turn now! Tell me all about what makes a beautiful, intelligent lady like you end up here, at the end of the world!" he exclaimed with a playful grin.

Amy blushed a little at Jake's compliment, her cheeks turning a soft shade of pink. She smiled warmly and began to tell her story to Jake, the porch bathed in the gentle glow of moonlight. They were engrossed in their conversation when a sudden, deafening *"CRACK!"* shattered the tranquility of the night. The sound echoed through the air, resembling the boom of a distant cannon shot. The atmosphere shifted around them as terror-filled screams and frantic shouts from Jenny and Bolo pierced the once-peaceful night.

Startled, Jake and Amy exchanged glances, their expressions tense as they instinctively knew something was wrong. Without hesitation, they ran together, their footsteps echoing on the path, towards the main house and the source of the disturbance. As they approached the yard's edge and the pier came into view, the moonlight revealed the harbor's water, agitated and churning as if stirred by unseen forces.

Meanwhile, beneath the harbor's surface, *he* swam with a purpose. *He* was a massive creature, his movements both fluid and powerful. *He* had been gliding near the shallows, his senses attuned to his surroundings, when he unexpectedly turned into what seemed like a small inlet. The creature had anticipated a chance to feed on the tiny creatures that dwelled there. Yet, instead of an inlet, he found himself at the entrance to the harbor.

As *he* moved forward, his muscles rippling beneath his sleek skin, he noticed a pair of bottle-nosed dolphins ahead. Instinctively, he gave chase, his determination propelling him forward. The dolphins were swift, but his sheer size allowed him to accelerate at an astonishing rate, closing the gap between them. However, as he gained ground, the dolphins abruptly veered to the side, causing him to overshoot his target.

With a force that belied his bulk, he collided with a solid obstruction in his path, sending shockwaves through his body. The once-sturdy supports of a section of the pier gave way under his massive form, and debris rained down upon him. His instincts kicked in, and he swiftly rolled and dove deeper, fleeing what he perceived as an assault from above. The debris hadn't harmed him but disrupted his feeding plan.

Navigating the underwater terrain, he approached the mouth of the harbor, a rocky rim rising sharply beneath him. His dorsal fin breached the surface, the moonlight glinting off the water as he struggled to maintain depth. Pushed by the rising bottom, he couldn't avoid exposing part of his back above the waterline, a clear sign of his presence. He continued his relentless movement, determined to reach the safety of the open sea beyond the rim.

Jake and Amy were racing toward the boat back on the pier, their footsteps quick and urgent. They were met by Bolo, his usually composed demeanor replaced by wild panic, Jenny trailing behind him in a similar state. "Boss!... Mister Jake! You've got to see over on the other side of the fuel tank there!" Bolo's voice trembled with fear, and Jenny's rapid breathing indicated her distress.

"Calm down, Bolo! Calm down!" Jake took hold of Bolo's arms, trying to steady him amidst the chaos. "Tell me what's happening, and what caused that loud crack?" Jake scanned the surroundings, his eyes searching for any visible signs of damage.

While Jake attended to Bolo, Amy comforted Jenny, her arms wrapped around the young woman as she looked out toward the harbor. Through the shifting moonlight, she spotted something that sent a shiver down her spine. A dorsal fin emerged briefly from the water at the harbor's entrance. Urgently, she tugged on Jake's sleeve, directing his attention to the same spot.

As Jake turned toward Amy, he followed her gaze and saw the fin just before disappearing behind the rocky walls framing the entrance. The realization hit him like a wave. His expression was that of concern and apprehension.

Bolo's frantic gestures and words pulled Jake's attention back. Bolo was waving his arms, trying to communicate something important. Jake followed Bolo's gaze, and his heart sank. The end section of the pier, where the old shed had stood, was obliterated. The support poles, typically unyielding, had snapped like toothpicks, leaving a scene of chaos on the water's surface.

"Mister Jake...Mister Jake!" Bolo's voice was a mix of urgency and desperation. Jake was lost in thought, his mind racing to grasp the implications of what they were witnessing.

Bolo's determined shake brought Jake back to the present. "Mister Jake, what are we gonna do now?" Bolo's voice held a note of helplessness that Jake had rarely heard from him before.

"Pray it isn't, old friend," Jake responded his words carrying a weight of solemnity. Despite the situation, his determination remained resolute.

Amid their apprehension, Jake's thoughts turned to Old Amos. He needed to warn the bush pilot about the potential danger before he landed. Jake and Bolo exchanged words, and Jake quickly decided on a plan.

With the night's events and conversations with Amy weighing heavily on his mind, Jake retreated to the main house, his weariness finally catching up. He laid down on the sofa, seeking a few hours of sleep to recharge.

When he awoke, the sun began casting its golden light over the horizon. Jake moved with purpose, brewing a pot of strong coffee to help shake off the remnants of sleep. He stepped out onto the porch, his gaze sweeping the surroundings as he assessed the situation.

Bolo appeared as he sipped his coffee, their exchange filled with a conversation of greeting and concern. The radio crackled to life, and Amos Scoggins' familiar voice filled the airwaves. Jake chuckled at Amos' unconventional greeting as he engaged in the conversation.

As the radio chatter concluded, Jake turned his attention to Bolo, a sense of anticipation in the air. "Well, Bolo, I guess that's all I can do. For now, we wait." Jake's words held a mixture of resolve and uncertainty.

Bolo settled into a seat on the porch, his gaze fixed on the harbor's expanse. He hoped fervently that the danger they had witnessed wouldn't return, but the unease lingered in the back of his mind.

JAKE AND BOLO WERE finally able to relax on the porch. The tension of waiting for Amos' arrival and the presence of the newcomers in their midst momentarily eased. The soft ocean breeze rustled the leaves of the nearby palm trees, and the air was heavy with a mix of salty sea scent and the earthy aroma of the island's vegetation.

As they settled into their chairs, the creaking of the wooden porch added to the soothing rhythm of their surroundings. The sun had climbed higher in the sky, casting a warm, golden glow over everything, and the occasional distant cry of a seagull echoed in the background.

Moments later, Amy and Jenny emerged from the yard, their faces reflecting a renewed sense of vitality compared to earlier in the day. They approached the porch with light steps, the anticipation of Amos' arrival evident in their expressions.

"Hi, guys!" Amy greeted cheerfully, her eyes flitting between Jake and Bolo. Jenny gave a small wave, her smile a bit more fragile but genuine. "Any word from Amos yet?" Amy inquired, her gaze shifting to the horizon where she hoped to catch the first glimpse of the approaching plane. A slight furrow creased her brow. Excitement and concern played across her features.

Jake noted the hint of worry in Amy's eyes as he responded, his voice reassuring. "Yeah, Bolo and I just got a call from him; he's about—" Jake checked his watch briefly. "Oh, about forty-five minutes out, based on his last call. I told him to check his landing area thoroughly for... uh... obstructions in the water that might have been brought in by the recent storm. Understand?"

Upon hearing the news, Amy's expression relaxed slightly, a visible weight lifting from her shoulders. She offered a thankful smile to Jake, a mixture of gratitude and relief in her eyes. She joined Jenny on the porch swing, settling in as they waited for further updates.

Meanwhile, Jake's attention shifted from Amy to the expanse of the sea beyond. His gaze wandered, scanning the horizon intermittently, a mix of contemplation and vigilance evident in his posture. He was deeply lost in thought, his brow furrowing slightly as his mind worked through the implications of their situation.

After several moments of silence, Jake spoke up, his tone slightly more serious as he addressed an issue on his mind since the decision to bring Lamar Toombs to the island. "Listen, guys. As long as we are all here, let's agree to keep the details of the past few days' events pretty close to the vest, okay? I mean, Toombs and his buddy are coming out here to take over this whole thing, and although I welcome his expertise, I would sure hate to have him begin bringing others of his ilk into the area to research this thing and, maybe, eventually, stand in the way of eliminating it."

Amy tilted her head slightly, her skepticism evident as she interjected, "Aw, come now, Jake! You don't really think that would happen, now, do you? Especially once they come face to face with what we all know is out there?" Her expression sought agreement from the others as she finished her point.

Jake's eyes met Amy's, a mix of conviction and caution in his gaze. He leaned back slightly in his chair, his hands resting on his thighs as he spoke. "Amy, let me tell you. I've seen a lot of guys like Toombs over the years, over-educated, in an academic rut, with a deep feeling that life is passing them by. They feel under-appreciated, and when something like what we have here comes to their attention, they feel like they deserve the exclusive opportunity to benefit from it."

Jake's voice carried a tinge of frustration as he continued, "No, our Professor Toombs is going to want to make sure that all his cronies know that this is his discovery... and his alone. That's why he will want to take over the show here and, eventually, bring his people in to show them how important he has become."

Amy's initial skepticism seemed to waver a bit as she absorbed Jake's words, her expression thoughtful. Jenny, who had been intently listening to the conversation, suddenly interjected with a direct question, her voice holding a note of suspicion, "Wait a minute! Tell me, Jake, are you actually beginning to have doubts that you've... we've... done the right thing in bringing Toombs out here and not calling the Navy to come to destroy that monster in the first place?"

Jenny's eyes bore into Jake with curiosity and concern in her gaze. Jake met her gaze steadily, his expression open and honest as he responded, "No, Jenny, that's not an entirely accurate hypothesis. I began to have second thoughts last night when our 'friend' out there found our lagoon here and destroyed part of our docks! Those were two-foot thick seasoned support timbers snapped in two like matchsticks!"

He paused, his gaze softening as he observed Jenny, "I've also talked about things to Bolo." Jake looked over at his friend, who had been listening attentively. "And he has told me of his own fears and deep concerns also, right Bolo?"

Bolo nodded in agreement, his face somber. He chimed in, "That's right, little missy! This thing isn't like notin' I've seen in any ocean I have ever been on! You bet I'm scared, but I know I got Mister Jake to be watchin' my backside... and, missy, that makes ol' Bolo feel a lot better! Do you get what Bolo be sayin', missy?"

Jenny's eyes shifted from Bolo to Jake, her skepticism giving way to a mixture of understanding and relief. She let out a small sigh as she clung to Jake's hand, the gesture seeking reassurance and connection. "Yeah, Bolo, I get you, and... well, thanks, all of you!" Her voice quivered slightly, a hint of emotion threading through her words. She regained her composure and continued, "I just knew I wasn't the only one here who felt really freaked out about all this!"

Jenny's admission seemed to connect the group, an unspoken unity forming amid their shared fears. As Bolo and Jake offered her supportive gestures, a sense of camaraderie settled over the porch, their worries momentarily eclipsed by the strength of their bond.

Amidst this atmosphere of solidarity, Amy's attention was suddenly drawn to a faint sound, a distant drone that grew gradually louder. Her gaze shifted from the conversation to the sky, where a tiny speck began forming against the blue expanse.

"There!" Amy exclaimed, pointing to the distant figure in the sky. The others followed her gesture, their eyes fixated on the approaching plane. The rhythmic beat of its engine resonated through the air, a palpable anticipation building as they watched its gradual approach.

As the plane drew nearer, Jake felt anxiety and hope on the horizon. He unconsciously held his breath and focused on the aircraft's progress. The creaking of the wooden porch, the gentle breeze, and the distant cry of seagulls formed a symphony of background sounds that accompanied their tense vigil.

The plane's silhouette gradually grew more defined against the sky, its wings cutting through the air as it executed a graceful turn. The engine's sound was now unmistakable, a constant presence in the foreground of their awareness.

The remote radio speaker crackled to life, Amos' voice breaking through the airwaves with his characteristic lack of radio procedure. "Hey! On the island! You there, Jake?" He asked with a feeling of urgency, reflecting the imminent landing.

Jake swiftly approached the porch, grabbing the mike cable as he walked. "Yeah, I hear you, you old bandit! The wind is out of the west, about fifteen knots, okay? Over!" He spoke into the microphone, his voice carrying a sense of purpose.

The plane appeared more distinct, its wings glinting in the sunlight as it maneuvered for landing. It descended gracefully behind the cliffs, momentarily disappearing from view before reemerging, its engines roaring as it taxied across the water.

Jake watched the plane's movements with rapt attention, gripping the mike tightly. The tension in the air was palpable as the aircraft's path took it closer to the pier. Finally, the engine died, and the door swung open, revealing Amos' figure as he emerged.

Amos' grin was infectious as he greeted Jake and Bolo with warm hugs, the excitement of his arrival evident in his eyes. "How are ya, boy? What was all this stuff about keeping my eyes open for... obstructions?" Amos' curiosity was genuine, his tone lighthearted.

Jake patted Amos on the back, his eyes flickering briefly to the plane's door as he whispered, "I'll tell you later, Amos." He watched intently as an older man, Lamar Toombs, stepped onto the pier. The man's appearance was as Jake had imagined, and his eyes locked onto Jake's with a hint of calculation.

"You must be Lamar Toombs!" Jake greeted with an upbeat tone, extending his hand in welcome. "We've all been looking forward to your arrival, sir! Your knowledge and expertise should really help us here! Thanks for coming as fast as you did!" Jake's handshake was firm, his words sincere as he offered his welcome.

Lamar Toombs' response was enthusiastic, his words bubbling forth with excitement. "Please, please, my good man, just call me Lamar! And, as for my coming this fast, well now, just how many times in a lifetime does one have an opportunity to, perhaps, view a living specimen of Carcharodon Megalodon! Why, my good sir, this creature has been thought wholly extinct by every accepted authority in the civilized world for over a million years at least!"

As Toombs spoke, his eyes gleamed with the passion of a dedicated scholar, and Jake couldn't help but be swept up in his fervor. The plane's door opened once more, and another figure emerged. This man was markedly different from Toombs, with a rugged appearance and a gaze that held a cold, assessing quality.

"You must be Darwin Graham," Jake stated, offering a polite nod as he observed the newcomer. "Welcome to Crandle's Keep. We're glad to have you here." His tone was less exuberant than with Toombs, but it carried the same genuine intention.

Graham's response was aloof, his focus shifting between Jake and the others before he finally turned his attention to his tasks. He began unloading items from the plane without a word, his actions speaking volumes about his nature.

The atmosphere shifted slightly as the group dispersed, each attending to their responsibilities. Amy and Jenny engaged Toombs in conversation, their excitement evident as they exchanged words. Bolo and Amos inspected the plane, ensuring everything was in order for the upcoming endeavors.

With lunchtime approaching, Jake decided it was time to begin preparations. He looked out at the vast expanse of the sea, his mind caught in a swirl of thoughts and emotions. A sense of foreboding tugged at the edges of his consciousness, a feeling he couldn't quite shake.

"Okay, folks," Jake announced, his voice carrying a sense of purpose. "Why don't we all go up to the main house and settle in before we get to... business?" He gestured toward the house, signaling for the group to follow him.

As they made their way to the house, the steady rhythm of their footsteps on the wooden porch seemed to echo the anticipation in the air. The sun bathed the surroundings in warm light, casting long shadows that danced along the path.

Once inside the main house, Jake couldn't shake his lingering unease. The arrival of Toombs and Graham had stirred up a host of conflicting emotions, and as he began to prepare lunch, he couldn't help but wonder if their intentions were truly aligned with his own.

CHAPTER 11
Instinct Keeps Him in Holding Pattern

He had been swimming in the deep water on the harbor side of the island, his constant need for sustenance somewhat abated, for the time being, by a chance encounter with a giant squid. As he finished the last remnants of the squid, he sensed a faint new sound vibration on the surface that caught his attention. He turned his vast bulk slowly toward this new sensation and moved toward it, anticipating perhaps another meal.

He sensed Amos' plane taxiing on the surface toward and into the harbor, and as he neared the sound's source, it suddenly stopped. Confused and lacking any direction to hunt, he slowly circled near the surface, keeping his towering dorsal below the surface and only a few hundred yards outside the harbor mouth. Instinct kept him in this holding pattern for several hours, continually looking for additional food.

Finally, he broke his current track and began following the warmer waters of the currents coming from the north. The old familiar burning hunger slowly returned as he swam in a generally northerly direction. He fed on numerous large fish and even a small whale, which had the misfortune of straying away from the pod in search of food, but he still maintained a primal lust to feed.

Several miles to the north, a small frigate, dispatched from a southern Chilean port, had joined the investigation of the small patrol craft he had destroyed about a week earlier. It generally sailed in a southerly direction, scanning the surrounding area for any signs of the lost boat or crew. This was a more formidable adversary than the small patrol craft. Its hull was made of steel plate and carried two deck guns and three machine guns. It would have given him a major test...had the captain needed to have his crew at general quarters. Tragically, he did not!

As he was swimming randomly in the depths, he sensed a giant "thing" moving across the surface to his front. His instincts kicked in, and he picked up speed, closing the distance between him and his "target." As he neared the frigate, he began to circle below until the "thing" was right over him, and then he dived down deeper, matching his speed with that of the ship. He then turned upward to attack his prey from directly below.

His mighty muscles accelerated his incredible bulk until he approached the frigate with the speed of a runaway freight train. On the frigate, the captain had just sent a report that all was normal and that he had found no sign of the patrol boat or anything else out of the ordinary to his headquarters. He was preparing to reverse course for his homeport when his world exploded!

He had collided with the frigate, almost dead amidships, and the massive cartilage of his snout, propelled by several tons of inertia, had caved in the ship's hull plates and practically lifted it out of the water.

The initial impact had killed several sailors, dashing them violently against bulkheads, hatchways, and other fixtures, and many were thrown overboard! The captain was lucky; he was mercifully killed on the bridge upon the first impact, and he was spared the maddening scene of his ship sinking rapidly while many of his crew were eaten whole by this monster from some prehistoric past.

So violent was the attack that all communications were knocked out immediately, and the fate of the ship and all on board would go undiscovered for many days. He circled the scene of the sinking frigate and all the life that he found there. Many sailors went to their deaths, unable to accept what their eyes saw. They just could not believe that something this mammoth and horrible could exist here in today's seas.....then, the enormous tooth-lined maw closed around them, one by one, until there was nothing!

He was satiated again, at least for now, and he began a wide, slow circle back toward the island his natural instincts told him was a constant food source. Meanwhile, back on the island, Toombs and Graham had stored their gear in their respective cabins and had come back to the main house, where they found Amos and Bolo commiserating in rockers on the porch and Jake inside, laying out cold cuts, bread, and condiments for lunch.

The girls were still in their cabins organizing their notes to present to Toombs now that he had finally arrived. "I say, my dear...uh...Jake, you have a fascinating setup here! My compliments!" Lamar gave Jake an overstated half-bow and walked around the main house's large living area as if he were in a department store looking to see what was on the "sale" shelves.

"Thanks a lot, Doctor...Lamar! I'm glad you could make it to the end of the earth to help investigate our sha....er..problem." Jake gave his best welcome smile as he glanced subtly from Toombs to Graham, who had been silently walking through the main house, poking and handling anything that caught his interest.

"How about you, Mister Graham?" Jake tossed at Darwin. "You think you can help us get rid of our problem?" Jake had stopped puttering with lunch and stared fixedly at Graham, waiting for his response.

The big Aussie stopped his snooping abruptly at the sound of Jake's voice, and as he returned Jake's piercing stare, he gave a small, humorless smile and answered. "Oh, dunno, mate! 'Might jus' have a trick or two tucked in me now! 'Know what I mean...mate?" It was Graham's turn to stare at Jake and await a return.

"Oh yeah!" Jake exaggeratedly raised his eyebrows as he started, once again, with the final arrangements for lunch. "I know exactly what you mean......mate! The sarcasm wasn't lost on anyone in the room, especially not on Graham, who pretended not to notice as he chuckled and returned to his poking and snooping.

Jake missed that Darwin showed more than a casual interest in the old radio set in the back room before he returned to the dining area to join the others, an oversight that would prove tragic and costly to the small group in the dark days ahead. Jake was about to send Bolo to fetch Amy and Jenny when they both appeared in the doorway.

"Hey, girls! I was just about to send Bolo for you!" Jake smiled. "Lunch is ready, and we can all share our part of this....mmm...phenomenon with Lamar here." Jake noticed that each girl carried a notebook and other papers as he turned his attention to Toombs. "That okay with you, Lamar?"

"But, of course, Jake! After all, I dropped all of my research projects and contacted Darwin here to collect his gear immediately. I told him to gather me up with all haste as soon as I got this from you!" Lamar laid a green velvet package on the table and gently unfolded it to show two almost identical teeth, presumably from some type of shark, of their unique triangular shape. The main difference was that one of the teeth was about two-thirds the size of the other, and the smaller tooth was apparently much older than the larger one because the smaller one was dull and had suffered some brittle fracturing along the edges, while the larger tooth was still bright and maintained its complete structure.

Notwithstanding small talk, they all ate silently, each staring, from time to time, at the two teeth lying on the side table. Toombs did, however, question Amy somewhat on the nature of her original research that brought her to the island in the first place.

"Tell me, my dear, how is it that you were drawn to this particular spot in the ocean? I mean, it is, after all, rather non-descript now, isn't it?" Toombs smiled rather engagingly as if to add..."Hmm?"...to his request.

Amy wondered at the question because she found it difficult to believe that a renowned academician like Toombs wouldn't be up to date on phenomena like the warming of prominent currents, occurring now in various parts of the traditionally cold, dark Southern Pacific basins, but she humored him, anyway, as he took a bite of his sandwich. "Well, Lamar, my dissertation is based on displaced species and how some survive while others become extinct. I was wrapping up my presentation when we received word that the large east-west currents west of here had reportedly increased several degrees in temperature. This really excited me because, if, in fact, this was true, many species in the marine food chain that would normally only survive in waters much farther to the north would apparently thrive down here for the first time. Thus, I packed my instruments and notes, found Jenny, who shared my interests in the marine phenomenon, and found my way here." Amy watched for Toombs' response.

Toombs still had a slight look of confusion on his face as he nodded his understanding of Amy's rationale. "Yes, yes; I understand your predilection for these possible expanded areas of food chain saturation and all that... but why here, specifically?" He looked at Amy directly for an accurate answer.

Amy returned the answer quickly. "Oh, I see what you're asking now. Well, this island is as close as I could get to the junction of two warming currents, one east-west, the other north-south, along the west coast of the mainland. This way, using Jake's boat," She smiled up at Jake, who, along with Bolo and Jenny, was listening to Amy's discourse with Toombs quietly as they finished their sandwiches. We could take measurements within a reasonable distance from a base where I could summarize my findings without staying at sea. Understand?" She saw that Lamar did seem to grasp her logic completely.

"I see. Yes, of course; it makes sense. Tell me, Amy, how much data have you amassed?" He seemed truly intrigued now as he queried Amy further with a smile.

Amy appeared to deflate then as her smile faded from her pretty features. She stared at the table between Toombs and her as she answered. "Not much at all since we were just starting our work when we ran across... the village!" She snapped a look at Jake, tears welling in her eyes, looking for some support.

"That's where we found the tooth we sent you, Lamar!" Jake interjected, watching Amy's tear-filled eyes.

Lamar caught Jake's look, and Toombs, too, saw how upset the young lady was. "Oh......yes, of course! I'm sorry, my dear! 'Terribly insensitive of me, what! Please forgive an old man's awkward probing!" He looked at Amy with raised eyebrows, silently awaiting her forgiveness.

"Oh, forget it, Lamar!" Amy wiped away tears that had crept into her cheeks as she pondered the apparent carnage they had encountered at the village earlier. "You really had no way of knowing everything we've been through around here!"

"Yes, to be sure, my dear... to be sure!" Toombs finished his lunch and retrieved the two teeth he had unwrapped before.

As everyone finished dinner, Jake and Bolo put the dishes in the sink and quickly cleaned the table to give Toombs room to lay out his drawing and the two teeth. Bolo volunteered to wash the dishes, but Jake told him to wait until later because Jake felt they needed to hear what Lamar would say to them.

Toombs spread a dark green cloth on the table and placed both teeth side-by-side in the middle of the fabric. "Very well, then!" Lamar motioned for everyone to gather around the table and began speaking in a "professorial" way. "What we have here are two teeth from what we call Carcharodon Megalodon, a creature dating back as far as the Miocene Era, or some forty to sixty million years. Please note that the smaller tooth on the right is an upper anterior tooth, measuring about seven and a quarter inches along the long serrated edge.

Now, what excited me so much about what we have here, you see, is that this tooth..." He indicated the smaller one. "... has been determined to be a tooth from one of the largest examples of Megalodon to have lived; that being... oh... I should say some sixty feet in length. This was, more or less, the norm for "Meg," as we paleontologists lovingly like to call her." Toombs laughed more than the others at his private joke.

"However, two things about the tooth you sent me have excited me so much that I couldn't wait to get here. One, of course, is the obvious size of your tooth." Toombs was becoming as giddy as a schoolboy as he continued with his explanation. "This tooth, I had measured a little over seven and a half inches across the cemented root, was one of the largest on record. Simple calculations tell us that the norm for "Meg" was around fifty to sixty feet long, with anterior teeth that have never measured larger than 7 ½ inches across the root!

Well, imagine my wonder and, I must admit, skepticism when I opened the box from you, and there, I found a tooth that measured almost 10 inches across! Good people! If these fish existed in these waters, he would be immense! Indeed, he would probably be more than one-hundred feet long, with a jaw width of about twelve to fourteen feet!" Lamar paused momentarily, looking from one person to another in the virtually silent room.

"Put this information aside for the moment. The truly amazing and unbelievable point that would set the paleontology community on its ear, should we choose to let it out..." He uttered that last phrase in a conspiratorial half-whisper. "...is that the root material taken from the smaller tooth is, as you can plainly see, totally calcified and dates back... oh... shall we say at least three to four million years; whereas, tissue samples from your large tooth are actually fresh, and I doubt if it dates back more than three or four bloody weeks!" Toombs' eyes were wide, and the volume of his voice had risen several decibels as he emphasized his point by holding the large tooth aloft.

Lamar put the tooth on the table, and his expression indicated deep thought. He began speaking again; this time, he was apparently attempting to rationalize his own conclusions to himself. "Oh, of course, we have all heard the stories about the Australian crayfish fishermen in the early 1900s who supposedly observed a gigantic shark devour their lot of crayfish pots, which were reportedly about three feet in diameter. They were said to be so distraught by the sighting that they hysterically refused to return to their jobs.

Then, too, there's the familiar tale of the famous Western writer Zane Grey, who reported not one but two sightings of massive sharks over four or five years from the late twenties to the early thirties. He swore the sharks were not whale sharks, as he knew the difference.

One thing that I keep dwelling on, however, is that experts throughout our field, for many years, declared emphatically that, just because modern scientists had never seen a given species, that species must be extinct!

Well... then, that theory was set on its proverbial ear in the seventies when two fishermen off the coast of Africa pulled in a living specimen of a coelacanth, a lobe-finned fish, which, until that time, of course, was thought to have been extinct for over fifty million years!" He snapped out of his self-rationalizing at this point and began to address the others directly once again.

"My friends, we know more about outer space than we know about what lies in the oceans of our own world, whether we accept or admit it or not." He paused for a sip of water, then continued.

"But, let's be realistic! If any of us were to report to the world that we had sighted Megalodon off the coast of South America, we would probably be laughed out of the room!" He paused again to take expected objections but slammed home his big point when he had nothing but close attention.

"No, no, my erudite companions; the only way anyone will ever believe us is... if we find and take this remarkable creature... ALIVE!

"Wait a second, Doc!" Jenny piped in, with a bit of hysteria in her voice. Amy recognized that Jenny was reacting badly to Toombs' unbelievable suggestion and jumped to try and calm the younger assistant before Jenny totally lost it again, but Jenny just glanced at Amy and waved her off. "Just what do you mean...'take?' Do you mean, like, ...CAPTURE?" Jenny just stood there in astonishment.

Toombs just smiled calmly and nodded... yes!

"Well, I don't wish to be the one to insult your intelligence...Doc. But just how in the Hell do you plan to...how did you put it?..."Take!"....a creature that is around a hundred feet long and must weigh... What?...about twenty tons?" Jenny was becoming mad now, and her attitude was disrespectful and nasty towards Toombs.

Lamar looked briefly at Graham and resumed his explanation. "My dear Miss... Landis, was it? I realize you must feel distraught by all you have been through..." Jenny just snorted derisively in response as Toombs continued. "....but let me assure you Charcaradon Megalodon is, at least, the first cousin of Charcaradon Charcarias, or, as you all know it, the Great White Shark!

Now, one of the things we know about the Great White is that it is a warm-blooded creature!" Lamar was a little taken aback by the fact that all the others nodded their understanding and prior knowledge of this little-known piece of information. "Yes... well... being a warm-blooded animal, we can surmise that its metabolism is somewhat advanced and, as such, we have developed some exciting compounds in our labs that we feel confident will thoroughly tranquilize the big fellow to the point that he will be as easy to handle as a baby dolphin!

"So, Miss Landis, what do you think? Have I adequately explained our little plan?" Lamar just smiled a sort of "Cheshire Cat" smile reassuringly at Jenny.

Jenny was about to voice her concerns and critique Toombs' scheme when Jake, who had been silent until now, finally spoke up. His voice carried a weight of experience and respect as he addressed Toombs.

"Doctor Toombs, I realize that I agreed to keep the lid on all this, and I have done just that... to the point that I have lied to the authorities from the mainland and convinced people I care about..." He glanced briefly at Amy and Bolo, a look that wasn't lost on Amy. "...to join in this conspiracy in the interest of scientific curiosity, but let me tell you that you are proposing pure lunacy. I know neither you nor your trained 'attack dog' over there..." Jake nodded in Graham's direction. "...can possibly pull this off."

Darwin Graham tensed, stepping toward Jake, but Lamar intervened, raising his hand to stop Graham's reaction.

"Very well, Mister Crandle; I admit that our task will be... uh... formidable, but we have given this a lot of thought, and..."

Jake cut Toombs off. His frustration was evident. "Hold on a sec, Doctor Toombs! Before we all get into a gigantic pissing contest here..." Jake shot a pointed look at Graham. "...I would like you and Darwin to come across the yard with me. There's something I want you both to see." He opened the front door and gestured for them to follow. The group filtered outside, except for Bolo, who hung back.

As the others moved outside, Bolo whispered to Jake, voicing his suspicions. "Mister Jake, I just don't trust that big fella who is with that Doctor man! He looks plum dangerous to me, and I be thinkin' dat I will just stay pretty close to him... if you are agreein' with me."

Jake nodded in agreement. "Good idea, old friend. You do that, Bolo, but stay close to Amos, too, okay? Whenever ol' Amos is this quiet, he doesn't like what's happening at all. He's liable to spout off something that will set Graham off like I almost did. Amos isn't... well, shall we say... 'equipped' to handle trouble like you and I are. Understand, Bolo?"

Bolo's dark eyes lit up with understanding. "Yeah, I am seein' what you getting at, boss! No problem; I will be staying close to my little buddy! Nothing be happening to him, Mister Jake! You can count on me, for sure!"

Jake patted Bolo on the shoulder before they joined the others in the yard. He led Toombs and Graham to the refrigerated part of the storage shed overlooking the harbor. They entered a dimly lit locker, and Jake uncovered a covered bundle, revealing a corpse.

Jake's voice trembled slightly as he spoke. "This was a seasoned naval officer. He literally died of fright, Lamar! He was someone's husband... and probably some child's father!" His voice showed his anger, not just at Toombs or Graham, but at himself.

Darwin Graham, however, studied the body with a detached demeanor. Jake continued with his frustration. "So, you see, Lamar, we are all guilty of at least some obstruction of justice and violation of moral codes... all in our selfish pursuit of scientific curiosity and personal recognition."

Graham finally spoke, challenging Jake's anger. "'Ere now, mate! Steady on! I've known the good Doctor, 'ere, for quite a while now, and I've helped 'im take many species in several parts of this world... I 'ave. I'll tell ya, mate, I'm good at what I do... excellent! So, ease up, mate; whaddya say? 'Ow about givin' us a chance before you start jumpin' on a bloody pulpit, okay?"

Amos stepped in, trying to diffuse the tension further. "Look, people, we don't know exactly what we're up against here, do we? Sure, Doc, we got one damn big tooth, and Jake, you guys have seen a big fin in the distance at night. I suppose this thing could be everything you all say it is and then some, but what do you all say I go up around here this afternoon, some, in my plane and see if I can spot something kinda strange?"

Amos' suggestion garnered attention, and he continued. "Then, if not this afternoon, I can spend a couple of days flying around the area here and see if I can spot your pet sea monster for you? How's that sound for a plan?"

Amos' approach helped ease the tension, and Jake took it further. "That's what we all discussed before you arrived, Amos. But I don't like the idea of you going up alone. What are we going to do if you actually find the thing? I don't think my boat would offer much resistance..."

"...Not to mention that it can probably move as fast as one hundred feet per second, at least for short bursts, right, Doctor Toombs?" Amy interjected, voicing a valid concern.

Toombs, seemingly unfazed, explained their countermeasure. "Under normal conditions, your synopsis would be accurate, my dear. But we have brought something that will... ahem... discourage our huge friend from having us for lunch. We have a unique sound generator that will surround the boat with a sort of wall of sound at frequencies that disrupt all sharks' hearing and neuro senses. We will be in a kind of 'safe zone' if we move slowly enough to give our 'friend' a chance to move away."

Amy and Jake exchanged skeptical glances, prompting Toombs' continued explanation. "So, you see, we will be in a kind of 'safe zone' if we move slowly enough to give our 'friend' a chance to move away. Do you grasp this idea, my dear?"

As the conversation continued, Amy and Jake remained cautious, but the decision was made for Jenny to join Amos on the plane. Tensions eased with laughter and discussions of plans for the future. Ultimately, they gathered on a hill overlooking the harbor, contemplating their actions. Jake took charge, suggesting that Lamar and Darwin start preparing the Maggie Mae with the sound generator. The group was set into motion with skepticism and a newfound determination to face the looming challenge ahead.

CHAPTER 12

A Call Comes in Over the Radio

A my and Jake had been going over the engines on the boat for only a little while when Jenny yelled from the porch of the main house that a call was coming in on the radio.

"Dammit!" Jake said, obviously irritated with himself.

"What is it?" Amy asked as Jake wiped his hands, hurried up on the deck, and jumped to the pier.

"I forgot to turn on the remote speaker when we left the house!" He shouted over his shoulder as he trotted up the hill and across the yard to the house.

"...Senor, Crandle!... Please respond, Sir!... Over!" Jake caught the last transmission, then flipped the transmitter switch from standby to "transmit."

"This is Crandle's Keep! Jake Crandle here! That you, Commandant?... Over!" Jake had gotten to know the old militia commander pretty well during the weeks he'd spent on the mainland before buying the island. In fact, the old man had tried to help Jake locate Johno, but to no avail. Jake hadn't heard from him since moving out to the island, but the old policeman had once sent Jake a large bottle of homemade wine with Amos as a housewarming gift.

Jake knew that Amos and the Commandant were very close friends, and Jake was sure that the two talked about Jake during their get-togethers.

"Si, Senor Jake, it's me! I'm still trying to keep all my "children" in line!" The Commandant had always referred to his militiamen as his "children" because they had been with the old man since they were raw recruits. Some had stayed with him all their lives. Jake admired the commander for infusing widespread loyalty throughout the ranks.

"Tell me, Senor Jake, did my old friend make it out to your island?... Over!"

Jake knew there was more to the call than just checking on Amos' arrival, but he played along. "Of course he did! That old bucket of bolts he flies knows its own way here by itself by now!... Over!"

"I'm delighted to hear it, my friend!" The old man's voice took on a more serious tone, at this point, even over the radio. "Please, Senor Jake, have you, by chance, seen any sign of one of our coastal frigates? It seems it was sent out on a search patrol for that small patrol craft we lost earlier, and it hasn't returned or reported in for some time!... Over!"

Jake was getting an icy, upset feeling in the pit of his stomach as he listened to the old Commandant's words.

Before Jake could respond, however, he noticed shadows moving across his desk. He looked over his shoulder and saw that Toombs and Graham had quietly entered the room.

"Please consider our prior agreement, Jake!" Lamar said, wide-eyed, with his right index finger pressed to his lips in a hushing sign, as Jake was about to broadcast his answer to the old militia chief on the other end.

Jake frowned deeply and turned back to the radio. "Uh....no, old friend, I haven't seen any boat in these nearby waters for some time, but I will watch when we go out tomorrow!... Over!" Jake hated to mislead the old guy, but he wanted to give him the idea that all was well.

"You say you plan to go out in your boat tomorrow?" There was more than a hint of concern in the commander's voice. "I would...

um... suggest... my young friend, that you exercise the utmost caution if you must go out! We have two of our boats missing already, and I would sincerely hate to have a third disappear as well!... Over!"

Jake felt ashamed that he had deceived the old fellow while the Commandant genuinely cared for him.

"We'll be cautious, my friend; please don't worry! We're just going out near the island so that the young female researchers can measure the new currents that have warmed our waters a few degrees recently.

Oh, by the way! Amos can't bear to leave my cooking so he will stay and relax for a few days, so don't worry about him, okay?... Over!" Jake forced a laugh as he ended the transmission.

"Very well, Senor Jake, and please pass on my warmest regards to Amos! ...Oh! And tell him that, when he does return, I have a nice rum from the northern islands that I wish to share with him, won't you?... Over!" The fondness in the commander's voice for Amos was very plain and genuine.

"You bet, Commandant! And, if we happen to see any sign of your boats," Jake glanced up at Toombs and Graham, a look of self-guilt and misgiving written all over him. "...we'll be sure to give you a call. Anything more, for now, my friend?...Over!"

"No... nothing I can think of! Just be very careful and....take care of my dear old friend! I couldn't bear it if anything were to happen to him!

Farewell, for now, my young friend!... Fiorino out!"

Jake just sat still momentarily, staring at the radio as static from the speakers broke through the room's quietness.

As Jake sat, staring at the radio, he didn't notice Lamar and Darwin exchanging questioning looks. Then Toombs spoke up. "Uh...Jake, my dear boy," Lamar had looked at the floor as he began, "you aren't, by chance, having any thoughts about reneging on our agreement, now...."

Jake snapped a cold, quick glance at Toombs over his shoulder, then returned his thoughtful attention to the tabletop as he interrupted Toombs' query. "No, no, Lamar, don't worry! We'll try to find your big fish!" Sarcasm had crept into Jake's voice, a point that hadn't gone unnoticed by Graham, who was very suspicious of Jake from the beginning. But Jake continued. "I just hate having to manipulate my friends and mislead the others, only to pursue an admittedly self-serving, ego-building goal like this!" He turned, then, and stood to face the other two men. "And let me tell you both something else! I will keep my agreement to find and document this beast's existence because I don't go back on my word!" The other two men looked at each other, the beginnings of a conspiratorial smile playing around the corners of their respective mouths.

"BUT!" Jake pointed a finger at each of them, which snapped their full attention back to Jake. "I promise you both that if anyone else gets hurt in any way, or anything happens to my island or boat...." He paused to make sure that they absorbed everything he was saying. ".... I will radio that old Commandant and get the Navy out here so fast, it will make your heads swim! Now, do we understand each other?" Jake stood, feet slightly apart, waiting defiantly for their answers.

Graham was the first to respond by taking a menacing step toward Jake. "Steady on, there, Crandle...." Toombs, simply staring back at Jake, restrained Graham with a firm hand to the big Aussie's chest.

"Calm down, Darwin! Our friend here is quite right! We mustn't risk damage to life and limb... er... just to study a fish!" Lamar had a condescending smile on his face as he spoke. "Granted, if it is Charcharadon Megalodon, as the tooth would seem to indicate, it has been thought extinct by science for over thirty million years! Nonetheless, I say we should abide by Jake's ideals!"

"'There now, Doc!" Darwin turned to Lamar now. He thought that Toombs had gone crazy. "You can't just let a bloody Yank's attack of bleedin' conscience....." Lamar jerked a cold, halting stare at Graham, cutting him off mid-sentence.

"You forget yourself, my boy!" Toombs spat with an uncharacteristic force and anger in his speech. "Of course, Mister Crandle, here, can dictate the conditions of our.....little research program!" Graham was transfixed, his expression of total confusion, as he paid strict attention to his employer. Toombs continued. "This is, after all, his island, his boat....and the find was his, after all! Agreed, Darwin?"

Still confused, Graham nodded slowly, agreeing, then Lamar went on as Jake listened intently, unsure of how much of this he believed.

"Splendid! Now, if you will be so kind as to get on the installation of the sonic equipment onto Jake's boat, we can all undertake the accomplishment of the project that brought us together in the first place....hurry on...there's a good lad!" Toombs motioned for Graham to go, waving both hands toward the front door.

`Darwin gave Jake one last resentful look as he picked up the two large suitcase-like cases, then turned and walked out to the pier.

Jake watched the big Aussie until he disappeared through the front door, then Jake turned his attention back to Toombs. "Lamar, your....associate...is really overstepping his bounds here! I've got a dead seaman!" He pointed out at the refrigerated shed. "I know that somewhere out there is a fish as big as a warship that could demolish everything in my harbor! I've got three other people, one a hysterical young girl on the verge of a nervous breakdown, though she doesn't know it!" Jake was letting the stress get to him, so he got angrier than usual. "I don't need some arrogant Australian soldier for hire coming on as a God damned enforcer and trying to intimidate me into something... anything... more than I agreed to in the first place!" Jake was practically yelling by this time. "Do I make myself clear, Lamar?"

Toombs, to his credit, was perfectly composed. He paused momentarily, allowing Jake to catch himself a little before answering. "My dear young... er... Jake, I've never believed otherwise! You have every right... nay... obligation to take care of your property and the priceless lives of the people in your charge! Of that, I am quite convinced.

Now then, as to what you choose as a fate for "Meg," should this, in fact, be such a creature," Jake missed the extremely brief look of unconsciously selfish lust that appeared in Toombs' eyes at the mention of Megalodon's nickname. "...I am confident that, at the appropriate time, you will decide on a course of action that you feel is in the best interests of all concerned. Am I not correct, my boy?" Lamar emphasized his point with a "Cheshire cat-like" smile and a slight professional bow.

Jake regained a good measure of composure and responded in a more or less normal voice. "Yeah, Lamar, you're damned straight. I will, and I hope I won't have any trouble with you or your bodyguard when the decision is finally made! What do you think, Lamar?" Jake's expression was intense as he stared directly into Toombs' wide-eyed face, waiting for the professor's expected commitment.

"Of course not, Jake! Darwin is very impulsive and sometimes over-zealous, but he will accede to my wishes in all things; I assure you!" Again, the cat-like smile.

Jake nodded and led the older paleontologist outside and onto the porch.

While the two men had been inside, Bolo and Amos had joined Jenny and Amy in the main yard. The two girls had obviously been in an animated discussion of their own, probably about Jenny's going with Amos. Jenny was now fiddling with the oversized binoculars, ensuring she could adjust the focus and zoom properly in the small plane.

"The plane's all ready, Jake!" Amos piped up. "If we get up pretty quick, we can properly search the nearby waters before that weather moves in there." Amos pointed at a line of dark, low clouds off to the west that promised to bring an unexpected gale by nightfall.

Jake looked back at Amos, then to Jenny, who had ceased playing with the field glasses and was fidgeting nervously in anticipation of the next flight. "Okay, Amos, but you better take care of our little girl here..." Jenny blushed a little at Jake's half-glib and half-serious remark. "... or I'll skin your old carcass and nail your hide to the outhouse door!" Jake was forcing a smile at this point.

"Okay! Okay!... nag, nag, nag!" Amos joked, dismissing Jake with a wave of his hand. He told Jenny to come along, shook hands with Bolo and Amy, and the two unlikely-looking aviators marched down the hill to the plane.

Toombs and Bolo proceeded toward their respective cabins to grab a little time alone to sort of decompress and rest while Jake and Amy stood side-by-side, almost transfixed, watching Jenny and Amos with a mutually shared uneasy feeling.

Graham continued to work non-stop on installing the sonic equipment on the "Maggie Mae" and didn't even look up as Jenny and Amos passed.

Jake hooked Amy's arm and gently led her to the elevated knoll, and they watched Amos and Jenny disappear behind the fuel tanks where the plane was moored. They listened for the rumble of the aircraft's engine, and after about five minutes, they heard it.

Jake noticed Bolo returning from his cabin about this time, apparently hearing the sound of the engine himself. As he approached Jake, he looked at the source of the engine sound and slowly shook his head.

When Bolo reached Jake and Amy, he turned to watch with them as the plane moved across the harbor toward the ocean entrance. "Mister Jake, if you don't mind me sayin' so, I've been thinkin' that we might have taken a little time... you know, ... to talk about what we're doin' here! What you be thinkin', Mister Jake?" Bolo looked at the big man at his side and waited for Jake's thoughts.

"Well, my friend," Jake began, reassuringly touching Bolo's massive shoulder. "I think that, sometimes, you show wisdom far more advanced than most of us!" Jake smiled.

The two men's attention joined that of Amy when they heard the engine run up to full power, signifying that it had begun its take-off run.

They saw the plane emerge from behind the cliffs to the left and could only follow the sound as it disappeared quickly behind the rock rim to the right of the entrance. Finally, they saw the small aircraft rise from behind the rim and climb slowly as it circled around the island.

Jake hugged Amy and indicated for her and Bolo to follow him as he turned and walked briskly to the radio in the main house.

As they neared the house, the remote speaker crackled to life again. "Okay, Jake! We're up and trimmed, and Jenny is puttin' the glasses to good use! Over!"

"Good, Amos!" Jake really meant it! "We'll stand by here. Call if you run across... er... anything of interest. Understand?... Over!" Jake didn't want some interested party on the mainland, who might catch some of their transmissions, to pick up anything that might cause them to get too nosey... at least, not yet, anyway.

Amos also seemed to have picked up on Jake's point because his response was guarded. "Will do, boy! If we happen upon any of those schools we discussed, we'll call it in ASAP!... Over!" Amos was now putting genuine effort into adhering to proper radio protocol.

Jake had noticed the horizon shifting, the once distant storm system now taking on a larger, more menacing form. "... Make sure you closely watch that squall line out there! It seems to be approaching quite a bit faster than it was earlier!... Over!"

"Gotcha, Jake! We have about forty-five minutes of cruising time before we need to head back! We'll be in touch! Scoggins out!" Amos switched the radio to the stand-by mode and began guiding the plane in a wide ellipse around the island.

"Well, Jenny, how's it going?" Amos asked a touch of amusement in his voice. "Those binoculars are nearly as big as you, little lady!" He chuckled softly, his gaze shifting between the instruments and Jenny's face.

Jenny was gradually getting the hang of using the powerful binoculars, her focus intent on the waters below. She would occasionally zoom in for a more detailed look whenever she spotted a shadow or shape in the water.

"I'm doing alright, Amos!" Jenny responded, a quick, nervous smile tugging at her lips as her eyes remained locked on the binoculars. "I'm not entirely sure if I want to see anything or not!" She glanced at Amos, her eyes seeking reassurance. "Do you understand?"

Amos looked up from the instrument panel, his voice soft and understanding. "I do, Jenny. I can't pretend to know everything that's happened out here or what you've been through... that's beyond me, isn't it?" He gently pats her arm to alleviate some of her tension. "But let me tell you this. No matter how many scary or tragic things you go through, if you manage to come out of them still standing, you become stronger, better even. You catch my drift, Jenny?" Amos' usually jovial expression turned serious.

"I think I do, Amos," Jenny responded with a touch of uncertainty, but a small measure of relief was settling over her thanks to Amos' comforting tone. "What you mean is that I'm stronger than I give myself credit for, right?" She nodded in agreement.

"Exactly, my dear," Amos said, his gaze warm. "Just let that strength shine through. Don't let the troubles of the past week or two defeat you... alright? Can you do that for old Amos?" His hand continued to pat her arm gently.

She nodded once more, reaffirming her determination. Realizing she had stopped scanning the waters during their heartfelt exchange, she took a steady breath and returned to the task at hand.

Yet, neither Jenny nor Amos noticed the massive, ominous fin that briefly broke the surface beneath the plane near the island's western end.

Underneath the water, the creature had been feeding in the deep, not far from the harbor entrance. It sensed vibrations above, akin to what it had encountered earlier, drawing it back towards the surface. Gradually, the vibrations started moving away, compelling the creature to accelerate in pursuit of this elusive sensation. Its cavernous jaws opened and closed, anticipating a potential meal. However, as it closed in, the vibrations suddenly ceased, causing the creature to slow and circle as it approached the surface.

The creature felt the rush of air as it broke through the water's surface, its primitive mind driven by a singular focus. Oblivious to the aircraft directly above, it made an erratic movement, churning the water around it before diving back down into the depths, leaving the surface calm once more.

Not known to Jenny and Amos, the enigmatic shadow of the creature had passed right beneath them during their heartfelt conversation, almost a whisper away from the island.

After completing their four spiraling circles around the island, Amos steered the plane for a smooth landing, then taxied it back to the docks where Bolo was waiting to secure it.

Emerging from the plane, Amos and Jenny saw Jake standing atop the hill, a surreal figure against the backdrop of encroaching storm clouds. The wind tousled Jake's hair, giving him an almost mythic appearance.

"Welcome back, you two!" Jake's voice carried over the gusting wind. "Did you spot anything... unusual out there?" Jake found it difficult to directly acknowledge that an unparalleled and dangerous fish might lurk.

Amos, never one for such subtleties, responded with a hearty tonc. "Well, boy, let's cut to the chase! Did we catch a glimpse of that oversized white shark?" A self-satisfied smirk accompanied his words.

Just as Jake was about to answer, Lamar's voice broke in. "Goodness, no, Mr. Scoggins!" Lamar had been alerted by the plane's return and had made his way to the porch from his cabin. "What we're dealing with is far more formidable than your standard great white." Bolo joined the group from the pier, and they all headed towards the main house, raindrops beginning to fall as distant thunder rumbled.

"Hold up, folks! Wait for me!" Graham hurriedly ensured the cover was in place on the Maggie Mae before catching up, eager to reach the shelter of the house before the rain soaked him.

"Ah, Darwin, my boy, how is the installation progressing?" Lamar had momentarily forgotten that Graham had spent the afternoon working on the sonic system's installation.

"Doing well, Doc!" Darwin responded, the others momentarily forgotten as he walked alongside Lamar. "A few stubborn problems as usual, but overall, it's shaping up nicely. I should have it finished and tested by tomorrow afternoon." He glanced over at Jake. "Is that timeline suitable for you, mate?" The mockingly casual use of "mate" was clearly a playful jab at Jake, who pretended not to be bothered.

As the others dispersed to their respective cabins upon arriving at the house, Jake stayed on the porch, gazing at the ever-darkening sky. He knew the storm would rage through the night. He prepared dinner and advised the others to stay dry in their cabins.

True to Jake's prediction, the rest of the group, except Bolo, emerged from their cabins and headed to the main house as they heard the horn blare, signaling that dinner was ready.

After shedding their wet attire, the group engaged in light conversation over wine as they settled around the table for dinner, served efficiently by Jake and Bolo. The conversation inevitably turned to the topic of Megalodon.

As the meal ended, coffee was served, and the group continued to discuss their experiences and concerns regarding the monstrous creature.

Lamar, the sole smoker, asked the others if they minded his pipe before lighting it. He began to speak, his voice thoughtful and measured, addressing the questions hanging in the air.

Before Lamar could continue, Graham interjected with his characteristic enthusiasm. "Listen here, Amy!" He addressed her, much to her chagrin. "I've dived with all sorts of sharks in every ocean... whites, makos, hammerheads. And I'm telling you, a spear gun with an explosive-tipped spear takes care of them just fine!" Graham turned to Lamar with an expectant grin. "Right, Doc?"

Toombs had been puffing calmly on his pipe as he waited patiently for his associate to finish making an idiot out of himself. His crinkled eyes and faint smile suggested a mix of amusement and exasperation. "If you're quite finished, my boy," Toombs spoke up, his voice carrying a tone of reserved authority, "allow me to enlighten you. If this is truly the specimen of Carcharodon Megalodon that I think it is, your favorite little 'pop gun' would only serve to make it angry, I'm afraid."

"But, professor," Darwin interjected, his brow furrowing in earnest, attempting to maintain his macho presence, especially in front of the two women, "this 'ere fish is just an overgrown shark, now, ain't he? He's just a great white with a few extra feet tacked on, right?"

Observing the interaction, Jake couldn't help but remain silent, his amusement evident in the quirk of his lips and the glint in his eyes. He savored the entertainment unfolding before him, aware of the absurdity of Graham's statements.

Lamar shook his head, a plume of fragrant smoke trailing from his pipe. "Darwin, Darwin," he began, his voice a mix of gentle condescension and faint amusement, "I'm amazed that you have always seemed to have such a practical grasp of the many dangers and mysteries of the seas... and, yet, display a seemingly total naivety of what we face at this time!"

Graham's bravado waned a bit under Toombs' patient explanation, and he settled back, realizing he might have oversimplified the situation.

Graham's subdued demeanor didn't escape Lamar's notice. "Ah, my poor deluded Darwin!" Toombs exclaimed, his voice carrying a tone of both affection and mild reproach as he blew a plume of smoke into the air. "Alas, you and I have encountered many of the seas' mysteries, monsters, and aberrations over the years. You are quite correct, but..." Lamar paused, momentarily letting his words hang in the air, his pipe dangling from his fingers. "We never have... never encountered a beast such as the one which is, quite probably, swimming a short distance from where you stand."

Toombs' words had a sobering effect on the room, and even Graham's stubbornness seemed to wane as he looked at the ground, grappling with the implications.

"As a matter of fact," Toombs continued, his tone shifting to a more informative cadence, "Meg's size and the tremendous need for food, to maintain his mammoth proportions, is what many say caused the species to become extinct in the first place."

With a sudden sense of gravity, the room fell into a thoughtful silence. Toombs' words had stirred unease, and the group sat rapt as he continued his mini-seminar on Megalodon.

"Bloody hell, Doc!" Darwin interjected, his voice betraying a mix of awe and incredulity, "See 'ere; I have been dealin' with the likes of bloody great whites in almost all the oceans, I suppose, and I don't see why I should be that afraid of some oversized 'white,' even if it is that much bigger! I mean, I got me, 'ere, all the tools I'll be needin' to handle whatever we got here, now, don't I?"

Graham looked at Toombs for some measure of assurance, but all he got was another cold, disappointed stare in return.

"Ah, my dear boy," Toombs addressed Darwin, his voice tinged with both exasperation and a hint of amusement, "you've certainly got the audacity that's befitting a sailor of your caliber. But you're underestimating the sheer terror that Megalodon can invoke. This isn't just a bigger shark. It's an apex predator of unparalleled scale and ferocity."

Jake, who had been listening intently to Toombs' explanations, chose this moment to intervene. "You really seem to know a lot about this particular fish, Doc! In fact, it's almost as if you... uh... idolize the thing!" He raised an eyebrow, looking at Toombs with a playful expression.

Lamar chuckled at Jake's remark and pointed the stem of his pipe at him. "My boy, you are absolutely correct! What paleontologist, in his... ahem... or her right mind, such as myself, wouldn't be somewhat obsessed with a chance to actually study a living specimen that was the absolute ruler of the seas over five million years ago and which has been thought extinct for almost as long?" Toombs' excitement was palpable, his voice almost trembling with anticipation.

Jake exchanged a quick glance with Amy, who caught his look and returned it with raised eyebrows, indicating her concern. "Of course, you're right, Lamar, but I'm sure that, once we have all seen this thing, kind of 'up close and personal'..." Jake paused to ensure that Bolo, Amos, and the girls were paying close attention, "... well, you're not going to have any objections to following through with our agreement to call in the authorities to get rid of it, right?" Jake re-emphasized the slightly hesitant confirmation of this point they had spoken of earlier.

"Well... I... uh..." Toombs hesitated, not expecting to revisit this point again. He was torn between his eagerness to study the creature and its potential dangers. But Graham jumped in, clearly attempting to keep suspicions at bay.

"Pardon, Doc, but I'm sure I speak for both of us when I say we surely recognize the need to eventually rid the ocean of this bloody terror. And, as agreed, when we all 'ave proof of its living presence, we will certainly do the honorable thing... now ain't that right, Doc?" Graham's broad smile was an attempt to quell doubts, but Jake and Amy were not easily convinced.

"That's great, guys!" Jake expressed a touch of feigned relief in his tone. He clapped his hands, signaling that the evening's discussion had reached a natural conclusion. "Well, I guess we should all be turning in since I expect we will all have a full day tomorrow, right?"

The group murmured their agreement and began to leave the main house. However, Amy remained behind to help Bolo with cleaning up. One expression prompted Amy to engage in a deeper conversation as they worked.

"Mister Bolo, are you feeling uneasy about all this too?" Amy's voice was gentle, her concern evident.

Bolo's eyes met hers, a mixture of seriousness and worry etched on his face. "Yessir, Miss Amy, I surely am. I have been feelin' it in my gut. This whole situation... it ain't sittin' right with me. There's somethin' unnatural about it."

Amy nodded, understanding his unease. "I feel it too, Bolo. It's like a storm brewing beneath the surface, and we're just starting to see the ripples."

Bolo's expression turned even more somber. "You're right, Miss Amy. And sometimes, the storm you can't see is the one that's the most dangerous."

As Amy and Bolo finished cleaning up, they gazed at the cabins where Toombs and Graham had retired for the night. The sea outside seemed calm now, but both knew something extraordinary and menacing awaited beneath that deceptive surface.

The night settled around the compound, the moon casting its silvery glow over the water. As everyone slept, a colossal fin glided silently through the depths, a living relic of a time long past, yet very much alive and hungry in the present.

CHAPTER 13

Testing the Sonic System on the Boat

The following day came swiftly, and the group gathered in the main house, where Jake had rustled up a hurried breakfast of French toast and hash browns. The collection of bloodshot eyes spoke volumes about the restless night that had passed.

Amidst the clinking of cutlery and murmurs of conversation, Jenny donned the oversized binoculars, slinging them across her body, ready for another day of searching with Amos. To the others, it seemed she was seeking her personal demons and the looming shadow of the megalodon.

At one end of the dining area, Toombs and Graham huddled in hushed conversation while the rest of the group chatted about the day's schedule at the other end. The atmosphere blended tense anticipation and a touch of nervous excitement.

As the group settled for breakfast, Toombs finished his meal and tapped his water glass with his knife to gain their attention. "If I might," he began, "Darwin here has informed me that he'll need a few more hours to complete and test the sonic system on your boat, Jake. However, I suggest that once they're ready and the plane is prepared, Amos and Jenny should head out ahead of us. We may need time to locate any signs of 'Meg.'"

Jake's head snapped up at this suggestion, his disagreement apparent in his tone. "Hold on a minute, Lamar—"

Toombs held up his hand, effectively cutting off Jake's protest. "Now, now, Jake," he interjected calmly, "I understand your concerns, but believe me, we'll have sufficient sonic defense to respond if necessary. Don't you think so, Darwin?"

Graham finally spoke up, breaking his silence. "Aye, sir. I've got about half the system up and running now, and I should have the rest of those bleedin' transmitter pods working in a couple of hours at most."

Jake's attention was keenly fixed on Graham, his skepticism evident. "So, you've got half of it working. Can it keep that beast off us if we have to assist Amos and Jenny out there? Can you guarantee that?"

Graham's response was direct. "Well, I've got it functional enough to give us a fighting chance. It should buy us a bit of time if we need it."

Jake's gaze shifted from Graham to Lamar, his distrust still evident. "All right, Lamar," Jake said firmly, "I'll go along with this plan, but I'm not exactly thrilled about it."

Lamar met Jake's gaze and responded sincerely, "I understand your concerns, Jake. This situation is filled with risks, but sometimes, achieving historical discoveries requires us to endure a certain level of danger. It's the essence of exploration, my boy."

Amy, who had been tidying up the kitchen, interjected with her thoughts. "I agree, Doctor, but we must prioritize safety as much as possible. Each of us has the right to determine the level of risk we're comfortable with."

Lamar turned his attention to Amy. "Of course, my dear. We'll proceed cautiously but are on the verge of uncovering something incredible. Sometimes, progress comes with its share of perils."

Jake nodded in agreement with Amy's sentiment. "Well, I suppose our philosophies differ a bit, Lamar. But let's get on with it."

As Jake and Amy headed out to the porch, Amos, Lamar, and Jenny followed. After receiving Amos' instructions, Bolo hurriedly made his way to the plane, and Graham begrudgingly trudged toward the Maggie Mae.

Amos and Jenny, now on the plane, went through the pre-flight checks. As Amos prepared to take off, everyone's eyes were locked on the aircraft as it taxied across the lagoon and eventually disappeared behind the cliffs.

Little did they know that a massive form was moving with purpose beneath the water's surface. The Megalodon sensed its prey, and with incredible speed, it surged toward its target.

Amos and Jenny's flight was short-lived. The plane jerked violently as the creature's teeth clamped around its rear, tearing it apart. Amos acted swiftly, unbuckling Jenny and pushing her out of the plane. He yelled at her to swim for shore before the beast's maw consumed him.

Jenny, adrenaline coursing through her veins, swam desperately towards the shore. She reached it, battered and shaken, just in time to witness the horrifying events that followed. The creature's jaws engulf Amos, silencing his screams in an instant.

Sobbing and in shock, Jenny dragged herself onto the rocky beach, her eyes fixed on the carnage in the water. The Megalodon turned away, its menacing presence haunting her, and she scrambled up the boulders to safety. The ocean that had once seemed so inviting was now a realm of terror.

The group watched back on the hill with bated breath as the plane emerged again, heading towards takeoff. But their hopes were dashed as the aircraft stalled and crashed into the water.

Jenny's cries of grief echoed through the air, and her body ached from the impact against the rocks. But she had escaped the beast's jaws, and now, from her vantage point atop the boulders, she watched as the megalodon retreated back into the depths, leaving a wake of devastation behind.

Tears streamed down Jenny's face as she murmured a prayer under her breath. The morning's events had left an indelible mark on everyone present, a reminder of the unimaginable power and danger that lurked beneath the ocean's surface.

"Sweet Jesus! Look... there!" Amy's voice trembled as she pointed towards the rising plume of steam and smoke, a stark contrast against the horizon, exactly where the aircraft should have ascended.

"Lord, no!" Jake's exclamation carried the weight of dread as he bolted towards the radio mic on the main house's front porch. He urgently grabbed the microphone, repeating his calls to Amos, desperately seeking a response that would never come. The others, except for Graham, who remained absorbed in his work on the sonic system, clustered around Jake.

"Amos! Amos! This is Jake! You there?... Over!" The words echoed futilely, each repetition a harsh reminder of the unfolding tragedy.

Tears welled up in Jake's eyes, his gaze fixed on the column of smoke that climbed higher into the sky. Amid the turmoil of emotions, he struggled to make a rational decision that would ensure their safety.

Lamar intervened, his voice a steadying presence amid chaos. "My boy, I regret to say this, but the system installation should be nearly complete. It might offer some measure of protection."

A tense pause followed Lamar's suggestion. "If one of us were to take the boat out there to see if anyone survived, it would minimize our exposure to whatever peril awaits!" Toombs' gaze rested pointedly on Jake, conveying the risky implication of his idea.

Jake's response was incredulous. "You're suggesting that someone risk their life and our boat on your unfinished system to check if they survived that?" He gestured emphatically at the growing column of smoke.

"Well, yes... I suppose so," Lamar conceded, fully aware of the audacious nature of his proposal.

A vehement retort was forming on Jake's lips when the sudden cries of Amy and Bolo shattered the heated conversation. Their fingers pointed wildly towards the rising smoke, commanding the attention of all present. The trio shifted their focus to the indicated spot, straining to perceive any movement. Initially, there was nothing, but then Jake spotted a subtle motion atop the stack of boulders that formed the rim wall.

Bolo hurried into the house, reappearing with binoculars that Jake seized. Adjusting the focus, he fixed on the point of interest, observing a lump on a flat boulder. It remained motionless for a moment before an arm lifted into the air, accompanied by a tuft of blonde hair. "My God! It's Jenny! She's alive!"

Jake's actions were instinctual. He raced downhill onto the pier and deftly secured the Maggie Mae. Climbing to the flying bridge, he fired up the engines without noticing that Bolo had followed closely behind. Graham emerged from below as the boat moved, puzzled by the commotion. "Bloody Hell, Jake! What are you doing? I'm trying to finish the sonic..."

Graham's words trailed off as he followed Jake's gesture, his eyes landing on the weakly waving arms atop the rim. Meanwhile, Bolo readied a rope and a boat hook at the bow, preparing to navigate the rocky terrain.

Darwin positioned himself at the ladder's base, acknowledging his intention to salvage what he could from the sonic system. Jake acknowledged him with a grim smile before focusing on steering the boat.

Journeying towards the opposite side of the lagoon, Jake's eyes scanned the water's surface for signs of the lurking menace. Prayers filled his thoughts as he hoped to avoid encountering the monstrous creature. Simultaneously, he wished, with equal fervor, for Amos' safety, though he knew the odds were slim.

Midway across, Graham reappeared on deck, hauling two cylindrical tubes attached to cables. He positioned them over the sides, explaining that they were sonic guns, part of a system that would eventually include six. For now, only two were operational. His hope was that they would prove effective should the need arise.

"Good work, guy!" Jake's shout expressed gratitude and a sliver of hope. As the boat continued its journey, Graham joined Bolo on the bow to keep watch over Jenny.

Amy and Lamar observed from their vantage point above the pier, abiding by Jake's instructions to wait. The boat's progress across the harbor's tranquil surface captivated Amy's attention. Its gradual slowing indicated a cautious approach to the rocky edges.

On the boat, Bolo stood poised on the bow, the boat hook extended. Jake, on the bridge, managed to wedge the vessel, allowing Bolo to throw a grappling hook-tipped rope over the rocky wall. The line caught, securing the boat, and Jake shifted into reverse. Bolo manipulated the boat hook to keep the bow clear of the rocky edges as the boat backed away.

With a turn of the throttle, the boat surged forward, carrying them back to the pier. Jake's eyes darted between the dock and the harbor entrance, each glance filled with apprehension. He knew that the sound of their engines could beckon the creature.

As he gripped the helm, he murmured to himself, his voice carried away by the wind. "Now... for the longest short trip of my life."

THE *"big boy"* had caught the 'surface thing' just before it had gotten away. *His* mammoth muscles had propelled *him* through the surface, where *his* vast jaws had seized the 'thing' out of the air.

He found that the 'thing' had challenged his strength to the limit as *he* closed *his* cavernous jaws on it in a death grip, cutting it, virtually, in two and pulling it down into the water.

While pulling the 'thing' down, *he* became aware of two smaller animals that came out of the larger creature *he'd* pulled out of the air, and the 'things' bore an unmistakable smell of food.

One of the new 'things' was too far for *him* to get to, but the other, slower, was very close on the surface. *He* turned and located the nearest disturbance and circled once below it; then, *he* came from directly beneath and opened *his* great tooth-lined jaws to receive *his* feeding.

On the surface, Amos had broken out of the plane just as it was pulled under, and he spotted Jenny nearing shore. "Good!" He thought. At least, she had made it clear. Then he figured he'd try for shore, himself. As he started to swim, he became aware of a large shadow moving over him and a row of unbelievably large teeth rising a few feet in front of his face. It would be the last sensation he'd ever experience.

His face went slack, and he quit swimming. Then he murmured his last words, closing his eyes. "Oh, God! Take me home!"

Then....blackness as Amos was crushed and torn out of existence!

He had not swallowed this 'thing' whole this time. Instead, *he'd* bitten down, crushed, and shredded the creature into tiny bits that filled *his* taste sensors with sensations that drove *him* into a feeding lust that set all *his* senses to high alert.

As *he* turned erratically on the surface, *he* picked up the residual spore of the other creature, which led *him* to rush toward the shore. At the same time, one of *his* saucer-sized eyes picked up motion near the water, at the spot where the smell of the other 'thing' was leading *him*. *He* zeroed in on the movement of Jenny and picked up speed again. So intent was *he* on catching this bit of food that *he* paid no attention to the rapidly rising bottom near *his* underside.

He was about thirty yards from *his* intended prey when *he* rolled slightly and opened his huge mouth, but at about the ten-meter mark, the sharp gravel of the bottom bit into *his* rough hide and slowed *him* up just a bit. That 'bit,' however, was enough to give the 'little thing' sufficient time to scramble out of the grasp of *his* closing jaws.

He rammed into the huge granite boulders with the force of a warship running aground, and even though *his* great snout was made of dense cartilage and the skin was thicker than an elephant's hide, *he* still sensed real pain for the first time in *his* life, and *he* rolled and recoiled frantically to back out into deeper water. After a couple of minutes of thrashing uncontrollably, *he* managed to work *himself* into deep enough water where *he* was able to swim rapidly away from the uncomfortable shallows.

As *he* swam away from the rim and into deeper water, his senses again picked up a now familiar sound from the surface. *He* reacted to the recent sound that had meant food and turned toward the harbor entrance.

Jake had the boat on plane and smoothly crossing the harbor, and, as the Maggie Mae gradually picked up speed, Jake caught Bolo's excited gestures out of the corner of his eye. Jake looked down to see what Bolo wanted, expecting that Jenny had a rough crossing. But, when he turned to look in the direction Bolo indicated, his blood ran cold as he froze momentarily at the sight of the unimaginably large fin that cut smoothly through the entrance on an intersecting course with the boat.

"Shit!" Jake muttered as he tried to get more speed out of the boat, but he knew they wouldn't make the pier before 'Meg' got to them.

Jake thumbed the intercom to the cabin below, attempting to get Darwin. "Oh, Gra – ham! Now would be a good time to hear from your system because our 'friend' is here!" No response came from the intercom below, only static. Jake turned to find that the Aussie had come up on deck with a small black control cubicle in his hand, which he held up for Jake to see.

"Remote!" Graham offered loudly over the engine noise. "It's partially online, and..." Darwin looked up at the approaching fin, only about two hundred yards away and homing in on the boat. "...I only hope it will be enough; it should be!" Graham looked at Bolo, then at Jake, then held the remote box at arm's length, pointed at the shark like he would with a pistol, and pushed a red button on the surface.

At first, nothing happened, and the distance continued to close. Bolo knelt over Jenny and shielded her from the vision to try and give the collapsed girl a few moments of peace before what he now was convinced was their inevitable deaths!

But, as if in answer to all their private prayers, the towering fin suddenly stopped, vacillated, rapidly, from side to side, and, with a spray of mist and waves that rocked the boat violently, turned and moved, with increasing speed, back through the entrance channel to the sea beyond and disappeared.

Graham leaned against the bridge ladder and hung his head for a moment before pressing the box's standby button and looked up at Jake with a smile that Jake readily returned.

"Thanks....mate! We all owe you a big one for that...but, say! I thought that the system wasn't finished yet!" The two men chuckled lightly despite the tragic mood and their previous antagonism toward each other.

"Neither did I....mate!" Darwin offered a wry grin at Jake as he patted the little black remote box in his hand. "But, see here, Jake," Darwin became serious again. "This bloody system will need much more calibration before we again run into that bleedin' animal. I'm gonna hafta get more juice into the water because, this time, *he'll* be a lot harder to keep off our bloody backs, he will!" Jake frowned and nodded his understanding, turning back to the job of docking the boat. He looked up briefly while Bolo ran from point to point, tying the lines and securing the vessel, to see Lamar and Amy running onto the pier.

"What happened out there?" Amy shouted excitedly upon reaching the boat and finding Jake and Bolo helping Jenny, who was still groggy and a half in shock, over the gunwale and onto the pier.

"Amos is dead!" Jake looked directly into Amy's eyes, his own eyes tearing. "The plane was destroyed by that thing before it could get into the air, and Jenny, apparently, just managed to jump clear and reach shore before the damned fish got her too!" He glared at Toombs momentarily before turning his attention back to Jenny.

Amy, now crying softly, jumped in to help Jenny ambled up the pier toward their cabins with Bolo's assistance on the other side.

Jake made sure that the girls were well on their way to the houses, then he turned back to Lamar, huddled in very animated conversation with Graham on the boat's rear deck. "Lamar, Godammit! I should never have gone along with this insane scheme of yours!

Lamar stepped behind Graham, who stood his ground and held out a hand in a halting gesture. "'Ere, Ere, Jake!" Darwin's tone was more empathetic now than belligerent. "I liked the old beggar, too! 'Reminded me of me, dad, 'e did! But Jake! 'Fess up, mate! We all knew there'd be bloody risks, didn't we?.....C'mon and admit it, okay?" Graham scrutinized Jake to see if there was any sign that a nasty confrontation could be avoided....there was a small one.

Jake's anger had, in fact, softened a little, but Jake kicked a cushion as he snapped out. "Oh, Hell! I hate to admit it one damned bit, especially to you, Darwin, but I guess you're right....to some extent! I wish we could've gone after that big fucker without exposing our friends to this tragedy! I blame myself, I guess, more than anyone else!"

"By the way, Darwin, I appreciate your coming through, in the pinch, with your system. For a moment there, I thought we had all bought it! Thanks!" Jake was plainly sincere as he wiped the residual tears from his eyes.

Graham really hadn't liked Jake much since meeting him, but he also possessed enough empathy beneath his tough man exterior to know that you don't kick a man when he's down...even Jake. "No problem....mate!" Darwin smiled thinly at Jake. "All in a day's work, ya know?"

Jake saw that Graham was trying to soften the tragedy of the moment and returned the smile, if ever so briefly.

Toombs saw that things were easing up a bit, and, thus, he relaxed somewhat and moved out to stand more beside Darwin than behind him. Bolo had also returned from helping the girls to their cabins and watched the exchange's last part. He had also moved his hand over a handy boat hook in case Jake needed help. Now that things seemed to be settling down, Bolo moved his hand to his back pocket, withdrew a rag to wipe his brow, and busied himself with tidying up the boat, lines, and such to hide the tears in his own eyes and the deep heartache he felt at the loss of his dear old friend.

Also, unheard by anyone else, Bolo murmured as he worked. "Amos, ol' brother! If you be hearin' Bolo up there, just sit and wait.

Bolo thinks you will see some of us up there with you soon! Yessir! We are coming to join you, I'ma-thinkin.'"

Jake sniffled a little and then spoke again, authoritatively this time. "Okay, I'm sorry for losing it, Lamar, but I guess we agree that we need to go ahead and call the Navy in now, right?" He looked inquiringly, with raised eyebrows, at Lamar for his concurrence.

Lamar's eyes widened, and he looked over at Graham, who gave a slight shrug. Then, Toombs turned to Jake, his presentation coming across as a bit confused. "I beg your pardon, Jake! I'm not sure I understand! I thought we agreed to verify and record 'Meg's' existence before we went to the authorities. Am I not right... Jake?"

Jake couldn't believe what he was hearing. "Jesus Christ, Lamar! What I'm talking about is that this thing has killed another person, a very dear friend of mine, I might add, and it's only thanks to Graham, here, that whatever was attached to that damned twelve-foot fin, under the water, was startled into a quick retreat, or we would have been lunch ourselves!"

Jake was rapidly reaching the anger level he'd experienced earlier, and he could feel his better judgment and self-control slipping away.

Lamar knew that, in the excitement of the moment, he'd said the wrong thing to Jake, and he also knew that if he were to have a chance in Hell of his plan working, he'd better diffuse the current situation.

"Jake! Jake! Please!" Lamar held up both hands, palms out as if fending off Jake's verbal assault. "I realize that my reaction must sound insane to you, especially in light of the tragic developments of the day!" Before Toombs could continue, Jake snapped.

"Certifiably!" Jake's rage hadn't calmed much, if at all.

"Yes,... ahem... well, be that as it may! I only want the chance to have a video recording of 'Meg!' Proof that will be indisputable! Surely, you can understand, Jake!" Lamar studied Jake's expression but wasn't finding any softening or cooperation. So, the professor continued imploringly. "Look, I fully accept the need to eventually destroy this creature! He's a *throwback*, to be sure, and there's no permanent place for him in today's world! However, I'm asking that you put yourself in my position! This is a finding of epoch-historical proportions, and any paleontologist would give his life, if necessary, to document such an evolutionary phenomenon! Can't you, at least, try to understand?" Toombs was practically groveling now, and Graham wasn't lifting a voice in support either.

The big Aussie would typically be fronting for Toombs, using his rough, intimidating style to force their common point on whoever was unlucky enough to be arguing with Lamar at the time. However, in this case, Darwin could still see the towering fin in his mind, and although he wouldn't admit it to a living soul, he had been absolutely terrified, as he had worked desperately to get the sonic generation pods working enough to drive the beast away!

"Here now, Doc! Maybe Jake, here, has a point!" He was almost sheepish in his response to Toombs' rationale.

"What's that, Darwin?" Lamar couldn't believe that his own long-time assistant was taking a position against him.

"Look, Doc!" Darwin jumped back. "I'm always your Mate! You know that! But, I gotta tell ya! Sittin' out there and watchin' that thing comin' for us, and not bloody sure that this sonic system was gonna fuckin' work!" Graham carried an unfamiliar tinge of fright in his tone. "Well....it just makes a gent think; that's all! .... 'Specially after we found the little 'Shiela' there, scared out of her head! Then, to find that the old man was... well... eaten!" Darwin paused briefly and looked quietly down at the deck before continuing. "I liked that old man, Doc!..." Graham was uncharacteristically emotional in his explanation to Toombs, and Jake was pleasantly surprised by this revelation.

Privately, Jake mused to himself. *"Maybe old Amos really did remind Graham of his own dad!... Hmmmm!"* His thoughts were interrupted as Darwin continued.

"This fish is different. It is! It's not just the size, Doc; it's the feelin' I'm getting! This is one nasty fish, Professor! I... I don't know how to explain it!" Darwin was looking at the harbor entrance as he took a couple of steps in that direction down the pier. "Listen, Doc! You knew me, what, ten years or so, and you've never seen me run from any creature in this world's seas, right?"

Toombs, with a confused look, just nodded in agreement. He had never seen Graham like this before, and it was beginning to unsettle Lamar.

Darwin went on. "Well, I gotta be honest, mate; this fish has our number, he does! If we try to take this thing on... even to study it..." He turned back to look Toombs straight in the eye. "... We will all end up in his belly!" Graham saw the blood drain from Toombs' face, and the Aussie moved his look to Jake and continued his chilling admonition.

"That's why I need to agree with Jake on this one! We should call in the Navy boys to handle this big rascal, right!"

Jake started to thank Darwin for his support when Bolo hollered from the boat's bow. "Smoke, Mister Jake!"

Jake looked over his shoulder at Bolo and at the plume of black smoke from the plane, which, by this time, had risen, in a streaming plume, several hundred feet into the clear sky. "Yeah, I know, Bolo. It's just the remnants of the plane. It will dissipate soon."

"No, no, Mister Jake; not that smoke... that smoke!" Bolo pointed to a spot on the horizon, and Jake made his way rapidly across the rear deck and up to the big man's side with Graham trailing him.

"Where, Bolo?" Jake asked when he reached Bolo's spot near the bow.

Bolo pointed, again, to a barely visible wisp of smoke, sitting atop a tiny spec on the far away place where the water met the sky, and it was almost perfectly framed by the harbor entrance as well. "There, Mister Jake! 'Looks to be some kinda boat!"

Jake pointed, in turn, for Graham, who had just come up to join Jake and Bolo on the boat's prow.

When Graham indicated that he had seen the black splotch painting the far-away sky, Jake jumped into the boat's cabin to retrieve some binoculars, and, meanwhile, Darwin shielded his eyes with his hand to try and see the object better.

Jake popped back on the front deck with the binoculars and sighted in on the smoke.

"That be a boat, Mister Jake?" Bolo asked.

""Yeah... uh... yeah, it is, Bolo!" Jake kept his eyes glued to the field glasses, trying to focus better on the small dot below the black vapor. "It's a boat, alright, but I can't tell what kind or anything else yet. It's still too far out... about a couple of hours." Jake took his eyes away from the glasses and faced Bolo and Darwin. "...And God help them if they come to see what this smoke is all about! Our 'friend' here..." Jake held a hand toward the water outside the harbor. "....will, undoubtedly, be drawn to the surface noise and destroy whoever is on that boat just like he did to Amos' plane!" Jake's eyes developed tears again at the recurring thought of losing his old friend.

"Now! Who the Hell is that, and what are they doing this far out?" Jake thought to himself as he gave the small dot one more scan with the glasses.

During the discussion among Jake, Darwin, and Bolo about the smoke in the distance, none of the three noticed Lamar stomping up the hill in a huff, talking to himself unintelligibly. Nor did anyone see Toombs check to see if anybody was watching him as he crept into the main house.

Meanwhile, Jake was more interested in completing the sonic generation system since it would probably be their only absolute protection should they have to put to sea for any reason. "Say, Darwin! How long to finish that system...so it's putting out at maximum?" Before Graham could answer, Jake added. "That beast won't be startled away as easily, again; you can bet on it!"

Darwin nodded in agreement while staring off in thought. "Oh, I dunno, mate; likely to take me another two or three hours." He looked up at Jake then and asked. "Tell me, Jake." He had a wry grin on his face. "What do you think our chances would be if we tried to somehow... capture that bloody fish rather than kill it?"

Jake's neck stiffened, and his eyes practically bugged out in total disbelief at Graham's question, especially given the events of the past couple of hours.

Darwin saw this and shook his head while he raised his hand, palm out, shaking it right to left as if to fend off Jake's threatening, violent reaction to his question. "Whoa, mate! Take it easy! I'm not suggesting anythin' of the bloody sort!" Jake's face softened just a bit; the look of anger was replaced by one of confusion and uncertainty. "Here now, Jake! I just wanted to see if you felt that we had a bleedin' chance of takin' this thing if we had to... alive or dead... if it became necessary....without the navy's help, that is?"

Jake took a few more moments to regain his composure, then, with a little tinge of anger in his voice, he explained his true thoughts to Graham, not seeing Bolo come up from behind to listen to Jake's words.

"Darwin, let's not misunderstand each other. When you both first arrived, I had deep reservations about my decision to invite you in the first place. In fact, I've got to admit that I had to fight the others, as well as my own better judgment not to call the authorities immediately and alert them to the monster they faced. Well, as we all know, this decision, on my part, most likely cost the loss of two vessels and several lives in the balance. Anyway, that's my cross to bear.

But that's all 'spilled milk,' to coin a phrase, and there's nothing we can do but try and correct things going forward.

Also, we've lost one of my best friends, and we have a young lady who's almost catatonic with fear!

And, finally," Jake looked intensely into Graham's eyes. "I'm beginning to feel that you want this thing dead almost as badly as I! I don't know why, but that's my guess! Am I right, Darwin?"

With a half glass of water in one hand, Graham thought for a moment, then, chuckling to himself, he responded to Jake's supposition. "You know, Jake, I'll be shafted, but I guess I gotta buy into your point!" Graham half-lifted his glass in a small toast. "But, let me set you straight on the good professor. He has only had a couple of passions, which I know of, in his life. One was his lovely Ethel, his wife of thirty years, whom he lost to pneumonia when he was away in Madagascar... oh... nearly six years ago. She was his life, and he always beamed when she was in the room, and since she's been gone, he's never been the same atoll!"

Darwin drained the glass and set it down very deliberately on a tray, in thought, before he went on. "I'd been kickin' round various ports 'o call, pickin' up divin' jobs as I found 'em when I met up with Lamar on a job for his school off of Indonesia, where they were lookin' for a rare type of shark.

When I dug one 'o the buggers out of a grotto that no one else wanted to go into, old Toombs was so happy that he started to hire me for all his excursions, which, at that time, weren't very frequent." Graham looked at the deck below in deeper reflection than before. Finally, he looked back up at the far-off horizon and began again.

"One day, though, while we were in Madagascar, he told me that he had just received word that his wife had died. He was so bloody torn up that he stayed in his room for four days, hardly taking anything to eat or drink.

Then, a queer thing happened. On the fifth day, he popped out of his room, dressed to the nines, and packed for a trip. He announced that his senior assistant would take over and that Lamar and I were off for home that same day."

Jake didn't want to interfere with this tale of enlightenment because he wanted to know what made Toombs tick. In this way, Jake would have some insight into what to expect from the professor regarding future decisions about Megalodon. So, he listened attentively as Graham went on.

"Well, when we got back to the States, Lamar gave me a check for my fees and then some and told me that, one day soon, he'd be requiring my services more frequently. I thought, oh sure, thanked him for his generosity, and went off searching for other things I did.

A few weeks later, though, I picked up, from a drinkin' bud and diver, that old Toombs had sold everything he owned, resigned his tenured position at his school, and had taken a research post in the marine biology department of a university in Brazil.

The rest is history, if you know what I mean, mate."

Jake perked up at this and asked. "That makes sense, Darwin, but you mentioned a couple of passions. What are the others?" Jake could guess the answer but wanted the Aussie to confirm his beliefs.

"Sorry, mate!" Graham recalled. "I forgot that you don't know much about our good Doctor. His only other real passion has been, and continues to be... prehistoric sharks; more precisely, long extinct mackerel sharks, mako and sand shark ancestors, and, of course, our lovely 'friend,' Megalodon, out there tops his dream list!

Jake, I'm solemn now. This creature has given Lamar's life a new meaning! He was a bleedin' 'rat in a rut,' just goin' through the motions until the day he received that tooth from you.

So, I guess you can see why he doesn't want to let 'Meg' be killed just yet. He's not a selfish or mean-spirited man, Jake, but... look... you destroy 'Meg;' you tear his old heart outta his chest! 'Get my drift, mate?" Darwin looked at Jake with a strained expression, awaiting Jake's reaction, but, deep down, knowing what Jake would say... what he'd have to say.

Jake scuffed his shoe on the rough planks of the pier, apparently thinking about what he'd just been told. "Look, Darwin, I don't want to come across like a heartless asshole here, but this fish is, arguably, one of the most dangerous monsters to ever swim in that sea, and you damn well know it! Right?" Graham raised his eyebrows and, hesitantly, nodded his agreement. Jake went on.

"Well, I'm sure I'm gonna pretty well devastate Lamar, but I just feel that it's time we call in the authorities and let them bring out whatever it takes to destroy this thing before it catches some other vessel unaware and kills again!" Jake wasn't filled with rage now, just with grim determination and total resolve... and it showed.

"So, tell me, right here and now, if you're against me, Darwin, because we might as well get to it if you are!" Jake stood straight and faced Graham, who stared unflinchingly at Jake for several moments. Then, Graham shook his head slowly and deliberately... no, he wasn't.

"Nah! I'm not against you, Jake, but I will tell you one thing....and don't take it wrong. I won't let you or any other bloody piker lay a hand on the professor... ever! I will protect him all the way!" At this point, Darwin stood, waiting for Jake's response.

"I understand completely, Darwin! Okay! I'm going up to the house and radio the mainland. It'll probably take about a day or so for their ships to arrive, but they may have planes overhead in a few hours. You okay with this?"

Darwin indicated that he was, and Jake turned to walk toward the main house, intending to end this whole mess.

CHAPTER 14

The Vibrations Diminish Almost Completely

He had just missed catching the other small creature when it scrambled out of *his* reach up the shore, but *the beast's* hunger was somewhat abated by the other, slower creature that *he* had caught in the water.

Meg was swimming slowly in a circle outside the harbor entrance when he heard what had now become a familiar vibration in the water off to *his* right. *He* began to move *his* monstrous bulk toward the spot, where *his* senses told *him* the source of the noise was coming. But, the monstrous beast encountered a submerged reef that prevented *him* from getting to the noise source. So, *he* swam back and forth, sensing the agitation moving across *his* front, from right to left.

Finally, the vibrations diminished almost entirely, but *he* continued swimming in random patterns until *he* chanced upon an opening in the reef, the channel leading to the harbor.

He started through the channel just as the vibration returned, coming from *his* left and moving diagonally to *his* right.

The gigantic shark felt a surge of lust as *he* rose toward the surface enough to remove the shallower bottom of the short channel leading into the lagoon, and, in doing so, about two-thirds of *his* huge fin was thrust into the air of the harbor above.

He then began to close with the surface object on an intersecting course, and just as *his* mammoth jaws began to open in anticipation of *his* next meal ...... *his* senses exploded, and *he* felt a coursing pain that *he'd* never experienced before! It seemed to assail *his* whole body, and *he* was startled into retreating, instantly, back the way *he'd* come, swimming rapidly out into deep water and away from the painful feeling just now starting to subside.

He slowed when the numbing pain went away and began to swim in lazy circles again, *his* primitive brain impressed with the feeling *he'd* just been subjected to. However, *his* instinct told *him* to return for the 'food' he had missed. As a result, *he* turned, slowly but deliberately, after an hour or so of recovering from the previous shock and headed back toward the harbor opening. This time, *he* wouldn't be quick to escape this new feeling!

He was about to enter the restrictive channel leading to the harbor when *his* heightened senses detected a new but familiar sensation coming from the opposite direction and from such a distance as to be barely audible, even to *his* keen senses.

He responded to the new source of agitation and, from habit, sought the depths of deeper water for *his* initial approach.

Meanwhile, Jake had reached the main house, while Toombs and the girls had, apparently, partaken of the refuge of their respective cabins to recover, in their own ways, from the traumatic happenings of the morning.

Bolo had stayed to perform preventive maintenance on the boat engines, and Jake knew that his big mate would find a bit of therapy in this activity for himself.

Graham had also remained at the boat because he, privately, realized that Jake was probably correct in calling for the Navy to assist, and, therefore, he decided to finish the sonic generator completely and tune it to maximum output, just in case the 'Maggie Mae' was needed for any sort of escape or rescue later.

Jake went into the house, to his office, and sat down at the radio set to transmit his call for help, but nothing happened when he threw the switch to send! He tried again... and again! Still nothing!

Jake felt a little gnawing in the pit of his stomach as he turned the set and unscrewed the knurled thumbscrews on the rear access panel, which opened to the small bank of circuit boards inside.

When he finally opened the cover, fully marked 'transmitter,' he began to lose all self-control at what he found and a primal rage that he hadn't felt since Vietnam took over! His behavior was because all the circuit boards from the plug-in tray inside the set were missing! Not just one, but all four panels!

Jake knew he didn't have replacement boards for all four slots... maybe one or two, but not all four!

He jumped up from the desk so violently that his chair flew across the room and turned over with a crash!

He threw the screen door open and stormed out to the porch, grabbing the small, gas-powered horn as he went.

He blew the horn several times and yelled... "Toombs!...Dammit, Toombs! You get your ass out here now!" Jake was screaming at the top of his lungs, and the tirade brought both girls running from their cabins and Bolo and Graham from the boat!

As the other four approached Jake, such was his rage that he ignored them and continued to look toward Lamar's hut and holler. "Godammit, Lamar! I know you screwed up the radio! Now, you get your big ass out here and face the music! You don't want to make me come and get you!" Jake's face was red as a beet and contorted into a mask of fury that scared the girls and upset the other two men!

Darwin displayed a look of both frustration and worry. He knew what Lamar had done because Graham had, initially, before he underwent a change of heart and mind, given Toombs a sketched outline of how to disable the radio....that is, if Graham, himself, was under scrutiny and couldn't have done it first! But that was before 'Meg' had killed Amos and others, destroyed the plane, and practically devoured Darwin in the process!

Darwin was, therefore, genuinely torn between helping Jake recover the boards or protecting his long-time associate and employer from Jake's wrath, which, at the moment, could prove to be hurtful at best.

Darwin took a deep breath and ran up to meet Jake as the big man descended the steps, focused on one thing... going after Toombs! "Easy on there, Jake!" Graham forced a smile. "Don't ya think we can handle this with a little calmer heads, mate?" Darwin knew he was just buying time, hoping Jake would cool just a bit before encountering the old professor... No such luck!

"Get out of the Goddamn way, Darwin!" Jake was tensed from head to toe, a formidable presence for anyone to confront, even Graham! "I don't want to go through you, man, but I will if I have to!... Now, move it, or we'll both be sorry!" Graham noticed that Jake shifted his stance slightly to prepare for a battle, so the equally intimidating Aussie, regretfully, did the same. Thus, the atmosphere became charged to a very hostile state.

Jenny saw what was about to happen and, as drawn and stressed out as she was, she jumped to grab Jake's right arm. "For Christ's sake, Jake! This just doesn't make sense! We all miss Amos; it hurts... it hurts a lot! Hell, I, above all, should want justice and push for help as fast as possible, and trust me, I do! But we all need each other, now!" Jenny was totally hysterical, but she was lucid and did make sense.

Jake looked down at Jenny with a shocked, disoriented, and angry expression. "Let me be, Jenny! Toombs has to face up to this! He's disabled the radio; do you know what that means? It's the only way we have to contact the outside here!"

Jenny persisted and tugged further at Jake's arm as she sobbed. "I know!... I know!..." She bowed her head briefly, then looked into Jake's eyes. "But Lamar isn't a bad man, Jake. He's just trying to delay things, in his own way, to fulfill his long-time personal dream! It's certainly not right, but you've got to try and understand. We'll get the parts back! Won't we, Mister Graham?" She caught Darwin off guard by shifting her plea to include him. Also, whether she knew it or not, she had, albeit imperceptibly, defused the stand-off between Jake and Darwin to allow further dialogue rather than a tragic fight that had been brewing between the two.

"What? Oh, you betcha, love! I know what he's done and can get him to return those parts. That's for certain, it is." Graham looked back at Jake. "Honest, Jake! I can get the old guy to give 'em back! I don't want no fight with ya, mate! It won't prove or solve anything!" Darwin held his arms out in an open stance of vulnerability.

Jake stared, briefly, off into space, obviously taking stock of everything. Then, he relaxed somewhat and replied to Darwin's logic. "Dammit, Darwin, you and Jenny may have a point, but..." He was interrupted by Bolo, who pointed out past the harbor entrance to the previous vessel that they'd seen before, only now; it was a little less than halfway to the horizon... much closer than before.

"The boat, Mister Jake! She is comin'! 'Lot closer, now! Could be help for us, ready enough, right?" Bolo's features reflected his hope for Jake, far different from Bolo's depressive state the past few days.

Jake glanced at each of the others, in turn, and thought to himself. "Lamar, you old reprobate, you'll just have to wait for now!" He turned and ran to the house to get his large field glasses, and upon emerging back onto the porch, he threw them up to his eyes and moved them back and forth until he acquired the boat's image.

The others came up to him as he focused on the sight picture. Suddenly, Jake stiffened noticeably and studied the approaching craft intently. Finally, he muttered, almost unintelligibly, under his breath. "Sweet Mother of Jesus! Haven't we been through enough? In all the seas, where he could have run and hidden..." Jake's eyes left the eyepieces and landed on Bolo! The bright red icon on the stack was unmistakable. Bolo read Jake's expression and nodded slowly...."No!"...in disbelief before Jake confirmed it.

"Tesoro!" Bolo jumped at this announcement.

"No, Mister, Jake! You are havin' hard time! It can't be that, fella! You be seein' things, I'm believin'. You look again, okay?" Bolo was upset now, and Amy, afraid to get between Jake and Darwin earlier, recalled the story Jake had told her about Tesoro and turned to look at the larger column of smoke and the slight outline of the approaching craft. At this point, she became frightened and turned back to Jake. "Bolo's right, Jake?" She took a swift look out at the boat. "There has to be a mistake! How about taking just one more look... you know... just to make absolutely sure, please?" Amy was very disturbed by everything else that had happened, and a group of thugs was something she was convinced they didn't want now, here on the island.

Darwin, not knowing the story at all, stepped up alongside Jake on the porch, and when Jake showed just a small hesitation, Darwin held out his hand, indicating that he would be glad to scan the oncoming boat one more time, himself. Jake shrugged and handed Graham the binoculars without taking his own focus away from the craft in the distance.

Darwin adjusted the focus, found the boat in the eyepieces, and described the vessel thoroughly, from stem to stern, including the distinct red insignia on the stack. "Well, is it the bloody piker you both said it was?"

Jake and Bolo looked down at the ground resignedly, leaving no doubt that Johno Tesoro's boat was coming to Crandle's Keep!

Graham saw that this guy, arriving on the approaching craft, must be someone awful for Jake and offered a suggestion. "Jake, I don't know who this bugger is to you, but, obviously, you don't want him and the other blokes with him to see you when they come into the docks, 'ere, 'cause it appears to me that, they see you, they either start shootin', assumin' they got guns, or, what's more likely, they turn and run like Hell, right?" Jake stood still, a fixed look locked on Darwin. Jake displayed a slight glimmer of appreciation as he thought through Dawin's logic.

"Damn! You know, Darwin, you're absolutely right! And, by the way, thanks, big guy; I owe you one!" Jake now had a plan, thanks to Graham's suggestions.

"I'll be over by the shed with a rifle! Darwin, you go down with Bolo, like you own the place, and welcome our guests, okay? .... Oh, take one of the pistols from the locker, Bolo! Got it?" Again, Jake was in a zone, thinking with cold calculation and tactical expertise.

"Yeah, I got it, okay, but this must be a badass bugger for you to set up an armed camp!" Graham barked as he headed to the main house, where he'd previously seen a small locker marked 'weapons.'

Jake didn't respond; instead, he trotted to his small cabin, where he kept his Weatherby three-hundred H&H! His body and mind were starting to feel the sharpened edge, unfamiliar to him for many years, and he didn't like it.

Bolo joined the two women, huddled near the porch, apparently confused about what they should be doing to prepare.

And, still... no Toombs!

Jake came out of his hut, and as he finished loading the rifle, he noticed the three. A short question crossed his sharpened mind... "Where the Hell is Toombs?".....but he dismissed it, for the time being, to complete preparations for Tesoro's arrival.

"Girls!" He looked pointedly at Amy. "Go to your cabins and lock the doors, and please, don't come out until I call! Okay?" He looked, for the ascent, at each young lady, and they both indicated that they would concur and together, they walked rapidly toward their dwellings.

"Okay, Bolo! You stand on the knoll and wave as they approach the pier. Then, go down to help Graham! And, old friend!" Jake said as an afterthought. "Don't be taking any unnecessary chances. If things begin to get really dicey, you grab Graham and run! I'll cover you from the top! Understand?" Jake had put a hand on Bolo's arm and looked questioningly into Bolo's eyes.

"Okay! Okay, Mister Jake! Bolo's a big boy!" The understatement from Bolo was punctuated by a broad smile as he shuffled across toward the knoll.

Jake stood alone and thought for a second. What had he overlooked? "Nothing except that damned Toombs!" His mind shouted at him.

"Oh well, it can't be helped for now." He muttered back to himself while moving over to the shed, the large binoculars dangling around his neck and one of the powerful '300' rounds chambered in his rifle.

His breath caught in his chest, a deep inhale as he fought to steady his racing heart. With every fiber of his being, he willed himself to calm the tremors coursing through his veins. Casting one final glance around the weathered corner of the shed, he adjusted the large binoculars, his gaze fixed on the vessel drawing nearer. The weight of anticipation hung in the air.

"Now," he whispered to himself, a mixture of determination and uncertainty simmering in his voice. His senses sharpened, attuned to the pivotal moment that loomed before him. He had meticulously orchestrated every detail, the culmination of meticulous planning leaving him on the precipice of action.

A bead of sweat trailed down his temple, a silent testament to the gravity of the situation. With the binoculars pressed firmly to his eyes, he tracked the boat's approach, each passing second a throbbing reminder of time slipping away. The lenses magnified the scene, revealing the contours of the vessel and the figures aboard.

Regardless, he knew that the lone person in the wheelhouse must be... Tesoro!

Jake and the others weren't the only ones 'observing' the approaching craft. Deep below the boat, *the big boy* circled in long, oval patterns, stalking the 'surface thing' until *his* instincts told *him* to attack.

He hesitated longer than expected due to *his* recent association of this same surface noise with the violent disruption that sent an unfamiliar and painful surge throughout *his* massive body's nervous system.

In that fleeting moment of hesitation, fate cast its dice, sparing a handful of souls aboard Tesoro's boat a few precious heartbeats longer. The tension hung thick in the salt-tinged air, a heavy pause stretching into eternity. With a decision forged in the crucible of primal instinct, Tesoro's resolve solidified, a predator sensing its moment to strike.

But nature's age-old rhythm, honed through epochs of predation, clashed with the modern pulse of human design. As his determination coalesced into action, Tesoro's sleek form sliced through the water, a hunter preparing to target the vulnerable underbelly of its quarry. It was a tactic etched into the annals of his lineage, a strategy that had felled whales and prehistoric leviathans alike, passed down through generations encoded in his very being.

The sea around him was a realm of dim luminescence and shifting currents. A dance of life and death played out beneath the waves. Yet, as Tesoro committed to his decisive descent, the boat moved. The vessel, a bastion of human engineering, entered the outer reaches of a channel, a passage that threaded the line between the open sea and the sanctuary of the harbor beyond.

Tesoro's calculated trajectory was foiled. His intended attack angle was lost to maritime geography's capriciousness. His prey had unwittingly outwitted him, a testament to human ingenuity intersecting with the age-old contest between predator and prey. The expanse of water that had seemed limitless suddenly took on the confines of destiny, shaping the course of the hunt.

The predator became a shadow, a stealthy pursuer trailing behind its quarry. The instinct to strike burned fiercely within Tesoro's veins, yet circumstance had imposed a new rhythm upon him—one of patience, of biding his time. He clung to the periphery of the vessel's wake, an enigma lurking just beyond the perception threshold.

The night shrouded him in obscurity, the moonlight glinting off the waves in a scattered dance. He moved with unhurried grace, each motion deliberate, every fiber of his being attuned to the ebb and flow of opportunity. He was a sentinel of the deep, the embodiment of relentless purpose as he followed the boat's path with unswerving determination.

Time was both ally and adversary, an enigmatic companion that quickened and slowed its pace. Tesoro's thoughts were a whirlpool of strategy and instinct, his senses locked onto the rhythmic pulse of the vessel ahead. He waited, the thrill of the impending strike intermingled with the restraint challenges.

And as the boat inched ever closer to the harbor's embrace, Tesoro's anticipation swelled like a tide reaching its zenith. The taste of triumph and the scent of salt hung heavy in the air, an electrifying fusion of ancient heritage and modern convergence. With every passing second, his predatory essence coiled tighter, the promise of the hunt drawing closer to fulfillment.

So, as the fishing boat proceeded through the passageway into the lagoon, *he* approached from about a quarter mile astern, maintaining as much depth as possible.

Eventually, Johno Tesoro eased his boat to a crawl upon emerging into the glassy harbor, and he saw two men waving. On closer scrutiny, he saw a black man standing on a rise above the pier, framed by several buildings in the background, while the other was a tall, muscled fellow standing beside another boat on the other side of the pier complex across the harbor.

Johno and all the others were focusing their total attention on the shore with the strange facilities on the bluffs across the way, where the two men stood, and no one bothered to look back astern to see a six to eight-foot portion of a much larger fin approach the vessel to within about a hundred yards, then vanish, quickly, into the deep water inside the lagoon.

Tragically, neither of the two men, standing on the shore, saw the fin either because it was blocked from their sight by the boat, and the glow from a full moon was in a position to cast a vision-hindering glare in the wake of the moving craft.

"Pino! You and Nacho stand by the ropes!" Johno barked at his deckmen. "Jojo,..." Johno addressed his first mate and close friend, whose build gave one the image of a fire hydrant with legs... short but stocky with strong, heavily muscled arms. "...take Petrino and Dolphano and get up front, and make sure you get in a position on the pier to handle that big guy if there's any trouble! Comprende, amigo?" Tesoro laughed out loud, and Jojo motioned for the other two to hustle up to the bow while Jojo lagged back to discuss plans with Johno for a few minutes.

Tesoro had been motoring north from fishing grounds to the island's southwest, preparing to head for a small island village just south of Valparaiso, Chile, where he had taken up residence. Earlier, he had seen the smoke rising from this island, and, since the normally productive fishing area had, inexplicably, gone barren on this trip, he thought that he and his men might stop and ..... uh ....'scavenge' something from this place that could help make the journey worthwhile.

With this thought in mind, Johno eyed the other craft sitting at the pier, and his ingrained larcenous nature brought a grin to his lips as he muttered. "Perhaps we can find a way to 'convince' these good people, whoever they are, to part with that boat! Whaddaya think, Jojo-sito?"

While he was joking with his stocky friend, he watched the two men and the boat, and as he drew closer and the details of the other vessel became clearer, Johno's eyes grew wide, and he started. "Wait a damn minute! Hijo de puta!" He squinted an intense stare at the boat now. He had come about two-thirds of the way across the harbor from the entrance, and the details on the other craft were now frighteningly distinct. Tesoro recognized the small brass plate he had installed on the hull, just below the wheelhouse, years ago. "Dios, mio!" He frantically scanned the shoreline for any sign of the one man in the world that he feared above any other but saw nothing.

A piercing screech tore through the air, a primal sound that jolted everyone on board. "Hold on, muchachos!" Johno's voice quavered with a mixture of urgency and fear, his words tumbling out in a frenzied torrent of his native Spanish. His eyes, wide and frantic, betrayed the rising panic within him, a tempestuous storm of emotions that threatened to engulf reason itself. His trembling hand reached out, fingers closing around the throttle levers, an instinctual response driven by a primal need to escape.

In the grip of his berserk state, language boundaries blurred, and his voice carried the weight of ancestral roots. The boat quivered beneath him, a vessel poised between the known and the unknown, its fate now tightly entwined with the hands of a man succumbing to his most basic instincts. As the throttle levers yielded to Johno's touch, engines roared to life with ferocious energy, propelling the boat forward with a surge that matched the turmoil in his heart.

The sea around them transformed into a maelstrom of possibilities, a realm where danger and salvation danced on the same treacherous currents. The boat's hull cut through the water, each wave a challenge to be conquered, every second a heartbeat that echoed the urgency of their flight. The wind howled in response, a cacophonous symphony underscoring the moment's chaos.

Johno's grip tightened, knuckles whitening as he clung to control with desperate resolve. The shoreline blurred as the boat hurtled forward, a streak of defiance against an impending cataclysm. The scent of salt and brine mingled with the heady aroma of fear, a cocktail of sensations that flooded the senses.

With every passing moment, the chasm between them and whatever pursued them seemed to narrow and expand in a macabre rhythm. Johno's eyes, once filled with panic, now smoldered with fierce determination. He was a man possessed, a guardian of his compatriots and his own survival, his actions fueled by a primal instinct to endure.

The throttle levers were not mere controls but conduits of salvation, bridges to a precarious sanctuary. As the boat surged forward, it carried the weight of their hopes and fears, hurtling through the unknown in a battle between human will and the tempestuous forces of nature.

Then!... the world around him began to explode, as the boat started to rise out of the water! He looked frenetically out over the side and briefly viewed a monstrous gray snout framing a row of enormous teeth that had sunk into the side of his boat!

A loud cracking sound was a precursor to the breaking of the vessel into two parts that flew in opposite directions; one part contained the wheelhouse, with Tesoro clinging to the doorframe, and two others were sent flying in the general direction of the pier, and the other, holding three deck men was pushed by the waves of violently agitated water, carrying it away from land and toward the harbor entrance from whence it had come!

Meg had, once again, come into the restrictive place where *he* had, a few hours before, encountered the senses-numbing attack earlier, but the lust for food was much stronger than the conditioning *he* had experienced from the sonic shot.

His prey lay above *him*, almost stationary, and *he* somehow knew that this was the time to strike! *He* spiraled down until *he* had the space to develop sufficient momentum. He turned up and strained *his* powerful muscles to accelerate to a rapid rate so that, when *he* drove into the bottom of the boat, with *his* massive jaws opened wide, *he* slammed into the craft with so much inertia that *he* lifted it entirely out of the water, and, upon closing *his* hydraulic press-like jowl, as *he* hit, *he* cracked the boat in two, sending part of the 'surface thing, and the food it contained, in one direction and part in the opposite direction.

He then circled the scene, deep enough to let *his* senses 'scan' the surface for possible disturbances, which would indicate food, and *he* detected two sources nearer the shore and three further out in deeper water, grouped tightly together.

Since the three, together, presented a small target in deeper water, *he* dived beneath them and, once again, instinctually, came straight up from below with *his* massive maw opened to the limit .....about thirteen feet in diameter, lined with several rows of the sharp, serrated teeth, some of which had been broken earlier in the encounter with the boat's hull.

When *he* neared his surface quarry, *he* rolled the protective lids across *his* cold, black, saucer-sized eyes and felt the three 'things' kick around in *his* jaws while *his* attack momentum carried a full third of *his* incredible body about thirty-five feet into the moonlit air of the harbor. *He* started to close *his* jaws over these three 'pieces' of food when one of them wriggled over the lead row of teeth and flew through the air toward the shore. *He* completed shutting *his* mouth over the other two 'things' and tasted their warm juices flowing down *his* throat!

Then, *his* body fell, like a giant tree trunk, back into the water, ironically saving the life of the crewman who had scrambled over 'Meg's' teeth and fallen into the lagoon because the wave, caused by 'Meg's' great body, carried the man and most of the surrounding debris, including the portion containing the wheelhouse, almost all the way to the narrow, rocky shoreline.

Johno, badly shaken, had held onto the door frame of the wheelhouse when the boat broke in two, but he jumped free as it sailed to one side and landed in the water near Pino and Nacho, who had leaped together to get clear of the wreckage, themselves.

In a tight group, the three dog-paddled, trying to get their bearings, and Johno started fighting the water closer to shore to try and make it. One of them appeared to Johno to be hurt because he wasn't making much headway, while the other looked like Dolphino was making fair progress.

In the tense and murky expanse of the sea, Johno's eyes were fixed on the horizon, his senses attuned to every ripple and nuance of the water. The air was thick with foreboding. A palpable tension hung over their ill-fated expedition like a shroud. Then, as if summoned by the darkness, a sudden eruption of furious spray and foam shattered the tranquility with a ferocity that defied imagination. Dolphino, a vital presence just moments before, was consumed by the maelstrom, swallowed by the very abyss they had come to conquer.

Johno's heart pounded, his mind struggling to process the horrifying spectacle that had unfolded before him. The chasm of the ocean had claimed one of their own, extinguishing life in a heartbeat, leaving only frantic bubbles and swirling currents in its wake. The abyss had shown its teeth, and panic seized the hearts of those who remained.

Johno's survival instincts ignited like a primal fire. He clutched the two companions who had managed to evade the watery wrath, his wide-eyed gaze beckoning them to follow him into the depths, away from the cataclysm that had descended upon them. But their flight was a fleeting hope, a desperate bid to escape an entity that defied all reason.

Before they could gain any semblance of safety, the sea erupted again, a violent explosion that shattered the surface like a vengeful force. Another man, injured and vulnerable, was consumed in the chaos, his fate sealed in the unforgiving embrace of the waves. Johno's breath hitched, a strangled cry of disbelief caught in his throat as he watched Petro's demise unfold before his very eyes.

And then, like a nightmarish crescendo, a sight emerged from the depths that froze the blood in their veins. A dorsal fin, a grotesque monolith of nature's horror, pierced the surface, its sinister presence casting a shadow over the very essence of their existence. Ten feet of primal terror rose defiantly, a manifestation of dread that dwarfed their wildest nightmares.

Transfixed by the harrowing scene, Tesoro felt a chill creep down his spine, an icy grip of terror that clenched his heart. This was a horror unlike any other, a confrontation with an apex predator that stirred primordial fears buried deep within the human psyche. The colossal fin, a macabre sentinel of the abyss, pivoted toward their group, a dire omen of their impending doom.

Then, with a malevolent grace, it plunged back into the murky depths, leaving only a void of silence in its wake.

The water settled, a deceptive calm blanketing the scene of devastation. The remnants of their ill-fated venture floated on the surface, remnants of lives shattered, and dreams dashed. Tesoro's mind reeled, grappling with the grotesque reality that had unfolded before him. Suspense clung to the air like a suffocating shroud, a prelude to further horrors that lurked just beyond the horizon, waiting to unleash their terrible fury.

A primal terror gripped Tesoro's being, his voice cutting through the chaotic symphony of panic that enveloped them. "Madre de Dios! Swim, hombres! Para tu vida!" His command echoed through the swirling abyss, a desperate plea that hung in the air like a prayer to any force that might listen. With every fiber of his being electrified by a surge of adrenaline, Tesoro propelled his body through the water, limbs churning in a desperate bid for survival.

Tesoro's form sliced through the water with fervent urgency, the weight of impending doom bearing upon them. His skills as a swimmer granted him an edge, a slight lead over his companions in this ruthless race against the unknown. But the cold tendrils of fear still coiled around his heart, threatening to paralyze even the most determined spirit.

As Tesoro stroked through the dark abyss, a grotesque tableau of horror appeared before his eyes. In a surreal twist of reality, the water around them seemed to defy its nature, warping and lifting into the air. His heart hammered in his chest, breath hitching as he beheld the nightmare unfolding around them. A line of colossal teeth, each as long as a human foot, rose from the depths, forming an encircling prison of death. The water seemed to solidify into a nightmarish cage, triangular teeth glistening with an otherworldly malevolence.

Time seemed to slow as Tesoro's mind raced, his instincts forged in the crucible of survival guiding him. With a reflex honed by millennia of evolution, he surged upward, muscles straining against the impossible force of fear. His body contorted, and the rough skin surrounding the teeth grazed his thigh, leaving a searing laceration in its wake. Pain merged with determination, a symphony of sensations that propelled him onward.

In a heart-stopping instant, Tesoro found himself atop this horrific edifice, a towering column of death that defied all reason. The realization struck him with a sickening weight, the gravity of their plight pressing down like a leaden shroud. But Tesoro was not a man to succumb to fate without a fight. Gathering every ounce of strength and courage, he braced himself against the rough, alien texture of the tooth-lined prison. With a surge of raw power, he pushed off with a primal scream, a sound that reverberated through the watery abyss.

The world twisted and spun as Tesoro hurtled through the air, his heart in his throat, his destiny hanging by a thread. The abyss, once his enemy, now became his fleeting ally, drawing him closer to the surface that seemed impossibly distant. The rush of water, the howl of the deep, the pulse of survival—all merged into a symphony of suspense gripping Tesoro's soul.

When Johno landed in the water, he fought to quickly regain the surface, and as he did so, he saw the terrifying gray monster flex at the top, and a red liquid that he knew to be the blood of his other two companions flew from the mouth, randomly, in all directions!

"Oh, Dios mío," he whispered, a breathy exhalation in the thick silence. His heart pounded like a relentless drum, the moment's weight bearing down upon him like a vice. The scene before him was a visceral tableau of horror, a cruel tapestry of violence that seared into his consciousness.

But, he snapped out of his shocked paralysis, jerked his attention to the shore, and began to swim, with frantic, panicked strokes, toward the sand and rocks ahead and his only chance at life! He knew it was over a hundred yards, and his odds of making it were slim to none, but he was gamely trying.....when 'Meg's' massive body hit the water behind him, creating a wave almost fifteen feet high! It picked up Tesoro's body like a leaf and carried him rapidly toward the rock-strewn shore along with the boat's floating rubbish.

At first, Johno was thankful to God that he had been delivered up from the creature behind him, even shooting a fist into the air and whooping, but upon his closer visual inspection, he saw that, at his present height and speed, he would, almost certainly, be dashed onto the rocks, rushing up in front of him. So, he dug both hands into the wave, submerged, and swam straight down with solid strokes, allowing the main part of the wave to proceed without him.

When he surfaced a few moments later, he found he had succeeded. The wave smashed ahead on the shore....still about twenty yards away!

Johno then became aware of three people standing on the island, waving and yelling at him. He looked over his shoulder, and the immense fin was about two hundred yards away! From his perspective, it looked like a shark's fin but over three times as big and high!

"Ah, shit!" he bellowed, a surge of raw adrenaline jolting through him. With renewed determination fueled by sheer desperation, he propelled himself through the water with a newfound ferocity, each stroke carrying him closer to the safety of the shore.

One of the three people, a huge black man, left the group and disappeared behind a shed, and a few seconds later, he emerged with a rope and ran to a point near where Johno would land. There, the man threw the rope down, and, through the water splashing in his eyes as he swam, Johno understood.

When he reached land, Johno scrambled upright and grabbed the rope. The big black man began to pull, and Tesoro, in a state of near-hysteria, tried to climb the rope away from the water below.

Most of the gargantuan back of Megalodon could be clearly seen as *he* approached the shore, but, this time, rather than run into the rocks, like *he* did while chasing Jenny, 'Meg' slowed, turned, and descended into the lagoon depths.

The water became still and returned to how it had always been, except for the debris left from the smashed boat that had been ripped apart by 'Meg.'

Jake had run to the knoll to join Bolo when he saw 'Meg's horrifying attack from his hiding place behind the shed.

He and Bolo were virtually frozen at the sight of the three men being carried over thirty feet into the air by the mammoth fish before one of the three scrambled over the edge of the cavernous mouth and flew to the temporary safety of the harbor surface. Seeing this opportunity to save at least one of the crewmen, Jake snapped at Bolo. "Bolo! Look there!" Jake pointed to the escaped seaman, unaware at the time that it was, in fact, Johno Tesoro he was pointing at! "One fought free! Go get..."

Then, the colossal fish closed *his* jaws on the remaining men, screaming and flailing in *his* mouth! "Oh, Jesus!" Jake could hardly catch his breath as he watched the blood and gore explode in all directions from 'Meg's' mouth!

"Mister Jake! For the love of all that's holy, save us! ... Mister Jake!" Bolo cried out, his voice quivering with a potent blend of terror and disbelief. "This can't be real, Mister Jake! There ain't no fish in the entire ocean that's this colossal!" Bolo's eyes were on the verge of popping out of their sockets as he desperately sought affirmation from Jake on this unimaginable reality.

"Well, old friend..." Jake glanced at his mate, his false calm betrayed by his large eyes and pale features. "... Apparently, there is now, and I'm afraid you can forget the Lord, at least, for now, because this thing is straight from the gates of Hell!"

Their attention was drawn back to the scene in the harbor by the loud smack and roar of 'Meg' crashing back into the water. Jake saw the ensuing wave pick up the man, who'd managed to get away from the monster and carry him toward the shore, where Jake knew, for sure, the man would be dashed on the rocks and killed. However, the seaman dug into the wave and escaped its frothy grasp.

Jake caught motion in his right periphery and looked to see Darwin running up to them. "Bleedin' shit, mate! Look over there!"

Jake and Bolo snapped their heads jointly in the direction that Graham indicated. There, off to their right, not more than two hundred yards from the boat and pier, 'Meg's' fin, or what appeared to be a small part of it, rose out of the water and turned in a slow, almost lazy, circle to head back for the area where the lone remaining man from the boat was paddling, seemingly somewhat disoriented, about twenty-five yards from the bank.

Jake's voice ripped through the air, a desperate shout, as he wildly gestured to the man, urgently conveying the need to make a desperate swim for the shore! Bolo and Graham's hearts raced as they joined in, their trembling fingers pointing at the sinister fin slicing through the water, its deliberate movement bringing it relentlessly closer to the man's vulnerable form.

Their signal was apparently received because the man looked over his shoulder and immediately began swimming frantically.

Jake saw that, without help, even if the man below made it to the narrow beach, he would never make it up the steep bluff fast enough to escape 'Meg's' lunge!

"Bolo, sprint to the shed, fetch a rope—swiftly! Position yourself above that man down there! Strive to yank him beyond the grasp of that cursed creature! Move with haste, Bolo! Don't waste a second! Go! Go! Go!"

"Yep!" Bolo's voice echoed with determination as he surged forward, defying his size and bulk with remarkable swiftness. He reached the shed, wrenching its door open, and plunged inside. In a matter of heartbeats, he reemerged, a hefty coil of rope slung resolutely across his shoulders. He raced along the jagged ledge behind the shed, bypassing the stretch directly over the pier. His strides ceased thirty feet above the water's surface, precisely where he predicted the struggling man would emerge from the depths.

Bolo threw the rope down the cliff, and when the beaten fellow finally crawled up on the narrow spit of beach, Bolo yelled. "The rope, man! Grab the rope! Do it now, or you're bound to die!" Bolo pointed out at the approaching monster.

The man struggled to his feet and wrapped the rope around him. Then, with the man clawing at the rope to try and climb, Bolo strained his mighty muscles and began to pull the rope up the cliff. By this time, Jake and Darwin had come from their observation positions and pitched in to help pull the seaman to safety.

As they made significant progress with the rope, Jake saw 'Meg' turn and gradually dive into the middle of the harbor again.

Meanwhile, unnoticed by the three men, Toombs had appeared from the path leading to the land bridge and lagoon on the other end of the island, and the old man had watched the last of the unfolding drama alone from the eastern edge of the harbor. His focus could have been perceived as almost worshipful, and his heart was beating so fast at the sight of this 'extinct' creature living and breathing....and killing.....right in front of him that he might have swooned in a dead faint at any moment.....but he didn't!

Such was Lamar's obsession that he blocked, out of his mind, the carnage and destruction being wrought by the giant fish, and, instead, he silently thanked God for the chance to realize this dream that other paleontologists around the world would give their lives to experience. He walked, trancelike, up the path, and when he passed the two girls' cabins, they came out to see what Toombs was staring at. Then, they, too, saw the last part of the action in the waters below.

Amy put her arms around Jenny, who had grabbed her head and begun to scream, and Amy shook Jenny gently but firmly until Jenny returned Amy's hug while crying softly into Amy's shoulder.

Amy's gaze snapped to Toombs, who remained in a daze, transfixed by the macabre display orchestrated by the creature that had haunted his adult life. "Professor!" Amy's voice pierced through the tense air, carried by urgency as she shouted into Lamar's ear. Despite the mere few feet separating them, he remained unresponsive, lost in some inner turmoil. Frustration and worry intertwined in Amy's voice as she refused to relent. "Dammit, Lamar! Look at me!" Her words escalated into an angry scream, a final act of defiance to shatter Toombs' trance.

He looked hesitantly away from the lagoon and encountered a furious stare, in return, from the lovely brunette standing off to his right. "Wha... did you say something, my dear?" He asked politely.

"Don't...'my dear'...me, Lamar!" Amy was livid now. "Look down there!" Amy was trying to make a point, but Toombs jumped in.

"Yes! Yes! I'm looking!" His eyes played over the harbor, hoping to acquire any sign of 'Meg,' but the surface was still and mirror flat for the moment. "Isn't *he* magnificent, Amy?" He went on without waiting for her answer. "A species lost for millennia, and we are here to witness it!" His eyes were glassed over as he stared at the reflective surface.

Amy realized that Toombs had finally surpassed all rational thought, but instead of empathy, she felt a wave of increasing anger, not specifically at Toombs, personally, but at Toombs, the icon of their recent, collective, and tragically ill-conceived courses of action....along with the horrible results!

"Godammit, Lamar!" Amy fumed. "Aren't you feeling the least bit guilty at what's happened lately?" She went on without waiting for his answer. "I mean, after all, this son-of-a-bitch has been directly responsible for, who knows, how many deaths, not to mention the hundreds of thousands, if not millions, of dollars in ships, boats, and property it's destroyed, to date! And, here, you have the unmitigated gall to say he's 'magnificent'....and with apparent admiration at that?"

Toombs stared blankly at Amy for a few moments, and then he responded as he would to a question in one of his classes at the university.

"Amy, my dear girl!..." He was, again, cut off in mid-thought by Amy's furious burst.

"Cut the fuck up with the damn niceties, Lamar!" Tell me where you stand on bringing in the mainland authorities as soon as possible! Are you going to cooperate and bring back the radio parts or not?" She stood, hugging the shaking Jenny, breathing deeply, with dark red cheeks, and staring coldly at Toombs.

Toombs stood, shoulders sagging, facial features impassive, and gazed calmly at Amy. His mind was waging an internal war of decisions between his deep-seated, decades-old desires and obsessions and his basically sound moral character.

Fortunately, the scene that had just unfolded in the harbor had given him a little more impetus to pursue the morally committed path, especially since 'Meg's' appearance had, to some extent, satiated his longings to actually encounter a live specimen of this prehistoric monster.

He smiled softly at Amy and sighed deeply. "My dear, what can I say? You're absolutely right....all of you! I've hidden the parts down the path, there, near the rocky bridge, and I shall be the one to go back and retrieve them myself! I...will be the one to deliver them, personally, to Jake. I trust that this will sufficiently warrant, at least, a small degree of forgiveness; do you think so?

Amy saw that Lamar was a beaten, guilt-ridden old man who, obviously, realized the magnitude of what had happened, and she also knew that all of them shared, to some degree, in the decision to delay calling the authorities. So, she dropped her angry demeanor somewhat and returned just a bit of a smile as she answered Lamar. "I suppose so, Lamar. Just get those parts now so we can call in some help before someone else is hurt or killed, okay?" Lamar gave a quick nod and shuffled off down the path. His head was down, and his shoulders continued to stoop, prolonging the image of a broken man whose spirit had deserted him.

Amy watched for a few minutes and doubted the professor would be the same again. Then, she patted Jenny on the back, and, with an arm around the smaller blonde's shoulder, they went to the knoll to see what was going on further down the edge of the harbor.

Back on the bluff, Bolo had gotten Tesoro about halfway up the hill, but Jake wasn't paying attention because he was watching the surface for signs of 'Meg's' return. Darwin had arrived from the boat and jumped to help Bolo bring the beleaguered boat captain the rest of the way up.

Jake, too, was about to help the other two when, out of the corner of his eye, he caught motion near the harbor mouth, and he snapped his entire focus on that spot as the large dorsal rose out of the water and cut, smoothly, through the gap, to the open ocean beyond. Then, as suddenly as it appeared, the fin dipped beneath the small waves and was gone.

Jake stared at the spot for an instant, thinking about it and the other time the fish had entered the harbor, and he abruptly thought of what was bothering him about what he'd seen but not understood until now. "Of course!....Shallow bottom in the entrance!" He barked to no one in particular. With this realization, he turned to Darwin and Bolo and was about to tell them of his revelation when he looked down and saw the face of the man he'd sworn to kill if he could ever find him again.....Tesoro!

"You sorry mother fucker! Now you'll die for sure!" Jake screamed, and before Graham or Bolo could step in, Jake grabbed Johno by the neck and lifted the smaller man, like a rag doll, up until he dangled limply in front of Jake.

Bolo and Darwin looked at each other, tremendously startled by Jake's explosive violence!

At the same time, Jake had begun to shake Tesoro brutally, from side to side, and, through a profoundly red visage, Jake yelled repeatedly! "Die, you motherfucker!... Just die!"

With Darwin's help, Bolo swiftly grabbed Jake's arms and tried to prevent the heavily muscled guy from committing murder immediately!

Along with their attempt to physically restrain the big man, Bolo tried to reason with Jake. "Please, Mister Jake! Please don't kill him! It won't bring them back, and you'll be taken away! Bolo won't have anyone, then! You don't want that, do you, Mister Jake?" Bolo was practically screaming himself as he and Graham had succeeded in getting Tesoro back on the ground, albeit with Jake's hands still on the more petite man's throat.

Jake finally let go, though, and Johno slumped to the ground at the three men's feet, rubbing his bruised throat.

Jake's gaze darted between Bolo and Graham, his eyes wide with intensity and determination. "Listen, fellas," he began, his voice carrying the weight of a long-held purpose. "This little bastard doesn't deserve to live." Each word was punctuated with unwavering conviction. "I trailed him from Puerto Rico to 'the horn,' and I swore he wouldn't escape justice for what he'd done."

The gravity of his mission hung palpably in the air. "There's no one else to hold him accountable. Think about it. Who will ensure he pays for snuffing out the lives of the only people who stood by him?" Jake's tone grew fiercer, his anger barely contained. "They treated him like their own son, and how does he repay years of unwavering devotion? He fucking killed them!" His control teetered on the edge, a storm of emotions brewing within.

Even Darwin sensed the imminent eruption. Darwin had almost lunged forward to extract the vulnerable figure from the line of fire, recognizing Jake's descent into unrestrained fury.

But then, a sound from the debris at the water's edge shattered the charged atmosphere—emanating specifically from the wreckage of the boat's wheelhouse, which now lay on its side. "What the...?" Jake trained the binoculars on the portion of the vessel that the moaning and sound of timbers being moved seemed to be coming from, and, at first, all he saw was wreckage. But, just as he thought they'd heard only sounds from shifting timbers rubbing against each other, he caught a slight movement from a small porthole. "Wait a minute!" He exclaimed, still looking through the field glasses. "It looks like there's someone alive down there! Look at the porthole on the cabin wall just aft of the wheelhouse... there... on the side!" Jake directed the others.

They all saw it then, including Tesoro, who was now regaining his composure. "It's Johno!" Johno sputtered, still a little breathless from the encounter with Jake. "He had sent the others forward and returned to my side, in the wheelhouse, when the world... she exploded!" Johno tried to reach his feet, but Graham grabbed him by the back of the neck with a mighty hand.

"Hey there, you! Hold on a second! Where do you believe you're headed?" Darwin's grip tightened, reaching the perfect balance between control and restraint as he subdued the restless young man.

"Listen up! You can't simply abandon him to blister in the sun down there! He hasn't caused harm to any of you, has he?" Tesoro's voice resonated with solid emphasis.

Jake thought for a second, then nodded to Bolo and picked up the rope, motioning for Darwin and even Tesoro to do the same.

With Jake, Darwin, and Johno securely holding the rope, Bolo descended, hand over hand, to the shore at the bluff's base.

Jake yelled after him. "We'll watch the entrance across the way, Bolo, and if we see any sign of a fin, you drop what you're doing and get back up the rope. Understand?"

Bolo waved to Jake, caught on to Jake's instructions, and lumbered down the narrow beach toward the vessel about forty yards away.

As it was, however, Bolo and Jake needn't have worried because, unknown to all on the island, 'Meg' had turned *his* attention to the western end of the island, near a rocky overpass and smaller lagoon, from whence *he* had picked up a minute scent of blood in the water.

Nevertheless, Bolo proceeded quickly to the cabin, lying part in and part out of the water, periodically casting glances across the harbor, himself, even though he knew that there were three sets of eyes up on the hill and two sets that, neither he nor the other three, knew about, watching from the knoll over by the pier... Amy and Jenny!

Bolo pulled away a broken mast and some netting, shouldered the cabin door open against some boards wedged against it, and looked inside. "Say, man! You be here?" Bolo spoke loudly and listened for a response.

"O-o-o-h-h-h! Madre de Dios!... Aqui!... Aqui!" The Spanish for 'Here!... Here!' came out of an overturned bunk and desk to the left and over in a corner!

Bolo had no flashlight, but the light from the porthole was sufficient to cast a dim, dusk-like pall on the room, and once Bolo's eyes adjusted to the gloom, he could make out a slight motion in the corner to go with the sound.

"Wait a moment, my friend! Bolo is heading your way! How are you feeling? Are you in a condition to move out?" Bolo carefully navigated through the obstacles in his path, approaching the man partially covered by debris and cradling his head in his hands.

"Yes, I believe I'll manage! Something struck my head, and I lost consciousness, I think! What happened to the boat, sir? And where is our captain?" The stout, muscular individual assisted Bolo in shifting aside the bunk, and together, they maneuvered towards the cabin's entrance and stepped out into the sunlight, emerging atop the towering cliffs that enclosed this side of the island, all the while showing deep concern for their situation.

Bolo helped the disoriented man to his feet, tapped him on the shoulder, and pointed to the men atop the ridge.

"Jojo! Aqui, companero!" Tesoro yelled down to them.

"Ola, Jefe!" The thick-set crewman waved back, a broad smile plastered on his weather-beaten face.

Bolo glanced over his shoulder at the harbor mouth, then took Jojo by the arm and guided him rapidly to the rope, where the two men began to climb up to the top.

When Bolo and Jojo reached the precipice, Jake looked at the new arrival and issued a directive in a robust and firm voice. "Bolo! You and Darwin, please, take our two new....ah...' guests' to the storage building behind my cottage over there! We'll keep them locked until I can figure out what's to be done with them, okay?" Then, he turned to Tesoro, whose voice carried an icy edge colder than any ice flow down south. "Now, you listen, Johno...." Jake grabbed one of the smaller man's arms in his calloused hand for emphasis. "...and I mean listen very closely! You aren't out of the woods on this thing by a long shot! You will stand accountable for your deeds; I promise you! Whether you face the laws of man or the laws of God doesn't matter! You will pay for what you've done! So, right now, you can do me a personal favor..." Jake briefly glanced from Bolo to Graham. "...and try to resist or run from these men." Jake turned his head slowly until his eyes unmistakably came to rest on the scoped rifle he'd propped against the side of the nearby shed. "That way, I've got an excuse to do what I've wanted to see done for a long time!... Or, you can go along with them, cooperate, and disappoint me a lot!

Do you understand?" Jake shook Johno's arm once, for good measure, and to let Tesoro know that Jake meant business.

Johno knew, full well, Jake's background and spoke with a slight tremble in his voice. "Believe me, Jake! We will give you no problems!" He looked meaningfully at his mate, Jojo, and got an eager nod of compliance from him, as well.

Bolo and Darwin pushed each of the two 'guests' to start them on their way, and the four moved out toward the little-used shed behind Jake's cabin.

Jake watched them momentarily and turned back to scan the ocean for any sign of 'Meg' when he noticed the two girls huddled, motionless, on the knoll, over by the path leading to the pier. He'd forgotten about them in all the riotous happenings of the past couple of hours.

He swiftly moved in the shadows behind the refrigerated shed and crossed the expanse that stretched ahead, approaching the two women cautiously. "Hey! Are you both alright?" As he inquired, his gaze locked onto Amy's eyes, a sense of tension filling the air.

Amy mustered a faint, half-hearted smile and affirmed her safety with a nod. However, her eyes shifted downward towards Jenny. In a subtle, almost imperceptible gesture, she slightly shook her head from side to side, signaling that the condition of the young blonde was anything but alright, shrouding the situation in an aura of suspense.

Jake caught her meaning and spoke gently to Jenny. "Jenny!... Sweetheart!... You shouldn't be out here; you should be resting. We will need you to be well soon to help, and you've got to rest in the meantime!" Jake smoothed her hair back as he smiled at her frightened expression.

While he was soothing Jenny's golden tresses, Jake studied Amy closely to assure himself that she was, in fact, okay and not suffering similar deleterious emotional effects as Jenny. When he felt convinced, he asked Amy. "Amy, have you seen Toombs anywhere?" He looked around the compound area and at the area surrounding the girls' cabins. "We've got to get that radio fixed and get through to the mainland. This thing has got to be stopped!" Jake pounded a fist into his opposite hand to drive this point home!

Amy glanced briefly at the ground, clearly in thought. "Jake, we just talked with Lamar a little while ago, and I believe he has come to his senses now. He must have taken the parts over by the lagoon before because after we talked, I think he returned to retrieve them and said he wanted to bring them to you personally. I think his conscience is eating him up inside, and he's searching for some degree of absolution."

Jake peered down the path that wound to the lagoon for about half a mile. "Maybe I'd better go find him. That's not a safe area for an old man like Lamar to wander around in." Jake appeared to be angry with, but, at the same time, actually concerned about the old professor.

"Jake, I'm begging you! Cut him some slack. I gave him a real tongue-lashing over everything, and he's pretty beaten down already if you catch my drift." Amy's petite hand clasped Jake's forearm, applying intense and deliberate pressure, intensifying her plea.

Jake enveloped the hand on his arm with his other hand, his touch gentle yet firm, as he locked his gaze onto her eyes with an intense focus. "Amy, let me make this crystal clear. I have no intention of laying a finger on Lamar, physically or metaphorically, any more than he's already managed to hurt himself."

Amy felt the warmth of Jake's hand on her own and smiled as she returned his gaze and slowly released his arm.

Jake held onto Amy's hand a moment longer, then tossed it back as an afterthought while he started down the trail. "Oh, get our little 'princess' there, something hot, and put her to bed! We will all need our wits about us to deal with 'our friend' out there... at least, until we can get some help out here!" Amy waved her understanding, and Jake turned and was gone.

CHAPTER 15
A Subtle Hint of Blood's Aroma

Our Big Boy had accomplished his grim task of feeding on four creatures from the surface, executing his strategy with precision. Two creatures were promptly dislodged from the larger entity during his initial attack. These he engulfed whole, their struggling forms disappearing down his cavernous throat. A few moments later, he ruthlessly crushed two more creatures in his massive jaws during a violent breach from below. This maneuver catapulted his prey and himself high above the water's surface.

Although he had somewhat quelled his insatiable hunger, there remained a nagging sense that another presence, a foreign entity, had disrupted the water's equilibrium as he descended back into it. An urge to pursue this interloper, to incorporate it into his meal, gripped him. Yet, despite his efforts, this enigmatic presence had eluded him, slipping away into the depths. Frustrated but undeterred, he focused on exploring the deeper waters, anticipating the potential for more excellent sustenance and the freedom to hunt more expansively.

As *Meg* cleared the harbor, *he* picked up a faint scent of blood drifting on the currents from *his* right, and *his* recent conditioning told *him* that this was where *he* had taken several of the large, agile surface swimmers in recent days.

Therefore, *big fish* responded aggressively to the scent, and the blood lust inherent to *his* species drove *him* to increase speed and focus.

When nearing the end of the island, *he* found the blood spore much more robust and the currents a bit warmer, stimulating *him* to dart back and forth in a random pattern, trying to locate the source of the smell that set *his* appetite to burning once again.

Meanwhile, unaware that his 'obsession' swam just a few hundred yards offshore, Lamar had made his way, through an often bush-lined pathway, to the lagoon, but, as he emerged near the spring, he almost fainted from shock, because he startled two large sea lions, one a larger-than-normal bull and, the other, a somewhat smaller cow, most probably the bull's mate.

The cow leaped into the lagoon and swam out to the middle, then in a wide circle, which would bring her, eventually, to her mate's side. He had been slower, though, and Lamar could see a fresh gash in his flank, probably caused by one of the other males in an earlier fight for the 'lady's' affections. He must have sought this spot to rest his wounds. Nevertheless, when startled by Lamar's arrival, he made a mad dash toward the inlet, running beneath the land bridge to be joined by his mate.

Unfortunately, the water under the rocky overpass was only four feet deep and ran over very sharp, jagged rocks strewn along the shallow bottom. This shallow channel proceeded for approximately thirty yards before dropping off dramatically on the ocean.

When the bull accelerated to a dangerously rapid clip and zipped under the bridge, his mate a few yards behind, their bulk caused them to displace too much water, and they both raked over some large sharp rocks sticking up from the sand. The result was several cuts in their thick hides, which caused a generous discharge of blood to flow in a long stream in their wakes.

The bull felt pain was more significant than the cow's; thus, the bull turned in an arc and returned to the lagoon to search for a covered area on the bank to rest his injuries before following after his mate. Lamar didn't see the bull make his way onto the shore and into some bushes bordering the spring, where the old sea lion stretched out and became motionless.

The female wasn't experiencing too much pain because none of her cuts had hit any artery or vital nerve, but... these cuts would have been just as potentially lethal had she had a knife pressed to her throat!

After Lamar had recovered from his initial shock, he watched the two sea lions until he lost sight of the more prominent male. Then he redirected his focus, moved carefully along the uneven path, and proceeded up and over the narrow rock bridge to a small, nondescript pile of rocks on the far side. The professor knelt and methodically removed the stones until he found a recently filled hole underneath. He dug the loose sand out of the hole, uncovering the plastic bag full of radio parts. He pulled the bag out and gently shook the sand off of it. All the circuit boards were still in good shape, and Toombs breathed a sigh of relief and resignation.

As luck... bad luck... would have it, Toombs' guilt and determination to right his past wrongs had caused him to be so intensely focused on the recovery of the parts that he was oblivious to the twelve-foot fin that silently rounded the rocky point just a couple of hundred yards from his location, nor the life-or-death drama that was beginning even closer, involving the female sea lion that he'd just watched.

Lamar rose with the bag and turned to start back when Jake came out of the bushes near the spring. "Hey! Lamar!" Over here!" Jake waved to get the old man's attention.

Lamar had just begun crossing back over the bridge when he heard Jake's yell, and, wanting to please Jake so much, Toombs paused in the middle of the bridge to return Jake's wave. He also held up the bag of parts to show Jake his reformed intentions when Lamar's universe exploded in a wave of spray and water!

As he rounded the final jagged outcrop, drawing closer to the island's edge, the scent of blood enveloped the surroundings, thickening the air with eerie anticipation. Determined, he initiated a broad, sweeping arc, his keen senses seeking out his quarry. Remarkably, locating his prey strategically between the shoreline and his current vantage point took only an instant.

Locked onto the presence of the sizable sea lion, his primal instincts surged to the forefront, propelled by the unrelenting allure of feeding driven by the ceaseless infusion of blood into the water. Without a moment's hesitation, he launched himself into an attack trajectory. His velocity surged as he plunged downward, aiming to strike from the depths below. Yet, the creature of the surface had sensed his approach, the specter of danger driving it to flee urgently, back toward the safety of the shore—more precisely, toward the shallow enclave beneath the land bridge.

The impending collision course between the fleeing sea lion and the lurking menace beneath the waves, all within the confined waters of the inlet, cast a chilling shroud of suspense over the unfolding scene, a moment poised on the precipice of dramatic consequence.

Meg increased *his* speed even more, *his* vast jaws opening and closing uncontrollably in frenzied anticipation, and as *he* overtook *his* quarry...*he* ran out of the ocean!

The sea lion was swimming faster than she ever had, filled with an unfathomable terror that gave her strength beyond any she possessed in her long life! As she approached the channel beneath the bridge, she felt strong turbulence and heard a roar of water being displaced at an unbelievable rate behind her, and, abruptly, she was being lifted and pushed, head over flippers, through the air and into the lagoon beyond. There, she struggled to regain her orientation and take in deep breaths of air!

He was so very close to the 'target creature' at that time, but, out of nowhere, the sharp, jagged bottom loomed in front of *him,* and *he* turned upward, narrowly missing his intended 'meal' by only a few feet, but sending the 'thing' flying on a giant wave, caused when *he* broke the surface at an angle, which propelled *him* into the side of the end of the rocky land bridge, holding Toombs and the precious radio parts!

Lamar's body was flung through the air with a sickening resemblance to the sea lion, a marionette manipulated by the monstrous wave thrust skyward by 'Meg's' massive breach. His trajectory was cruelly determined by the roiling forces, and he crashed into the lagoon's water, a grisly puppet landing in the darkness. The unforgiving bridge channel embraced his impact, roughly twenty-five feet from its entrance. Meanwhile, the bag of parts he had clung to was wrenched violently from his grip and propelled backward toward the bridge's exterior. A cruel dance of fate saw it collide with 'Meg's' immense form before tumbling carelessly into the churning surf at Lamar's side. The tumultuous currents greedily claimed the bag, carrying it beneath 'Meg's' colossal body as the waters receded, a cruel fate sealing its doom as its contents were mercilessly crushed and obliterated against the unyielding seabed.

Jake's eyes remained fixed on the unfolding horrors at the bridge, his limbs immobilized by the suffocating grip of silent dread. Yet, a primal instinct, an internal force honed by survival, suddenly overpowered the paralysis of horror. In a frenzied surge, his body transformed from statue to motion, his mind veering away from the abyss of terror as he propelled himself into a frantic and urgent reaction.

"Lamar! Oh, God!" Jake's voice shattered the air, his words laced with desperation, as he tore off his shoes and plunged into the lagoon. The sight before him was a tableau of suspenseful dread:

Lamar lay motionless, a spectral figure some twenty yards away in the water's expanse. Casting a quick glance towards the looming presence of 'Meg,' Jake's determination surged, propelling him through the water with an astonishing burst of power. The seconds stretched into an eternity as he bridged the distance to Lamar's lifeless form, his every muscle working in a symphony of urgency.

Upon reaching his stricken comrade, Jake wasted no time. With a deft movement, he turned Lamar over, his heart pounding as he sought signs of life. Fearing the worst, he looped his arm under Lamar's armpits and secured it across his chest, his powerful side strokes cutting through the water in a frantic race toward the safety of the shore.

Their gasping figures finally found refuge on the slender strip of sandy land that bordered the lagoon. Jake's hands moved with a practiced urgency as he dragged Lamar from the water, the atmosphere thick with tension. Swiftly transitioning into action, he initiated the rhythmic motions of CPR, his words a constant stream of encouragement and desperation mingled.

"Come on, Lamar! Fight back!... Damn it, Lamar!" Jake's voice wavered between a fervent shout and a strained plea, his open palms delivering gentle yet urgent slaps to Lamar's pale cheeks. The scene unfolded in a suspended state of suspense, the outcome uncertain, as hope and fear waged a fierce battle against time itself.

Finally, Toombs coughed and turned his head from side to side, spitting frothy water from his lips. He rolled his eyes wildly and eventually recognized Jake's face hovering above his own. "Oh!... Jake, my boy!... Where?... uh... what happened?" The old man suddenly tensed and felt around him, looking all around. Then, he felt his body, like a man who's offered to pay the check, and realized he'd forgotten his wallet. "The parts, Jake! Oh, dear me! I wanted to give them back! I truly did! Please, believe...!" Jake put his big hand on Lamar's flailing arm to try and calm the professor.

"Easy, Lamar! I saw the bag in your hands... just before 'Meg' hit the rocks behind you!" Lamar's eyes widened at this news.

"You mean Megalodon was here?" Toombs sat up straight, helped by a shot of adrenaline caused by hearing about his near encounter with the monster. "Where?" Over his shoulder, he looked at the waters on the other side of the bridge, which had sustained some damage from the collision with 'Meg' but was still standing. "My heavens! I guess that was a bit too close! You say you saw it happen, Jake?" Lamar had turned back to his savior.

"Yeah, I did. I'd just come out of the path over there. I was looking for you to try and get everything resolved between us... you know, but just as I saw you holding the parts up for me to see, *Meg* shot out of the water and rammed into the rocks near the far end of the bridge. *He* rose up so violently that the combination of waves and impact threw you over here, right out there," Jake pointed at the lagoon. "The parts for the radio weren't so lucky. They were ripped out of your hand, and the last I saw, they went to sea under that Goddammed fish!" Jake lapsed into a look of disappointment and pensiveness at recounting this part of the story.

"Oh my! Jake, I'm so sorry... really! If I'd only controlled my preoccupation with 'M....!" Jake placed a hand on Lamar's shoulder to stop the elderly gentleman's self-recrimination.

"Stop it, Lamar! What's done is done!... I'm unsure, but given the same background and experience, I would most likely have done the same thing!" Jake stood, smiled, and offered Toombs a hand to help him to his feet. Lamar took Jake's hand and rose a little unsteadily. The two men turned, then, as one, and started slowly back up the path to the compound.

Toombs grasped Jake's forearm a few minutes into the walk and turned to address Jake. "Wait a moment! Jake! The boat has a radio on it...I saw it before!... Doesn't it?"

Jake was, strangely, deflated as he responded. "Yeah... yeah, it does, Lamar, but it's pretty old, and the range has really been shortened over the years. I think the transmitter is all but worn out. I've only used it around the island to call back to the base or nearby supply ships when I am out with rare charters. I'm afraid we're out of luck there.... And, even if it were stronger, the harbor wall and cliffs block any transmission unless we had a tall antenna like the one at the main house." Jake just shook his head and began walking up the path.

Toombs, however, stayed where he was, bringing the fingers of one hand to his lips in apparent concentration. "Wait a minute, Jake! What if the boat was taken out of the harbor... ... and up toward the mainland? At some point, the transmitter has got to get through! Right?" He beheld Jake with a brightened expression, which 'shouted'.... "Agree!... Agree!... Agree!"

But Jake just gaped at Lamar, his jaw a little slack when hearing what Jake thought was pure lunacy!

"No!....Not right! It's suicide, Lamar! You forget that there's a fish out there who, apparently, likes to have any boat in the vicinity for lunch! What makes you think anyone would survive long enough to reach a place where the signal would go through?" Jake waited patiently for Lamar's response.

Toombs, on the other hand, wasn't to be dissuaded. "Please! Please, dear boy!" Lamar sighed deeply and presented his thoughts to Jake very slowly and beseechingly. "I realize that you are very committed to the welfare of your charges..." Jake jumped in.

"Not just my charges, Lamar; you and Darwin, also! I don't want to see anything happen to anyone that can be avoided!"

Lamar smiled softly and continued. "Yes, Jake; I know this is a trait of a true leader, and I truly admire this about you... I do! However, I'm asking you to be a bit more pragmatic about this. Just consider! 'A'... through my childish actions, we don't have any way to contact the outside, and who knows when they are likely to become concerned about not getting a response from their radio calls and come out to investigate... two weeks... three?"

"I've gone a month at a time, on occasion, before needing to call in, but usually, two to three weeks won't worry them very much," Jake interjected, listening responsibly to Lamar's logic.

"Very well; let's say three weeks to a month before they feel anything is wrong and send a boat or plane to check.

'B'.... Based on the current occupancy here on the island, how long will our current provisions last?"

"Oh... probably about two weeks, or so, on the food and, maybe, a little longer with our fresh water tank....that is if we all conserve. Take GI towel baths rather than showers and things like that. But, our supply ship should be here before.... shit!" Jake snapped his fingers angrily. "That bastard will make short work of this vessel before it ever reaches the island, and there's nothing we can do about it!"

Lamar put his hands together in a prayer-like pose and nodded his head up and down as Jake made Lamar's point for him.

"Holy Christ, Lamar! There'll be fifteen to twenty people on that ship, not to mention the potable water, food, and other supplies that we will definitely need!" Jake took in Lamar's reaction and froze momentarily, contemplating Toombs' logic and realizing, his stomach becoming knotted, that there was no way around it! Someone had to risk it and take the 'Maggie Mae' on a potential suicide run to reach the naval people on the mainland! This had to be done immediately to save the people on the island and those aboard any vessel unfortunate enough to venture into the waters around this ocean area.

Jake exhaled as if deflating, the tension of the situation palpable. "Alright, Lamar. Your point has hit home, crystal clear. I'll take the 'Maggie Mae' out tomorrow, and..." Jake's words trailed off as Toombs intervened abruptly, his tone carrying an uncharacteristic urgency.

"No, Jake! That's not an option. You're irreplaceable to the survival of everyone here, especially if things go awry. It can't be you out on that boat," Toombs's grip tightened unconsciously on Jake's sleeve, a desperate plea beneath his forceful words.

Jake's hand found its way over Toombs's, his touch a calming reassurance amidst the rising tension. "Alright, Lamar, then who?" Jake's voice held a mixture of resignation and genuine curiosity. "Who else can I ask to set sail into those waters, likely becoming nothing more than a meal for that monstrous creature?"

Stepping away from Jake, Toombs walked a few deliberate paces up the path before returning to face him. His voice softened, carrying a sense of quiet determination. "Me," Lamar's words hung in the air, a declaration imbued with an unexpected pride, painting his elderly frame with an aura of courage.

Jake's reaction was one of shock, his words escaping in a disbelieving tone. "No way! Lamar, you can't be serious! Think about it. This mission would probably be a one-way trip, and I don't mean just a journey to the mainland either." Lamar remained silent, his weathered face etched with a gentle smile, his response expected yet allowed Jake to voice his objections.

The suspense thickened, a silent tension hanging in the air as their words lingered, the weight of Lamar's proposition grappling with Jake's disbelief, the outcome of their conversation shrouded in uncertainty.

Jake saw that Lamar wasn't going to say anything, for the moment, in his own defense, so the big fellow drove his point home. "Look, Lamar! If we decide to do this crazy thing, it will take one of us who is physically fit, in case we may encounter some... uh.....problems along the way... and not, necessarily, the 'Meg' type of problems, at that! What if the boat has engine problems... or the radio needs to be 'tweaked' when you try to use it? And... and the sonic system itself! What happens if it needs to be quickly repaired while you're using it? Even if you can work on it, you can't do that and navigate the boat simultaneously! No, no, Lamar! It's just plain suicide!" Jake finished his tirade without taking hardly a breath. He was breathing deeply from the emotion the old man had elicited from him.

Toombs observed that Jake was finished and countered Jake's argument calmly and controlled. "Yes! You're probably right about this being... how did you put it?... oh, yes, a 'one-way ticket! I'm under no illusions to the contrary, dear boy! However, my dear Jake, look at me. I'm a beaten old man who has lived a very long, fulfilling life. I've been fortunate enough to have been granted the love of a great lady, completed a long, rewarding career in an area of interest that rewarded me with daily intellectual treasures that, I venture to say, no other man will ever enjoy... and, now, my deepest lifelong desire has been realized. I am, perhaps, the only academician who has ever seen a prehistoric creature like this, and the fact that this is Megalodon Carcharadon is... well, it's the crowning moment of my life, Jake.

Let's face facts, my boy! Should things require decisive action, I won't be much good to you from now on. You know that! Granted?" He stared at Jake quietly, shaking his head slowly up and down.

"Good!" Lamar started speaking from habit, like he was presenting his thesis to one of his classes. "Now we're making progress!

Insofar as my operating the boat and the sonic system at the same time is concerned, I've been thinking. You know those two unsavory young men from the fishing boat?" Jake again indicated that he did, but he was beginning to become suspicious. Lamar had been watching the goings on in the harbor longer than Jake thought.

"I watched, from a distance, how you seemed to have a serious issue with one of them! Correct?" Again, Lamar paused for Jake's confirmation.

"You're pretty observant, as well as astute, Lamar. Yes, that was the man I chased all over this hemisphere, the guy I swore to kill if I ever caught him! Is that what you wanted to know? Jake was a little put out by Lamar's line of reasoning, but he decided to let Toombs finish his case.

"As I surmised. Yes...yes...ahem. I don't know whether you noticed, but the other man's mannerisms... oh, the short, stocky one, that is... his mannerisms were of someone who was, I guess, very devoted to his leader, the skinny one."

Jake jumped in. "Okay, okay, Lamar! But, I don't see what all this has to do with..."

Lamar cut Jake off in return. "Patience! Patience, Jake! I'm getting to the crux of my point.

I'm betting that if you were to offer the skinny fellow, your nemesis, that is, deal, whereby, you would... ahem... set them both free at the end of all this..." As he thought, Lamar couldn't get his plan out on the table before Jake exploded.

"Are you out of your mind! For Christ's sake, Lamar!" Jake's voice carried a fervent mix of incredulity and anger, his restraint teetering on a knife's edge. "That damned little bastard was the reason behind the deaths of two elderly folks who practically raised him and me too, or at least they tried! And now... now you want me to set them free?" The effort Jake put into maintaining his composure was a feat of monumental willpower, barely containing his fiery emotions that threatened to erupt.

"Please! Just give me a moment, Jake!" Lamar's voice, normally gentle and measured, had risen to an intensity he rarely heard. It was the only way to cut through Jake's rising tirade, a shock tactic to invoke a moment of silence. "I'm not suggesting something reckless. Listen, just hear me out!" Lamar's words rang with a desperate plea, the urgency in his tone trying to bridge the gap of understanding.

"All I'm proposing is that we strike a deal," Lamar continued, his gaze unflinching as he met Jake's intense stare. "Make an agreement with the stout one. If he assists me in piloting the boat, navigating the treacherous waters while I monitor 'Meg's' movements and manage the sonic generators as needed... Then, once it's all said and done, you release them. We set them free on a skiff offshore, near a mainland town. It's a compromise that ensures their cooperation and justice while achieving our goal." Lamar's words held a fervor and conviction that matched the gravity of their situation, an intensity that sought to bridge the gap between Jake's righteous anger and a practical solution.

Of course, once I get a message to the military, they will, most likely, react and be here before we can return... even if we are incredibly fortunate enough to actually get back! In that case, you won't be able to fulfill your part of the bargain, will you?" Toombs capped his rationale with raised eyebrows and a flat conspiratorial grin.

Jake eased off his emotional peak and smiled sheepishly at Lamar in return. "I suppose, but wait a minute!" Jake snapped at a point he'd just recalled. "This will still be a suicide trip, and even though you have, at times, been a pain in the ass, Lamar; I still don't think I can live with myself if I knowingly let you go off to become well-educated 'fish food!'" Jake half-smiled and half-frowned. "Besides, I doubt, very seriously, that Darwin will stand for this! He'll want to go with you, personally."

Lamar shook his head, looking at the ground while walking up to Jake and putting a hand on the bigger man's shoulder. "I can handle Darwin, Jake; believe me, and, as to your repetitive point about this being a suicide mission, please try to understand. I have encountered and accomplished everything a man could possibly want! Do I want to die? Of course, I don't! However, Jake, we've got to come to grips with the hard, cold facts at this stage of the game. I am the most expendable one here!" Jake started to object, but Toombs held up a finger and shut him off. "No! Please don't insult my intelligence by trying to deny it!

Furthermore, after this experience, for which I am deeply grateful, anything else in life would be supremely anticlimactic." Jake just kept eye contact with the old man and listened, helpless to protest for the time being.

Lamar continued morosely. "Between you and me... I'm tired, Jake... emotionally... exhausted! I miss my wife tremendously!" He paused briefly, staring, misty-eyed, far off, at nothing, and chuckled lightly. "I can admit it to you, now; my Sarah was the one thing in this world that meant more to me than my encounter with 'Meg' ever could! Does that sound crazy to you, lad?"

Jake saw that Lamar's eyes were filling with tears at the discussion about his wife. "No, my friend; it sounds wiser and more logical than any idea philosophy I've ever heard... I mean that!" Jake patted Lamar's arm with a big hand.

Toombs caught himself, then, and adopted a firm, controlled tone for his summary. "Frankly, the one thing that concerns me about this trip would be the risk of losing our only boat!"

Jake's eyes widened at this realization, and he replied. "Dammit, you're right, Lamar! That could be catastrophic, especially if you don't happen to get a message through!" Jake lapsed into thought with this new challenge and peered down at his boots, the fingers of his right hand tapping softly at his lips. "I just don't know. Before presenting it to the group, I must think about this."

Lamar nodded his agreement but offered. "To be sure! But please recall that until we can notify the outside of what is out there, more vessels and many more unfortunate souls are at serious risk! You agree?"

Jake's hand landed firmly on Lamar's arm, his grip warm and familiar, as he guided the professor along the path that wound its way toward the compound. A sense of camaraderie was palpable, underscored by the tension that had ignited their conversation. "You're right, Lamar. Knowledge is a burden in its own right, but it sure as Hell doesn't make the choice any simpler."

The two figures moved in tandem, their steps synchronized, tracing the path together. Their silhouettes were framed against the backdrop of the surroundings, a moment frozen in time as they continued their journey, each lost in their own contemplative thoughts. The atmosphere was rich with unspoken reflections, a quiet symphony of emotions and uncertainties echoing beneath their shared silence.

IT WAS LATE AFTERNOON when Jake and Lamar emerged from the path in front of the two girls' cabins and moved into the extended open area leading to the main house.

On approaching the long porch, they saw Darwin and Jenny deep in an animated discussion. "Hey there, on the porch!" Jake yelled, making Jenny and Darwin break off their talk and jump up to greet the two new arrivals.

"Bloody Hell! Where 'ave the two 'a you been?" Darwin was legitimately concerned, but a small smile played briefly across his lips at the sight of Lamar holding onto Jake's arm. Jenny said nothing; she stood quietly behind Graham, projecting a meek, intimidating demeanor.

Jake exchanged glances with Lamar, then replied. "Oh, we both felt we needed a little swim, so we went to the lagoon for a... uh... dip!" Toombs gave a slight titter and managed to control a further outburst.

"A swim, you say?" Darwin scratched his head, baffled by Jake's explanation. "A swim... a bloody swim?" Graham was fit to be tied, and Jenny's eyes were wide with disbelief and surprise.

"I just can't believe you, two, would go off the bleedin' rocker enough to do that! No! Not for a minute, Jake!" Darwin was now suspicious and pressed the issue with Toombs to a greater extent. "'Here now, Doc! 'How 'bout a straight answer? What happened out there, and where are the radio parts?"

Before Lamar could answer, Amy and Bolo, who'd been trying to organize some semblance of a dinner meal, came out onto the porch in Jake's absence. They had heard the voices and come to see what was going on.

Lamar acknowledged them and took a couple of steps forward, effectively taking center stage. "My friends, I want to confess a terrible injustice that's been visited upon you all! In my selfish pursuit of self-gratification and personal glory, I have deprived all of us of the means to readily contact people outside for assistance in dealing with this most terrible crisis.

Further, I wish to express my deepest gratitude to Jake, here, without whose generous support at the lagoon a short while ago, I would not be standing, humbly, before you now!

In short, dear people..." Lamar paused to stem his rising emotion. "...the precious radio parts were...er...accidentally destroyed in an unfortunate encounter with 'Meg' at the lagoon!"

A murmur and shocked looks were passed among the others, but they all looked back to Toombs for an expanded explanation.

"In all fairness, I was, sincerely, in the process of retrieving and returning the parts....please, believe me on this point! However, as

I was bringing them back, across that rock bridge, at the lagoon, 'Meg' was, apparently, attacking a sea lion below me and lunged into the rocks near the bridge, knocking me into the lagoon and the parts somewhere, into the ocean beyond." From face to face, Lamar looked and saw a mixture of fear and reproach in each.

"I understand that I must be quite the object of your resentment, even you, Darwin, my dear boy," Graham's voice held a weight of acknowledgment, his gaze fixed with a mixture of longing and apprehension on Toombs.

Darwin's response came as a huff, a mere breath that carried complex emotions, a blend of exasperation, hurt, and a glimmer of unresolved tension. His gaze remained locked onto Toombs, unwavering and searching.

Graham's voice held a tone of humility laced with a plea for understanding. "Yes, I can sense the resentment and don't blame you. But I hope, perhaps against hope, that you might find it within your hearts to forgive an old man's foolish actions and selfishness. I wish to extend my sincerest apologies and attempt to rectify my wrongs," his words held a vulnerability, a raw admission of wrongdoing, as he contemplated the notion of redemption.

He was poised to delve into the details of the plan he and Jake had hatched, but a second thought reined him in. It was a decision born out of wisdom; he recognized that Jake was better suited to present the proposal, a gesture that carried its own subtle note of humility and acceptance, signifying a willingness to let others take the reins of redemption.

"And pray, enlighten us, Professor..." Amy's interruption carried a perceptibly sardonic edge, manifesting her skepticism. "...how exactly do you plan on making up for your blunders, if I may ask?"

The professor hesitated, momentarily caught in the crossfire of Amy's pointed sarcasm. A nervous smile crept onto his lips as he responded, his words carrying an air of both humility and eagerness. "Indeed, my dear, well... you see, I have a proposal in mind. With your permission, I believe Jake here might be the ideal person to elaborate."

The weight of Lamar's introduction caused Jake to stir from his contemplative silence, his gaze lifting from the thoughts that had held him captive. A sense of unexpected attention settled on him, a task he had been pondering now thrust into the forefront. However, Jake's response bore a hint of unease, still uncertain about how to unveil the plan to the others. The "cat was out of the bag," a phrase that held a sense of inevitability, and Darwin, the observant one, was quick to catch the shift. A question etched across Darwin's features, the trajectory of his gaze moving between Lamar and Jake, a silent demand for clarity emanating from his eyes.

Lamar's eyes squinted slightly, trying to communicate privately to Jake that this was the time to do this. "Nonsense, my boy! I think this is a perfect time, and I want you and all present..." He moved his arm in a wide circle, indicating his inclusion of everyone in his pronouncement. "...to know I am one hundred percent committed to the plan! As a matter of fact, Jake, I think that all these fine people should know that I plan to carry out this plan personally!" Lamar was a lousy actor, and anyone watching him could tell the old man was highly nervous despite his surface-only smile.

This comment from the professor brought an immediate reaction from Graham. "Eh...what's the plan, if I may ask, Doc?" Darwin looked from Toombs to Jake suspiciously.

Jake avoided eye contact with any of the others as he began to lay out the details of what had to be done. "Uh...before I get into this thing, let me tell all of you: if you can think of a more logical, practical, or just plain, better plan... I'm all for it; believe me!" No one replied, waiting for Jake to put the facts on the table.

"Okay, then! Here goes! It's a fact that the base radio is shot! Without the proper parts or control circuit boards, it just won't work. Now, everyone, please understand. Lamar has admitted to taking the parts...." Lamar stood, shoulders slumped, eyes fixed on the ground at his feet in sincere shame. "I believe him when he says that he had realized how wrong and, potentially, tragic his actions were, especially after a discussion he'd had with Amy and Jenny earlier." The two girls smiled, in understanding, at Lamar, and Jenny put a small arm around the old man's shoulders in knowing support.

Jake continued. "Nevertheless, during his attempt to return the components, Lamar, as was mentioned before, had an 'up close and personal' run-in with 'Meg,' and the bag of parts was lost.

So, this leaves us with minimal options. Of course, we can always wait and hope for help, and it may come. However, let me remind you that we are entering a very stormy season, and that storm we had the other night was like a spring shower. In comparison with some, we will very likely be getting. The people on the mainland know this, and it may be as long as a month before they get around to sending a patrol boat or plane out to check on us."

Jake shifted his gaze to Lamar, mustering a deep breath as he steeled himself for what lay ahead. With a resolute determination, he took the reins and laid out their plan's full scope. "More immediate, however, is the impending arrival of the coastal supply ship. It's set to reach our shores any day now, carrying crucial provisions, sustenance, and clean water. On top of that, about two dozen diligent individuals are on board, all of whom are counting on this delivery. But here's the grim truth: if we fail to devise a way to alert and communicate with them, if we cannot bridge the gap to the outside world, the lives on that ship, and ultimately our own, are perilously poised on the edge of uncertainty. The sunrises we take for granted might very well dwindle in number." Jake's words carried the gravity of the situation, his tone infused with urgency.

Before Jake could continue, Darwin interjected with characteristic promptness, seizing the opportunity to contribute to the unfolding discourse.

"Okay, Jake! You've just quoted the bloody obvious! So, what's the answer?"

Jake held a hand in a 'stop right there' gesture, then continued explaining. "Patience, Darwin! This is hard enough to admit, much less explain, but there is one other radio!" Jake paused and thought momentarily, then changed his tack a little.

"But first! Bolo, are our two... uh... 'guests' comfortable?" Bolo nodded grimly that they were well secured. "Good! Next, Darwin, please tell me that the sonic system is fully operational and dependable."

"Aye, Jake! This contraption is as ready as a bloke at a ball, itching to dance the 'Waltzing Matilda'!" Graham's words conveyed assurance, enthusiasm, and a hint of swagger. The confidence in his voice was unmistakable as he spoke with a touch of bravado, ensuring Jake that the contraption was fully prepared for action.

Jake let out a hearty chuckle, amused by the Aussie's playful sense of humor. "Well, mate, you've certainly got a way with words," he remarked light-heartedly. "But you've hit the nail on the head. Those two elements are absolutely critical to the success of this plan."

"The only other radio is the small one on the 'Maggie Mae,'..." Again, Graham jumped in prematurely.

"Hey there, Jake! That contraption you're calling a 'radio,' does it even have enough juice left to send a signal?" Darwin's skepticism was evident as he raised the concern.

"No, Darwin, unfortunately, it doesn't," Jake replied, pacing a restless dance within the circle formed by the others. "And that right there... that's the crux of the matter!"

To get the radio on the boat to effectively contact the coast, someone will have to take the boat about halfway to the beach and transmit the message for help, and then either try to return with the vessel or keep on going to overall safety!"

Darwin indicated his understanding while Jake was elaborating, and he picked this time to interject his logic. "Aye, mate! 'Makes sense; so, when do we leave?" Graham assumed he would be the natural selection for an apparently 'suicidal' mission.

Jake glanced again at Lamar and proceeded to the hard part. "Well,...uh...you're not, Darwin! That task will be....Lamar's!"

A dissonance of objections erupted from the assembled group, each voice clamoring for attention, yet Graham claimed the spotlight. "Hold on a minute, pardon my bluntness, but you two are daft! Both of you!" His assertion was resolute, taking in the scene with an air of exasperated disbelief. A quick glance at Lamar confirmed that the old man shared his sentiments. "Let's start with you, Doc. You can't steer the damn boat, and let's not forget that the sonic generator isn't exactly a walk in the park either."

Jake, exercising patience, allowed Graham to vent his frustration, understanding the need to clear the air. Once the initial outburst subsided, he resumed the discussion calmly yet steadfastly. "Secondly, Graham, let's be realistic here. Your brain is a damn treasure trove of knowledge, and what am I?" Darwin gestured toward himself with a dramatic sweep of his hands. "Just a washed-up soldier whose smarts are thanks to rubbing shoulders with minds like yours!" Jake's gaze held a deep respect, his lips curving into a small smile as he acknowledged the display of humility from Darwin.

Graham kept on with his subject. "See 'ere, Professor! People... lots of people... need you. They do! And, who needs the likes of me? No one, that's who!" Darwin was speaking from his soul, now, an action triggered by Lamar's shocking revelation, coupled with the reality that the old academician was, in fact, one of the few people in the world that Darwin truly respected.

Lamar could see that Graham was baring his heart, and the elderly man wanted to spare his friend further embarrassment, so he jumped in at this point. "My boy!... My boy!... My boy!" Toombs' own eyes were tearing as he began. "What you are saying touches an old man to his core, but... in the interest of all present... more rational logic needs to prevail!

In the first place, you have known for some time... actually, since my dear wife died... that my heart just wasn't in my teaching. Therefore, your admonition that lots of people need me anymore is really a trifle erroneous, and, insofar as my being here required, well, I've imparted as much knowledge, as I possibly can, to all of you....at least, when it comes to the nature of the beast we are currently facing! Ergo, my usefulness to the group's survival is minor at best.

You, on the other hand, my dear Darwin," Graham listened intently, trying to grasp some flaw in Toombs' reasoning, which Graham could exploit to substantiate a veto of the trip. Tragically, he found none. "You're an accomplished diver and warrior who could significantly contribute in a final struggle with Megalodon, should it become necessary.

So you see..." Graham snapped his fingers, interrupting Toombs' presentation.

"Diver! By all the stars in the sky, that's it!" Graham's excitement was palpable, his energy igniting as he began to pace back and forth rapidly, almost frenzied. He punctuated his words with forceful gestures, his clenched fist meeting his opposite palm in a series of emphatic impacts that underscored the urgency of his revelation. "Doc, remember those spears? The ones we rigged with the explosive tips?" The words tumbled out of his mouth, each one carrying a surge of renewed insight and determination.

Jake perked up at this and thought for a second. Then... "Nice thought, Darwin, but one of those going off in this hundred-foot monster, would only tear a small plug out of him and thoroughly piss him off! You agree, Lamar?"

"I'm afraid so, Darwin," Toombs replied directly to Graham, and as the others looked on, Graham held up an index finger to call everyone's attention to his main point. "Yeah, Doc... that's if you fire it from a distance and hit somewhere on the fleshy part of the body...But!... What if some lunatic were to fire at the soft spot behind the eye... from right next to the bastard? What then?" Darwin crossed his arms and waited for the emotional explosion he was sure would come.

"Lunacy, plain and simple!" Jake's response came with a touch of suspicion, his skepticism evident before Toombs could even voice his thoughts. "Darwin, have you stopped to consider that each of those high-powered 'sticks' you're proposing has the concussive impact of a stick of dynamite? If, and that's a big if, someone could survive the blast at close range... and that's a monstrous if... the repercussions on their eardrums and, quite possibly, their internal organs, would be nothing short of substantial and irreparable."

"Nevertheless," Jake continued, a shroud of private reservations lingering beneath his words. He did not want Graham to become a sacrificial lamb more than he wanted Lamar to sail into the unknown. "Even if you were to ensure an accurate shot, which would mean getting up close and personal with that beast without becoming its next meal, for heaven's sake! The odds just don't add up, Darwin. Chances are, we'd lose one of us and still have no choice but to send the boat out at the end of the day, anyway." As he concluded his fervent speech, Jake's breath came in heavy exhalations, each word laden with the weight of his emotional plea.

Darwin could see Jake's point and put his closed fist to his mouth, tapping it lightly in intense thought. After a few seconds, he waved his finger at Jake and blurted out an idea, countering Jake's hypothesis.

"Alright, 'here's how it goes!" He looked briefly at the opening between the two rocky walls leading out to the sea, nodded to himself that he was convinced his idea was workable, and laid it out for everyone. "You charge the sonic system and take me, complete with my tanks and spears, over to the entrance, yonder, and drop me off! I dive down to the bottom and wait! Meantime, we know that the 'brute' is attracted to the sound of boats, like a bloody dinner bell! Right! So, you bring the boat back across the pond, here, and gun the engine. When 'our boy' comes to see what's what, he has to go right past me, and I nail him! And, pow! No more 'Meg!'

What do you think, mate?" Graham pasted a less than convincing smile on his ruddy features and waited for someone to offer their thoughts.

Lamar answered first this time. "Uh....it sounds like you have a way to actually achieve the goal, my boy! However, I don't see where you are protecting yourself from the underwater blast effects that Jake alluded to... or... ah... did I miss something?" The old man looked deeply worried as he finished.

"Bingo, mate!" Jake added with a knowing, mirthless smile on his lips.

Graham allowed a moment of silence to stretch between them, contemplating the gravity of the situation. Then, in a voice unusually soft, he spoke up. "I can't deny the challenge that's there," he conceded, his tone carrying a sense of quiet determination. "But I firmly believe this risk is one worth taking. You've got to see it, Jake..." Darwin's words were directed at Jake, a plea beneath his intent gaze, urging him to consider his perspective over Toombs'.

"...that I stand a much better chance of surviving the explosive impact from my spears than Doc would have, exposed out there on open water against that monstrosity," Darwin's voice held an earnest sincerity, his argument crafted with a fervent hope that Jake would be swayed by the logic.

Jake's thoughts churned briefly, his gaze flickering between Darwin and Lamar. With a quick glance towards the professor, he finally spoke up. "It's difficult to admit, Darwin, but you have a point. A small one, mind you, but a point nonetheless."

With a decision reached, Toombs and Graham separated from the group, each retreating to their respective cabins to collect their thoughts and emotions.

As they walked away, Jake watched them, acknowledging the growing weight of the path he was choosing to tread. He recognized the necessity of giving Darwin a chance to prove his plan, albeit with considerable misgivings. But he also knew he couldn't disregard Lamar's arrangement as a backup, a safety net against the uncertainty of the sea.

"Hey, Bolo!" Jake called out, his voice breaking the momentary stillness. The tall, ebony figure of Bolo sprang up from his perch, swiftly crossing the distance to stand before Jake.

"Whatcha need, Mister Jake?" Bolo had always felt that Jake was one of the smartest and most determined men he had ever known, and to say that he would follow Jake blindly into any situation wouldn't be much of a stretch.

Jake placed a big hand on Bolo's shoulder. "Tell me, my friend, how are our two 'guests' doing?" Jake was dead serious, even though his question was tinged with a bit of humor.

"They are fine, Mister Jake. As you say, we have locked 'em up over there and gave 'em coffee and some of the leftovers from lunch. That be okay for you?"

"Yeah, that's fine, Bolo, but I want you to bring them both to the main house in... oh..." Jake looked at his watch to see that the day was almost gone. It was about four-thirty in the afternoon, and the shadows were lengthening, indicating that evening was fast approaching. "...about thirty minutes. Damn! I didn't realize how late it was getting. I'd better get up to the house and start dinner. Oh, by the way, Bolo...." Jake had started across the open area but turned back. "Please run and catch up with Lamar and Darwin and ask them to return to the house in twenty minutes, okay?"

Bolo's brow furrowed with confusion. The exchanges between Toombs and Graham at the pier had left him puzzled. "Mister Jake, they just went to their huts. You want me to fetch 'em back?"

"Yeah, that's right, Bolo," Jake affirmed. His tone was concerned as he explained, "I forgot a few things I need to discuss with them before dinner." Bolo nodded in understanding, his cap tilting slightly as he acknowledged the instructions before swiftly heading off.

Making his way up the porch steps, Jake's peripheral vision caught a movement to his left. He turned to find Amy, her arms crossed, hair tousled by the wind, and one eye half-hidden beneath a cascade of hair. With his curiosity piqued, he approached her. "Hey, Jake, can I have a word with you... privately?" Amy's voice held a bit of uncertainty and seriousness.

With a nod, Jake stepped away from the house and gently took Amy's arm, leading her around the side of the main building to a narrow footpath. The path wound its way to a secluded spot at the base of the hills, about one hundred and fifty yards away. The journey unfolded in silence, the touch of Amy's hand on Jake's arm a reassuring anchor. Upon reaching their destination, Jake released her arm and seated himself on a boulder, positioning himself across from Amy.

"Alright, Amy, usually I'd pay top dollar for a moment alone with you," Jake's playful grin tugged at the corners of his lips, earning a shy flush from her. "But given the circumstances, I'm curious to know what's on your mind." His eyes held a genuine concern as he sought to delve into the reason behind their private conversation.

Amy met Jake's gaze, her own searching and laden with unspoken thoughts. After a few moments of tension-filled silence, she finally spoke up. "Jake, tell me. If we can't count on the Navy's help, what's our plan? Let's be honest; how long can we hold out without re-supplying? I don't want my fate sealed on this island, Jake... though I must admit..." A soft chuckle escaped her lips as her hand found its way to her mouth, her eyelashes casting a delicate shadow over her gaze. "...I'd have to say, you're at the very top of my list of men to be marooned with!" A burst of shared laughter followed her confession.

Returning to a more serious demeanor, Jake regarded Amy intently, struggling to articulate his response to her concerns. "I... uh... Look, Amy, you've got to believe me. I'd never let anything happen to you... or anyone else here, for that matter." Amy's grin softened the tension in the air, her amusement evident at Jake's slightly awkward words. "But the truth is, to ensure we get any help from the mainland and guarantee the safety of the upcoming supply ship, we need the 'Maggie Mae' close enough for them to receive our message. That's if Darwin's efforts against 'Meg' tomorrow don't pan out." A touch of apprehension and somberness colored Jake's tone as he broached this final point.

"So, Jake?" Amy's gaze remained locked on him, her perceptive eyes capturing every nuance of his expression, even as the late afternoon shadows deepened. "What do you really think Graham's chances are? Do you believe there's any shot at all for him to put a stop to that creature?"

Jake picked up a handful of pebbles from a crevice and threw one at a time against a boulder about ten feet away while pondering his true feelings. "Amy... I just don't know! This is a fish with the mass of a small destroyer... *he's* bigger than any fish there's ever been in any ocean on this earth! However, *he* would appear to have the same weak spot that any large shark would have, a soft spot just behind the eye that is susceptible to real damage from a focused attack or, in this case, an explosion!" Jake paused again, in a transient state of deep concentration. "Yes, Darwin could injure the beast badly... maybe, even kill it, with those 'beefed-up' spears he's brought. My real concern is that the explosive charge on those things will be going off very close to Darwin, and I don't know whether or not he can survive the concussive effect when they do! Now, don't get me wrong! There are times when a personal sacrifice of one to save many is called for... and this may be one of those times, in which case, I would say that Darwin is to be respected and admired for such a selfless act.

But, this would only be warranted if we could be sure... absolutely sure... that doing this would, undoubtedly, stop 'Meg' and not just hurt him... and make him madder and, therefore, more challenging to deal with at the end of the day! Understand?" He broke from his faraway reverie and established eye contact with Amy again.

Amy's eyes burned into Jake's, like she was, in fact, seeing him for the first time. "Yes, Jake...yes...I understand."

Then, Amy changed topics completely, catching Jake off balance. "Jake, tell me; why is it that, in the story, you told me about yourself, you never mentioned any 'special' person in your life?" She smiled wryly as she finished the question.

Jake's squirming body language betrayed his uneasiness with this personal questioning line. "Uh... well... I... I guess I just never, really, thought about it; that's all." He hadn't kept his previous eye contact with Amy nor attempted it, once, with Amy, during his response.

"That's complete nonsense, and you're well aware of it!" Amy's unexpected comeback surprised Jake, her confident retort jolting him out of his comfort zone. "Listen, Jake, if I'm touching on something sensitive here, just let me know. But I've got to say, even if it seems forward, I've found myself growing rather attached to you. And I can't help but wonder why a man of your caliber isn't involved or hasn't been in the past." She paused, her gaze steady as she awaited his response, half-expecting him to shut her down or tell her she was meddling.

But Jake's reaction was quite the opposite. He rose suddenly, casting aside the remaining rocks with a forceful throw, and began pacing, a surge of energy propelling him forward. "Alright, Amy, you're about to become the only living soul privy to this part of my life." He seized her arms firmly, his grip unwavering as he locked eyes with her, the intensity in his gaze a clear indicator that what he was about to reveal was something he might never discuss again.

"I met her right after college, fresh out of training, just when I received my commission," he began, his voice carrying a sense of introspection. "It was during a period of specialized training before heading overseas, and she was starting her teaching career at the base where I was stationed.

Fear of the uncertain path ahead plagued both her and me. Hindsight reveals that we both yearned for a solid presence to lean on during those times, and our connection was undeniable. The flames of our passion burned fiercely and swiftly, perhaps quicker and hotter than they should have. We decided to tie the knot about three weeks before my scheduled deployment.

Her parents flew in from Kansas to meet me. Everything seemed to be going smoothly. That is until my inebriated best man let slip to her mother that my primary skill, in essence, was taking lives. The aftermath was far from pretty, and once the storm passed, she vanished with her parents in tow."

Jake stood close to Amy, his gaze fixed on her. As she looked up from the ground, his hand found its place on her shoulder, a gentle reassurance. She reciprocated by covering his hand with her own, their connection solidifying as he continued. "Months later, after a long silence, a letter reached me. The quartermaster delivered it, and I noticed the four different postmarks it bore. It had been written about a month prior, forwarding through each location I'd been stationed for training since leaving my initial base and before arriving in-country.

"In the letter, she confessed her enduring love for me, acknowledging the irreconcilable differences that kept us apart. She mentioned a Baptist minister she had been seeing, admitting that while her feelings for him would never match what she felt for me, she was leaning toward a more secure future with him due to the inherent safety it held. I was shattered emotionally, and this devastation led me to fully immerse myself in my... unique skill set. I became numb to emotional attachments, engaging in physical relationships over the years without letting anyone penetrate my heart... until now."

"What?!" Amy was caught entirely off guard by this revelation. "Jake, I... I don't even know what to say! I..."

Jake wouldn't let her finish. With a determined motion, he pulled her to her feet, taking hold of both her hands before firmly gripping her arms, locking their intense gazes and compelling them to confront each other head-on. "I'm aware there's an age gap between us, Amy, and we've only known each other briefly, but something happened that day. I..." Before he could continue, Amy intervened. Throughout his words, she shook her head slowly in disbelief.

"Enough of that, you big lug!" Her command punctuated by a chuckle, she wrapped her arms around his neck and pressed her soft lips fervently to his, a passionate kiss that spoke volumes about her own sentiments for him.

The embrace lingered for several minutes, the world around them fading into insignificance. When they finally broke apart, they stood in silence, their stillness resonating with the intensity of newfound passion and longing that both craved and sought to capture within one another's souls.

Eventually, Jake ventured, "Amy, I wasn't sure if you felt the same way. I kept telling myself not to hope for this, considering you're from a different world and time."

Amy playfully placed a finger to his lips, signaling him to hush. Then, she offered him a broad smile and retorted, "Mister Crandle, you have much to learn about a woman who's intelligent, knows her mind, and is mature enough to act on it!" She sealed her words with another kiss, followed by heartfelt dialogue transcending the physical. Afterward, they strolled to the compound, hand in hand, savoring the unhurried moments together.

They exchanged small talk and mutual reassurances for the future along the way, and as they entered the main house, they found all the others gathered, including Tesoro and Johno. They sat, apart from the primary group, over in the corner, with Bolo overseeing them.

"You told Bolo thirty minutes, Mister Jake, and it is almost an hour! Bolo was getting worried!" Darwin watched Jake and Amy come in; their actions and glances told him a lot. As a result, he quietly laughed a knowing laugh when Bolo unintentionally delivered his 'straight line.'

Jenny hadn't come up yet, so Amy told Jake that she'd go fetch her young assistant, and she went back out of the door.

This left the men alone to 'talk' over their plans with Johno, his friend and crewman.

Despite Jake's strong emotional feelings, to the contrary, he shot a quick look at Toombs and Graham, both of which nodded approval and began. "Okay, Johno, here's how it's going to work! Unless we all work together, we are all in danger of not getting off this island alive."

"Man! What you sayin'?" Johno fired back before Jake could elaborate. "All we need to do is sit here, and someone gonna come, man! So, I don't see what the big thing is!" Tesoro sat, staring defiantly at Jake and the others.

Jake's restraint kept his hand from smacking Tesoro, though the urge was almost overwhelming. His better judgment managed to prevail, at least for the time being. "Normally, you'd be spot on, Johno," Jake began, his tone laced with a controlled irritation. "But, in this particular scenario, we've already contacted the authorities and informed them that everything is under control. Given these circumstances, receiving further communication from them could take three to four weeks. Now, I need you to really focus here, Johno." A touch of sarcasm found its way into Jake's explanation, his response to the younger man's skepticism.

"As of now, we have food and water for the group, enough to sustain us for maybe ten days at best. That's a grim reality right there. But, if you add to that the mainland navy losing at least two boats, maybe even more by now, and then factor in the very real probability that our supply ship, carrying ten to fifteen lives, could become prey for that monstrous creature unless we act—well, that's the horrifying situation we're facing. A situation that might cost us our lives and theirs out there as well." Jake's gaze turned steely as he extended his arm, rigidly pointing out towards the treacherous expanse of ocean beyond the island. "They have no idea what awaits them down there." His eyes locked onto Tesoro's, awaiting the pivotal decision of whether to cooperate or not.

However, it wasn't Johno who responded first to Jake's reasoning; it was Jojo, Johno's mate, who offered a glimmer of hope. "Por favor, Jefe! I've been with you for a long time! We've done a lot together—caught many fish, had our share of whiskey!" Jojo's voice trembled with fear. His eyes bulged, and his gestures were those of a man confronted with his own mortality. He clutched one of Tesoro's arms and squeezed as he continued his plea. "But, Jefe! I don't want to die in this place!" The stocky seaman scanned the room, making eye contact with each person. "We help them... yes?" Johno regarded his friend, his expression a mix of understanding and perhaps even sympathy.

"Easy, 'Primero!' We will not die here! You hear me, Companero?" Tesoro's voice carried a tone of reassurance and determination. "I promise! But, let's see what my 'Soldado' friend, Crandle, has in mind." Johno turned his gaze from Jojo, his hand still resting on the shorter man's shoulder, and directed his questioning look toward Jake.

"Okay, here's how it's going down, Johno!" Jake's confidence grew, believing that he could make this plan work if it came to that. "You will stay here and help figure out a way to take the beast down in these waters while your man there goes with Professor Toombs." Jake pointed at Lamar, who acknowledged the introduction with a solemn nod. "On the 'Maggie Mae,' they'll get close enough to the coast for the boat's radio to transmit a message for help. Your man will... " Tesoro surged to his feet, restraining Jojo with a firm hand on his shoulder.

"You fuckin' crazy, mano? You just told me that anybody going out there gets to be fish food, didn't you? Well, my 'hermano' no goin' to be no fish food for no big-ass shark! You can fuckin' forget it!" Johno was practically hysterical, causing Bolo to tense his hold on the pistol in his belt.

Toombs spoke up before Darwin or Jake could. "Young man!... Young man, if I may?" He waved his pipe to get Johno's attention, and it worked because Tesoro stopped yelling and looked at the professor. The young man's face still contorted in fear, however.

I realize you don't want to subject your friend, or yourself, to certain death! Well....I'll be absolutely candid! Neither do I! What we have done, therefore, is equip the boat, out there, with a powerful sonic generator, which is capable of assaulting 'Meg'... uh... the... uh... big-ass shark, as you so colorfully describe him... with an intense sound pulse that is, of a frequency and intensity, sufficient to drive our creature away. We believe, therefore, that this will give us a significant degree of protection from 'Megalodon.'"

Lamar could see that Johno was skeptical, so he explained further. "My boy, we have designed our system to scramble 'Meg's' highly sensitive nervous system, thus discouraging him from attacking us! Do you understand what I'm telling you?"

Jojo's face displayed utter bewilderment as he turned to Tesoro, seeking his leader's interpretation of these seemingly extravagant claims. Meanwhile, Johno, though he managed to grasp most of Lamar's statement, wasn't entirely sold on the concept, his incredulity evident in his skeptical snort. "Crandle, come on now! I know you, man. Are you seriously telling me you're gonna take down that monster... with sound? You're gonna convince me that some noise will halt 'El Diablo' out there?" The edge of challenge laced Johno's words, daring Jake to genuinely support what Tesoro saw as a ludicrous plan that would lead the boat and the men aboard it to certain doom!

Jake was starting to lose what little patience he had left with Tesoro. "Look, Johno! Try to get it through your thick skull that we wouldn't let Professor Toombs here go on the trip unless we were very confident that this system works! We know it works because we've already chased the thing away with it once, and that was before the system was fully functional." Jake caught himself and softened his retort a little. "It... will... work, Johno!" He turned to Jojo to add. "What about you, my friend? Are you willing to do this?" Jake tried his best not to be intimidating to the short seaman.

"Si, senor! If mi Capitan, he believes it! I will go with the old man! But, senor! Jojo no wanna die in the belly of some large fish! You know?" The smaller crewman was, understandably, frightened a lot, and Jake didn't want him to panic. So, Jake's response was kind and understanding.

"Yes... companero, I do understand, and we've done all possible to make sure that neither of you will come to any harm. Believe me!" Jojo made a half-bow, with a slight smile, to Jake.

"Gracias, Senor; gracias." Jojo said and sat down close to Tesoro.

Jake looked around at the other men and, finally, brought his attention to Darwin. "Okay, we have our backup plan in place, so Darwin, I guess we'll come to you!" Jake smiled encouragingly at Graham, who, try as he might, just couldn't show any levity that night. He was extremely nervous, and Jake knew it. Therefore, Jake continued with the plan for the following day.

"Darwin, over there, has volunteered to set himself up by the harbor mouth tomorrow and attempt to take 'Meg' out with the explosive spears he brought with him." Tesoro was listening and pounced on this logic, interrupting Jake's explanation.

"Man! That's nothin' but crazy! The size of that fish! No spear, explosive or not, gonna take it down! It's like shootin' an... an... elephant with a fuckin' .22 long rifle!" Johno looked at Graham as if the Aussie was a certifiable suicidal lunatic.

"Wait just a minute, Johno!" Jake interjected assertively. "Our theory is that if Darwin can get up close from the side, he might be able to target the vulnerable area just behind the eye and breach the creature's brain with the explosive tip. In principle, that should bring it down, don't you think?" Jake's tone was impatient, yet he sought to convey his point to Johno.

"Darwin," Jake addressed, "we'll transport you to your designated position in the morning and ensure everything's in order. Once confirmed, we'll return the boat to a central point near the pier, which aligns with the harbor's entrance and exit. There, Bolo and I will rev up the boat's engines, alternating between forward and reverse, to lure 'our adversary' to investigate us. This maneuver should expose its flank and eye, allowing you to take the shot."

Darwin and Jake shared knowing stares and barely perceptible, mutually understanding nods before Jake finished explaining the plan. "Darwin, be close, enough, to be sure of your shot... but, do me a favor; will you? Take the shot as far as possible to try and minimize the concussion, okay?" Jake was deadly serious because he knew Darwin's chances of surviving the 'beefed-up" explosive tips on the spears were slim.

"Aye, mate!" Graham gave a grin that belied his true feelings of dread at what the next day held. "You won't be gettin' rid of me that easy, mate! How would you ever get along without my bloody sparklin' personality, now?" It was a good try, and Jake played along, but he knew the next day would be a culminating experience for everyone!

"Alright, everyone! Now that we've arranged things well, what do you say we grab a bite?" Jake suggested, gesturing for everyone to sit at the long dining table. He then headed over to assist Bolo in finalizing dinner preparations. As he helped, he couldn't help but think to himself, *"Yeah, like anyone's going to get a proper night's sleep tonight."*

A short while later, when the meal was ready, Amy entered the room with Jenny in tow. She nodded to everyone before the two women took their place at the table. Although Jenny appeared visibly distressed and distant, she tried to engage in the conversations swirling around her.

Jake and Bolo distributed dinner to each person. The room was mostly quiet except for some hushed exchanges. When Jake reached Darwin's spot, he leaned in as he set the plate down, whispering into Darwin's ear, "Hey, big guy! You aim to be a hero or something?" A grin accompanied Jake's words, followed by a friendly pat on Darwin's shoulder.

"Not bloody likely, Jake!" Darwin muttered back. "I just want to solve a huge problem, and the future will take care of itself, I'm believin'!" He drained his drink glass. Both men smiled openly at that.

They let the two outsiders join dinner this evening, leading to spirited dialogue.

Conversely, Amy was becoming quieter and more withdrawn as dinner progressed. She stared at Jake, on occasion, for several minutes at a time, and Jake was becoming a bit concerned.

Nevertheless, dinner came off surprisingly reasonably, with everyone sharing small talk and points of trivia as if they all wanted to shut out if only for a little while, the events that would transpire on the morrow!

After a couple of hours of pleasant discourse, Graham, with Toombs in tow, announced that they would turn in to check his diving equipment and try to get some rest. "'Night, all! 'See you all tomorrow!" He forced a smile as he walked through the door and tossed one final thought before he disappeared, with Toombs, into the dark. "It's gonna be a Hell of a day tomorrow, I'm bettin'! Then, waving, he was gone.

Jake looked meaningfully at Bolo and Amy and told Bolo. "Bolo, if our two 'friends' here are finished eating, please take them back to their quarters and see that they are... uh... *'tucked in'* for the evening, okay?"

Bolo understood and stood up from the table, and the big revolver, which had been invisible during the meal, reappeared in the big man's hand. "Gotcha, Mister Jake! Okay, you two fellas be comin' with Bolo!" He unmistakably motioned with the gun, and Johno and Jojo, frowning, stood and quietly led Bolo out of the front door to the building they had been secured in since arriving.

This left Jake alone with the two women, and all three sipped at after-supper coffee quietly for perhaps ten minutes as they each fidgeted with their respective coffee cups, lost in their thoughts and worries about what would come.

Amy finally broke the heavy silence, her cup trembling slightly in her nervous hands. She darted anxious glances from her cup to Jenny and then to Jake. "Jake," she began hesitantly, "Jenny and I have been discussing things, and I hope you won't take this the wrong way... but we're genuinely afraid that what Graham and Toombs are attempting on that boat is putting us in danger. The danger of losing not only the boat, our one chance of escape, but also the potential loss of Lamar, Graham, or, worse yet, both of them." Throughout Amy's statement, Jenny's silent agreement was evident in her continuous nods. In response, Jake's expression twisted into one of pain and helplessness.

"Listen, ladies," Jake started, his voice gentle and reasonable, trying not to escalate the distress already present. "I truly understand your concerns, honestly. But think about it for a moment. Don't you both believe I would have chosen it instantly if any other option was available?" He paused, giving them a moment to let his words sink in. "You know very well I would."

Jenny's voice trembled as she raised her concern. "What about just waiting for the Navy? If we don't communicate with them in a few more days, won't they come to check on us?" Jake noticed the fine line between rationality and emotional breakdown that Jenny was teetering on, and he empathized.

"Jenny, you're likely right," Jake began gently. "But consider this: how many lives and vessels could be lost in that time? Can we truly live with ourselves knowing that our inaction might contribute to further losses?" As Jake posed this question, Amy and Jenny cast their gazes downward, grappling with the weight of his words. Jake continued, his sincerity shining through. "I thought as much. Please try to understand and support what we're doing here. I promise each of you that I'll do everything in my power to ensure we all make it out of this in one piece, alright?" He reached across the table, placing a hand on each girl's arms to underscore his heartfelt commitment.

Amy covered Jake's hand with her own, and eyes welling with tears, she answered his logic with a shaky voice filled with reconciliation. "I suppose you're right, Jake! It's only that we... uh... Jenny and I have just seen so much death and don't want to see it anymore! But, when you put it like you have, I guess..." She looked at Jenny for support and received a barely discernible nod. "... I... that is, we can see the need to take these calculated risks, right Jen?"

This time, Jenny gave a broad movement of her head and a sympathetic response. "I suppose so."

Jake was convinced that Amy was okay with everything, at least for the time being, but he had serious reservations about Jenny, mainly due to her fragile emotional state. "Good! I'm glad, ladies, because, to be frank with you, I will need everyone here to be together as a team!

I can tell you that I believe we will still have to face some rough times before this is over, and we won't have anyone to lean on except each other. 'Make sense?" Jake patted the girls' arms. Finally, in unison, they both indicated that they were with him.

With this, the three stood and walked out onto the porch, where Jake put one of his large calloused 'paws' on each of their backs and wished them a good night.

Amy and Jenny intertwined their arms and walked away from Jake, their footsteps echoing softly on the wooden decking. The night air embraced them as they crossed the open space. Just as they began to vanish into the shadows, Amy turned back, casting a glance of profound emotion at Jake. His response was a faint smile and a brief wave. With that, the two women disappeared into the darkness.

As Jake was about to re-enter the house, Bolo emerged from around the porch's corner, exchanging words with Jake on his way to his cabin. "Oh, Mister Jake... looks like everyone's settling in for the night. You should get some rest, too, now." Bolo studied Jake closely with concern and camaraderie in his gaze. Jake offered a weary wave in response, acknowledging his friend's advice.

"That's where I'm headed, my friend," Jake replied, his voice tinged with fatigue. "Thought I'd bunk in on the couch tonight. Don't feel much like going to my cabin. Probably won't get much sleep either way."

"I'm with you there, Mister Jake! I am thinkin', tomorrow gone be one of them days that you no be forgettin' long as you be on this big ol' world! What you be thinking, Mister Jake?" After digesting Bolo's pure philosophy, Bolo had a deeply wrinkled expression, and Jake could only shake his head from side to side and answer with, "Yep... I'm afraid you're right on, Bolo." With this, Jake turned to go inside, but not before saying. "Good night, old friend!"

With this final exchange, both men drifted apart toward their beds and silently made their preparations to try and rest for the night. Each of them knew, however, that the rest would be tough to come by this night!

CHAPTER 16
Beneath the Descending Moon

A s anticipated, **Jake's sleep was restless,** broken into short, fitful intervals lasting only about four hours. Around three forty-five in the early morning darkness, he awoke with a start, his body drenched in a cold sweat. It felt as though he had barely slept at all. Knowing that sleep wouldn't return, he heaved himself off the old, sagging divan that had served as his makeshift bed for those few hours. His muscles protested as he stood, and he had to shake off the numbness in one leg.

With determination, he poured water into a basin and gave himself a brisk "sailor's bath," scrubbing away the remnants of discomfort from his restless slumber. He selected a fresh shirt, jeans, and clean underwear from their designated spots behind the door and in a nearby trunk. As he dressed, he couldn't ignore the weight of the day ahead – a day that would seal their collective fate, no matter the outcome.

Moving with a purposeful resolve, Jake began the morning rituals. He set a large urn of coffee to brew and traversed the yard through the misty pre-dawn atmosphere to retrieve eggs and bacon from the chilled shed. There, amidst the cool air, he cast a contemplative glance at the covered form in the corner, lost in somber thoughts of the tragic events that had brought them to this crucial juncture. With a deep breath, he left the shed and retraced his steps to the house.

Back on the porch, he took a moment to gaze out at the expanse of the sea, shrouded in the early morning haze. His thoughts turned to "Meg," the looming presence that dominated their concerns. The uncertainty of its current whereabouts weighed heavily on his mind as he stood between the dim light of dawn and the fate of the day ahead.

While he was standing on the porch, he heard a short cough off to his left, and, emerging from the darkness, he saw Darwin, dressed in swim shorts and a T-shirt, with dirty sneakers, striding up the path. "'Mornin', mate! I see there's been another bloody soul who couldn't sleep any better than I could!" Jake grinned at Graham's attempt to lighten the atmosphere of the moment.

"I guess you're right... mate!" Jake smiled and shook Darwin's hand as the big Aussie approached him.

Jake continued while wheeling to lead the way into the house. "Coffee's almost done. Help yourself! I've got some eggs and bacon for anyone with an appetite." Jake raised his eyebrows at Darwin in an unspoken question.

"Naw, mate! This Aussie won't be able to eat a bleedin' bite until this thing is damn well done and in the books!" The two men were alone, and Darwin felt no need for any bravado or show of machismo today.

Jake took a mug and followed Darwin's lead by filling it to the brim and sipping the hot liquid without anything added.

The two walked outside, and both stood, without saying a word, for several minutes, casting worried looks toward the vast ocean, visible under the setting moon, through the harbor's entrance....neither knowing what the next twelve hours would bring.

While Jake and Darwin spent the next two hours over coffee, mainly exchanging small talk, the hundred-foot object of their pre-occupation was occupied with *his* target, about a mile east of the giant cliffs forming the tall side of the harbor portal.

Meg had patiently fed on stragglers from a large pod of killer whales for several hours and trimmed the group down to four young adults, three males, and one colossal female.

The whales were swimming in a much tighter grouping by this time, too, instinctually, to form a more effective defense against the vicious attacks that had severely thinned their numbers during the night.

The colossal beast swam parallel to the pod and off to the side, watching for any opening to provide *him* with *his* next feast. It came when one of the larger males moved on a path that would take him further away from the leading group, thus making him vulnerable to the deadly jaws waiting in the gloom. *He* sensed this and closed on *his* prey with exceptional speed.

He neared the young whale and quickened his pace even more while, at the same time, opening *his* trap-like, tooth-lined maw. When *he* made contact with the 'killer,' *he* half-closed *his* mouth over the black and white body, and *he* literally sheared the large mammal in two, swallowing, whole, a large chunk of meat that had remained in *his* mouth following the attack.

The three surviving members of the pod were rapidly turning back to the west, hoping to elude this 'terror' that they'd never experienced before.

As they cut sleekly through the water, their vision became clearer because daylight had begun to evolve from the east, and the pitch-black water all around them had started giving way to a murky lucidity that would help them detect the danger before it struck.

On the other hand, he was also assisted in detecting his quarry sooner, so he spent the next couple of hours methodically picking off the remaining two males.

This set up a fatal struggle between the large female and 'Meg' that would, ultimately, involve others in a life-or-death confrontation!

BACK ON THE ISLAND, everyone had gathered for breakfast, and Jake could only sell his bacon and eggs to Lamar and Bolo. The rest only had coffee, claiming they were too focused on the coming events to have much appetite.

Darwin left the group and went to his cabin to gather his gear and double-check all of it one last time. Toombs accompanied Bolo to the boat to run a diagnostic on the sonic generator and get a preliminary demonstration on how to operate the 'Maggie Mae's' controls, should it become necessary at some point.

Jake, joined by Amy and Jenny, took two plates of food to Tesoro and Jojo, along with a small thermos of coffee.

When Jake unlocked the door, he stood back and let Amy push it open.

Both seamen were still seated on their bunks, and neither made any move to be confrontational when Jake brought the food to them.

Johno and Jojo wolfed the food, poured a large paper cup of coffee, and washed down their meals. After stretching, Tesoro asked. "Senor Jake, I think today smells..." He took a deep breath. "....like a bad day, no es verdad?" He looked at Jake purposefully, waiting for his reply.

"I certainly hope not, Johno. In fact, if luck is on our side, this might be one of our better days in a while. Now, have the two of you finished your breakfast?" Jake's question hung in the air briefly before he began gathering the plates and cups. His intention was apparent despite not waiting for a response. Moving to the door with Amy, he prepared to close and lock it.

However, Jojo's voice broke the silence before the door could shut, his words stumbling in broken English. "I don't know everything happening, sir, but I spent many years on the sea, sir, and I have a feeling today someone will die." The declaration carried an eerie weight, especially from someone who was usually a man of few words.

"What's that?" Jake halted in his tracks, swiveling to face the typically reserved Jojo sitting beside Johno. "What makes you say that?" The unexpectedness of Jojo's comment caught Jake off guard. He instinctively placed a reassuring hand on Amy's shoulder, signaling her to remain by the door. With a slow and deliberate pace, Jake retraced his steps into the room, his gaze fixed on Jojo. Standing before him, he repeated the question in a softer tone, now more intrigued than taken aback by the statement. "Could you tell me, Jojo, is it? What leads you to say something like that? I'm genuinely curious."

Jojo's attention was riveted on the floor at his feet because he was very introverted and felt uncomfortable and intimidated by Jake's imposing presence in front of the shorter man. "Por favor, senor Jake; I no speak very good the English, but I just know the ocean, and this thing, out there; it's no belong there! No 'popgun speargun,' dynamite or not, gonna kill something that can't be killed! It is a... how I can say... a devil fish!... Permiso! I am just a simple man of the sea, who, maybe, talks too much, I think! Me hope you no think Jojo is crazy, senor! I just afraid!" Jojo never looked up from the floor the whole time he was talking.

Jake stood still for a few seconds, his internal conflict evident in his furrowed brows. He couldn't decide whether to dismiss Jojo's words as baseless superstition or acknowledge the weight of his fear. "Jojo, I wish I could tell you that you're just being superstitious and fearful, but the more I think about it, the more I believe you have a point."

Jojo looked up at Jake as he spoke, their eyes meeting in a moment of solemn understanding.

Jake continued, "This creature, this fish—it's like something from the past, something out of place in our world today. None of us have seen anything like it because it doesn't belong here. So, my perceptive friend," Jake adjusted his language to connect with Jojo, knowing some words might not translate, "even though I'd prefer to disagree with you, you might just be onto something. In any case..." His gaze shifted to Tesoro, who maintained a steady look, "Both of you will stay here and see how things unfold. Understand?" Jojo nodded, eyes downcast, while Johno mirrored the acknowledgment but locked eyes with Jake.

"Alright, then!" Jake concluded with a hint of irony before leaving the room. Amy smiled knowingly and secured the door after him. In the background, Jenny stood behind Amy, seemingly lost in her thoughts. Her eyes didn't seem to focus on the present; they were fixed on something unreachable.

Walking back to the main house, Jake was bottomless in contemplation, his mind mulling over the impending events. Amy linked arms with Jenny, deliberately placing the young woman between herself and Jake.

Jenny shifted her gaze slowly from Amy to Jake, her voice almost childlike, as if her words came from a younger version of herself. "Jake, I want to go home now. When will someone come to take me back? I really need to be home, Jake. Can you make that happen?"

"So... Jenny!" As they stopped in front of the main house, Jake tried to get Jenny's fragile attention. When they paused, she seemed to snap back to the here and now and turned back to Jake, and he explained. "As I said, sweetheart, we would all like to go, wherever it is, we now call, or, in some cases, would, eventually, like to call home, and forget the past couple of weeks... and we will... I promise, but we must first deal with this menace that threatens us! Are you okay with this, honey?" He softly grasped both of Jenny's upper arms with his large hands to put importance to his question and to get her to concentrate on a sincere answer.

Jenny had difficulty establishing eye contact but indicated she was all right with this plan.

"That's my girl!" Jake's voice held a bit of fondness and reassurance as he hugged Jenny before gently passing her into Amy's care. "Amy, how about taking Jenny to the cabin? Both of you should try to get some rest while we handle what needs to be done, alright?" There was an unspoken understanding between Jake and Amy, a shared awareness of the difficult task ahead. Despite her wish to remain by Jake's side, Amy nodded in agreement, allowing herself to play the role Jake suggested.

Amy put her arm around Jenny's shoulders, providing a supportive gesture as they started down the path together. She glanced back at Jake, her gaze carrying both determination and concern. "That works for us," she declared with a hint of forced cheerfulness, the gravity of the situation not escaping her. With a final wave to Jake, they continued on their way, heading towards the cabin.

Jake stood motionless and watched them go, his mind racing through mixed emotions. Most of his feelings were aimed at the events ahead, but a private corner of his mind...and heart.... kept reminding him to face his newly-released sensations regarding Amy. He'd have to come to grips with these once this overpowering dilemma was resolved....supposing they all survived the confrontation with 'Meg!'

Then, as quickly as the thoughts flooded his consciousness, they were suppressed, and he snapped back to the reality of the moment with a sharp shake of his head.

He returned to his office and retrieved the formidable hunting rifle and large field glasses. With a somber determination, he stepped out of the house and crossed the verdant expanse, heading towards the meeting that held their fate.

As Jake approached the boat, he saw Bolo and Toombs engrossed in some activity involving the sonic tubes mounted on the sides of the 'Maggie Mae.' A sense of concern immediately prickled Jake's thoughts. "What's going on, you two? Please, don't tell me there's an issue with this setup now," he exclaimed, his apprehension clearly evident. The entire concept of the sonic system had been met with skepticism from the start, and any indication of a problem only heightened his unease.

Seeing Jake's worried expression, both Toombs and Bolo exchanged amused smiles. Toombs took the lead in addressing Jake's concern. "Easy now, my dear boy. I was merely elucidating the intricacies of our equipment to our friend here," he nodded towards Bolo, "in exchange for his invaluable lessons on operating your splendid vessel. Rest assured, our equipment is functioning perfectly. No need for alarm." A flicker of relief passed through Jake's eyes at Toombs' assurance.

"Thank goodness for that," Jake quipped, a slight grin forming as the tension in the air lifted slightly.

"'Allo, everyone!'" Darwin came down the hill with his diving gear in two large, multicolored duffel bags, and Jake reached to help him load it onto the boat. "So! I guess it's time to go bloody shark huntin'! Aint it?" Graham's tone was light, but his expression and body language betrayed volumes in contradiction.

"See here, Darwin!" Lamar rose to his feet at Darwin's statement. "Megalodon isn't..."

"I know! I know, Doc! 'E's not a shark! Okay! I understand! How about...let's see...we're goin' huntin' for a damn big fish, then? That all right with you, then?" Darwin was doing his utmost to stay loose, and keeping a little humor in the mix was his way of doing so.

Jake chuckled and helped get Graham rigged up. Finally, all was prepared, and Jake reviewed the plan one final time. When he finished, he added one small change. "Bolo, I think you'd better stay over by the fuel pump, and when we finish, we'll come over to top off the tanks and dock the boat there for the time being, okay?"

Bolo couldn't have appeared more hurt if Jake had walked up and slapped his face! "Mister Jake! I'm always on your side when the boat goes out! You know that! What you doin', Mister Jake?" The black man-mountain was practically in tears, and it cut Jake to the quick.

"Bolo, listen closely. The plain truth is this: if our plan falls apart and, in the worst scenario, we can't fend off that creature from the boat, I would find some semblance of peace knowing you're here to watch over the girls. Do you understand what I'm getting at?" Jake's words held a blend of earnestness and intensity, his voice carrying the weight of his concerns.

Bolo met Jake's gaze with his own blend of seriousness, nodding slowly. "I reckon I'm starting to grasp it, Mister Jake. But I won't pretend I'll be comfortable letting you head out there..." He trailed off, motioning towards the harbor channel. "Without me by your side. It just doesn't feel right."

Jake responded firmly and empathetically, saying, "I understand your feelings, Bolo. But I need you here, holding down the fort, so to speak. Your strength and presence here are vital, my friend." He paused, letting his words sink in. "Besides, it's not just about me. I need you to keep Amy and the others safe and grounded. Can you do that for me?"

Bolo's expression softened as he took in Jake's words. He exhaled slowly, a sense of responsibility in his eyes. "I can do that, Mister Jake. I'll look after them. You can count on that."

Jake clapped Bolo's sturdy shoulder, his grip firm and reassuring. "I know you will, Bolo. And believe me, I'm not taking this lightly. We're all in this together, each playing a crucial role."

Bolo nodded, his resolve solidifying. "You just make sure you return in one piece, alright?"

Jake managed a half-smile. His gratitude was evident. "Deal. Now, let's get back to our preparations. We've got a long day ahead."

Jake felt terrible about his decision to leave Bolo because Jake's long-time companion was right about always being on Jake's side, but, in truth, Jake wanted to avoid placing his long-time friend in harm's way... this time. "Bolo, buddy; just trust me. It's for the best, in this case; believe me." Jake finished with a friendly pat on Bolo's back.

Bolo merely made a slight head gesture of agreement, gathered his things, and stepped up onto the pier. He helped Jake disconnect the lines and trudged off across the pier toward the fuel tanks and pump at the other end of the dock. As he walked, his head hung low in disappointment at being left alone while the others made the short, perilous trip across the sound.

Jake leaned over the railing momentarily, then called down to Toombs and Graham. "Alright, guys! Engines are primed and ready! How's our 'armor' holding up?" He deliberately used the metaphorical term, knowing they'd understand the reference.

Graham ascended the stairs, already suited up in his wetsuit, minus the cowl. "The system's performing perfectly, Jake," Darwin's usually laid-back demeanor replaced by seriousness. "If we need it, it'll deliver."

Observing Graham's focus and the gravity of the situation, Jake decided against lightening the mood. "Good. Do you need any assistance with your gear?"

"Nah, mate. I've got it all sorted... but I appreciate the offer," Darwin replied, extending his hand for a firm shake. Their hands met, conveying mutual understanding and respect.

"Things might get pretty intense out there in the next hour or so, Darwin," Jake's words carried deep emotion. "I just wanted to say..."

Darwin cut him off, maintaining their handshake. "Easy there, mate. I'm with you all the way. No need for words. Let's just get the job done, yeah?" Their shared smile spoke volumes.

Graham went downstairs to join Lamar while Jake took a calming breath, offered a silent prayer, and turned the ignition switch. The robust diesel engine roared to life, and Jake maneuvered the boat away from the mooring, each calculated movement bearing the weight of their impending mission.

During this time, the *Big Boy* had been patiently closing in on the female Orca for a couple of hours, and *his* senses were telling *him* that *he* was almost in a position to launch *his* attack, albeit a quartering assault from the side, this time, rather than *his* more natural run from below.

Ahead, a sense of dread surged as the seasoned, mature killer whale perceived the encroaching menace behind her. Responding instinctively, she veered sharply, her sleek form slicing through the water towards the shallower, labyrinthine waters near the coral-studded shoals of the island. A flicker of hope sparked within her, hoping her seasoned agility could somehow outmaneuver the monstrous presence closing in with each passing minute.

The predator trailing her sensed the shift in the killer's trajectory, noting the surge in her speed. Swiftly recalculating his approach, he adjusted his course, determined to stay relentlessly locked onto his target. Amid his pursuit, his acute auditory senses registered a sizable surface entity's distinctive, resonating notes. This strangely familiar sound from recent encounters now echoed through the water. The predator's finely honed discipline allowed him to bookmark this new auditory prey for later while he continued his pursuit of the substantial quarry just ahead.

Meanwhile, the female whale also intercepted the distant, captivating symphony. To her, these auditory vibrations triggered memories of dolphins and massive schools of fish congregating in an underwater harmony. Despite the unknown threat stalking her, the inner echo of her kind's communal feeding needs still resonated. She propelled herself deliberately toward the outer entrance of a channel to her front right. This calculated movement was driven by her instinct, a belief that this passage would inevitably lead her toward the source of the enigmatic aquatic chorus beckoning from the distant end of the channel.

The monstrous shark's conditioning told *him he* was entering familiar waters... and so was *his* quarry! This caused *him* to increase speed slightly and close the gap with the creature he was stalking.

Jake checked to ensure the boat was clear of any obstructions and pushed the throttle about three-quarters of the way open. The vessel increased speed smoothly until it played out on an even track on the other side of the harbor. As it approached the edge of the rocks bordering the right side of the opening, Jake decreased speed to a crawl and edged up to the nearest rock. At the same time, Toombs appeared on deck with the red remote button for the sonic defenses, followed by Darwin, who had his black air tanks and pneumatic spear gun assembly, complete with two explosive spears.

Toombs held the button assembly up to show Jake he was ready.

Jake jumped onto the front deck and tossed a small claw anchor over to the rocks, pulling the line until it caught in a shallow crevice, where Jake could shake it free quickly.

Turning swiftly, Jake's eyes locked onto Darwin, who was fastening his weight belt and tank pack. Jake moved purposefully, stepping to assist the diver in completing his setup. "Darwin, turn around. Let me give you the once-over," Jake commanded, urgency lacing his tone. "Lamar, head up to the flying bridge with that gadget. Keep your eyes peeled for that monstrous beast, you hear?" The directive was clear, and Lamar nodded before scrambling up the ladder with the binoculars.

"Appreciate it, Jake!" Tension hung palpably in the air as Graham's gratitude carried a weight of nerves. In response, Jake sought to maintain a composed routine as he inspected Darwin's gear. "No worries, Darwin. Everything's good to go. From how you're rigged up, you've got some military experience, haven't you?" Jake queried, trying to establish a connection amidst the heightened atmosphere.

Graham's pause was marked by a wry smile tugging at his lips. "Takes one to know one, huh, mate?" The camaraderie was acknowledged with a handshake, a silent understanding that passed between two individuals facing a shared peril. Adjusting his mask and spitting in it before placing it on his face, Graham took a final breath before plunging into the water from the stern of the 'Maggie Mae.'

As Darwin's bubbles dissipated into the expanse, Jake waited for the appropriate distance before climbing up to the bow and freeing the anchor. Swiftly hauling it aboard, he ascended the ladder to join Toombs at the control panel. Toombs, field glasses pressed to his eyes, was vigilantly scanning the surrounding waters.

"Reverse!" Jake ordered tersely, and the boat moved away from the perilous rocks. Maneuvering with precision, Jake oriented the vessel so that its bow aligned with a point on the pier near where Bolo stood. Without hesitation, Jake pushed the throttle to its maximum, the boat lunging forward and nearly throwing Lamar off his perch as it accelerated swiftly across the lagoon.

In his quest to generate the most potent sound and vibrations, Jake harnessed the full power of his twin engines and propellers, determined to create an enticing commotion that the lurking menace could not resist.

Darwin was making preparations at the harbor entrance about thirty feet below the surface. He'd located the channel and positioned himself off to one side and behind a large outcropping of rock and coral. He found a flat block of granite and sat on it to wait. He would only have a few seconds of warning should 'Meg' come by because the same ledge that hid Darwin from detection also screened most of the approach route from Darwin's view.

The cacophonous reverberations of the boat's return journey reached Darwin's ears, setting his heart pounding in anticipation. He knew it was only a matter of time before the colossal menace cruised by his position. Darwin double-checked his gun in tense anticipation, ensuring every detail was in place. He meticulously examined the spear, ensuring it was securely seated in the firing assembly. With resolute focus, he extracted the ring pin from the charge's base, arming the explosive. Now primed, the detonation would be a forceful blast, equivalent to the power of an entire stick of dynamite—a level of destruction more than sufficient to take down, or grievously wound, even the massive 'Meg.'

Meanwhile, as the boat's sound echoed in the distance, Darwin had stealthily closed the gap on the female killer whale. He found himself within a mere three hundred yards of her. The primal hunger that had driven him earlier once again surged, propelling his body into heightened states of alertness. Ahead of him, the black and white female sensed his presence, triggering a burst of adrenaline-fueled energy. She surged through the channel, her twenty-eight feet of bulk brushing against the channel's contours, as a surge of urgency coursed through her. The prospect of eluding the "silent death" spurred her to push her physical limits, achieving speeds she had never attempted before. With each powerful thrust, she raced towards the harbor ahead, the gap between them narrowing as the relentless "silent death" drew nearer.

In contrast, Darwin remained unfazed by the killer whale's frenzied acceleration. He had not yet reached his maximum potential attack velocity. Gradually, methodically, he continued to narrow the distance between himself and his intended prey. Following her through the channel, he navigated the underwater terrain with expertise honed over years of experience. As the gap between them diminished to less than two hundred yards, he encountered occasional widening due to the constrictive geography below the surface, a natural consequence of his massive form navigating the waters.

Darwin was on full alert, gun ready, and his finger on the trigger! He'd only have one chance; therefore, he was poised, with all his senses at combat levels. He had tuned out the incessant noise of the boat's engines, racing up and down and reverberating through the water as the vessel sat at the distant pier. His only conscious focus was the imaginary spot in the gloom before him, where he felt 'Meg's' eye would pass. When *his* body started gliding by, his finger would fire a 'snapshot' at this area and, hopefully, kill or seriously disable the enormous beast!

Jake had docked the boat at the pier, and Bolo had tied it off securely while Lamar stayed up in the tower above the main deck to watch for any sign of 'Meg's' approach.

When Jake was sure that all the ropes were tied, he went to the main controls and began gunning the throttle, conveying the sounds into the water and, as all hoped, attracting the big fish they were trying to ambush. "Oh, Bolo!" Jake yelled loudly over the sounds of the engines. "Crank up the pump and top off the tanks while we have the chance, okay?"

Bolo's hand trembled as he waved and swiftly operated the fused switch, connecting the filling pump to the generators up the hill. The pump roared to life, its mechanical heartbeat thrumming through the hose. He inserted the nozzle into the filler orifice on the 'Maggie Mae,' watching with a mix of trepidation and urgency as fuel began its journey into the boat's waiting tanks.

Jake's fingers were tight around the engine controls as he kept the revs high, his eyes straining to capture any glimpse of movement in the choppy waters.

But Lamar first spotted it, his voice a tremor of terror as he called out to Jake. "Jake! Over there! Coming through the opening... It's coming!" Jake killed the engines and sprinted to the aft deck, his pulse pounding in his ears. He raised his own field glasses, desperation in his eyes, only for Lamar's next words to freeze his heart. "Wait! No... that's a killer whale, Jake! It's big, but it's not Megalodon!"

"Jesus Christ!" The exclamation escaped Jake's lips, relief and frustration warring in his tone as he lowered his glasses. He continued to watch the approaching fin, his silent plea a desperate whisper carried by the wind. "Darwin, please, don't shoot."

Then, as if mocking their hope, Lamar's scream shattered the air anew. His voice trembled as he pointed past the whale's fin towards the lagoon entrance. "Jake! Out there, beyond the whale's fin, I see it... It's 'M...'!" But Lamar's words were truncated by a deafening explosion. The killer whale, approaching the harbor, had triggered the blast, the water erupting in a violent burst of red-tinged flesh and spray, launching debris high into the sky before it rained down into the agitated waters, setting off ripples that surged in all directions.

Stunned, Jake muttered in disbelief, grappling with the enormity of the explosion. "Jesus Christ!" Adrenaline surged through him, animating his actions. "Bolo, untie us! Quickly!" His orders were urgent, charged with the intensity of the moment. "Lamar, get the sonic system ready. We might need it now!" As Bolo released the lines, the engines roared back to life, the fuel nozzle discarded as he planned to leap onto the boat. But Jake was a step ahead, engaging the propellers and guiding the ship away from the pier.

As the boat shifted, the explosion's aftermath continued to unfold underwater, a spectacle unseen by the surface world but reverberating in the depths with chaotic turmoil.

Darwin had anticipated 'Meg's' approach from his close vantage point, his senses coiled like a spring, finger poised delicately on the trigger pad of the spear gun. The anticipation hung in the air, a tense moment before the storm.

Abruptly, a torrent of small fish, a vibrant collage of species, surged past him in a chaotic display of fear. It was as if the very water had become electrified with panic. In that electrifying instant, Darwin's heightened senses screamed, "Here it comes!" An assumption that triggered a sequence of events that would, tragically, mark his final moments.

His finger tensed, and the spear was propelled precisely at the area where instinct told him the eye should be. A colossal shadow whisked across his line of sight, and with an instinctual burst, the spear was released, finding its mark in the creature's massive form.

Yet, in the following suspended heartbeat, reality crashed upon him like a tidal wave moving slowly. This wasn't 'Meg'—this massive creature wasn't the target of their pursuit. Before realization fully cemented, the world detonated around him, a violent explosion that hammered his senses, temporarily knocking him to the threshold of unconsciousness.

In that disorienting space between wakefulness and oblivion, Darwin fought against the pull of darkness that threatened to engulf him, to drag him under the surface and into the abyss. Amidst the chaos, his mind replayed the words, "That damn whale! Where's 'Meg?'" A desperate plea tethering him to reality as he battled to regain his grip on the present.

Gradually, the throbbing in his head began to subside, and Darwin clawed his way back to a semblance of consciousness. The world around him was a hazy mixture of movement and disarray. He felt immobilized, limbs unresponsive, his body a symphony of pain. His vision gradually cleared, revealing a scene of destruction and horror.

Roughly twenty to thirty yards away, the torn, bloody remnants of the killer whale lay in a nightmarish tableau. The water was clouded with a thick haze of suspended gore, the once-mighty predator reduced to a macabre tapestry. Darwin's heart pounded with grim realization resulting from his impulsive shot. Despite his injuries, remorse and guilt gripped him as he struggled against his bodily limitations, a silent promise that he would be ready when help arrived.

Abruptly, his left shoulder was brushed by a large mackerel that tore past him at full speed, and his legs were bumped by other fish that sprinted by him in full flight and, from all indications, extremely terror-stricken!

Darwin fought and labored to get his beaten, rebellious body turned around, but as soon as he'd done this, he wished he hadn't!

"Oh!... Bloody Hell!... Not like this!" Darwin's mind screamed, a maelstrom of horror and regret flooding his thoughts. But despite his mental anguish, the harsh reality of his impending fate loomed inescapably before him. Struggling to reorient himself in the water, he was met with a nightmarish sight—an immense, obsidian tunnel lined with tiers of triangular teeth, a monstrous maw hurtling toward him with relentless velocity. The teeth, an embodiment of death itself, seemed to close in from every angle, a macabre labyrinth he could not navigate, even with his agility.

Having distanced himself slightly from the colossal predator, the separation of around 250 yards was a stroke of luck. The tighter confines of the shallower waters and rocky obstacles saved him from an even more dire confrontation. As he maneuvered through the outer harbor channel, the water seemed to fight against him, an invisible force forcing him to deviate from his path before relenting and allowing him to continue.

The scent of blood flooded his senses as he entered the main channel leading to the lagoon. His primitive instincts ignited, propelling him forward recklessly, his jaws opening and closing involuntarily, a cruel dance of anticipation. A darker form flickered in his vision—a smaller creature darting erratically in his path. Ignoring it entirely, he lunged forward, jaws agape, eager to capture it on his way to his ultimate prize.

Darwin's mind raced with fractured thoughts in the throes of his final moments. Religion, never a cornerstone of his life, had little place here. The gaping abyss of darkness descended upon him, the jaws inexorably sealing his fate. A muted scream expelled from his lungs as he relinquished his last breath. Amidst the impending embrace of oblivion, one coherent thought pierced through his terror: a plea to the man who had orchestrated this dangerous gamble. "Jake... You better kill this bloody motherfucker..."

Then, in an instant, his existence was extinguished. The last remnants of Darwin Graham were reduced to a twisted pair of black air tanks, ejected by 'Meg' and drifting lazily in the murky depths, a silent testament to his valiant but tragic encounter.

CHAPTER 17
Agitated Presence of Unwelcome Company

Jake aggressively jammed the throttle of the 'Maggie Mae' to its maximum, a surge of anger fueling his actions as he steered the boat directly towards the heart of the explosion. Dread gnawed at him as he spotted that chillingly familiar fin, the emblem of his worst nightmares, slicing through the water as it emerged from the channel mouth. Without a moment to spare, 'Meg's' tail followed, thrashing erratically amidst the chaos of the blast's aftermath. The water seemed to churn and boil like a furious river crashing over jagged rocks.

Jake's grip tightened on the helm, knuckles white as he fought against the rising panic. He barked into the intercom for Lamar, his voice laced with urgency. "Doc! Get up on deck with that damn button box! We've got some uninvited company, and he's not in the best of moods!"

Before the echoes of his words had even faded, Toombs appeared on deck, clutching the sonic remote control cubicle with determination. "I've got it, Jake!" Lamar announced, his gaze scanning the tumultuous harbor behind the boat. "Ah, there he is! The big guy's making quite the spectacle."

Curiosity battled fear in Jake's mind, prompting him to query, "You think he's feeding, Doc?" The situation seemed unusually intense, even for 'Meg.' To keep 'Meg' at bay, Jake carefully navigated the boat at a crawl, wary of arousing the beast's curiosity.

Lamar stepped forward, his gaze locked on the chaotic scene ahead. A tinge of bitterness crept into his voice as he confirmed

275

Jake's suspicion. "Yeah, Jake. He's definitely feeding." The weight of the revelation hung heavily in the air, their fears crystallizing into a horrifying reality.

Jake recognized all the signs now. He wasn't sure before, due to 'Meg's' size, but he'd seen many normal-sized sharks in feeding frenzies in the past, and this was the same, only much larger and more assertive action. "Yeah! I see it now!... Lamar! Do you think Darwin could have escaped?" Jake knew the answer deep down before Lamar turned a saddened visage toward him in the flying bridge.

Still, Jake continued. "I guess we can always hold some hope, right? Darwin was... er... is a competent diver, and...!" Jake was rambling, grabbing at whatever small straw he could.

"Jake, my good lad! I'm afraid that there's only a slight possibility, in the very least, that my dear associate could have evaded all this," He waved his hand at the turbulent waters off the bow quarter. "...but first things first!" The professor had snapped back to the actions at hand. "Jake! Be a good lad and, ever so slowly, edge the boat a little closer to 'Meg' for the sonic pulse to have the maximum effect.....and then pray for the dear boy!" Toombs made his way to the furthest point forward, where he could still find a rail to hold on to.

The violent feeding activity was calming a bit, illustrating that 'Meg' was finishing the remains of the Killer Whale. The boat was within two hundred yards of the monster by this time, a proximity much closer than Jake liked, and Lamar motioned to proceed closer, still not taking his eyes away from the beast in front of them for an instant.

As they drew closer, Lamar signaled for Jake to bring the boat to a halt at around one hundred and fifty yards from the unfolding spectacle. Jake obediently eased back the throttles until they were at a complete standstill.

"Alright, here goes nothing," Lamar muttered, a mixture of anxiousness and determination in his voice. At that moment, 'Meg' abruptly abandoned his frenzied behavior, transitioning into a calculated quartering course that brought him across the bow of the 'Maggie Mae.'

"Whenever you're ready, Lamar! He's getting too close for comfort!" Jake shouted, his focus split between the imposing fin and tail that towered before them.

"Hang tight, Jake," Lamar cautioned, extending the black box with both thumbs poised over the ominous red button. "Be prepared for a powerful reaction when this hits him."

Jake gripped the deck cover frame and the throttle stick as he watched Lamar, his anticipation rising to a crescendo. "Alright, do it!"

'Meg' had ravaged the whale's carcass, tearing through it in a frenzy and gorging himself until his appetite was satiated. His meal had dulled his awareness of the faint commotion on the water's surface, a disturbance that paled compared to the feast he had just enjoyed.

However, as he retreated from the scene of gore, 'Meg' was seized by an unprecedented paralysis. A numbing sensation surged through his colossal form, causing involuntary convulsions and a momentary loss of control. The pain was a foreign concept to him, yet this strange experience jolted his senses, compelling him to thrust his muscles to their limits, propel his immense body at maximum speed, and escape to the safety of the open sea.

Above the surface, Lamar initiated the sonic discharge, and the ensuing reaction was as violent as he had anticipated. A maelstrom of foam and spray exploded around 'Meg,' the towering fin racing away through the harbor's entrance and vanishing beneath the waves. The speed of the retreat was astonishing, even to Lamar.

278 SIDNEY ST. JAMES AND JEREMIAH SHERMAN

"Damn... how can something that colossal move so fast?" Jake marveled, taken aback by the unexpected swiftness of 'Meg's' departure.

Lamar squinted as he tracked the fin's retreat, maintaining visual contact for as long as possible before turning to Jake. "I reckon our surprise packed quite a punch. He must have been thoroughly rattled by it." Lamar scanned the expanse between the boat and the horizon, his voice tinged with resignation. "Well, I'd say he's had enough of our sonic therapy. Let's see what's happened to Darwin, shall we?"

Jake nodded in agreement, his heart heavy with worry as he gently guided the 'Maggie Mae' forward, carefully scouring the waters around them for any trace of Darwin, though his efforts yielded nothing.

Toombs, too, was scanning the surrounding waters, but, like Jake, he also failed to discover any clue as to Graham's fate...at first. After they had completed their first pass through the search zone, however, and were starting back, Lamar caught sight of a shiny glint of light on the surface, where the water met the rocks of the wall, and he shouted at Jake. "Hold it, Jake!" He pointed at the edge of the water as he continued. "Over there! Next to the rocks! A reflection of something, I think!"

Jake turned the vessel around and followed the line indicated by Toombs' pointing arm. When they

The old man's sobs echoed, raw and uncontained, as he gazed upon the contorted diving equipment. He wiped his nose with a trembling hand, his voice heavy with emotion as he offered the closest thing to a eulogy Darwin would ever have. "May the good Lord watch over you, my dear friend."

Jake's gaze remained fixed on the heart-wrenching scene for a moment. After confirming that 'Meg' hadn't regained his senses sooner than expected, he expertly guided the boat around and engaged the twin engines at half-power, steering them back toward the pier. Once the vessel was safely docked, nestled against the timeworn planks near the fuel pumps, Jake cut the engines.

Bolo's eyes locked onto the battered tanks strewn across the boat's deck. He cast a mournful glance toward Jake, who could only offer a slow, sorrowful shake of his head. Bolo's spirit seemed to deflate, the weight of despair evident as he tied off the 'Maggie Mae.'

"Fill her up quickly, Bolo. We might be embarking on a long journey..." Jake exchanged a solemn look with Lamar, "...tomorrow. Alright?"

"Of course, Mister Jake," Bolo replied, his voice tinged with anguish. He muttered softly to himself, words expressing disbelief and acceptance. "Bolo understands. The devil takes us one by one. He's coming for all of us."

Though the words were muffled, Jake could sense the melancholy tone in Bolo's voice. Meanwhile, Lamar had managed to make his way up onto the weathered planks, his grief evident in every step. He barely acknowledged Bolo's presence as he moved, lost in his own world of sorrow.

Bolo recognized Lamar's profound sorrow and offered a simple condolence. "A dark day, Mister Toombs."

Lamar halted his slow shuffle and turned back, addressing Bolo's words. "I'm sorry, young man, could you repeat that?"

Bolo clarified his sentiment, his voice carrying the weight of truth. "I said it's a dark day, sir. The devil has taken my old friend before; now he's taken your friend. A truly dark day."

Bolo stood there, a picture of vulnerability and helplessness. Lamar looked down at the worn planks beneath his feet, contemplative. After a moment, he met Bolo's gaze with a somber yet understanding smile. "My young friend, have you ever considered a career in philosophy?"

A faint chuckle escaped Lamar's lips as he turned and continued his slow ascent toward his cabin. Jake observed the exchange while securing the boat, and Bolo turned to him with a curious question. "Mister Jake, what he means by... 'filof...' ... 'filsof'...?"

A slight smile crept onto Jake's face, even amid such a solemn day. "What he means, Bolo is that he believes you possess wisdom beyond your years... Oh, and don't ask me to explain 'astute.' Just accept it as a genuine compliment, alright?"

Bolo shrugged, accepting the answer, and tended to the pump nozzle as he finished topping off the boat's fuel tanks.

Jake went below to make sure all was well with the engine, and when he came back on deck, Bolo was wiping his hands and waiting.

"Mister Jake, the boat; she be ready. Where we be goin'?" Bolo queried, a little frightened.

"Bolo, old buddy-." Jake stood directly in front of Bolo with both hands in his pockets. "...you and I won't be taking the 'Maggie Mae' out...this time." The giant ebony visage displayed a perplexed frown at this comment because, since he and Jake had formed their relationship a long ago, Bolo had naturally 'adopted' the vessel, along with her master.

Jake held up one hand to fend off the expected questions and objections from his mate. "Bolo, listen! This time, I'm letting Lamar take the boat out!"

Bolo's eyes widened in understandable shock, but he said nothing.

Jake continued quickly, knowing Bolo was becoming tormented at realizing what Jake had decided to do. "Lamar has pleaded and rationalized with me, Bolo, and I've decided that his plan makes sound sense."

"But, Mister Jake!" Bolo jumped in. "He no can operate de boat, himself! I need to be with him, don't I?" The big mate asked dejectedly.

"No, Bolo; you don't!...Not this time! Lamar will have Tesoro's man, Jojo, with him to operate the 'Maggie Mae,' while Lamar controls the sonic generation system if needed. And... if... uh... when they get close enough to contact the mainland, Lamar will work the radio to get a message through for help."

Bolo's eyes narrowed ever so slightly, revealing his lingering doubts. "But, Mister Jake! 'That Devil' will surely catch them. You know what it's done to the other boats before."

Jake avoided direct eye contact with Bolo, feeling the weight of the decision. "I understand the possibility, but Lamar and Jojo are aware of the risks, and they've both chosen to proceed." He had to assert his authority to prevent Bolo from challenging the decision further. "So, it's settled, my friend. They're going, and we'll stay and wait."

Bolo's countenance shifted with a blend of resignation and defeat on his face. "Whatever you think is best, Mister Jake." The big, imposing figure of a man turned and walked away, ascending the slope at the head of the dock. Jake watched his departure with unease, regretting the harshness he had shown to his longtime friend.

Alone on the pier by the boat, Jake gazed out at the open expanse of the ocean beyond the harbor gate. He half-expected the ominous gray silhouette that had become hauntingly familiar to emerge from the depths at any moment. But this time, it remained absent.

As Jake contemplated the empty waves, he noticed a line of dark clouds forming on the distant horizon, a sight that had become all too common at this time of year. He knew that another strong southern gale was on its way. *"Damn,"* he muttered to himself, quickening his pace toward Amy's cabin. "We really don't need a storm right now." The urgency was apparent in his thoughts. He understood that any delay in sending word to the outside world could result in more lives lost.

Jake knocked on Amy's door, and after a short wait, she opened it. Her hair was wrapped in a towel, and she wore a sleeveless T-shirt and cutoff shorts. It was a side of her he hadn't seen before, and despite the somber atmosphere, he found himself drawn to it.

"I... uh... just wanted to check in on you and Jenny," Jake stammered, a slight blush creeping up his cheeks. Amy chuckled warmly, tugging him into the room by his strong arm.

"Jenny's resting. She's pretty worn out, so she's taking a nap. And I've still got to stay clean, no matter what's happening around us." Amy gestured to the towel on her head. "When my hair gets dirty, I've got to wash it. Silly, I know."

Jake smiled and shook his head. "Not at all. In fact, I find it quite appealing." He tried to lighten the mood with a playful remark, but his smile faded as he settled into an old armchair. His gaze locked onto Amy's, and though his lips remained still, his eyes revealed a depth of emotion he struggled to put into words.

Sensing his difficulty, Amy recognized that something significant was troubling Jake. She had become attuned to his nuances over time and had a hunch that he was grappling with the news about Darwin. She had thought about venturing out to see what was happening in the harbor, but she couldn't bring herself to confront more death. Her ritual of washing her hair had, over the years, become a way to escape or find solace in times of distress.

Jake simply nodded, his expression heavy with the weight of the news he was about to deliver.

"No!" Amy's voice trembled with disbelief and anguish as her hand covered her mouth.

Jake felt a wave of weariness wash over him, the years showing in his tired eyes as he looked down at the floor. "We found his tanks... severely dented... near the rocks. He's gone, Amy." He lifted his gaze, revealing tears glistening in his dark eyes. Amy walked over to the chair where Jake sat and perched on the arm, wrapping one of her delicate arms around his neck.

"Jake, look at me," she gently coaxed, lifting his chin until their eyes locked. The intensity of their gaze held a silent understanding. "You said it yourself. He knew what he was getting into. We all knew the risks were high. Hell, he might not have even survived the blast. We don't know."

Jake reached up, his fingers intertwining with hers, offering a faint, appreciative smile. "Thanks, Amy."

"For what?" She furrowed her brows, puzzled.

"For trying to ease the pain a little, for me," Jake whispered, his voice tinged with gratitude. "But losing Darwin, on top of everything else that's happened, it's tearing me apart... deeply. And not knowing what might come next is driving me crazy."

Amy listened intently, allowing Jake to pour out his feelings without interruption. But now, she saw an opportunity and leaned in, pressing a soft, brief kiss to Jake's dry lips. "I think you're incredible, doing everything you can to save as many lives as possible with your limited resources." She playfully tapped the tip of his nose with her fingertip before planting another kiss, longer this time, still gentle yet conveying the depth of her feelings.

After they reluctantly broke the kiss, their eyes held a mixture of sadness and confusion as they gazed at each other for a long, heavy moment. Jake cleared his throat, trying to find the right words. "Amy, I... um..."

Amy gently raised her index finger, a bittersweet smile tugging at her lips. "Shh. There'll be time for many conversations once this is behind us. As much as I'd like to share my feelings with you, Jake now isn't the right moment. You know what I mean?"

Jake nodded, his emotions still a jumble. "Yeah, I understand." He stood up, offering a faint smile. "Alright then. Let's go check on how Jenny's doing, shall we?" He seemed to have pulled himself partially out of the emotional turmoil he had been grappling with, although not entirely.

Opening the door for Amy, Jake let her go first. Just as she was about to step out, Amy paused and turned back, reaching out to cup Jake's face with both hands. She kissed him again, this time with a fervor that conveyed longing and uncertainty. "There. Hopefully, you won't forget that we must have that conversation once this ends."

Jake's expression showed his surprise, and his silent promise assured her he wouldn't forget.

They entered the adjacent cabin, and Amy knocked firmly on the door.

"Come in! It's open!" Jenny's voice came from within.

Amy led Jake into the room, where Jenny was lying on the small sofa, absorbed in a paper she held in a blue plastic folder. Despite her apparent composure, there was an underlying nervousness in her voice and actions, evident to Jake.

"What about Darwin, Jake?" Jenny's question seemed to carry a sense of foreboding as if she was expecting the worst.

Jake observed her closely, and when he shook his head slowly, her reaction was almost stoic. "Yeah, I had a feeling it might not work out," she said matter-of-factly. "So, the next step is sending Lamar and the fisherman out on the boat, right?"

Jenny's unusual nonchalance was both confusing and concerning to Jake, as well as to Amy.

"Jenny, please understand. I'm not sending anyone out anywhere," Jake explained, his tone a touch more assertive. "I honestly don't want anyone else taking the 'Maggie Mae' out except me."

Jenny began to ask another question, but Jake interrupted her, finishing his point. "However, letting Lamar and Jojo take the boat this time makes sense. It limits the risk, and Lamar is the only one who can operate the sonic protection system. If anyone can get the word out, it's him."

Amy and Jenny started to see Jake's reasoning as the conversation unfolded, although Jenny's inconsistency troubled them both.

"But what about Amy and me?" Jenny's gaze shifted between Jake and Amy.

"You both will be of great help if the supply ship arrives," Jake reassured them, his sincerity evident in his demeanor. "You can assist in settling the crew, and you'll help keep me focused. Emotionally, I'm pretty drained right now." His words seemed to resonate with the girls, especially Jenny.

Yet, beneath his explanation lay Jake's underlying motivation: to keep Amy and Jenny away from the dangerous waters ahead.

"So!" Jake tried to lighten the mood, seeing that Jenny had calmed down. "Shall we head over to the main house? I'll cook dinner with your assistance, and we can discuss our plans for the next phase of dealing with 'Meg.'"

Neither woman moved immediately, both lost in thoughts of what lay ahead. Jake interrupted their contemplation, clapping his hands together. "Alright then, let's go!" He swung the door open with a flourish.

Jenny got to her feet, and Amy followed while Jake ushered them towards the central cabin, thoughts churning in their minds. As they approached, Jake instructed the ladies to go inside while he went to fetch Tesoro and Jojo from the shed.

He walked up to the weathered structure and unlocked the door. "Alright, Jojo! You and your partner come out. We're meeting at the main house, and we'd like you both to be part of it." Stepping back a few paces, he waited for them to emerge.

Johno came out first, with the shorter Jojo on his heels. He drew up in front of Jake with too much swagger for Jake's taste. "So, tell me, Jake! Did the other big 'gringo' kill the devil fish or not?" Jojo said nothing, but one look would tell anyone that the stocky little seaman was more concerned about the answer to Tesoro's question than Johno himself.

Jake's expression was dark and somber when he forced himself to say the words. "No, he didn't! He didn't make it back, either, Johno!"

Johno turned reflexively to Jojo, knowing what was in the offing now but staying outwardly calm while addressing his mate. "Companero, I am truly sorry! Are you going to be okay to do this thing?" Tesoro sounded as sincere as Jake had ever heard him.

Jojo, on the other hand, was anything but calm. His eyes were the size of saucers, and his bottom lip quivered, just slightly, as he made the sign of the cross. He took a deep breath and was barely audible when he responded to his captain. "Si, mi jefe! I am okay!" Then Jojo addressed Jake. "When must we leave, Senor Jake?"

Before answering, Jake took note of the darkening line of clouds moving noticeably closer, and he tried to gauge the thickness of the approaching mass to, more accurately, estimate the duration of the pending torrent. He nodded in the direction of the ocean. "I would say, oh... sometime tomorrow morning, but, from the looks of those clouds, we may be in for a real 'blow,' and it depends on how long it lasts! In the meantime, let's go to the house and get some dinner!"

Both Johno and Jojo were practically drooling because they were tired of the sandwiches that Jake had Bolo leave with them that morning. Most of the extra ones had gone pretty stale by now, and the two men were becoming famished in the 'cage.' So, the two trotted ahead of Jake, around the house, onto the porch, and into the main room, where they met up with Amy, Jenny, and Bolo. Jake popped in a few seconds behind them and saw that Bolo had gone ahead and thawed a box of frozen chicken parts for dinner. When he caught Bolo's attention, he motioned for the big fellow to come to the door for a private sidebar discussion.

Jake told him in a hushed voice when Bolo approached him, "Bolo, could you please run down and get Lamar for me? He'll probably be lying down because today's events are bound to have drained him pretty badly!"

Bolo grunted his compliance and moved off quickly to fetch the old man.

Then, Jake took up his position at the sink and picked up where Bolo had left off. He noticed the women holding a muted conversation in one corner while Jojo and Tesoro were doing the same in a different part of the room. Therefore, for now, Jake decided to let them alone until everyone was gathered, and he focused on the dinner preparations instead.

A few minutes later, the door opened, and a very disheveled Lamar Toombs came in, with Bolo close behind. The professor's eyes were noticeably red-rimmed, indicating that the elderly gentleman had likely been crying.

"I'm terribly sorry, everyone! I apologize for appearing for dinner, looking like some street urchin, just in from the slums, but, to tell the truth, I am feeling a bit emotionally stripped at the moment!" As if to confirm this point, Lamar was visibly wobbly as he took a chair at the dining table, and Bolo had to help him get settled.

Jake studied Lamar for a few seconds; then, he went over to the locked cabinet in the corner, unlocked the door, and took out an ancient, expensive bottle of cognac. He poured a stiff snifter and sat it before Lamar while the others looked on. "Here ya go, Lamar! This will help a little, I think!" Lamar started to object, but Jake wasn't hearing it. "I insist, Lamar! We will have to discuss the implementation of your plan tonight, and I will need your mind here, with me, and not out there with our lost friends!... So!... Down the hatch!"

Toombs smiled softly and raised the glass to Jake in a mock toast; then, he downed the whole drink in one gulp. He sputtered and coughed a couple of times, but he bobbed his head up and down when he sat the glass down. "Thank you, my friend. It does feel a trifle more bearable now!" Lamar took a deep breath and continued. "Very well! You won't have to worry about me, my boy! Undoubtedly, I shall be focused on the here and now when needed!"

Jake patted Lamar's shoulder and went back to cooking.

Amy set the table, and Bolo poured the wine into all the glasses.

Jojo had come over and was talking, mutedly, to Lamar, of course, about the forthcoming trip, and Tesoro had gone to stand in front of the screen door to look out at the silent ocean in the distance.

And Jenny....she was curled up in a ball on the old sofa in the corner, deep in meditation about her inner scourges and torments.

As Jake meticulously finished his preparations in the kitchen, he absorbed the atmosphere in the room, a sense of unease hanging heavily. With everything ready, he called them to the table, a somber gathering where the weight of unspoken words seemed to press upon them. The discussion they knew was imminent, which carried the gravity of their next moves, hung in the air like a cloud of anticipation.

As the meal progressed over the next hour, the conversation remained minimal, everyone too preoccupied with the unspoken topic that loomed ahead. Amy and Jake exchanged meaningful glances, their silent connection not escaping Jenny's perceptive eyes. The subtle bond between them brought a smile to Jenny's lips; she harbored her plans for the upcoming day, which would prove to be fateful for everyone involved.

When everyone had eaten their fill, Jake shifted the tone of the evening as he broached the much-anticipated conversation about their planned mission. "Alright, I hope you've all had your fill because now we need to address our final opportunity to bring about the eventual demise of that creature and secure assistance before we face even greater... um, inconveniences and discomfort," he began, his tone laden with gravity. A silence settled over the room as he paused, waiting for any initial input, though none was forthcoming.

Seeing the reluctance to speak, Jake pressed on. "Bolo, it's crucial that you ensure the boat is well-stocked with provisions and water for the anticipated four to five days of the journey. Include flares, nautical charts, and communication frequencies we possess for reaching mainland authorities, understood?" His gaze fixed on Bolo, who nodded in agreement.

"Good!" Jojo, you will probably need to help Bolo and have him familiarize you with the boat's controls and the charts for the coastal waters... when you reach them. Think you can handle that?" Jake was all business by this point, and Jojo detected it.

"Si, Senor Jake! I do not have any problem working your boat! I know the type very well, but I will get with the big man here, and we'll get it done!" He smiled up at Bolo, who returned the smile.

Jake liked what he heard. "Good man! I know you will!" Jake then turned his attention to the young women. "Ladies, as we discussed earlier, I will need you to stand by, ready to assist with any emergency that might occur. This, of course, includes helping with securing the crew of the supply ship, should it arrive, as expected, in the next day or two. Alright?" He smiled genuinely when he finished his remarks.

Both women nodded in agreement, signifying their willingness to align with Jake's directives. However, behind Jenny's affirmative expression, a hidden agenda took root in her thoughts, a plan she guarded closely, unwilling to reveal to anyone else. In the depths of her mind, she had made a quiet resolve—to venture home the following day. This decision, cloaked in secrecy, was her own private pact, one she was determined to keep from the others for now.

AFTER A LENGTHY DISCUSSION on the details and probable courses of action each should be prepared for, the meeting broke up.

Tesoro, whom no one addressed during the entire evening, except for some small talk with the girls, early on, sat silently, not wanting to risk Jake's ire by butting in. However, when the gathering did adjourn, he picked up his opportunity and asked Jake privately. "Jake, I know your feelings for me, but,... honestly... I would like to help in some way! Please!"

Jake read a genuine sincerity on Johno's face for the first time, which surprised him. So, after pausing for a second, Jake responded with a degree of congeniality. "You're right, Johno! You should help out, but know one thing!" Jake's tone took on a severe, almost ominous, demeanor. "Your cooperation, in no way, relieves you of your guilt or responsibility in all that has happened before! Understand?" There was no mistaking Jake's bitterness.

"Si!... Yes, Jake! I know that I can't live it down! I ain't no saint; far from it... Never will be! But I also know we must make the best of this whole thing, right?" Jake nodded his agreement. "So, I look at it this way!...' We don't make it off this island; I go out with some class at the last... doin' something right!

On the other hand, if we do get outta here, I'm gonna hafta face up to what I did, anyway! So,... ya see?... why not pitch in... it can't hurt my chances in the end! 'Make sense?" He watched Jake for the tough man's reaction.

Jake had to give it to the younger man. For someone who'd been rotten most of his life, Johno made surprisingly good sense. "You know, Johno! I almost believe you!... In any event, we're stuck here together, and chances are good that we'll all have to face up to worse challenges before this is over.

So!... Why don't you stick close to Bolo and do everything he tells you until this thing is over. You think you can do that?" Jake capped his point with an intense questioning expression, set directly on Tesoro.

"Si, Jake!" Johno walked over to Bolo, who'd moved to the doorway. "I help Bolo good!" Johno smiled at Bolo, who quickly glanced at Jake, rolled his eyes up, and scuffled out of the house with Lamar, Johno, and Jojo in tow.

The girls pitched in and helped Jake prepare and pack the food and provisions for the boat. Once finished and everything was packed, they cleaned up and walked down to the 'Maggie Mae.' There, they gave the food, water jugs, and other items necessary for the long journey to Bolo, who passed it to Jojo to store forward and below.

Jake scanned the skies for the first time since going in for dinner and saw lightning, broadspread, along the horizon.

"Damn, Bolo! 'Looks like a big one coming in!" Bolo acknowledged Jake without looking.

"Yessir, Mister Jake! I saw that weather a while ago. 'Don't know how much is comin'!' 'Could last a long time, from all that lightning!" Now, Bolo looked at the gathering thunderheads. "What you be thinking,' Mister Jake?"

"Hmmm! If it was you and me, Bolo, I'd be more inclined to take a chance and go out at first light." Jake rubbed his chin, struggling with a decision. "... But, with Lamar and Jojo taking her alone, I'm more inclined to wait until it passes." He studied the gathering storm closely before continuing. " We may have to wait until the day after tomorrow if it's too bad."

Jake gestured for Lamar and Jojo to join them from the forward deck, and the two women, Amy and Jenny, also walked over, their curiosity piqued by the gathering. Jake's index finger extended to indicate the distant flashes of light. "See that storm front on the horizon? It looks pretty formidable, and the odds are it's heading our way. Given the size of the system, Bolo and I were discussing the possibility of postponing your departure for a day. We might have to take the risk and let you set off the day after tomorrow."

Lamar began to voice his objections, but Jake swiftly interjected. "I understand your urgency, Lamar, but rushing into a storm won't do us any favors. Going out and getting sunk won't help anyone either."

Sighing, Lamar turned his gaze downward, his frustration evident. He acknowledged that Jake's reasoning was valid, which didn't alleviate his disappointment at the delay.

"Alright, Bolo and I will stay here and monitor the radio again. The rest of you, especially you and Jojo, Lamar, need some rest," Jake instructed authoritatively.

Amy gently led Jenny away, their steps carrying them into the enveloping darkness of the night.

Johno and Jojo lingered near Jake, their eyes expectant. Johno inquired, "You do not want to lock us up, Jake?"

Jake shook his head. "No, Johno. You both know the situation well enough to take care of yourselves. Find an empty cabin near Bolo's and get some sleep, alright?"

The two fishermen exchanged words expressing gratitude and made their way down the hill toward Bolo's cabin.

Lamar patted Jake on the back and offered a frail smile. "Good night, my dear friend. A troubled sleep awaits me, I fear. But, such has been my fate for countless years. Good night!"

"Good night, Lamar," Jake and Bolo responded in unison, watching the elderly professor retreat to his abode.

Left alone, Jake and Bolo meticulously reviewed every control and function of the equipment. Jake paid particular attention to the radio transmitter, his fingers adeptly manipulating the knobs. After some adjustments, he managed to squeeze about fifty percent signal strength. His apprehension was palpable, etched onto his weathered face like lines on a map.

"Mister Jake, I can tell from that look that you're doubting their chances," Bolo noted, recognizing the worry in Jake's eyes.

"I honestly can't say, Bolo. Unless that sonic scrambler down there..." Jake pointed below the deck. "...can fend off that massive creature longer than I expect. Their chances are slim. Damn it, I wish there was another way!"

Bolo's massive hand touched Jake's shoulder lightly, a comforting gesture from behind. "There ain't no other way now, Mister Jake, not if we aim to save those other lives you're concerned about. The old professor is also right; you must be here if this doesn't work either. You know that, Mister Jake." Bolo's voice carried a mixture of support and reality, his grip on Jake's shoulder providing strength and solace.

"I know, Bolo...Dammit! I know!" Jake's level of frustration increased by the minute.

Finally, Jake rubbed his face with both hands and breathed a deep sigh. "If you're finished, Bolo, let's go try to get us some rest. Mornin's gonna come soon enough." Jake stepped up onto the pier and pulled Bolo up with him. Then, the two men walked wordlessly up the hill and split toward each one's abode.

Jake washed off with a wet cloth and bowl of water and put on a fresh set of underwear. After this, he lay down and tried to sleep. This night, however, sleep was elusive, and Jake rolled and turned, dozing fitfully for only three hours. Eventually, he got up, donned a fresh pair of worn jeans, and walked out to check on the weather.

The sky was now adorned with thick, ominous clouds that hung ominously overhead, occasionally illuminated by bursts of lightning. Thunder rumbled intermittently, creating an eerie symphony of nature's forces. The wind bore down from the south with newfound intensity, carrying a cold bite that sent shivers down spines.

"I'd better go make sure the boat is buffered and secure," He thought out loud. While he crossed the dark, soundless yard, he subconsciously peered out into the blackness, wondering if a towering fin was waiting for him to venture too close.

Suddenly, as he approached the incline leading down to the wharf, he was startled by a motion off to his right in the vicinity of the little knoll. "Who's there?" He barked, bristling a little.

"Sorry, Jake!" It was Jenny. She was bundled in a blanket, standing on the small overlook. "I didn't mean to alarm you! I just couldn't sleep and thought I'd come out where I could watch the coming gale and think." Her blonde hair was tousled by the wind.

Jake walked over to her and smiled. "I understand what you are going through, sweetheart, but you must return to your cabin. That's a big wind coming..." He pointed at the most active part of the approaching system. "...and you'll catch your death of a cold!

So, go back and, at least, try to sleep, okay?" He smoothed the younger woman's hair back with his hand.

"Alright, Jake, but... ah... I want to ensure I'm here in the morning to see Lamar off!" She squinted at Jake through the building gate, awaiting a response to her unspoken question.

"Well, it doesn't appear that you'll have to worry about that, Jenny. If this weather system is half 'the beast' it looks to be, Lamar won't be going out today...at all!" Jake ushered Jenny along to a good start down the path, then he trotted down and ensured the bumpers were all out along the sides of the 'Maggie Mae,' and the lines were tied off well. This being done, he made his way back to the porch of the main house. He had just started up the steps when the first raindrops fell on his head and shoulders. Within a few minutes, the light shower became a torrent, underscored by frequent lightning flashes and the intensifying roar of thunder, which were very near and covered the sky in all directions.

Jake stood for a while, gauging the progress of the storm, and after he saw that the wind was whipping and swishing non-stop, he made a rational decision to forego Lamar's mission for a day.

Jake went inside, turned on the lights, and put a pot of coffee on because he knew he would never get back to sleep, so why not just make coffee for himself and any of the others who might be insomniacs like him.

The coffee had been boiling for about five minutes when Jake heard heavy steps running onto the porch. The door opened, and it was Lamar, looking like a drowned rat, but at least he was dressed in a black slicker suit that had been used before.

"Ah! Hello, good sir! The coffee smells wonderful, indeed! May I share in a cup?" Lamar's jittery mannerisms indicated he was stressed out and trying not to babble too severely to hide the fact.

"It'll be ready in a few, Lamar! Did you manage to sleep at all?" Jake didn't want to postpone the trip, but the deck was stacked against Toombs, even in the best weather! Even experienced seamen would hesitate before tackling these waters in weather like this.

Lamar was rubbing his hands together briskly, and his eyes were glued to the coffee maker. "Good! Good! I can use a cup to ward off the effects of no sleep, believe me!" He selected a cup and poured powdered sugar and creamer into it. Seeing the coffee wasn't quite ready, Lamar sat at the table with his mug in front of him, fidgeting nervously while he waited.

Jake broke the ensuing pregnant silence when he saw that Toombs wouldn't. "Lamar, I suppose you've seen..." Jake noticed the puddles of water forming around the old man's feet, caused by the water running off the slicker bottoms, and smiled. "...and experienced just how badly it's blowing out there!?"

"Indeed, I have, Jake! I was almost bowled over on my way here from the cabin!" Toombs reported. "So..." Lamar squinted suspiciously at Jake, catching the inference in the bigger man's line of questioning. "...am I to understand that our little excursion will have to wait until the storm has passed, my boy?" Lamar asked apprehensively.

"I'm afraid so, Lamar." Jake hated to delay things, knowing, full well, that Toombs' nerves, already poorly frayed, would take an immense emotional battering. "Believe me, my friend! If I thought you two could pull this off without any significant risk of sinking at the outset, I'd send you off with my blessing! But look out there! You can barely see your hand in front of your nose!"

"Yes, yes, my dear Jake! I can see this, of course! But don't you think canceling for the day is a bit premature? I mean, mightn't it blow itself out in relatively short order? If it were early enough, we could travel most of the daylight hours anyway!" Apparently, Lamar wanted to get on with it before losing his nerve.

Jake saw that the coffee was finally ready, and after filling his own mug, he took a pot full over to the table and filled Toombs' cup. "I suppose so, but from my experiences here, I think this will stay with us for most of the day, hopefully, not longer." Jake went back and set the pot on the stove.

Lamar was, understandably, upset with Jake's outlook, and he just sat glumly, staring at his coffee on the table in front of him.

The door opened then, and Bolo led Johno and Jojo into the room. Bolo wore a slicker suit, but the other two looked like two waterlogged rodents.

"Mister Jake!" Bolo spoke out. "I see that you could not sleep any better than me. 'You neither, professor?" Bolo began stripping off the wet rain suit.

"You're quite right, Bolo. I don't think I closed my weary eyes for more than two hours the entire evening." Lamar answered.

Jake simply shrugged and shook his head, 'no,' while he sorted out breakfast.

Johno and Jojo, on the other hand, headed straight for the coffee, and each poured a steaming mug to ease the wet chill they were enduring.

Jake reached a point where he could pause in his preparations, and, grasping his mug, he turned to talk with the other men.

"I'm sorry, guys, but, like I was telling Lamar, it's looking like we may have to scratch the mission for today." The only person in the room who didn't display a noticeable deflated expression was, understandably, Jojo.

"I know this is a bit disappointing, but we simply cannot risk losing the 'Maggie Mae' before she can get Lamar within certain radio proximity of the mainland." Jake saw that Jojo was relieved at the potential 'reprieve' and smiled to himself.

"Lamar, we can be productive during this delay by educating you and Jojo on the correct use of the fish finder on board. Bolo, after breakfast, why don't you take the guys down to the boat and teach them the fine points of reading the 'finder's' display. Oh, and while you're at it, take the dummy from the shed and drop it in so that you can calibrate the 'finder,' too, okay?"

Bolo gave Jake a mock salute, indicating a friendly acknowledgment of Jake's wishes.

The next hour or so slipped by as the conversation flowed into sporadic small talk and contemplative silence. Jake deftly carried out his morning routine, preparing breakfast while the storm outside maintained its furious assault on the landscape. Beyond the windows, the thick clouds hinted at the imminent dawn with a subtle tint of light on the eastern horizon.

Slowly, the sky transformed from an inky blackness to a subdued gray, and the men migrated to the porch shelter, cups of coffee in hand. They watched as rain-lashed waves crashed upon the harbor, their white crests stark against the backdrop of the tempest.

After about twenty minutes, two blurred figures navigated through the downpour from across the yard. Amy and Jenny emerged from the curtain of rain onto the porch steps, their heads shielded by old fishermen's rain hats they must have found in their cabins. They were clad in lightweight rain suits that kept them dry despite the weather's assault.

"Hey, guys!" Amy's cheerful greeting cut through the storm's din. Her gaze settled on Jake, a spark of humor glinting in her eyes as she addressed him.

Jenny, on the other hand, remained more subdued. She slipped indoors, presumably to get a cup of coffee, followed by Bolo, who seemed to have taken on a protective role toward the emotionally unsettled young woman.

"That's right, Amy," Jake affirmed with a nod. "We've discussed it, and the consensus is to wait until this system blows over. Plus, it's a good opportunity for Lamar and Jojo to familiarize themselves with the 'fish finder.' It can't hurt and might help them navigate without encountering difficulties during the trip."

With Jenny and Bolo rejoining the group on the porch, Jake gestured for everyone to follow him inside. The presence of the two women signaled that it was time to move on to breakfast.

After the meal, Amy and Jenny graciously offered to tackle the cleanup and tidying of the room. Meanwhile, Jake and the other men, each donned in various rain gear, trudged their way through the deluge to the boat. They huddled beneath the shelter of the zippered canvas deck cover, assembling around the fish-tracking transponder.

"Go ahead, Bolo. Show them how it's done," Jake preemptively answered an unspoken query from Bolo.

Bolo nodded in acknowledgment, and for the following forty-five minutes, the rain continued its unrelenting percussion on the cabin roof. Bolo took charge, walking Lamar and Jojo through the procedures for interpreting the readings on the scope. He even demonstrated the approximate size of the blip they would see on the screen if they happened to detect a hundred-foot target, such as the massive Megalodon.

Following the initial demonstration, Bolo delved into a thorough operating explanation for Jojo while the remaining three descended below decks to review the operation of the sonic defense system one final time. Once Bolo had concluded the concise yet comprehensive training, he queried Jojo on his understanding of the material. Positioned next to the boat's wheel and controls, the transponder itself would be Jojo's responsibility, ensuring he could navigate the 'Maggie Mae' and oversee the sonic defense system when they ventured into open waters.

The little fellow recounted what he had learned, in broken English, to Bolo with a surprisingly high degree of accuracy, and Bolo gave Jojo a firm pat on the back and a hearty laugh.

"Boy! You learn 'this thing very well! You can find anything in the water, now... 'specially that 'Devil Fish,' if he comes near!" With this comment, their mutual levity disappeared, replaced with somber expressions and two sets of grimly set lips. They shook hands, closed down the controls, and both moved over to peer down into the cabin, where Jake, shadowed by Johno, watched as Lamar went through each operation necessary to check out and fine-tune the sophisticated sonic equipment. Once satisfied that all was fully operational, the professor switched off the power, turned, and pronounced.

"All right! It's as ready as we're going to get it! I only hope it scrambles 'Meg's' senses and repels *him* when needed."

"What you be meaning,' professor?" Bolo piped down from the top of the hatchway. "Didn't we see it work already?"

Lamar snorted a derisive laugh, not at Bolo's question but at the prospect of the unit's previous operational success. "Oh, I'm quite certain we did, my dear Bolo!... I'm quite sure we did! However, the more they encounter them, the more animals have a knack for overcoming such disrupting effects! In short, we scared *him* the first time and probably will again, but on any subsequent encounters, we might find ourselves in severe trouble! Do you follow me, my boy?"

Bolo gave a quick indication that he understood and stepped back from the hatch to allow the others to come up and join Jojo and him on deck.

The canvas deck cover snapped in and out from the wind, and their hearing was made difficult by the incessant battering of the rain on the top. They all shared their feelings about what lay ahead, and Jake finally recommended that they make their way to their respective cabins and wait for what would probably be a highly stressful morrow.

Everyone donned the rain clothes they had removed in the shelter of the boat's cover, went out into the storm, and disappeared into the blinding rain. Jake and Bolo went to the main house together, where the two women were just finishing the cleaning and straightening up.

Amy smiled brightly when Jake walked in, followed by a drenched Bolo, who didn't believe in wearing a complete rainsuit, just the bottoms. "Hi there! 'Everything okay with the boat?" Amy asked.

"As well as we can get it!" Jake answered while he stripped off and hung up his oilskins.

"How about some fresh, hot coffee?" Jenny piped in. "I just made it....and it's strong!"

Jake and Bolo jumped at the offer, and the four of them sat around the table and discussed nothing in general as the tempest continued to rage outside.

Eventually, however, the topic came around to the next day's trip.

"Do you truly believe Lamar and the other fella can make it through, Jake?" Jenny's inquiry carried a pointed edge.

Jake took a moment to contemplate his response. "I believe they have a shot at getting a message across...yes. As for their chances of making it safely hinges on how effective Lamar's 'little black box' sound system proves to be." Concern etched itself unmistakably across Jake's features as he spoke.

Amy detected this undercurrent. "But Jake, what are their real odds, do you think?" Her expression left no room for evasion; she sought a candid response rather than a sugar-coated reassurance.

Jake's reply was frank. "I'd say, at best, about fifty-fifty." His words carried sincerity.

Amy nodded her thoughts deep in contemplation. "I had hoped for better."

The conversation gradually waned, and they eventually found themselves on the porch. They settled into a contemplative silence, watching the rain whip almost horizontally across the landscape. Each grappled with their own individual fears and apprehensions, lost in their thoughts for a time.

By mid-afternoon, Amy nudged Jenny, and the two of them stood, announcing their intention to retreat to their cabins to collect their thoughts and seek some rest. It was also a chance for Amy to distract herself from the intense stress by delving into the notes they had taken earlier about local currents.

After their departure, Bolo informed Jake that he, too, would be heading to his small dwelling, with plans to return in a couple of hours to assist Jake in preparing dinner.

Jake acknowledged Bolo's plan, watching the big man fade slowly into the curtain of rain that continued to batter the island.

Alone on the porch, Jake felt the weight of solitude more acutely than ever. Settling into a rocking chair, he gazed into the mist as a rush of recent events flooded his mind. He rocked gently back and forth, lost in thought, and offered a private prayer for God's protection over the living and His embrace for the departed souls. As he finished, Jake reclined in the rocker, intending to rest his eyes for a brief moment. However, the next thing he knew, someone was shaking him awake.

"Mister Jake! It's time for dinner!" Bolo's gentle shake roused Jake from his slumber, leaving him somewhat bewildered, as he had believed he'd only dozed off for a few minutes.

"What... What time is it?" He asked, his mind still foggy.

"It's after six o'clock, Mister Jake and the rain has moved on." Bolo pointed towards the fragmented clouds and the patches of blue sky peeking through.

"Damn! I've been sleeping for three hours here, on the porch, Bolo, and it seems like I just closed my eyes!" He rose from the rocker and turned to go inside and prepare dinner. Over the next two hours, the others filtered in, and dinner came off in a very somber mood, with no one saying much. Afterward, no one wanted to hang around and converse because, with the clearing weather, each one was becoming increasingly stressed or depressed about the next day. So, after a cup of post-dinner coffee, they disbanded unceremoniously and drifted off into the night.

Amy wanted to stay and talk privately with Jake, but she saw that the big man wasn't in a very talkative mood. Therefore, she ushered Jenny back to their hovels for the evening.

After washing up, Bolo helped Jake put the dinner things away, and, with a quiet 'good night,' he left Jake in the kitchen.

After a few minutes of laying out some of the items he would need for breakfast, Jake headed out for his cabin, but as he emerged onto the porch, he found Lamar, Jojo, and Johno whispering at one end of the platform, obviously about the mission. They looked up when he came out, and, after a 'good evening' gesture from Jake, they returned it and returned to their discussion. Jake left them to their caucus, went to his cabin, and immediately fell asleep!

Such was Jake's exhaustion that his usually dependable 'body clock' failed to wake him. Once again, his friend, Bolo, shook him awake around three thirty in the early morning. After rubbing his face with some water from a pitcher, Jake turned and addressed his big mate. "Okay, Bolo, it seems like we just ate dinner." He looked at his watch. "I guess we'd better go and get breakfast started for those that want to eat anything. I doubt that many will want to eat much because it will be a very long and eventful day. I'm sure!"

Bolo agreed, and the two men walked over to the big house and began the preliminary preparations for the morning meal.

After they had things well underway, Jake told Bolo. "Okay, it's about a quarter to five, Bolo. You'd better go round up the others and get them on up here because we must get Lamar and Jojo fed and on their way as early as possible."

Bolo had just gotten back from the cold locker with eggs and a slab of bacon, and he tipped his 'imaginary hat' to Jake and hustled toward the door.

Jake stopped him as an afterthought, though. "Oh, on your way back, why don't you stop at the locker and bring me a few cans of those rolls. I may, as well, throw them in the oven, too, okay?" Bolo waved and shuffled off into the pre-dawn darkness.

When Bolo returned, he put the fixings Jake had requested on the counter and announced. "Mister Jake, we near out of eggs and getting real low on slab bacon and near everythin' else, too! I hope that supply ship gets by that devil fish and arrives here soon! We gonna be needin' it!

Jake glanced up at this information. A look of grave concern crept across his wrinkled countenance. "I know, Bolo, but unless we give that thing something else to concentrate on, *he* will almost certainly go for that ship when it gets close! There's no doubt about it!"

Bolo's anxiety was palpable; he nervously bit his bottom lip as he turned his attention to aiding Jake in meal preparation. The concern for their friends weighed heavily on the big man's mind despite his efforts to push it aside.

CHAPTER 18
Foreboding Worries are Foretelling

Jake and Bolo's shared apprehension seemed eerily prophetic as events unfolded. At that very moment, the 'Rising Star,' a supply vessel, had concluded its series of coastal stops and navigated resolutely towards 'Crandle's Keep.' This sixty-two-foot ship had conquered approximately half the expanse of open water, spanning the mainland and the island, while the crew battled relentlessly against an unrelenting gale.

With the tempest gradually subsiding, Captain Roberto Ponce, a seasoned seafarer of over three decades, ordered most of his crew to take a break and find some rest. He asserted that he and a select few of his team would manage the remainder of the voyage. This decision showcased his remarkable leadership style, a captain who prioritized the welfare of his crew.

As the storm's intensity waned, tranquility enveloped the 'Star.' Amidst the early morning obscurity, a stillness permeated the vessel.

It wouldn't continue this way very much longer!

SEVERAL NAUTICAL MILES ahead, delving to depths exceeding five hundred feet, our Big Boy executed a series of intricate maneuvers, moving through the abyss with calculated unpredictability. In the dim aquatic twilight, his path crossed that of a colossal giant squid. He instantly pounced upon this formidable adversary, engaging it in a fierce contest of strength.

Triumph was his as he emerged victorious, the squid succumbing to his mastery.

After this underwater duel, his formidable appetite consumed the vanquished cephalopod, relishing its immense flesh. Yet, his innate senses detected distant tremors, vibrations echoing through the water – a signature indicative of a presence from the world above, the surface realm that intrigued and beckoned to him. Setting his course with a languid grace, he navigated toward the source of the disturbance, his curiosity piqued by the approaching unknown.

Back on board the 'Rising Star,' a sense of tranquility prevailed. The ship's captain, Roberto, muted the radio, ensuring his two loyal companions on the bridge remained undisturbed in their slumber. A decade of camaraderie bound them together, but little did they know that their serene journey across open waters would turn into a nightmare they couldn't fathom. Misguided by a false sense of control, Roberto allowed himself to be lulled into a dangerous complacency.

In the depths below, 'Meg' drew nearer to the unsuspecting freighter. The usual vibrations caused by his presence grew markedly stronger, signaling a heightened disturbance from this colossal predator. An adept hunter, he circled the ship cautiously, assessing his potential prey with a blend of calculated observation and primal instinct.

Meanwhile, on the bridge, Roberto wrestled with sleep's encroachment. His efforts to remain awake were hampered by the hypnotic rhythm of the vessel. Seeking respite, he stepped onto the walkway, perched precariously over the dark expanse of water. Suddenly, the ship convulsed violently beneath him as if colliding with an unseen force. Caught off guard, Roberto's weight shifted, and he was sent hurtling over the railing, disappearing into the inky abyss below.

The ship's two mates, jolted from their sleep by the abrupt upheaval, scrambled to their feet, their confusion mounting. The vessel's abrupt halt and unsettling lurch defied explanation, but more pressing was the absence of their captain. An air of foreboding enveloped the scene as they grappled with the inexplicable circumstances unfolding before them.

Meanwhile, below the waves, 'Meg' continued his relentless pursuit. Instinct seized control, driving him into a frenzy. He plummeted downward, then surged upward with a purpose, his monstrous snout colliding with the ship's hull. The initial impact left his nose marred and torn, but it didn't deter his determination. Rising again, he targeted the crucial juncture where keel met side, his massive form striking with a force that belied his aquatic grace.

Catastrophe ensued as the hull buckled and the sea surged into the hold. This unfortunate area happened to house Jake's meticulously stored provisions, a grim irony in the face of impending doom. 'Meg' wasn't done. He struck again, ferocity rending through metal and men alike. Chaos reigned as crew members, struggling to comprehend the turmoil, were flung into the churning waters below. The night, already thick with overcast shadows, was plunged into deeper darkness, further amplifying the terror gripping the scene.

On the bridge, the first mate's voice pierced the air, strained with urgency, as he sensed the perilous tilt of the ship. "Abandon ship! Abandon ship!" His frantic command echoed through the power megaphone, mingling with the ship's intercom. The first mate's efforts seemed almost redundant as bodies hurled themselves into the water, accompanied by the occasional orange life raft.

As the first mate confirmed the escape of those below deck, he scanned the decks rapidly, slipping into his life vest before launching himself from the sinking vessel. Amid the imminent disaster, Roberto clung to a rope line on the hull's side, his gaze frozen on the grim spectacle. One by one, his crew members were cast into the abyss, their desperate flight punctuated by the sporadic appearance of life rafts that struck the water's surface.

Roberto's grip on the rope was a lifeline to his waning hope, his heart pounding as the ship continued its inexorable descent. Desperation radiated from his expression as he witnessed his crew's frenzied exodus. His eyes locked onto a life raft bobbing about thirty yards away, and with determination, he abandoned the rope, plunging into the frigid depths to reach it.

Arriving at the life raft, Roberto found solace in the presence of his crew members, who had also sought refuge there. He joined them, his voice trembling as he inquired about their distress signal. A collective shrug communicated the failure to transmit their SOS amidst the chaos.

Roberto's heart constricted with fear as he observed additional life rafts dotting the distance, realizing the possibility of their isolation and the ominous prospect of rescue efforts being delayed. However, his worries would soon be overshadowed by an even greater terror.

In the depths, 'Meg' circled the wounded behemoth, his every move calculated with predatory precision. Satisfied with the impending demise of his colossal rival, he prepared to tighten his deadly loops for the final kill. But new vibrations diverted his attention; smaller creatures joined the tableau, altering his strategy.

As he continued his vigil, 'Meg' observed the sinking creature descending below him. Despite his earlier strikes, the massive prey slipped deeper, provoking 'Meg's' relentless pursuit. Frenzied strikes yielded only disappointment; the quarry remained lifeless. Frustrated, 'Meg' spiraled upward, surveying the surface where only four smaller 'creatures' remained. His keen senses detected no movement, rendering them seemingly lifeless. He swam cautiously toward the potential prey, each surface ripple guiding his approach.

Terror erupted on the raft as one of Roberto's crew members pointed at something behind the captain. Horrified disbelief etched across their faces, they watched as a colossal fin broke the surface, casting a terrifying shadow over their small haven. Roberto turned, incredulous, his voice trembling as he wrestled with the impossible sight. "Oh, good Lord, protect us! It can't be... There are no sharks in the sea this big!"

The nightmarish reality revealed itself as 'Meg's' immense form drew nearer. His monstrous fin churned the water, causing the raft to teeter perilously. A narrow escape ensued as 'Meg's' colossal tail swept by, Roberto and his crew clinging desperately to the raft.

Meanwhile, 'Meg' shifted his attention to three clustered rafts, hungry anticipation guiding his every move. But just before his assault, a disturbance behind him captured his attention. Urgency spurred him to dive beneath the surface, leaving the terrified men on the rafts paralyzed. As 'Meg' disappeared beneath the water, his towering dorsal fin nearly grazing the lead raft, the men clung to their fleeting lives, ignorant of the fate they had narrowly avoided.

Conversely, Roberto and his men considerably hastened the forfeiture of their lives by trying to paddle wildly away from the scene!

He had corkscrewed down and reversed *his* course, taking *him* underneath *his* splashing target. *He* didn't circle or swim in patterns this time. Instead, *he* turned up at a forty-five-degree angle and sped up in keeping with *his* instinctual feeding practices.

The water's surface erupted in turmoil around the boat, a maelstrom of chaos that sent shockwaves through Roberto and his crew. Their terrified screams blended into a collective high-pitched wail as the abyss's nightmarish jaws gaped before them. The gaping maw, a cavern of nightmarish teeth, rose menacingly from the depths, its insatiable hunger evident in every menacing tooth. In a horrifying instant, it lunged, swallowing both the raft and its occupants with a malevolent ferocity that defied comprehension. Then, just as quickly, it retreated with a resounding crash, flinging the remnants of the raft into the unforgiving sea.

In the aftermath of this sudden and violent calamity, a deathly stillness settled over the scene, punctuated only by the haunting echoes of the encounter. The first mate, one of the survivors in the remaining raft, witnessed the monstrous tragedy. His voice quavered with awe and terror as he issued a desperate command, a plea for survival amidst the unimaginable. "No one moves a muscle or makes a sound! It will attract him! Be very still... and pray." A potent silence descended as the survivors clung to his words, immobilized by fear and an instinct for self-preservation.

Amid the chilling aftermath of his deadly strike, 'Meg' reveled in his conquest. Sated for the moment, he returned to the site of his earlier attack, a macabre tableau of destruction and lifeless debris. He swam near the surface, his senses on high alert for any sign of movement, any trace of potential sustenance. Yet, the ocean around him remained devoid of life, an eerie void that failed to trigger his insatiable hunger.

After aimlessly traversing the scene for what felt like an eternity, he gradually altered his trajectory, his movements taking on a sense of purpose. The massive creature embarked on a determined course, a broad arc leading him toward his familiar feeding grounds—Crandle's Keep.

In the shadow of an encroaching dawn, the survivors clung to the remnants of their rafts, eyes locked on the implacable fin that continued its ominous glide through the water. Fear constricted their chests, and terror etched deep lines on their faces as they collectively witnessed the relentless advance of their predator. Among them, individuals shivered uncontrollably, fear manifesting in stark physical reactions. Yet, their resolve held, forged in the crucible of desperation, as they remained utterly motionless in the face of impending doom.

As the night receded, the first light of dawn washed over the sea, revealing a tableau of dread. With the growing illumination, the first mate mustered the courage to initiate movement. A wordless gesture prompted his fellow survivors to pick up their paddles, moving the raft towards the east. They drifted away from the horror that had consumed their companions, casting their fate on the shifting currents of uncertainty.

In the wake of that fateful night, the survivors were forever marked by the horrors they had witnessed. The trauma would haunt them for years, manifesting in sleepless nights punctuated by nightmarish screams. But for now, propelled by an instinctive desire to escape, they paddled eastward, their resolve unshakable, their collective will striving for the distant light of hope and the prospect of home.

IN THE MEANWHILE, JAKE served breakfast to somber faces all around. Not much was said or needed to be throughout the meal.

As the dawn slowly unfurled its canvas of light, a clear sky painted the horizon with delicate hues, casting a tranquil glow over the compound. Though yet to crest the craggy silhouette of the cliffs, the sun began to weave threads of brilliance through the dusky tapestry. In the soft embrace of this dim twilight, their hands cradling the last remnants of their coffee cups, they found a moment of serenity amid the encroaching daybreak.

Lamar was softly conferring with Jojo over in a corner, and Jake couldn't help but notice the deep lines etching the older man's weary complexion.

"I'm not feeling at all, well, Jake..." Jenny's words startled Jake, pulling him from his reverie. Her voice carried an undertone of discomfort that caught his attention. "...so, I think I'm gonna go lay down for a while. Say my goodbyes for me, will you?"

Amy overheard Jenny's announcement and approached them, her concern etched in her expression. She draped an arm around Jenny, offering her support. "Would you like me to go with you.....in case you get to feeling worse?"

Jenny shook her head gently, appreciating their concern. "No...no! You stay and help Jake get straightened up." A faint smile touched Jenny's lips as she addressed them both. "I'm going to try and nap for a while."

Then, turning her attention to Professor Toombs, Jenny's tone became more formal. "Oh, Professor!" Lamar paused his conversation with Jojo, and Johno joined their huddle in the corner.

"Yes, my dear? What is it?" Toombs responded, his voice carrying a mixture of curiosity and warmth.

"I'm going to my cabin and may not see you off, in which case, Jake will say my goodbyes at the dock. But I... uh... want to wish you the very best of luck, and may God keep you... both... safe on your journey." Jenny's hands gently cradled the professor's, her words sincere. She then extended her hand to Jojo for a polite handshake.

"You're very kind, Jenny! I will diligently try to assist the Maker in assuring our survival and success, as you have wished for us. Right, Jojo?" Toombs turned his gaze to the stocky seaman beside him.

"Si! Many thanks for your blessings, Senorita!" Jojo offered a respectful nod to Jenny.

With nods and smiles exchanged, Jenny began her departure towards the door. Her hand reached for the doorknob, but Bolo burst into the room just then, returning from provisioning the boat.

"Ah! Many pardons, Missy Jenny!" Bolo apologized quickly as he almost collided with the young blonde. "Bolo didn't see you!"

Jenny waved off his concern with a forgiving smile. "That's all right, 'big guy!' I'm not feeling well, so I'm on my way to lie down for a couple of hours to try and shake it off! 'See ya later!" She moved past Bolo, who turned and stopped her gently.

"Wait, Miss Jenny! Maybe Bolo needs to go and help the young Miss!"

"Nah, that's okay. Besides, Jake will need your help to get Lamar and Jojo off on their trip. I'll be fine... my good friend." Jenny patted his arm affectionately, her smile a mixture of gratitude and reassurance, before she continued down the steps toward her cabin. Bolo watched her momentarily, then headed inside to join the others in their preparations.

Everyone in the main house was so busy discussing last-minute details and straightening up the room that they overlooked that Jenny stopped where the path to her cabin intersected with the trail leading to the pier... and the boat moored.

She turned and checked to see that no one was on the porch or watching from the door, and, confirming this was the case, she bolted, in a sudden dash, down the hill, and onto the pier. She scrambled onto the 'Maggie Mae' and went directly below. She paused, deciding the best place to hide from notice. She noticed the forward storage compartment and crawled inside. She slid under a tarp and lashed to some of the supplies. When convinced she was adequately concealed, she made herself as comfortable as possible, relaxed the best she could, and waited!

An hour later, Jake, Lamar, and the others emerged onto the house's porch, scanned the horizon together, and made their way down to the vessel that held their collective fates in its hull.

Jake and Toombs immediately went downstairs and powered up the sonic system. When charged, Lamar hit the 'Test' switch, and the unit emitted a sonic bolt into the surrounding harbor. Satisfied that the unit was working, Lamar set it on standby, with Jake observing closely.

"Well, my boy! I suppose the time has come to sail forth to meet our destiny!" Lamar was visibly tense, and Jake knew the old man was as nervous as he could remember seeing him.

"Just make sure Jojo keeps a careful eye on the fish finder, alright?" Lamar nodded. "It's the one up-to-date 'toy' on this tub!" Jake tried a little levity to try and put the professor somewhat at ease.

Toombs thanked Jake and cracked a little humor of his own. "I'll try to bring your craft back in working order, my friend! But, in the event, I don't... I suppose you will have to keep my damage deposit!" Lamar chuckled, and, receiving a short laugh in return, he turned and led Jake up the stairs to the main deck, where Bolo and Jojo were checking the boat's controls and the fish finding sonar, with Johno looking on quietly.

"Oh, Mister Jake! How be the .....um.....'sound gun?'" Bolo had glanced up from watching the controls over Jojo's shoulder at the sight of Jake and Lamar emerging on deck.

"It's fine, Bolo! It should keep the thing off of them....hopefully, all the way across..." Jake looked meaningfully, from Lamar to Jojo... and even at Tesoro before he went on. "... But, at the very least, until they can get a confirmed message!" This reality caused the mood on the boat to become more somber than in the house.

Toombs' expression turned dark, his features etched with defiance, as he faced the possibility of this grim fate. His lips pressed tightly together in resolute determination.

Amy, on the pier, observed the preparations with increasing unease. But eventually, her concern overcame her restraint. She couldn't just stand by and watch the departure of the man she deeply respected despite his recent mistakes. She leaped onto the boat with a sense of defiance, striding up to Lamar and enveloping him in an unexpected embrace. "You be very careful out there, Lamar! Don't take any unnecessary chances!" Her words came out fervently, her anxiety evident.

Lamar was taken aback by Amy's sudden concern, but a warm smile spread across his face. He reciprocated the hug, his hand gently rubbing her back. "Listen, Lamar! At the first sign of that thing, you 'zap' him and run like Hell... you hear?" Amy's eyes glistened with tears, her emotions brimming over. She held Lamar at arm's length, her grip firm. "I won't forgive you if you don't come back... I mean it!" She tried to inject a hint of humor, wiping away her tears with determination and self-deprecation.

Lamar's voice was soothing as he replied, "There, now, child! I don't intend to let this magnificent beast anywhere near these old bones!... I'll come back, Amy! Count on it!" He sighed, embracing Amy again, before returning his attention to Jake. "And so, my dear Jake! The time is neigh! We must be off! What say you, Master Jojo? Are you ready to ride our 'white charger' into one last fateful crusade?"

Jojo's face registered confusion and determination at Lamar's poetic rhetoric, but he answered with resolute bravery. "Si, Senor Toombs! Jojo..." He thumped his chest, a gesture of defiant bravado. "...is ready to do this thing!"

Observing the conversation from a corner of the control space, Tesoro felt a twinge of guilt at Jojo's apparent courage and exclaimed. "Lo siento! I am very sorry, my old compadre!"

Jake examined Johno and was convinced that his long-time nemesis was sincere in his misgivings.

"It is okay, mi Jefe!" Jojo pronounced and crossed over to Johno, giving his younger captain a hug and a final pat on the back. "Besides, Jefe! Jojo will be home, having a long, cold drink...long before you get there!" The short, muscle-bound man stoically laughed and returned to crank the two diesels to life.

All the goodbyes having been said, everyone climbed out of the boat, upon the wharf, and, in a small cluster, they waved as Bolo threw the mooring lines aboard, freeing the vessel.

Jojo expertly guided the boat away from the pier, the motion feeling almost slow and deliberate as it turned toward the harbor entrance.

In her snug corner within the canvas-covered bow storage, Jenny felt a shiver run through her as the engines roared to life. As the boat glided beneath her, her cheeks glistened with tears. She whispered, her voice tinged with uneasiness, "Goodbye, Amy... Take good care of Jake." With tightly closed eyes, she tried to fend off the mounting sense of impending dread and, perhaps, even calamity.

Jake masked the uneasiness on the island and silently watched the 'Maggie Mae.' His gaze remained fixed on the vessel until it disappeared behind the cliffs into the open water expanse.

Stepping away from the group, Jake turned to address them. "Okay, people! It's begun! If any of you are God-fearing, I suggest you say a private prayer for those men because that sonic generator... and our prayers... are all that stand between them and... well, you know!" With those words, he headed towards the house, followed by Johno and Bolo. Amy called out as they walked away.

"Oh... Jake!" He halted and glanced back at her over his shoulder. "I'll be along in a minute! I want to see how Jenny's feeling!" Without waiting for his response, she headed towards her cabin next to Jenny's.

Inside the main building, Jake, Bolo, and Johno each poured a cup of strong coffee brewed hours earlier.

Amy reached the cabins, making her way directly to Jenny's. Wary of disturbing her if she was sleeping off her nausea, she peered through the window. From her vantage point, she spotted what appeared to be Jenny's form wrapped in a blanket on a bed at the far side of the room. Content that her friend was resting, Amy didn't enter. Had she gone inside, she would have found only a makeshift bed with cushions stuffed under the blanket.

Relieved about Jenny, Amy rejoined the three men, preparing for the long wait ahead, punctuated by sporadic prayers.

As the companions endured the wait, occasionally invoking prayers, 'Meg' glided leisurely beneath the waves near the rocks inhabited by sea lions at the island's far end. These large, awkward creatures had returned in recent days, driven by instinct to seek refuge among the boulders, which offered them a sense of safety. Consequently, the humpback knoll was now teeming with these sea lions' blubber-covered bodies and flippers, leaving hardly an inch of space unoccupied.

Continuously, Meg circled the small isle, his massive form sometimes close to the surface, where his distinctive dorsal fin broke the water's surface, serving as an unmistakable proclamation of his presence. At other times, he plunged deeper, rendering his movements undetectable by the crouching seals that sought refuge on the rocky shores.

His recent activities had involved capturing three of these seals as they attempted to cross to the larger island. Meg devoured them with an insatiable appetite, the abundance of prey in this area capturing his focus so thoroughly that even the distant rumbling vibrations of a surface vessel initially escaped his notice. For a time, his relentless pursuit of this more convenient source of sustenance overshadowed his awareness of other disturbances in the water.

Lamar glanced at his watch, noting that they had maintained a three-quarters throttle for approximately five hours. Consulting the charts, Jojo indicated that it would be until the following morning before they reached the outer reaches of their broadcast range, a parameter calculated by Jake before their departure. He pointed out the red circle Jake had marked on the map to Toombs, signifying this boundary.

Meanwhile, back on the island, the sun descended into mid-afternoon, casting elongated shadows. Amy and the three men had enjoyed a light lunch, and as Jake and Bolo attended to cleaning up, Amy prepared a plate of sandwiches to bring to Jenny, who had seemingly "slept" through the meal.

"Jake, I will take this plate to Jenny and wake her. She really needs to eat something, don't you think?"

Jake looked up from the sink. "Sure! Go ahead, Amy. She can't sleep the whole day without getting something in her stomach. It will just make her sicker in the long run."

Oh, and tell her to come on up and join us. It will make her feel better; I know it."

"Will do!" She tossed when she walked out, balancing the plate of food in one hand.

When Amy reached Jenny's cabin, she knocked on the door and shouted. "Jenny!... Jenny, wake up!... I've got some lunch for you!" Amy stood and waited, but there was no response from within. She beat, more heavily, on the light wooden door and repeated her prior information....still no answer.

Finally, Amy tried the door. It was wedged with a piece of cardboard but unlocked, and Amy forced it open by backing into it.

When her eyes adjusted to the room's dim light, she saw that the form she thought was Jenny hadn't moved since her last glance a few hours earlier. Amy placed the plate of sandwiches on a nearby table and approached the bed. She tugged at the corner of the blanket, ready to rouse her sleeping friend. "Hey, sleepyhead! Time to wake up..."

Her words trailed into a strangled gasp as the blanket revealed something unexpected. Her heart began to race uncontrollably, and her eyes widened like saucers as the truth sank in. "No! Oh, God, no!" Amy's voice trembled with panic, her instincts screaming at her about what had transpired. Her fingers fumbled as she reached to pull the blanket further back, revealing that Jenny was nowhere to be found.

Amy's mind spun into overdrive, racing through possibilities, each more terrifying than the last. "Jenny! Oh, Jenny, what have you done?" She snapped back into reality, her breaths coming in ragged bursts. Forcing herself to accept the fact, she forced her mind to focus on what she had actually seen.

Rushing to the screen door, Amy flung it open and darted across the open space, her voice piercing the air with desperate urgency. "Ja a-a-a-k-e! Oh, Ja a-a-a-k-e!" The sound of her screams echoed through the stillness of the island, reaching the ears of Jake and the others, who hurried out to the porch to find her.

Jake bounded down the steps, catching Amy as she practically fell into his arms. Her words came in a frenzied rush. "She's gone, Jake! She's on that boat! Out there!"

Confusion and disbelief clouded Jake's face. "What? How? Are you sure?"

Amy's breathing was rapid, on the brink of hyperventilation. "She made it look like she was in bed, covered rolls of cloth and canvas to look like her! Then she stowed away on the boat!"

Jake's mind raced as he tried to piece it together. "Probably hiding in the storage hold up front," he mumbled, more to himself than anyone else. The question still hung heavy in the air: why would Jenny take such a dangerous risk?

Bolo, silently listening to the unfolding crisis, spoke up with his own assessment. "Bolo thinks he knows why young Miss go on the boat. It is simple, I'm thinking... Young Miss Jenny, she just wants to go home! That's all!" A glance between Jake and Amy confirmed that Bolo's explanation held a plausible truth.

They stared at the horizon as if Jenny and the 'Maggie Mae' might miraculously appear. The reality, however, crashed down around them, and with the island's radio out of commission, there was little they could do but hope and pray.

On the boat, it was getting late in the day, and Lamar and Jojo were thankful that nothing on the fish scope had come close to 'Meg's" size thus far throughout the day! Lamar had conducted a trial run of the sonic unit based on a simulated alert from Jojo, and the professor was satisfied with the response time, as well as the short recharging time of the equipment.

Lamar read a book while Jojo sat at the boat's wheel, nursing a cup of stale coffee and occasionally glancing at the fish scope. Toombs checked his watch and saw that the time was close to six o'clock, and he realized that the excitement and stress of setting out on the trip had caused Jojo and him to forget to eat all day!

"I say, lad!" Lamar piped up. "I have just now realized that we've not had a thing to eat since leaving this morning, and I am famished! What about you?"

"Si, professor! I no think about, til' you say something! I, too, am hungry!"

"Okay, my boy! You stay at the controls, and I will go up front and unpack one of the coolers Bolo packed for us!"

"Si, mi Jefe! I wait!" Jojo kept, unconsciously, peering in all directions, not fully trusting the hi-tech sonar device next to him.

Toombs made his way down the stairs and through the cabin. When he opened the door to the storage area, it took a moment for him to focus in the dark.

Then, he lifted the edge of the canvas covering at several points until he found the food coolers and pulled the nearest one out. It was heavy, so he dragged it across the floor to the door.

All the while Lamar was searching for the food, he was unaware that, not ten feet away, under the canvas, in the cover, Jenny huddled, motionless, not wanting to be discovered until they were past the point of no return. She figured this would occur the next day, so she remained hidden.

Meg had feasted on sea lions several times throughout the day, but with the setting sun, the creatures' forays off the rocks virtually ceased, and after swimming in random patterns around the small island for almost two hours.

He turned from this area and headed, without haste, on a diagonal course, past the big island and out to sea. *He* was going to the spot where, *His* senses told *Him,* the orcas had been a couple of days before. It was also near where the "Maggie Mae" had traversed only a few hours earlier!

If all things had remained as they were, *he* would never have detected the boat... but this was not the case!

The night was pitched black, a function of some low-hanging clouds and a partial moon.

Jojo was uncomfortable with the speed at which they were traveling, and after a while, he asked Lamar if it would be okay to cut their speed down to compensate for the very poor visual conditions.

Lamar thought for a moment, and after concluding that they had made good time this day, coupled with the fact that there was no sign of *'MEG'* thus far, Toombs approved the speed reduction. This would prove to be a monumentally tragic decision, indeed!

Swimming through the night, Meg had maintained a steady course, occasionally feasting on large tarpons, various fish, and even a sizeable Mako shark that had crossed its path at an inopportune time. As dawn approached, the creature finished devouring the remnants of a giant squid in the deep waters. Its finely tuned senses picked up a faint disturbance through the water, signaling an occurrence far off. Responding purposefully, Meg increased its speed slightly, heading towards this distant signal.

On the 'Maggie Mae,' Lamar and Jojo had taken one-hour shifts to rest through the night. As the first light of dawn touched the eastern sky, Jojo adjusted the throttle to three-quarters, propelling the boat forward.

Jenny managed to sneak out at night to use the bathroom in the adjacent room. Returning to her hiding spot, she quietly rifled through containers and found a box of sandwiches. She settled back under the tarp in her makeshift hiding place.

As dawn arrived and the boat's engine sounds shifted, Jenny roused from her uncomfortable hiding spot. Gazing at her watch, she realized it was approximately six-thirty in the morning. *"Only a few more hours, and they won't be able to turn back,"* she whispered to herself, resigned to her decision. Unable to sleep any longer, she pondered their chances of avoiding 'Meg,' but little did she know that luck would not be on their side that day.

Closing in on the source of the surface disturbance, Meg was preparing to stalk and circle the presumed target when it detected sounds from another direction. A slower and more accessible meal beckoned, diverting its attention.

Jojo's eyes were fatigued from hours of watching the scope and lack of sleep on the boat's upper deck. But it wasn't his exhaustion that caused him to miss the large blip on the screen's edge; it was Toombs' voice from the flying bridge, where the professor had stationed himself since dawn.

"Jojo, if you please!" Toombs called out, and Jojo left the wheel momentarily to see what had captured the professor's attention.

"Si, Jefe! What is it?" Jojo emerged from the wheelhouse and looked up the ladder.

Amidst this exchange, Jenny decided it was time to face the consequences of her actions and emerge from her confined hiding place.

Lamar pointed off to the right and slightly behind, clearly excited. "There! Look there, Jojo, about a mile out!" Jojo used his binoculars to scan the indicated area, initially seeing nothing but open water. And then he saw it, almost slipping past his notice. "Si!... Si, Senor Doctor! I see them! It looks like two... no, three... lifeboats! Maybe ten people! It seems they've spotted us, Senor!" When something caught his eye, Jojo was about to look back at Lamar for direction.

Lamar was on the verge of giving commands when he caught sight of Jojo's reaction. "Santa Maria!" The exclamation rang above the engine's roar, and Toombs couldn't ignore the urgency in Jojo's voice. "What's the matter, Jojo?" Concern crept into Toombs' question, but it transformed into shock as he witnessed a tuft of blonde hair and a slender figure emerging onto the deck from below him. "Good Lord! Jenny! What in the world are you doing here?" Frustration tinged Toombs' tone, interwoven with a deep sense of worry.

As Jenny looked up at Lamar, a mix of guilt and embarrassment played across her features, her smile attempting to disarm Lamar's obvious displeasure. "Ah... just hitching a ride home, Lamar." Her nonchalant attempt fell flat, her words unable to pacify Lamar's evident irritation.

"A ride home?" Descending the ladder, Lamar's gaze bore into Jenny's. As he reached the main deck, he confronted Jenny directly. "Good God, child! Do you understand the risks? We might not even make it across, let alone back home."

Jojo broke in, attempting to steer the conversation toward a solution. "Senor Toombs, what about those lifeboats?" "To be sure! Alter our course, and let's offer assistance. Although, I fear our boat won't have enough room for all of them," Lamar replied, addressing Jojo but talking past Jenny.

Rushing to the controls, Jojo adjusted the boat's heading, maneuvering in a wide arc until they were set on a direct path toward the frantic figures paddling in the distance, some three-quarters of a mile away. While Jojo deftly handled the navigation, Toombs turned his attention back to Jenny, whose tearful expression reflected her regret. Despite his irritation, Lamar couldn't maintain a stern demeanor in the face of her emotional vulnerability. "Alright now, my dear! You've put yourself through quite a situation. I suppose I can understand why you took this reckless action. But, I need you to do exactly as I tell you in case we encounter any trouble," Lamar spoke, his tone a mixture of exasperation and care. He gently grasped her arms, ensuring direct eye contact. "You comprehend what I'm saying, don't you?" His raised eyebrows questioned her understanding.

"Yes, professor, I understand. I'll assist wherever needed, and I won't be a burden," Jenny replied, her voice tinted with sniffles.

"That's the spirit!" Lamar smiled, patting her arms before releasing them. "Now, you can help by heading below and brewing a large pot of coffee. I have a feeling those folks out there will be needing it." Lamar gestured towards the people in the orange life raft, steadily approaching as the boat drew near. Jenny nodded, mustering a smile, and descended the stairs towards the galley and cabin, leaving Lamar contemplating her presence.

A nagging unease still lingered, but Lamar shrugged it off, ascending the ladder back to the flying bridge. Just as he reached the top, a sharp scream from Jojo cut through the air, laden with terror. "Hijo de Cristo! Professor! Come quickly! You must see this!" Jojo's voice trembled with fear. Lamar nearly stumbled, his haste evident as he hurriedly descended the ladder and entered the wheelhouse.

Puffing slightly, the old man inquired with urgency, "What? What is it, my boy?" Wiping his brow with a blue handkerchief, Lamar's eyes darted toward the screen.

"Right there on the scope, professor!" Jojo's wide eyes were like saucers as he motioned frantically toward the fish finder.

Lamar already knew what he would find, but his heart raced all the same. As he laid eyes on the small screen, a deep gulp of air involuntarily escaped him. The disproportionately large blip on the screen was moving in a wide circle around them at a depth of about two hundred feet. Gazing up from the screen, Lamar spotted the three life rafts and the individuals within, paddling desperately to meet the approaching boat.

Lamar snatched the power megaphone without hesitation and ascended the stairway to the front deck. Before using the megaphone, he issued rapid instructions to Jojo. "Jojo, lock the wheel, reduce our speed, and head below to charge the sonic system as I showed you." Seeing Jojo comply, Lamar directed his focus back to the people in the life rafts.

Through the megaphone, he bellowed a warning. "You there! People on the rafts! Listen to me!" However, their frantic paddling continued unabated. "You people on the rafts! Cease paddling and listen!" This time, his words pierced through, prompting one person on the nearest raft to signal the others. Soon, all paddling ceased as they awaited Toombs' instructions.

Lamar saw this through the binoculars and mumbled a short... *"Thank God!"* to himself before taking a deep breath and resuming his cautionary advice.

"Very good! Now listen very carefully! There is a monstrous creature swimming directly beneath you... " This brought a panicked response, as expected from those on the small orange floats, but none of them resumed any action that would agitate the water around them... "and *it* reacts, quite aggressively, to any sound in the water! Therefore, you will assure yourselves of a much better chance of survival if you remain absolutely motionless!" Toombs was silently grateful for their cooperative response to his words. He continued.

"We have a device on board our vessel, which should offer us some measure of protection from the creature. We will maintain a distance from you to discourage its approach. If you understand me, wave your arms!" Lamar brought the binoculars back to his eyes, scanning the rafts, and observed a few individuals on each raft waving their arms.

"Excellent!" He projected through the power horn. "Now, if you all remain perfectly still, we might make it through this day. And perhaps a prayer to whatever higher power you believe in would also be prudent."

Lamar didn't linger to check if they were complying; he knew fear would compel them to do so. He turned, almost bumping into Jenny, who stood closely behind him, offering a cup of hot coffee, her tears flowing freely.

"I thought you might need this," she began, but her words faltered as the cup slipped from her grasp, and she almost crumbled into sobs in Lamar's arms.

Lamar sensed that Jenny was teetering on the edge, her composure shattered by the news of "Meg's" presence. He gently patted her back and whispered soothingly, "There now, my dear. We'll manage. Why don't you go below and monitor our sonic equipment? It's the sizable electronic box beside the radio, with an array of red and green lights."

"But, professor!" Jenny protested amid her sniffles. "I have no idea about that equipment. What could I possibly—"

Lamar held up a finger, silencing her. "Tut, tut! You don't need to know the details. Just keep an eye on the row of lights at the top and let me know if any fail to turn green after use. Can you manage that for me, my dear?" He held her at arm's length, locking gazes with her reddened eyes.

"I think so, but that creature, professor..." Lamar gently squeezed her arms, interrupting her again.

"No more words on that subject," he reassured her with a smile. "We're completely shielded, I promise. Our 'Meg' won't come near the sonic field we're generating around the boat. It's been effective on sharks worldwide... it works, without a doubt." He observed a hint of relief in her demeanor and wrapped up the conversation. "Alright then, off you go, and let an old man do his job." He held up the remote control box, emphasizing his point.

Jenny wiped away the tears from her cheeks and descended the steps into the cabin.

Jojo had been watching the intermittent 'blips' on the edge of the scope, indicating that 'Meg' wasn't closing yet, and he didn't want to interrupt the exchange between Lamar and Jenny.

However, the large splotch of light began to cut an arc across the top quarter of the screen... and the depth indicator showed that it was moving nearer to the surface. "Professor!... Por Favor!... The shark, she comes closer!" He looked over his shoulder to make sure that Toombs was there with the trigger box. Indeed, Lamar stood directly behind him, watching the fish finder intently over Jojo's shoulder.

"I see it, my boy!" Lamar absent-mindedly touched Jojo's shoulder, never taking his attention away from the screen.

The rafts, carrying the terrified seamen, floated silently, about a quarter mile off the bow. Toombs felt slightly relieved that they hadn't made any noise or sudden movements. *"Maybe there's a chance they'll make it,"* he thought.

Then, in a nightmarish instant, the all-too-familiar fin broke the water's surface to the right of the rafts, gliding ominously towards the 'Maggie Mae.' Lamar's grip tightened on Jojo's shoulder, and the shorter man shut his eyes, breathing in ragged gasps.

"Alright, Jojo, just like we practiced, cut the engines and stop here," Lamar instructed his voice tight with apprehension.

"Si, senor!" Jojo responded and eased the throttle to idle, causing the boat to slow down to a near stop.

Lamar's gaze was fixed on the enormous dorsal fin slicing through the water, drawing nearer and nearer. He raised the sonic control box at a distance of two hundred yards and pressed the large red button on its face.

Meanwhile, beneath the waves, the massive predator had been closing in on three potential prey targets on the surface. Just as it was about to shift its focus and attack one of them, all signs vanished. Its senses strained, but it failed to reacquire the targets. Spiraling upward, it breached the water's surface, its massive fin exposed to the cooling winds as it desperately sought any trace of its prey.

Failing to find its targets, the predator turned its attention back to a more significant sound signature it had previously disregarded for the closer prey. But as it zeroed in on the distant vibrations, those sounds disappeared. It continued in the same direction, sensing no other stimuli to divert its course.

Suddenly, its entire body was assaulted by a cacophony of high-pitched frequencies, causing its nerves to erupt in pain. Disoriented and struggling, the creature's movements became erratic as its senses were overwhelmed. Its jaws opened and closed involuntarily, its vision clouded.

In its ancient existence, it had never experienced such chaos or terror. Instinctively, it commanded itself to escape the onslaught as quickly as possible.

Lamar pressed the 'Maggie Mae' deck button, but there was no immediate feedback. The colossal fin continued its inexorable approach for a few agonizing seconds. Then, the water around the fin erupted in a maelstrom of foam. The monstrous head surged from the depths, the gargantuan fish arching its back and convulsing violently from side to side.

Following this frenzied spasm, 'Meg' snapped its body and shot away from the boat and rafts with astonishing speed.

"Professor! The fish—it's disappeared from the scope! The sound device, it worked!" Jojo exclaimed, his voice excitedly trembling as he operated the control console.

"My word, Jojo! It seems the device did the trick, at least for now!" Lamar's exhilaration was evident in his beaming smile and rapid breathing.

"What do you mean... 'for now,' Professor?" Jenny had climbed the stairs to join them, her eyes wide with anticipation and anxiety. She came to inform Lamar that the lights on the panel had momentarily turned red and then, except for one, returned to green.

Lamar's brow furrowed slightly at the lingering red indicator on the panel, a trace of worry flickering in his eyes. Nevertheless, he addressed Jenny's question with a reassuring tone. "You see, my dear, our 'Meg'—much like other sharks—is guided by instinct, not memory. Likely, the primal drive to feed will ultimately override any recollection of its encounter with our defense system here." His words were delivered with a sense of matter-of-factness, yet he was acutely aware that his explanation once again unsettled Jenny's already fragile emotions. Sensing her unease, he sought to provide her with further clarification.

"Here now, dear girl!" You don't suppose we will wait while that creature regains its composure, do you? Heaven forbid!" Toombs patted Jenny on the back and issued a command to Jojo.

"Jojo! Keep an eye on the scope and move swiftly to meet those rafts. We'll throw them a line and tow them behind us," Lamar ordered, urgency evident in his voice.

Jojo nodded in agreement but turned back to address Toombs with concern. "But, Professor, I respect you greatly as Jefe, but don't you think towing those rafts could slow us down? We might risk the 'Devil Fish' catching up before we can even talk to the people on land."

Lamar weighed Jojo's point tensely, his aged forehead creased in deep lines. He took a deep breath, exhaling in exasperation. "Jojo, I'm torn by this, but... you're right." His words hung heavy in the air as he grappled with the impending decision. But before he could continue down that path, Jenny grabbed his arm, her eyes reflecting a mix of desperation and determination.

"Lamar, you can't seriously be thinking of leaving those people out here!" Jenny's voice held a mixture of pleading and disbelief. Yet, the resignation on Toombs' face indicated that this was, indeed, the course he was considering.

"Child, believe me, the weight of this decision is not lost on me... but we must consider the dire consequences if we fail in our mission. Our lives are at stake, as are the lives of those men and countless others who will navigate these waters in the future."

Lamar's voice wavered with a mixture of regret and necessity. He looked into Jenny's eyes, realizing he needed to convey the gravity of the situation.

"If they remain still, as they are doing now, they can evade 'Meg's' detection. We, on the other hand, will likely draw the creature to us. Then, with luck, five of our six sonic pods will keep the monster at bay. You see, Jenny, by leaving them there, we stand a better chance of saving their lives. Do you understand?" Lamar raised his white eyebrows in a gesture of seeking comprehension.

"I suppose, Professor... I apologize for my panic. I'll do my best to stay composed," Jenny replied, her voice steadying as she wiped her nose.

"Don't blame yourself, my dear. You've shown remarkable resilience, considering the traumas you've endured. You're doing just fine," Lamar reassured her with a pat on her forearm, his tone gentle.

"Very well then. If you'd be so kind as to return to monitoring the control panel. I have a feeling we'll need it again soon. All right? You're doing wonderfully." Toombs watched Jenny head back below deck to oversee the system's readiness.

Lamar turned to Jojo next, a hint of urgency in his voice. "Excellent, Jojo! Please take the bullhorn to the bow. Once we're close enough, use it to communicate with those poor souls in English and Spanish. Instruct them to stay completely still, as we will draw the 'Devil Fish' away from their area. Let them know that a ship from the mainland Navy will be dispatched to pick them up. Understand?"

Jojo nodded in confirmation, already grabbing the power megaphone and moving toward the front of the boat. "Got it, Jefe. I'll make sure they get the message."

"Perfect! Then, ask if they need any supplies. If they do, we'll toss them provisions as we pass by slowly. However, we can't risk stopping right next to them. We must avoid making noise that could attract 'Meg.' Clear?"

Jojo was already making his way to the bow with the power megaphone in hand. "Crystal clear, Professor. I'll do exactly as you say."

Toombs shuffled quickly to the opening, which led below, and spoke loudly! "Jenny! Would you run to the forward cabin and put about half the rations, including... oh... perhaps a dozen bottles of water, in a large piece of netting and wrap it soundly so it won't come apart when tossed to the rafts?... That's a good girl!" He ended without waiting for her answer. It didn't matter because the little blonde jumped into the forward hole and began sorting through the stacked ration boxes.

Lamar turned his attention back to the rafts, particularly the lead one, which was a good thirty yards closer than the other two.

Jojo was finishing his announcement, and as Toombs expected, the reaction was somewhat less than cordial. Nevertheless, they settled back after some colorful expletives. Resigned to the fact that what was being done was probably the best for all of them. Besides, all the men in the rafts welcomed any plan to draw the beast away from their vicinity.

As the boat drew within ten yards of the lead raft, Jenny appeared on deck with a well-tied bag stuffed with rations. Jojo took the bag and made a sign that he was about to throw it. Then, the dark, unusual little man swung the sack around like a throwing hammer in track, and, timing it perfectly, he let the bundle fly through the air. It landed only four feet from the nearest float, and the men aboard paddled the short distance quickly and fished the package out of the water.

Meanwhile, The boat continued, and Lamar raised the bullhorn, which he'd taken from Jojo, for one last reminder.

"Remember! Stay in a tight group! Make no sound or motion in the water; remain completely still, and *we* will most assuredly draw the 'thing' away from you! Good Luck! And may God be with you all!" He punctuated his comments with a wave joined by Jojo and Jenny.

The men on the rafts returned the salute as one, and the 'Maggie Mae' departed the scene, heading northeast.

Jojo returned to the controls and pushed the throttle fully forward. The boat surged forward, climbing to its maximum velocity and planning out at a rapid speed of twenty-five knots. Jenny had returned to her system monitoring duties, and Lamar struggled to calculate the lost time at the rafts.

Finally, the old man concluded that if there were no more deviations, they would need to cruise, at their present speed and heading, for at least two more hours before they reached what had been determined to be the outer limits of the old transmitter. Therefore, Toombs crawled up into the perch above the wheelhouse and used the large binoculars to frequently scan the surrounding waters for any sign of the gargantuan creature that, he was sure, would approach them again sooner or later.

But, at that moment, in the obsidian blackness, over a thousand feet below the rafts, *he* had dived to rid *himself* of the unfamiliar, numbing agony caused by the sonic shock, and even as the effects started to wear off, *he* swam in circles, maintaining this depth. *His* base instincts reacted to the recent conditioning on the surface and kept *him* from proceeding to the light above... at least for the time being. This defensive hesitancy on 'Meg's' part allowed Toombs and his party to widen the distance from *him* and have a reasonable chance to get through the precious message for help!

Toombs was concerned. He stood beside Jojo and pressed the shorter man to squeeze every bit of speed out of the big twin diesel below. His attention alternated from watching the fish scope to studying the area they'd come from through the large binoculars.

"I don't know how long our luck will hold, Jojo. I expected to see our 'friend' on the scope again by this time." Jojo just stared ahead and kept the pressure on the throttle handle as if he would gain a little more speed by doing so.

Lamar could barely make out the rafts anymore. They were only small orange dots in the distance, even through the powerful field glasses.

"Please, Dear Lord!" Lamar muttered while still scanning the horizon. "Give us just one more hour unmolested, and I will be yours forever more!..." And so, the boat drove on across the waters.

On 'Crandle's Keep, ' Amy had just prepared lunch for Jake, Bolo, and Tesoro; after she had served the men, she poured herself a cup of five-hour-old coffee and walked out onto the porch. Jake noticed her, left the other two men talking at the table, and followed Amy outside.

"Worried?" He asked sincerely, sipping his own drink.

"Yes, I suppose I am... to some extent." She turned and cocked her head at Jake. "But, to tell the truth, I'm wondering if they've run into 'Meg' and, if so, how effective that sound gun has been?... Or, even if they are still alive and in one piece!" Amy moved into Jake's arms and buried her face in his shoulder at this thought.

"It's okay, Amy! You've got to have faith! I do!" Jake whispered into her ear as he softly stroked her hair. "Old Lamar is a brilliant and resourceful old bird, and that little fella, Jojo, really seems to know the sea, so I wouldn't count them out! I'm confident they are caring for Jenny and ... "He looked at this watch. "They should reach the outer fringes of the transmitter's estimated range in about twenty minutes." Jake held her out at arms-length and peered into her watery eyes. "So, whaddya you think? You gonna have faith in me?"

A faint smile tugged at the corners of her lips as she said, "Yes, I agree. But I don't think a little prayer would hurt either, do you?" Her words hung in the air as she looked up at Jake, who responded with a chuckle. He wrapped his arms around her waist, leading her back inside the house to rejoin the others and endure the wait.

Lamar's gaze flicked to his watch for the umpteenth time in fifteen minutes. Jenny, who had joined him on the deck, picked up on his growing impatience. She couldn't help but comment, her tone a mix of lightness and encouragement. "Come on, Lamar. Let's go ahead and start transmitting. It can't hurt at this point." Her suggestion was accompanied by a rare smile, emphasizing her point.

Those words were enough to push Toombs into action. He shrugged with a mild exclamation. "Oh, well then! Here goes nothing!" With a deliberate movement, he picked up the microphone from the radio set and flipped the power switch to the 'on' position. He swallowed, his eyes focused on the equipment before him. With a deep breath, he pressed the 'push-to-talk' switch and began transmitting their distress call.

"Mayday! Mayday! This is the Maggie Mae! Crandle's Keep under attack! Naval assistance is urgently needed. Please respond! Over!" Toombs and Jake had deliberately chosen to withhold the exact nature of the threat attacking the island. The thought was that revealing the truth might lead to disbelief and dismissing the call as a prank. Instead, by linking the boat's name to the island, Lamar lent a sense of credibility to the plea for help.

For the next two hours, Lamar repeated the distress call tirelessly, with Jojo periodically broadcasting the same message in Spanish. The only response that came back was static, punctuated by sporadic and unintelligible vocal snippets – likely skip transmissions bouncing unpredictably off the atmosphere.

Time moved at a crawling pace, and the sun gradually shifted past its zenith, casting a reminder that it was now early afternoon. Jenny emerged from below deck, carrying sandwiches and coffee. Lamar welcomed the hot liquid as it soothed his parched throat after hours of calling for help.

Just as they finished their lunch, Jojo jerked around in his seat, alerting everyone. "Senor Lamar! Come see! I think he's approaching again!"

Toombs exchanged a worried glance with Jenny, whose eyes widened in fearful anticipation. Swiftly, he got to his feet and hurried over to Jojo's side. As he feared, the substantial blip had reappeared on the scope, meandering erratically along the outer edge of the sonar's range.

"You're right, my friend. I should have anticipated this. I hoped the sonic system's effects would last longer," Lamar admitted with a sigh. His gaze shifted to Jenny, who stood on the deck, visibly entrapped by fear. "Jenny, my dear, would you please resume monitoring the instruments below? Your help would be invaluable."

Jenny blinked, breaking free from her fearful trance, and nodded in agreement. With a wave of her hand, she hurried back below deck to resume her monitoring duties.

Toombs rechecked the scope and saw that the giant 'blip' was slowly, yet surely, closing in on their position, and he began to transmit his message again.

Jojo was coaxing every bit of speed possible from the boat, but he knew that whatever velocity he produced... it wouldn't be enough. Whenever "Meg' wanted them badly enough, *he'd* get them!

"Oh Jenny, my dear!" Lamar yelled down the stairs between transmissions. "Can you please tell me the status of the system?"

A voice emerged from the dimly lit cabin, carrying a hint of trepidation. "There are... still five out of six that are green, professor," Jenny reported.

"Good, very good. That should hopefully be enough to deter our friend," Lamar responded, trying to sound more assured than he felt. He attempted the radio several times, each effort yielding only static and the occasional indecipherable 'skip.' But as the fruitless attempts continued, the old man's composure unraveled. "Bloody Hell! Where are those people? The radio signal strength shows we're broadcasting clearly, but still no response!" He made several more frustrated attempts, his frustration evident in his reddening face and the beads of sweat forming on his brow.

"Senor Professor!" Jojo's voice trembled as he beckoned Toombs over to the fish finder. "The fish! I think she's coming again!"

A quick look at the screen confirmed Lamar's fears. 'Meg' rapidly closed the gap between them, approaching quicker than before. "Very well! Jojo, keep the throttle wide open, no matter what! Do you understand?" Lamar's voice was tense and urgent. Jojo nodded, responding quickly and firmly on the speed control lever as if coaxing every ounce of speed from the 'Maggie Mae.'

Lamar retrieved the sonic remote trigger from the cabin below, instructing Jenny to watch the control panel for any change in the status lights. A sense of concern gnawed at him, knowing that with one station already down, the system's ability to repel 'Meg' repeatedly might be in jeopardy.

With his attention divided between the screen and the distant horizon, Lamar's gaze searched for the ladder leading to the flying bridge. The blob on the repeater screen was drawing nearer with each passing second.

The old man's eyes strained, looking for the unmistakable fin that would signify 'Meg's' formidable presence. It didn't take long before he spotted it, about a thousand yards off the stern quarter, slowly but surely drawing closer. With each heartbeat, Lamar's realization grew more dire; unless a miracle intervened, their chances of survival were slim. He knew that 'Meg' would become progressively more relentless and conditioned with every hit from the sonic guns. A shiver of desperation ran through him as he mumbled, *"Lord help us."*

Lamar watched for nearly twenty agonizing minutes as the monstrous fish closed the distance, coming within five hundred yards. He held his ground, unwavering, as 'Meg' drew even closer, the ominous shadow of her fin cutting through the water. When the distance had narrowed to two hundred yards, Lamar lifted the sonic remote trigger with both hands, his fingers poised over the red button.

CHAPTER 19
Sensing the Drone of the Surface

The colossal beast had been swimming in the deep, black abyss for over two hours, randomly moving from one underwater peak to another. Gradually, the numbing effects of the sonic blast were wearing off, and *his* voracious hunger was beginning to drive *his* instincts once again.

The beast was still sensing the drone of the surface 'thing,' but the vibrations were very faint and far away. Nevertheless, *he* ceased *his* aimless patterns and proceeded on a more direct track, slowly gathering speed to narrow the distance between *his* current target and *him*.

As *he* plunged into the darkness, *he* began to slant a small bit toward the surface, and what *his* instincts told *him* was food. *His* primordial brain had already forgotten the devastating effects of the sonic assault, and *he* was back on *his* never-ending search for nourishment.

After almost two hours, *he* detected a much more prominent noise above, and *he* adopted a parallel course with *his* prey until *his* conditioned reflex told *him* to attack this elusive creature!

Finally, *he* felt the need and dived into a path that would intersect with the target.

Once *he* came near the vibrations, *he* turned upward and moved into *his* attack speed, or roughly, that of a runaway freight train, with every bit of the mass.

His gigantic jaws began to once again open and close, involuntarily, in anticipation of *his* approaching feeding and, then, the painful hammering, all along *his* nerve endings returned but not quite as severe as before... and *he* twisted and contorted, violently, in the water and, as with the other sonic assaults, broke off the attack! *The Big Boy* headed swiftly for the proven safety of the deep and waited for the pain to subside. This time, however, *he* didn't go so deep or need to wait so long for recovery.

Up on the surface, Jojo saw the large green 'dot' turn away from the center of the screen and race rapidly for the edge, getting smaller in size as it went. This indicated that 'Meg' was going deeper as he retreated.

Lamar was also watching, over Jojo's shoulder, as the old man activated the system and patted the Hispanic mate on the shoulder. "Good show!" Lamar snapped. "We've bought ourselves a little more time, my boy!" Jojo nodded and continued to lean on the throttle, although it was wide open already.

"Jojo, I suggest you go below and switch the fuel flow to the next drum."

He noticed the indicator getting relatively low. "I'll watch things for you up here!"

"Si, Jefe! I do!" The squatty seaman shuffled to the stairs and went down to the engines.

A few moments after he had disappeared, Jenny came up, on deck, and over to Lamar. He noticed the worried look on her face and addressed her about it. "I can see you have something on your mind, my dear!" He smiled reassuringly. "So, out with it! What can I do to set your concerns to rest?"

"To tell the truth, Professor, I'm not sure you can do anything! Since this last shot, another light is staying red on the panel!"

Lamar's features went slack, and turned at her. "Let's go see what we have, shall we?" He said without expression and brushed past Jenny to hurry down the steps.

In the cabin, Lamar examined the system's controls, and, as Jenny had reported, two of the six lights remained red. He performed the automatic diagnostics and found the unit to be operating perfectly.

Jenny watched over his shoulder and saw the old man's shoulders visibly sag following the tests. Lamar turned slowly to Jenny and, with a very somber expression, gently laid a hand against Jenny's cheek. "My dear girl, I'm afraid you've cast your lot with the losing side this time!" His look of resolution and defeat spoke volumes.

"I guess you're implying that our defenses won't hold up for much longer with this diminished system, right?" Jenny's voice held a touch of helplessness, her eyes reflecting concern.

Lamar sighed, his expression somber as he replied, "I'm afraid you're right, Jenny. Even with a fully operational system, holding 'Meg' off for much longer would be challenging, given his past exposure. With a thirty percent reduction in effectiveness, you can imagine." He offered a sympathetic half-smile, hoping to convey his understanding.

"Yes, Professor, I do," Jenny nodded, straightening herself, a brave front concealing the vulnerability in her eyes. "But, you know what? If this ends up being... well, my time, I suppose it's comforting to be surrounded by friends." Her voice wavered slightly, a hint of tears threatening to surface.

Lamar laid a hand gently on her shoulder. "Thank you, my dear. But let's make sure we give this 'gentleman' a run for his money before—" His words were cut short by Jojo's urgent shout.

"Professor! Come quickly! The radio!" Jojo's excitement was palpable as Lamar rushed over to the console.

"Listen, Jefe!" Jojo's finger pointed at the crackling sounds emanating from the small speaker.

Toombs held his breath, his heart racing, as fragmented vocal reports filled the airwaves. "Hello... ship broadcasting... ever...! Please report your loca...? Your sig... very weak and bro...!" The message itself was barely coherent, plagued by interference, but it was undeniable. A reply to their transmission had finally come through!

Lamar grabbed the microphone, his voice determined as he tried to relay their approximate position to the mainland.

As Lamar spoke into the microphone, Jojo refocused on the scope. About twenty minutes later, he nudged Toombs in the ribs, his eyes wide with urgency. "Madre de Dios! He's returned, Jefe!" His hand motioned towards the scope.

Lamar released the transmit button and turned his attention to the screen. "Oh, can't we just have a bit more time?" he thought, silently pleading, as the familiar shape once again materialized at the edge of the scope, moving steadily into its range from the right side.

Lamar's swift leap carried him to the cabin door, where he hollered urgently to Jenny. She had descended back downstairs to monitor the severely weakened sonic system. "Jenny! Maintain a vigilant watch on the control panel, if you will! Our 'guest' has returned, and I suspect his determination will be significantly heightened this time!" Lamar's attempt at injecting some humor into the situation was eclipsed by the solemnity of the circumstances.

"I've got it covered, Professor!" Jenny's courageous reply wafted up from the lower deck.

Lamar's lips curled into a private smile. He recollected the trials the blonde had weathered in the past weeks and couldn't help but admire her tenacity in the face of their dire predicament. After a brief reflection, he returned to the present and rejoined Jojo's side. There, he extended the microphone cord to its limits, fixating his gaze on the blip on the screen as he recommenced transmitting their coordinates.

This time, Lamar's senses regained their clarity far more swiftly. His simple brain has adapted to the recurring sonic disruptions. Its interaction with the colossal host had conditioned it not to recoil from subsequent jolts. This innate response and mounting hunger propelled him to chase the object on the surface with renewed purpose and heightened focus.

The vibrations emitted by the target grew more pronounced and resonant, compelling him to accelerate his pace to close the gap more rapidly. Finally, close to his prey, he dove at a steep angle, positioning himself slightly ahead and around five hundred feet below the intended victim.

Executing his preferred attack pattern, he twisted upward, intent on rending into the vulnerable underbelly of the creature. Lamar had keenly observed the "blob" passing by and diminishing in size. Aware that "Meg" had plunged deep in preparation for an assault and considering the reduced effectiveness of their unit, Lamar grasped the necessity of timing. He knew he had to wait until the last conceivable instant to have any chance of repelling the colossal creature once again.

The blip on the screen expanded, maintaining its central position below them. Lamar clenched the box housing the red button, his right thumb resting resolutely on the button's prominent cap. The phosphorescent pattern grew larger and larger until Lamar's brain issued a decisive command, prompting his thumb to depress the button.

As before, the craft's occupants heard no audible indication, but the reaction beneath the water's surface, a mere hundred and fifty feet beneath them, was decidedly different. Zeroing in on the gargantuan creature above him, his robust musculature engaged, propelling him with escalating velocity as he instinctively honed in on a fatal collision with his intended quarry.

His enormous jaws began their rhythmic opening and closing cycle, indicative of an imminent attack, when he once more experienced the nerve-jangling shock he had encountered multiple times prior. However, this instance differed markedly from its predecessors. Rather than incapacitating him, the blast triggered a contraction and a sharp jerk to the left. Unlike the prior cases in which the sonic assault halted and repelled him, this time, it merely veered him off his direct course of attack, albeit slightly.

This diversion ensured that upon impact with the hull of the "Maggie Mae," he avoided colliding head-on with the central midsection, instead tearing through the aft portion. The impact tore away the open deck and inflicted a brutal gash along his lower jawline as he collided with the spinning propeller.

This searing, slashing counterattack from the surface-dwelling "creature" prompted him to release his grip on the aft portion, retreating temporarily to regroup below the surface.

While "Meg" gathered himself, the dire situation on the distressed vessel above escalated with an intensity that dripped with fear and terror.

Lamar's gaze remained fixated on the merging green target displayed on the scope, his hopes pinned on the tenuous thread of luck as he pressed the ominous red button. The blip on the screen hesitated a brief pause that raised a flicker of hope. Yet, that hope was dashed as the blip, after a momentary shift to the left, hurtled towards the center of the scope at an alarming pace.

"Sweet Mother! Jojo! Cling to something, boy!" Lamar's warning was accompanied by a desperate turn towards the aft end, his hands desperately grasping the ladder's side. Before he could secure himself, the ocean erupted in an earth-shattering explosion of water and sound.

In a harrowing struggle against implacable forces, Jojo fought for his life. A diminutive figure in the grand scope of the abyss, he writhed with desperate urgency, every instinct urging him to defy the impending doom. His frantic contortions drove him toward the corner of "Meg's" mouth, where he imagined a fleeting hope of salvation might linger – a chance to scramble over the lip and onto some other fractured fragment adrift in the ominous darkness below. His sinews strained, muscles flexed, and sweat mingled with the salt of fear on his skin.

With a supreme effort, Jojo's upper body barely escaped the gaping maw of "Meg," his gaze plummeting into the dread-inducing abyss below. The expanse yawned open, a realm of immeasurable depth and terror. He peered into the abyss, the water below beckoning with a ravenous, insatiable appetite. His heartbeat thundered in his ears, a stark counterpoint to the abyss's silence.

But fate's cruel twist was unrelenting. In a heart-stopping instant, "Meg" snapped his colossal jaws shut with a bone-chilling finality. The world around Jojo exploded into darkness and pressure, his vision obliterated by the engulfing maw. His scream metamorphosed into a choked, gurgling plea, a desperate symphony of agony and despair. Blood mingled with the brine of the sea, his tortured form devoured by the monstrous maw. The upper half of his body plummeted, a mere puppet cut free of its strings, while his lower half remained trapped, a grotesque offering to the merciless jaws above.

In that heart-wrenching fraction of time, the void within "Meg's" mouth offered a gruesome tableau. Jojo's eyes, wide with horror, glimpsed at his body's disarrayed fragments. The macabre scene, illuminated by the faint glimmer of bioluminescence, etched itself into his consciousness. Death's icy grip descended, his consciousness slipping away as he surrendered to the abyss.

The sea claimed its own. Jojo's remains tumbled into the depths, a final descent into the watery unknown. "Meg" wasted no time, his monstrous form a nightmare weaving through the wreckage in a terrifying ballet. A perverse hunger drove him, seeking to fill itself on whatever grim offerings the sea might bestow. His primal instincts guided him, an embodiment of terror, a predator that haunted the darkest recesses of the ocean.

Yet, to this day, destiny's tapestry unfurled in unexpected ways. By some eerie twist of fate or cosmic design, the sea denied "Meg" further sustenance. The currents offered no more morsels for his insatiable cravings. The ocean, tinged with an air of dread and suspense, had other plans.

The aftermath bore the scars of this relentless dance of terror, the waves whispering secrets and stories untold. The wreckage, a testament to the unyielding fury of nature, spread its remnants across the surface, fragments of wood and cloth afloat in the aftermath of the chaos. A twisted bow section, battered and half-flooded, drifted silently, a forsaken relic of the past.

Meanwhile, a motionless figure lay sprawled in the murky half-light within the vessel's shattered interior. Once vibrant with life, Jenny's form was now a tableau of stillness, her body resting atop provisions that would never serve their purpose. The encroaching shadows of twilight seemed to mirror the uncertainty in the air.

As daylight waned and evening's veil descended, the last chapter of this grim saga played out. The darkness cloaked the fragment of wreckage and the fragile figure it cradled, shrouding them in a mystery that would linger in the annals of the abyss.

After scouring the area for hours, "Meg" abandoned his grim quest, deliberately embarking towards the familiar waters he had recognized as his hunting grounds – Crandle's Keep.

With "Meg's" departure, a deceptive calm settled over the ocean again. The only remnants of the unspeakable tragedies that had unfolded were an expanding field of debris, fragments of wood, and cloth that had once constituted the "Maggie Mae." Yet, a couple of miles away, carried by the relentless current, the substantial bow section of the shattered vessel remained unnoticed by "Meg." It floated half-submerged, caught between the gentle swells.

Deep within the vessel's remains, Jenny's motionless form lay sprawled, her legs dipped in a pool of water while the rest rested atop bags of provisions that would never find use.

As daylight gave way to evening's encroaching shadows, no movement emanated from the seemingly lifeless form within the last remaining fragment of what was once Jake's pride and joy. Night eventually descended, and the engulfing darkness swallowed the fragment and the fragile figure it contained, sealing their fate in the cold embrace of the unknown.

ON THE ISLAND, TWO whole days had passed, and Jake was becoming more and more drawn and haggard from sleep deprivation brought on by worry over the unknown plight of the 'Maggie Mae' and his friends aboard her.

Amy had seen this condition coming over Jake and the brooding withdrawal that accompanied it. She, too, was worried about the mission's fate; more specifically, she worried about Jenny. Amy knew that Jenny was emotionally unstable and that, in this state, the young woman could very well flip out and cause damage to others or herself. So... Amy worried and lost sleep, too.

On the other hand, Bolo had taken Tesoro in tow, and the two of them had performed needed maintenance on various equipment items around the compound that had needed it for some time. Most notably, they had torn down the two diesel generators and cleaned and oiled the moving parts before reassembling and calibrating the two sets for maximum output.

It was now lunchtime of the third day since the boat's departure, and the four were finishing lunch.

Jake stood by the door, his gaze locked on the distant horizon as he cradled a steaming cup of coffee in his hands. His words pierced the air, carrying the weight of observation. "Looks like we're in for another gale later," he mused, his free hand gesturing vaguely to the tumultuous sky beyond.

Around him, the rest of the group occupied their respective places. Some were seated at the table while Amy diligently cleaned up the remnants of their midday meal. Bolo chimed in with a touch of Caribbean charm, ever the sage of maritime lore. "That always happens this time of year, Mister Jake! Ol' man summer... he is flexin' his muscles, I think."

Having softened his demeanor since Jojo's departure, Tesoro joined the conversation with a sense of camaraderie. His curiosity hung in the air like a question mark. "I wonder if that's going to affect our guys. What do you think, Jake?"

Jake's response came without a complete turn. A sidelong glance tossed Johno's way. A simmering resentment still colored their interactions, but a begrudging sense of teamwork had emerged from the depths of their animosity. Resigned to their shared fate, Jake knew working together was in everyone's interest.

"Dunno! It looks like a pretty spread-out system, so I suppose it might catch up to them, depending on how far they've gone. They should be nearing the mainland by now, though..." His gaze shifted, colliding with Amy's, their unspoken concerns mingling in the air. "...that is if nothing has happened to them along the way."

His cup met the counter with a soft thud, a punctuation mark underscoring his words. Amy's inquiry flowed seamlessly, a masterclass in feigned casualness. "Jake, along those lines, you mentioned that the supply ship was due in here today, didn't you?"

Jake, his attention back on the harbor, confirmed her inquiry. "Last night, actually! It's never been late before... has it, Bolo?"

Bolo's eyes flitted between Jake and Amy, his surprise evident. "No, Mister Jake... It's always here on time! Never run so late!"

Their collective anxiety began manifesting as they faced dwindling provisions and a brackish taste of urgency in their water. Jake's voice, a thin veneer of reassurance, attempted to mollify their concerns. "No need for too much concern... just yet! They're probably running late because of the frequent storms this time of year."

Like a whisper in the wind, Amy's skepticism didn't escape Jake's perceptive gaze. He spoke again to preserve the facade of optimism, his words calculated to bolster their spirits. "Besides... worse case, even if something has happened to the supply ship, I feel sure our boat has been in contact with the mainland by now, and there is help on the way!... Hell, we should have welcome company tomorrow!" A theatrical clap punctuated his statement, an attempt to infuse their gathering with an air of positivity.

But the room's unease refused to dissipate, lingering like a shadow cast by doubt.

Bolo's head hung low, eyes tracing patterns on the floor. His demeanor was a blend of sadness and uncertainty. On the other hand, Amy continued to fix her gaze on Jake, her expression a tableau of resignation and deep-seated worry. Johno, in stark contrast, muttered unintelligible words in Spanish before striding outside, his hands shoved deep into his jeans pockets. He stood there, rigid and watchful, eyes scanning the horizon for the monstrous fin that seemed poised to break through the surface at any moment.

Meanwhile, far from this hushed and fearful tableau on the island, "Meg" began his instinctual return to the tiny dot of land he had claimed as his dominion. His circuitous yet purposeful journey was punctuated by his predatory pursuits, a feast laid out by the ocean along his path.

The last attack was still fresh in his mind. He had been closing in on the boat's underbelly when the sonic disruption struck him again. This time, however, its potency had been dulled by the malfunctioning stations, mitigating its effects. Yet, it wasn't without consequence – the sonic shock had compelled "Meg's" colossal head to jerk involuntarily to the left, causing a minor deviation in his trajectory. As a result, his initial point of impact with the "Maggie Mae" shifted from amidships, his intended target, to the aft third of the vessel.

The sheer force of his assault cleaved the open deck from the ship, flinging the remaining section into a chaotic spin as "Meg's" immense form breached the surface. Clutched within his formidable jaws, the wreckage left a trail of destruction in its wake, accompanied by a haunting red ribbon of blood that traced the cut on his undersides. The spinning sensation and the discomfort of the sizable gash caused by the propellers biting into his jaw sent "Meg" into a hurried dive, seeking refuge in the depths to nurse his wounds.

Meanwhile, "Meg" had resumed his silent and methodical circling beneath the waves. Days had passed since his last attack, and his patience was rewarded as the sound of multiple paddles reached his senses. The source of his attention was the men on the orange life rafts, survivors of his previous onslaught. Deprived of provisions, their orange life rafts bobbed on the water's surface as they paddled toward an uncertain fate.

These men, seasoned seafarers, rationed their dwindling resources. Their strength lay in their unity. The three-engine room crewmen of the third raft have separated from the stronger groups to ensure their survival. As the distance grew between them, a sense of impending doom settled upon them, a premonition that their reunion would never come to pass.

The predator closed in on his prey, darkness descending as the day waned. A murky light filtered from the surface, casting a somber glow on the scene. A predator's instincts honed to perfection, "Meg" prepared for his final assault. Diving and resurging with a frenzied fury, his cavernous jaws oscillated in anticipation of the feast unfolding.

In seconds, the water boiled and erupted around the two leading rafts, and the seven men's anguished screams became a symphony of terror. Chaos reigned as the monstrous entity devoured its prey, leaving only fragments of orange foam in its wake. Across the expanse, the lone raft bore horrified witnesses to the grisly spectacle. Driven by an insatiable hunger, "Meg" struck with an unstoppable fury.

Meanwhile, the machinist's mate and two companions clung to their raft, frozen in terror and awaiting their doom. Silence enveloped them, punctuated by their pounding hearts. Yet, as the night deepened and the new moon shrouded their surroundings, they remained oblivious to the colossal fin passing nearby. Amid their terror, destiny unfurled its tapestry, weaving their fates with four others on a distant island, a shared horror uniting them across the expanse of the abyss.

CHAPTER 20
Supplies Run Low

As the morning sun stretched its fingers across the horizon on the sixth day since their trio had embarked on the perilous mission, Jake was tangled in a web of guilt and anxiety. The weight of responsibility pressed heavily on his shoulders, and his attempts at hopeful words were long lost in the abyss of uncertainty. Joined by his fellow island-dwellers, he was ensnared in a deepening cloud of despondency.

The dwindling supplies cast a pall over their situation. Hunger gnawed at them, yet their apathy towards food surpassed any longing for sustenance. Their collective psyche had shifted, and the pervasive gloom seemed to dull even the most fundamental instincts.

The urgency for sustenance remained, however. Food was necessary, and potable water was paramount for surviving in the days to come. Jake had combined half-used coffee grounds with the remaining fresh ones in a makeshift effort, brewing a bitter elixir that brought some semblance of warmth and momentary comfort. Amidst their grim reality, he had scraped a pot of creamed wheat, a meager offering from their dwindling provisions, symbolizing their tenuous grasp on sustenance.

Bolo and Tesoro shuffled into the main house, nodding to Jake, and took their seats at the table, where Jake poured them a mug of coffee each.

As he finished pouring, Amy walked in, her hair disheveled and wearing the same outfit she wore the previous day.

They all presented individual pictures that told Jake one thing: they'd given up all hope!

Jake had seen this coming and decided to offer an idea he'd wanted to avoid.

"Listen up, everyone!" Jake's voice trembled with urgency and fear, his gaze landing squarely on Amy as he began. "I know we're all sinking into this darkness, but we can't afford to let our strength wane any further. We have to try to eat something."

Johno's voice cut through, his apprehension evident. "But, Jake, man! We're running on empty, and that damn supply boat..." He trailed off, casting wary glances at Amy and Bolo. His voice wavered as he continued, anticipating Jake's wrath. Jake's response was surprisingly measured; he stared at the table before him, absorbing Johno's words.

"No, Johno, you're right." The admission tore out Jake's throat, a truth he had been avoiding. The weight of their dire circumstances hung in the air. "I think we're all feeling the same." Nods of agreement rippled across the group.

"I understand that none of us have much of an appetite right now," Jake continued, his tone heavy with understanding. The unanimous acknowledgment sent a ripple of agreement through the room. "But we can't let ourselves weaken any more than we already have. We need to maintain our strength, no matter how long this takes, and that's why we have to find a way to get some food."

Bolo, ever practical, chimed in. "But, Mister Jake! There's no fish left in these waters after that monster paid us a visit! How can we find something to eat?" His furrowed brows betrayed his confusion and concern.

Amy, too, seemed confused but chose not to say anything and see where Jake was taking this.

Jake stood erect and pointed at Bolo. "You Bolo, you're right, as well!" Then Jake quit speaking and stood silently in a manner that suggested he was giving his idea one last consideration before laying it out for them.

"It's not fish we're going after; it's sea lion!" ... He waited for their backlash and was not disappointed.

Johno was the first. "You crazy, Jake? Sea lion no good for eating man!"

Jake snapped back. "How do you know? Have you ever tried it?" He watched Amy and Bolo shaking their heads emphatically in the negative, supporting Johno's retort.

Tesoro thought for a second. "No!... No, I never ate it, but I just don't believe it tastes good!" He was followed immediately by Amy.

"Besides, Jake, sea lion... seals... what have you... are highly fat-saturated and wouldn't seem to be very nutritious at all! Don't you agree?" She challenged.

Jake indicated that he disagreed with her and addressed their concerns. "First of all, no, Johno, it won't taste good, but to your point, Amy, it won't be nutritious, but it will provide us all with the energy we'll need should we be here for any extended period."

Tesoro started to object again, but Jake motioned for him to back down. "Okay! I've got... oh... maybe half a box of shells for the rifle, and ..." He formed a grim, uncharacteristically cold set to his jaw. "..I can guarantee you that I can bring down a 'bull' with it!" His look was a little disconcerting to Amy, who'd not seen this heretofore guarded side of Jake.

"I'll go down to the far end of the lagoon and try to catch one of them swimming, but I'll need Johno to come with me and help tote the meat back in some cloth sacks for the refrigerator, okay?" They all agreed, decidedly skeptical about the whole thing. Tesoro wasn't looking forward to being alone with Jake... who would have the rifle... for any extended time.

But, the matter was settled, and they each forced down the cream of wheat breakfast with their coffee.

Bolo handled this private turmoil differently. He busied himself around the main house and didn't even walk out to acknowledge Jake's departure.

Jake didn't notice. He, too, was self-absorbed as he led Tesoro down the path leading to the island's far end.

Jake's gaze fixed upon the familiar rocky bridge formation as they entered the lagoon. The memories of Lamar's recent encounter – the catalyst that had thrust them into this unrelenting ordeal – flooded back, tormenting his already burdened mind. He motioned for Johno to join him, setting off along the water's edge towards the weathered overpass.

Abruptly, their movements were shattered by a sudden eruption of activity from a nearby thicket of reeds. A large brown form burst forth, a streak of motion that darted before them and vanished beneath the surface of the watery channel beneath the bridge. Johno's urgent voice pierced the moment, his excitement palpable. "There's one, Jake! Can you catch it?"

Yet, Jake's attention was elsewhere; he knelt at the point where the creature had entered the water. His weathered fingers traced over the ground, detecting a telling sign. "Hold on, Johno." His voice was steady, absorbed by the discovery. "Blood... here. Some fresh, some caked and crusted." His gaze fixed upon the evidence, a grim understanding settling over him. The lingering and unhealed wounds spoke of painful encounters, likely with the same predator that had set them on edge. "These poor sea lions, they've suffered, probably from our 'friend' out there." His words held a mix of sorrow and grim resolve, realizing that "Meg" had likely mutilated or devoured these creatures in his pursuit of sustenance.

Reality snapped back, and Jake rose from his examination, eyes scanning the water beyond the stone archway. He had to refocus on the task at hand. A healthier specimen for their sustenance awaited. Along the edge of the crystalline pond, they spotted a young male sunning itself on a large rock. Reluctance tugged at Jake's heart, but he steeled himself, carefully aiming and firing. The creature jolted, a sudden movement followed by a lifeless collapse onto the stone.

Without hesitation, Jake and Johno set to work. The process was swift, a blend of necessity and sorrow. They cleaned and butchered the animal, carefully wrapping the meat in cheesecloth bundles for the journey back. Each slice cut was a heavy reminder of the stakes they faced. Jake's heart ached for the life taken, but the survival of their group took precedence – a choice made with the weight of responsibility in each deliberate action.

As they made their way back to the compound, Jake gave a fleeting thought to 'Meg's' focus on the sea lion colony, and he shuddered inwardly at the mental picture of the slaughter that had taken place around the rocks from the tip of the island.

Johno noticed Jake's preoccupation and asked, "What you thinkin' about so hard on Jake? You don't like killin' these things, do you, man?"

Jake continued to focus his attention on the path ahead as he answered Tesoro. "Hum! There is that, Johno... but I was just wondering how many of these sea lions that big son of a bitch has either killed or eaten and how many have survived!" He looked up briefly at the smaller man to emphasize his point, then back at the trail. "It's almost like genocide... ya know?" Jake shook his head to himself. Of course, Johno didn't understand the real meaning of genocide, a fact made clear by the confused look that the other man was giving Jake. So, Jake elaborated in simpler terms. "What I mean is it's very possible that 'Meg' has virtually wiped out all sea lions... none of the species have survived! That's 'genocide,' Johno... when a whole race or species is killed off! Understand?

Johno mulled over Jake's words, a brief moment of contemplation crossing his features before understanding dawned in his eyes. He acknowledged his grasp of the concept they discussed with a sharp nod.

Their journey continued for a short while until Tesoro's forehead creased in deep thought and voiced an unsettling piece of logic. "Hey, Jake! As long as that colossal creature has its own territory, just like that massive seal colony out there, it's not likely to abandon these waters, right?"

Jake's face contorted in response to Tesoro's observation, a manifestation of the genuine concern that had taken root within him. The remainder of their trek unfolded silently, each man grappling with his fears and anxieties.

Upon arriving at the house, they were met with a scene of Amy and Bolo engrossed in a tense conversation, seemingly consumed by their own distress. Amy sprung up from the table as Jake and Tesoro entered, hurrying towards Jake with a hug and a sigh of relief. Bolo remained seated, his gaze locked onto his tightly gripped coffee cup, his expression heavy with despair.

"Jake, do you think we'll ever get off this island?" Amy's voice trembled with uncertainty, the desperation in her eyes evident. "It's been almost six days since Lamar left. Shouldn't we have received some help by now?"

Jake held her at arm's length, his gaze steady and comforting. "Amy, try to stay calm." He offered a soothing tone amidst her anxiety. "Yes, it's been a while, and ordinarily, help would have come, but we can't jump to conclusions. Lamar might have encountered unexpected challenges in getting his signal through. Or perhaps they're organizing a stronger rescue effort. There are many possibilities."

Johno's voice pierced the tense air, his words heavy with impending doom. "Or that damn thing has obliterated the boat and devoured our friends!" Hysteria tainted his exclamation, the tone bordering on madness. "Maybe the signal never even reached anyone!"

Amy's eyes betrayed a growing fear as she absorbed Johno's words. Anticipating the escalating panic, Jake stepped in to quell the rising tension. "Johno, that's enough!" His frustration mingled with anger, his hands clenching and unclenching. However, Amy's touch on his arm halted the brewing storm, a gesture that spoke of her calming influence. "You're right, Amy. We're all adults here. We can handle our emotions. Right, Bolo?" She turned her gaze to the despondent Bolo, seeking assurance.

Bolo nodded solemnly, excusing himself to the stove and busying his hands to avoid brewing conflict. Tesoro also recognized the need to step back, raising his open hands placatingly. "Okay, okay, Jefe! I'll be quiet from now on. But, please, Senor Jake, can you tell us... all of us... what we'll do if, God forbid, the message didn't get through? Can you tell me that?"

Jake's anger simmered as he looked from one face to another in the room. Slowly, he realized that his frustration stemmed more from his own feelings of helplessness rather than Johno's words. With a sigh, he softened his stance, acknowledging the weight of Tesoro's question. "Honestly," he began, acknowledging the fear in their eyes. "At this moment, I'm not entirely sure."

Instantly, fear overtook the room, replacing dependency with sheer terror as their minds raced through the implications. The trio exchanged anxious glances, searching for a spark of hope that seemed to elude them. But Jake wasn't finished. "However," he continued, determined to be truthful despite the bleak situation. "We do have some resources. As long as we have diesel for the generators—and I think the storage tank is about a quarter full, right Bolo?" Bolo nodded in agreement. "And as unappealing as it might be, we have a source of food," Jake gestured towards the bag of seal meat in the sink. "And we have fresh water from the spring by the lagoon. We'll survive, folks. Even in the worst-case scenario, they will send someone to investigate if they don't hear from us in another four or five days. Makes sense?"

Amy and Bolo slowly nodded, reassured by Jake's words. However, Tesoro's face remained a canvas of confusion and dread. "Yes, Jake, you're right. If they send a plane," Tesoro agreed with a hint of skepticism. "But what if they send a boat? That creature out there is a ship killer. Do you think they know what they're up against?"

Tesoro's simple yet logical question hit Jake like a bolt. "Damn it, Johno! You're right," Jake admitted, berating himself for not considering this crucial aspect. He lifted his face from his hands, addressing the group with a newfound gentleness. "Well, folks, all we can do is hope they send a plane because Johno's right. If they dispatch a frigate or something, it won't stand a chance against that monster if it's anywhere near."

The look of helpless anguish etched across Amy's otherwise composed face spoke volumes. They were trapped in a situation where waiting was their only option, a reality that weighed heavily on their shoulders.

FINALLY, MEG FOUND his way back to the familiar waters of the island, where he encountered a massive school of tuna. The silver fish darted frantically along the newly warmed currents, a journey leading them to the bountiful feeding grounds near the South American coastline. Unknown to them, their journey was about to be cut short brutally.

Meg burst through the school, tearing through them from below in a flurry of motion. In just three swift passes, he devoured nearly all of the sleek creatures, quelling the intense hunger that had gnawed at him. With a temporary sense of satisfaction, he continued his slow, meandering journey toward the island he had claimed as his private hunting ground.

Meg's massive form breached the surface as he neared the shallower waters surrounding his destination. His towering dorsal fin sliced through the night air as he moved, a silhouette against the dark backdrop of the ocean. However, he was met with an unexpected assault—powerful waves from an approaching stormfront began to pummel the island and the sea around it.

Reacting on instinct, Meg dove deeper in search of calmer waters. But to his dismay, the sea floor rose abruptly, leaving him with fewer options for shelter from the relentless waves. Desperate to escape the battering swells, he veered sharply to the right and surged forward. At this critical moment, fate intervened, setting into motion a chain of tragic events that would alter the course of this horrific tale.

His rapid movement along this new course led him to a strangely familiar, narrow, less turbulent channel. He slowed his pace as he progressed, the water gradually opening up into a broader expanse—the harbor of 'Crandle's Keep.' Submerging to the bottom, he navigated in slow, methodical patterns, attuned to any signs of potential prey.

Meg's immense form came tantalizingly close to the piers jutting out from the harbor's edge during some of his passes. In fact, one pass took him directly over the sunken remains of Johno's boat, which lay silently on the seabed, not far from the end of the wharf. Importantly, Meg maintained his depth, ensuring that anyone scanning the surface from the island remained blissfully unaware of his ominous presence.

Meanwhile, the four individuals on the island—unaware of the lurking danger—sought refuge in the safety of the large house.

They huddled together, enduring the unexpected fury of the storm surrounding them, completely unaware of the monstrous menace lurking beneath the waves.

Jake and Bolo stared out of the windows, both expecting that one of the older window frames would succumb to the near hurricane-force winds at any moment and crash in to allow the wind and rain to invade their quarters.

Fortunately, this did not occur, but while they were watching the sheets of precipitation and repeated flashes of lightning, Jake saw an expected anomaly... sparks... emanating from the vicinity of the fuel tanks on the docks, or more precisely, the filling station pump near them.

Bolo saw this, too, and a memory jolt hit the big man. "Oh damn! Mister Jake! I messed up. I did!" Bolo ran his hand nervously through his hair, obviously highly agitated.

"What, Bolo? What were those sparks down there... the light on the pier?" Jake paid full attention to his friend now.

"Yessir! That!... But, worse, I forgot and left the pump switch on when I last filled the boat; I just now remember!..." His eyes were wide, silently pleading for Jake's forgiveness.

But Jake was only concerned with an explosion, not mad at the big fellow in front of him. "It's all right, Bolo!... Just go on down and turn it off! Oh, and use the rubber gloves in the trunk, over there, because that's 220 volts, and I don't want you to get thrown into the pond...not on a night like this!" Jake forced a smile, despite his concern, to help calm Bolo.

"Okay, Mister Jake! I'm going!" Bolo said as he hustled over and pulled a long pair of yellow gloves from the trunk. Then, the huge black mate threw a slicker over his shoulders and charged into the storm.

Jake watched Bolo as he blended into the rain-whipped darkness, uneasy about Bolo's mission... Jake didn't know why, so he paced nervously, from window to window, watching for his big friend to come back up the hill.

Amid the escalating storm, Bolo had reached the switch box mounted on the pier post, only to find it stubbornly stuck. Frustration surging within him, Bolo's gaze landed on a four-foot crowbar nearby, conveniently resting next to the open valve of the diesel tank, which also supplied fuel to the generators atop the hill.

With rubber gloves removed, he seized the long tool and pounded on the weathered door of the switchbox. The reverberating clangs triggered a series of unexpected events. The door yielded, revealing the energized circuitry and the knife switch within. Meanwhile, Jake, alerted by the clamor, stepped onto the porch. His curiosity was piqued, and he started going toward the pier to investigate the commotion.

Unknown to both men, metallic reverberations had drawn another presence. An unwelcome visitor, this beast had been lurking beneath the surface, traversing the sprawling harbor for hours, his hunger intensifying with every passing moment. With a slow and purposeful trajectory towards the ocean, he had covered about two-thirds of the lagoon's expanse when a faint, intermittent noise reached his sensors.

Intrigued, the creature altered his course and ascended toward the water's surface. His massive dorsal fin emerged from the rain-beaten waves as he breached, casting an ominous shadow. Although the sound that had initially caught his attention faded, his predatory instincts took over, urging him to accelerate in pursuit of the source of the disturbance.

Tragically, this sudden surge of speed granted his colossal body the momentum akin to a runaway freight train. As he surged forward, his colossal mass bore down upon the pier. Like fragile matchsticks, the supporting poles snapped and splintered under the force, sending a shockwave of destruction through the wooden structure above.

From a vantage point up the small hill leading to the pier, Jake spotted Bolo working on the fuel valve, seemingly oblivious to the impending danger. A gesture of acknowledgment passed between them. However, just as Jake was about to descend to join Bolo, a seismic crack resonated through the air, and his world spiraled into chaos.

The pier, once a solid structure parallel to the shoreline, rose suddenly and dramatically, lifted by a colossal swell. It shot upward twenty feet, carrying the three imposing storage tanks. The tanks hurtled upward and outward, crashing onto the cliffs to Jake's left. Diesel and gasoline spewed forth, engulfing the compound in a volatile mist, their pungent fumes staining the air.

As this chaotic scene unfolded, Jake's focus zeroed in on Bolo, the unfolding disaster temporarily eclipsed by his concern. The immense force of the pier's eruption had catapulted Bolo into the air, a helpless figure suspended in the storm's fury. Thirty feet above, he flailed and twisted, his high-pitched screams mingling with the tempestuous winds. The descent was inevitable, and Jake watched in sheer terror as his friend plummeted from the zenith of his unsettling flight.

Amy and Tesoro had heard the commotion and were running across the yard in front of the house. They saw Bolo shoot into their line of sight before falling back toward the water, and Amy froze, with the back of her hand pressed to her mouth in abject horror at what she was seeing.

Meanwhile, Tesoro sprinted toward Jake's position to see what was happening!

At this point, Jake was immobilized by fear and shock! He watched helplessly while his longtime friend and companion fell into the cavernous, tooth-lined jaws that had emerged in the center of the splintered opening in the pier below.

Jake screamed... ' *N-o-o-o!*" at the top of his lungs! And again..."*My God,*...B-o-o-o-l-l-o-o-!...N-o-o-o!"

As Bolo's screams and desperate struggles vanished into the closing jaws, the creature's insidious maw swallowed him whole, its monstrous form retreating into the depths of the harbor. The place that had once been a sanctuary for Bolo, nestled alongside Jake, now became the haunting scene of his tragic demise.

Jake's countenance contorted, transformed into an agonized visage, unlike anything he had experienced before. The collision of sorrow and seething hatred painted his features with an eerie intensity, every emotion etched deeply into the lines of his face. A surge of determination gripped him, propelling his feet down the hill toward the unfathomable depths below. Grief had consumed him, eclipsing rational thought and leaving him driven only by the wild torrent of his own anguish.

Beside him, Tesoro stood as a steadfast contrast, a beacon of clarity amid chaos. His connection with Bolo had been different, less profound, allowing him to retain a level-headed perspective even in the face of this horrendous tragedy. Recognizing the trajectory of Jake's desperation, Tesoro sprang into action without hesitation. His lithe form launched toward Jake, limbs wrapping around the larger man's knees as he tackled him to the ground, a desperate attempt to curb Jake's frenzied descent toward the abyss.

Amid the turmoil, Jake's mind had abandoned all reason. He flipped over in a wild frenzy, his immense fist clenched and poised to strike Tesoro, a potentially devastating blow that would have inflicted severe harm had it landed. But just as Jake's muscles tensed for the assault, Amy surged onto the scene, her voice cutting through the chaos like a clarion call of reason.

"Jake, for God's sake, come to your senses!" Amy's voice carried a potent blend of fear and authority, a plea to pierce through the madness that had enveloped him.

Time slowed to a crawl, and a mere second of hesitation hung in the balance. Jake's wild eyes snapped toward Amy, their frantic intensity catching a fleeting glimpse of her plea. The rapidly evolving dynamics of the situation demanded swift action.

When 'Meg' had backed out of the splintered wharf, *he* had caused the light pole and pump control box, which was still open, to fall over and smash against the jagged mass of twisted piping across the hole.

This caused the breaking lamp and control relays in the box to emit a shower of sparks and burning insulation that touched off the fumes from the surrounding fuel oil and caused a massive explosion and fireball, generating a concussion that threw the three through the air, some ten feet to the far side of the grassy knoll that had served as an overlook for all of them.

This time, however, the small hill served as a lifesaver for the stunned people behind it. The fireball expanded rapidly, consuming all the fumes in the surrounding air and either burning or scorching everything in its path. As it hit the knoll, the rise blocked its effect on the motionless individuals behind it and thus saved them from certain fiery death!

Several minutes dripped by, an eternity in the realm of suspended consciousness. In the slow passage of time, the first glimmers of awakening manifested in Johno. He twitched, his body shivering off the veil of unconsciousness that had enshrouded him. His eyes fluttered open, blinking against the harsh light filtering through the swaying palm fronds. Disoriented and disheveled, he struggled to piece together the fragments of his awareness, a puzzle strewn with scattered thoughts.

Then, like the ripples of a pool disturbed by a fallen leaf, the stirrings of consciousness spread to Jake. His massive frame shifted, a deep inhalation filling his lungs as he groaned, the echoes of his awakening mingling with the sounds of the rustling leaves above. Slowly, his eyelids peeled apart, revealing the depths of his dark eyes, glazed with remnants of a dreamless slumber. Muscles that had been slack now tensed, each fiber sending signals of regained vitality to his foggy brain.

As the moments dragged on, the grip of unconsciousness released its hold on Amy. Her form was a sprawl of vulnerability amidst the tangle of palms and undergrowth, tendrils of her hair coiling around leaves like ivy. Her fingers twitched, the dainty digits furling and unfurling as she fought back to awareness. Through the haze, the world beckoned her with its muted hues and distorted shapes, and the symphony of chirping insects and rustling leaves began to seep into her senses.

And then, almost synchronously, they sat up, their collective consciousness shaking off the lethargy of their shared slumber. With each passing second, the tendrils of grogginess receded, revealing the harsh reality they had been cast into. The scene before them sent a jolt of sickening dread coursing through their veins, every nerve ending tingling with primal fear.

As their bleary eyes focused and the veil of confusion lifted, the sight that greeted them was enough to send shivers of terror down their spines. It was an image that congealed in their minds, a tableau etched with the stark lines of nightmarish horror, an image that seared itself into their memory with an intensity they would never forget.

The eastern half of the compound roared in an inferno of chaos, a devouring tempest of flames that consumed everything in its path. The refrigerated storage shed, the generators, and every structure in its wake became a writhing dance of red and orange.

Amidst the crackling blaze, their senses sharpened by the urgency of the situation, the trio stumbled to their feet, reeling from the shock of the unfolding disaster. Yet, as they rose, a surge of sound broke through the cacophony of flames—a furious whoosh that heralded a fresh burst of fire, now engulfing the eastern edge of the main house.

"Damn it all!" Jake's voice rang out in frustration and fear as he bolted across the fiery landscape toward the house. His strides were driven by desperation, his heart pounding with adrenaline as he leaped onto the porch and dashed into the building. Smoke and sparks greeted him, ominous signs of the encroaching blaze that threatened to consume everything they held dear.

Inside, as Jake moved with a sense of urgency, Amy and Tesoro reached the room. Their eyes widened as they witnessed Jake tearing through chests, ripping open closets, and grabbing whatever items he deemed essential. Rifles, ammunition, coats, scuba gear, binoculars—anything that could be salvaged was thrust into duffel bags, which Jake passed to his companions swiftly.

"Take these and get to safety!" Jake commanded. His voice was firm with authority and desperation. Amy and Tesoro obeyed, each clutching a bag, dragging them away from the encroaching fire as fast as their trembling limbs would allow. The adrenaline coursing through their veins drowned out the heat and chaos around them, fueling their determination to escape the growing conflagration.

Meanwhile, with a deep breath and a quick glance around, Jake's hands snatched up his journal, a fragment of 'Meg's' tooth, and the evidence of the grim truth unfolding on this cursed island. Gripping his precious cargo, he turned and retraced his steps, his path back through the room obscured by smoke and uncertainty. Every inch gained felt like a battle won against the raging fire that threatened to consume everything in its path.

Suddenly, he stopped short and focused on a closet in the corner near the wall of spreading fire! His mind flashed back to the morning Darwin had brought his gear up to the house before the Aussie's fateful dive! Jake put the other things on the dining table and bolted to the closet. He threw open the door and tore out the hanging wet suits! Behind other paraphernalia was Darwin's extra spear gun... and the two extra explosive spears he'd left behind! Jake grabbed the weapon, spears, and what other items he could carry and piled them on top of the other boxes. Even to Jake, the resulting load was a challenge, but he managed to stagger outside and make his way across the grounds and away from the spreading inferno.

He saw Amy and Tesoro, near Amy's cabin, waving at him, and he saw Johno running to meet him!

Jake gladly relinquished part of his load to the smaller man, and together, they made their way to where Amy was waiting.

They piled everything they had salvaged along the trail and turned to survey the tragic scene before them.

The flames raged on relentlessly, their insatiable hunger consuming the heart of the headquarters' house, leaving only memories and ashes in their wake. The once-familiar structures were now eerie silhouettes against the backdrop of destruction, painted in shades of burning orange and midnight black. The compound, once a sanctuary, now lay in ruins, a grim testament to the forces that had torn their lives apart.

Amid the devastation, the weight of the tragedy bore down on Jake's shoulders with an intensity he could no longer suppress. As the flames devoured the last remnants of their home, a flood of memories rushed in, punctuated by the image of Bolo. The pain of his loss cut deeper than Jake could have ever anticipated, and his knees buckled beneath the weight of grief.

Collapsed on the charred ground, his sobs mingled with the crackling of the flames. His heartrending cries reverberated through the night, a mournful lament for a dear friend lost to the merciless jaws of fate. Jake managed to choke out words of anguish between ragged breaths, his voice a raw testament to the profound sorrow that consumed him.

"Oh, my God... Bolo!" His words were a desperate plea, a heartbroken inquiry into the unfairness of life. Amy and Tesoro stood at a distance, watching as Jake's grief poured forth. They understood the depth of his pain, the ache of loss that refused to be contained.

"He was such a kind soul," Jake's voice cracked, the weight of his emotions too much to bear. He looked skyward, his tears mingling with the ash that filled the air. "Never harmed anyone, never meant any harm... Why him?"

The silent night seemed to echo his words, a cruel reminder of the void left by Bolo's absence. With his face cradled in his hands, Jake wept, his sorrow an unabated river.

Amid the heartache, Amy approached her, touching a gentle balm on his anguished soul. Her words trembled with understanding and urgency, a plea for him to find the strength to carry on. The tension in her voice was palpable, reflecting the dire situation they now faced.

"Jake, we know how much it hurts," she said softly, her hand resting on his neck. "Bolo was a remarkable person, and his loss is devastating. But right now, we need you to gather yourself. We need your strength and clear-headedness to get through this." She exchanged a meaningful glance with Tesoro, who silently affirmed her words.

Jake's grief was a heavy burden, but the survival of those who remained depended on his ability to rise above it. Amid the ruins of their world, they clung to one another, seeking solace and strength in the face of overwhelming loss.

Jake's understanding of Amy's words was apparent as he mustered the last of his sobs into his palms, pushing himself to his feet. His face, once contorted with grief, transformed into a visage of icy resolve, a chilling determination that sent shivers through those who witnessed it. With his heart still heavy, he took a few deliberate steps toward the harbor, his voice cutting through the night air like a blade.

"Count your hours, you colossal bastard!" His words were a defiant challenge aimed at the unseen creature lurking beneath the surface. He held his ground, undeterred by the unseen danger in the depths. "Your time is running out. I'll find a way to end you, personally... and soon!"

With clenched fists and a seething intensity, Jake's voice turned into a low growl as he continued, his every word dripping with the venom of his hatred. The anger radiated from him like a palpable force, and Amy and Tesoro could feel the raw energy of his determination.

"I swear it," he hissed through gritted teeth, his eyes gleaming with dangerous fire. "I'll see you dead for what you've done. I swear it on my friend's soul!"

With a swift pivot, he shifted his attention to the pile of equipment and supplies they had salvaged from the fire. The flames, now a consuming inferno, illuminated the scene, casting eerie shadows that danced on the wreckage. Amid the chaos, Jake began to sort through the items, creating a makeshift arsenal with methodical precision.

Amy and Tesoro exchanged glances, the realization dawning upon them as they witnessed Jake's purposeful actions. Amid their tragedy, Jake had forged a path fueled by vengeance and a burning determination to make the creature pay for the lives it had taken.

372   SIDNEY ST. JAMES AND JEREMIAH SHERMAN

The devastation around them seemed to mirror Jake's inner turmoil, and yet, within the wreckage, a fierce determination had ignited. The flames that had consumed their home were now reflected in Jake's eyes, a reflection of the fire ignited within him.

With the promise of vengeance hanging in the air, they stood together amidst the remnants of their former lives. The path ahead was uncertain, fraught with danger and uncertainty, but they were united by a shared purpose: to confront the terror that had taken so much from them.

The items included diving tanks, fins, masks, and associated paraphernalia. Also, the spear gun and explosive spears, a cheesecloth packed with chunk meat from the sea lion, had been in one of the boxes they dragged from the burning house. The high-power rifle was also in the mix, as well as a box of ammunition, field glasses, a small gray can of gasoline, and a small cloth bag; Jake checked the rifle's scope and set it down. He picked up the small cloth bag and opened it, removing the contents carefully to inspect it.

During the unfolding scene, Amy and Tesoro find themselves in a state of helplessness, mere observers of the enigmatic actions of their leader. What lay ahead seemed fraught with uncertainty, and dread gnawed at their hearts as they watched Jake's preparations unfold.

Jake's movements were deliberate and calculated as he extracted three small, ominous objects from the bag. Amy felt her breath hitch, a feeling of foreboding creeping up her spine. The weight of the situation settled heavily upon her chest, and her eyes remained transfixed on the objects in Jake's hands.

Beside her, Tesoro's reaction mirrored her own unease. His sharp intake of breath and the whispered exclamation that followed underscored the gravity of the discovery. Amy turned her head to see Tesoro's eyes widen, a mixture of shock and realization flashing across his features.

"Detonators!" Tesoro's words carried a tremor of disbelief, a stark recognition of the perilous nature of their situation. "Madre de Dios! He has detonators!"

The word hung in the air, a testament to the mounting tension surrounding them. The implications of Jake's possession of such devices were chilling, raising more questions than answers. The atmosphere crackled with suspense, leaving Amy and Tesoro to grapple with the uncertainty of what lay ahead and the ominous possibilities that Jake's actions had unveiled.

He spoke loudly enough for Amy to hear, and she looked at Tesoro. His eyes were as wide as saucers, and his jaw sagged open as the color drained from his face.

Amy saw this and felt a tightening, churning feeling rising in her stomach.

They both surmised that Jake intended to go after 'Meg"...in 'Meg's' backyard!

Amy was the first to speak up. "Jake? Just what are you going to do?" Her tone pleading yet demanding a response!

Jake took a moment, away from the stack of equipment he was working over, to look at Amy and answer. "I'm going to kill that goddamn fish, Amy ... or die trying!" He spat out the words, each one dripping with deliberate venom.

Johno jumped in at this point, emboldened by Amy's success in getting Jake's attention. "But tell me, Senor Jake! Just what you got there that can kill it? I don't see nothin'!" Jake's eyes narrowed, and his nostrils flared at Tesoro's arrogant tone, but he quickly calmed down and addressed the other's point.

"Ya know, Johno! I'm not sure I have what it takes, but I've got to try, or I'll go nuts!" He turned back to the pile of articles in front of him and began to assess each piece.

Johno looked pleadingly at Amy for her support and then blurted out. "Senor Jake! I know where we can get 'somethin' that will, for sure, kill that big motherfucker. The slim young man stood defiantly and waited for Jake's outburst! Jake didn't disappoint him.

The big man froze and snapped an angry, disbelieving glare at Tesoro. Then, Jake threw the things in his hands down roughly onto the pile and took two enormous strides that brought him up close to the other man. He grabbed Johno by both arms, squeezing off the circulation, and yelled. "Just what the fuck do you mean, Johno? Don't be jerking me around, boy! Now's not the time!"

Amy looked on in shock and knew that Jake was on the verge of losing control again, but she could only watch helplessly while the scene unfolded.

To his credit, Tesoro stood his ground as Jake grabbed him. "I ain't jerkin' you around, Jake!

For Christ's sake, you knew where we could get something before now? You might have saved Bolo's life!" Jake's eyes were wide and crazy! "Why the fuck didn't you say it before... you rotten little -?"

Jake didn't finish his expletives because Johno shouted out! "Because, Jake, it's going to, most likely, be suicide for someone, man!" He paused, taking a deep breath. "And that someone has got to be me! I'm the only one who can get to it! Besides, I didn't know how to get it to work, even if I could get it... not till I saw that bag of detonators you got there!"

Jake nor Amy said a word. They waited, expectantly, for Tesoro to elaborate.

"Now look! I had about eight pounds of plastic explosives on the boat's supply locker when it sank! Enough to blow 'our friend' out there to Hell! But we got to get it! And..."

Again, Jake anticipated Johno. "Explosives! You've got plastic?! And... It's at the bottom of the harbor! Damn! I see what you're saying! But hey! It's a better idea than I've got!" Jake quipped.

Amy's jaw dropped incredulously. "You can't be serious! Either of you! For all we know, that thing is out there... in this very harbor! This is insane!" She was borderline hysterical.

"I'm open to any better suggestions, Amy!" Jake interjected his voice firm between her tirades.

Johno didn't let her answer, though. "Amy, you know there ain't no better way! In Hell, this is the only way we've got a chance of taking him out!" His posture was challenging Amy to come up with a better solution. All she could do, however, was cover her face with her hands and sob, shaking her head back and forth.

"C'mon, Amy! This isn't the time to break down! You'll have to keep it together to help us on this!" Jake was obviously formulating a plan. "Johno, can you get me into that locker if I get you down to the boat in one piece?" With wide eyes, the other man gave a curt nod in the affirmative.

"Good!" Jake was bringing his ideas together into a solid action plan. "You and I will go down there when the sun rises." Jake surveyed the scene, spreading out in front of him. The fire was burning itself out, but the sky was filled with thick black smoke to such an extent that the thinning storm clouds were totally blotted out overhead. To the south, he could see some stars in the distance as the heavens cleared, and the seas were becoming much calmer. "...when we reach the wreck, I will go into the locker while the other watches for any sign of that bastard! Think you can handle the dive?" His eyes drilled into Johno's, trying to read the younger man's courage level.

Tesoro hesitated for a few seconds before responding. "Si, Senor Jake!" He pounded on his chest with a clenched fist. "I do what must be done! You don't have to worry about Johno!"

Jake stared silently as he tried to decide whether or not he could trust the other man. Finally, he decided that he really had no choice. So he acknowledged, "Okay! That's enough for me!"

Jake then turned his attention to Amy. "Sweetheart." He began with an uncharacteristically intimate address. "I know we'll be leaving you alone up here, and I know that you're going to be... uh... a little afraid, but..." He was interrupted by a surprisingly in-control Amy!

"Afraid?... Hell, Jake! Why would I be the least bit afraid?? Just because you and 'Cisco, here..." Tesoro winced slightly at Amy's sarcasm but managed to smile a little at the reference to a legendary Mexican folk hero. "We are going to take a swim in that monster's swimming pool! Hey! Why should I be afraid?"

Jake listened calmly, fully understanding her natural ire, and after she had seemed to come to a stopping point, he jumped in with the rest of his plan. "I know! I know! But, if you will let me explain, I think you'll see how we can, at least, minimize the risk... to some extent!"

Amy stood defiantly, hands on hips, and nodded for Jake to proceed.

"Okay! While Johno and I are down there, Amy, you'll take a piece of pipe about six to eight feet long, tie it to the end of the pier, and hang it down into the water. Then, keep a hammer handy and..." Amy took over, her eyes widening in understanding.

"And, since sound travels much better in water than in air, if I see 'Meg,' I beat on the pipe as an alarm, right?" Jake's smile confirmed her interpretation.

Jake shifted his gaze from Amy to Tesoro and back. "Well, that's the plan: get down there, get the explosive, and get back to high ground before he returns for lunch. What do you think?"

Tesoro spoke first. "I think it's the only way! I just hope to swim fast enough to keep up with Jake."

Jake grinned and responded in a slightly condescending tone, "Don't worry, Johno! You'll be fine. How about you, Amy? Are you on board?"

Amy's expression was somber, teetering on the edge of sullenness, as she replied, "I suppose. But with deep reservations, Jake. I don't want to lose you too." Her eyes welled up with tears, and her lip quivered slightly. "You've become pretty special to me, 'big guy.' You know what I mean?" She couldn't hold back any longer and collapsed into Jake's arms.

He held her tightly, whispering words of comfort. "I have no intention of leaving you, sweetheart, especially not to wind up in that fish's belly." He held her at arm's length, locking his gaze on hers. "I'll be back; I promise." Sincerity and determination shone in his eyes, and Amy slowly nodded her belief.

"Now that this is settled, we've got about three hours until sun-up. I think we should all try to rest. Johno, why don't you take Jenny's cabin over there, and Amy, if you don't mind, I'll use your old sofa to try and relax a bit."

"Are you kidding?" Amy looked surprised at Jake! "Of course, you can come in with me! C'mon." She started for her porch while Tesoro entered the other small house.

Jake followed Amy into the darkened room and shut the door behind him, plunging the room into blackness. He'd forgotten that there was no electricity since both generators had been destroyed.

"Damn! I forgot that we don't have the generators anymore! There should be some candles in the..." His words were cut off by the press of Amy's warm lips on his own, and the next kiss lasted for a full two minutes as the desperate need for both people boiled to the surface!

Amy lost herself in Jake's arms, and, for the moment anyway, Jake disregarded the age difference between them and matched Amy's passion with his own. Finally, Jake broke the kiss and managed some semblance of reason through the fog of mutual desire that had taken control of them both.

"Amy! Amy!" Her eyes were closed in a swoon of feeling that she didn't want to surrender, but she did at Jake's sharp exclamation. "This is crazy, Honey!" I want you a lot right now, but this is definitely the wrong time and place!... And we both know it!" He was breathing rapidly while presenting his plea for her understanding and restraint.

Amy looked intently at Jake's face through the darkness, and slowly, the serious nature of their overall situation replaced the sincere feelings of affection for Jake, which she had wanted so badly to release. "You're right, of course! It's just that... well..." Amy wasn't sure what to say or how to say it, considering the moment's awkwardness, but she stammered on. "I... uh... I think... no... I know I'm falling in love with you, Jake! I know!" She held up a hand, blocking any potential interruption on his part. "This isn't the right time! We may not even make it off of this island alive! I'm too young!.." Jake grabbed her in midsentence and crushed her lips to his in another long, deep kiss that took her breath away, and when he broke away, he whispered in a heartfelt tone that Amy hadn't heard from him before.

"Okay, listen. I'm not entirely sure. It's been a long, long time... But I think I feel the same way about you, Amy. I just didn't want to admit it, not to you or to myself, because I had this gut feeling that there was a real chance I wouldn't make it out of this mess. Call it a premonition. But I can't hold it back anymore," Jake confessed, his words punctuating the darkness. He couldn't see the joyous smile that lit up Amy's face amidst the blackness as he continued. "When all of this is over, if we both come out of it in one piece, I want to pick up this... uh... conversation where we left off. What do you say?" He pulled her into a tight embrace, waiting for her response.

Amy planted a soft kiss on Jake's neck and whispered, "You're on, big guy. And I'll hold you to that promise."

"So, we should try to rest for a bit, huh?" She gently slipped away from his hold and settled onto the small bed.

Jake sank into the sofa across the room, and despite both feeling far from sleep, they were snoring softly within ten minutes. Unknown to them, the familiar presence of the great gray dorsal fin rose from the harbor, slicing through the still waters in a large oval pattern around the entire perimeter. Finding no suitable prey, the fin eventually retreated to the white-capped sea beyond, leaving the trio oblivious to its presence.

CHAPTER 21
Exploding Fuel Oil from the Tanks

Meg's fury was palpable. **Hours had** passed since he had entered the familiar waters surrounding the island. After feasting on a bountiful school of king mackerel, he navigated the narrow channel into the sheltered harbor. The water was eerily calm and clear in this confined space, shielded from the storm's tumultuous waves.

Diving to the harbor's bottom, he languidly cruised in haphazard patterns, his primal instincts guiding him toward his next meal. Amid this tranquil interlude, a sharp banging sound reverberated through the water, setting off alarm bells within him. Breaking the surface, his eyes fixated on the pier, illuminated by scattered lights and intermittent movements. His innate response was to attack, to unleash his wrath upon this perceived threat.

Yet, the pursuit led him astray. The collision sent his colossal form barreling through the pier's telephone pole superstructure, splintering it like matchsticks. Triumphantly, he seized his target, a sizable creature that had stumbled into his grasp. But this victory came at a cost; an eight-foot fragment of sharp, broken pole impaled itself deep into his side, piercing through sinew and fat. Agonizing pain coursed through him, a foreign sensation causing him to convulse violently to dislodge the intrusive shard.

Unbeknownst to him, as he thrashed in anguish, the fuel oil from the ruptured tanks spread rapidly over the water's surface. Each movement carried him through the fiery slick, coating his immense dorsal fin with a blazing veneer. In the harbor's obscurity, the fin became an infernal beacon, a searing emblem slashing through the night with terrifying speed.

This new painful sensation was more severe than the large piece of timber protruding from the wound in *his* lower right side, and by the time *he'd* traversed the shallow channel leading to the sea and was able to dive into the depths, the nerves running through the surface tissue of the fin were telegraphing continuous pain signals to his primitive brain.

Of course, sadly, neither injury was life-threatening, but they caused the behemoth to be even more dangerous and unpredictable than *he'd* ever been!

To try and run away from the agony, *he* dived unusually deep, where the numbing cold of the surrounding water had deadened the pain to some extent. Here *he* remained for some time. As luck would have it, *Meg* had brushed against a massive outcropping, and it had jerked the length of the wood beam out of his side, leaving the cold salt water to cleanse and cauterize the remaining wound.

Over the next several hours, as daylight broke above, *he* remained in the murky depths, swimming slowly as the pain subsided, eventually returning to *his* habitual ways of hunting for the vast amounts of food necessary to sustain *his* energy and life force.

Amid the battered landscape of the island, the trio of survivors was poised on the precipice of a perilous undertaking. Oblivious to the unfolding developments that would temporarily detain 'Meg,' they prepared for their dive into the depths of the harbor, a venture that would soon intertwine with the unpredictable course of the colossal predator.

Johno meticulously inspected the diving equipment, his brows knitted in a worried expression, while Jake methodically assessed the spear guns and the spears armed with explosive tips. Across the charred expanse of ground, standing atop a small knoll that bore the scorched traces of the previous night's inferno, Amy wielded a pair of binoculars. Her gaze was unwavering, locked on the turbulent waters beyond the harbor's entrance, a vigilant search for any sign of the relentless force known as 'Meg.'

Johno's concern etched deep lines on his face as he raised his gaze from the equipment he'd been scrutinizing. "Senor Jake! I think you should take a look at these tanks! The gauges indicate only about half a tank of air in each."

Jake halted his inspection and cast his concentration on the ground between them. He then raised his eyes heavenward and snapped his fingers, a gesture that seemed to punctuate his realization. "Damn! We must've forgotten to refill them after the last dive. I remember now—those guys I took out had to cut their trip short due to an emergency in Buenos Aires. Bolo and I were rushing to help them pack and get ready to leave." His voice trailed off as he relived the memory.

Amy interjected, addressing Jake directly, a hint of desperation coloring her voice. "Well, it should still be enough, shouldn't it, Jake? A half tank should get us down and back with the C-4." She was clearly seeking reassurance from Jake, seeking an anchor of hope.

Jake took a moment to ponder, his gaze shifting from the ground to Amy. "Well, theoretically, it should suffice if we locate the wreck swiftly and can access the locker Johno mentioned without complications." He allowed another pause to linger. "However, it won't leave us much leeway for unexpected hurdles."

His gaze shifted from Amy to Tesoro, his tone growing more serious. "And there definitely won't be enough air to retrieve the plastique and confront our 'big friend' out there." He locked eyes with Johno, his tone turning frosty and determined. "Johno, I need you to understand this clearly: if that behemoth appears before we secure the C-4 and return to the boat, we abort the mission and high-tail it to shore. Do you comprehend?"

Johno nodded, his face displaying a mix of understanding and apprehension. "Yeah, Jake, I'm with you. Survival comes first."

"Good!" Jake returned, "Oh, Amy! I noticed that we have a couple of tins of coffee and a few bags of powdered eggs in one of the boxes we saved! Can you start a little fire over there while I finish checking everything out?" She indicated she would and hustled to clear a spot near her cabin to prepare the fire pit.

While this little drama was playing out on the island, a much more deadly scenario was unfolding, only about fifteen miles to the east. The destroyer escort, the 'Hijo del Rey,' steamed toward the island at top speed in response to the broken distress signal from the 'Maggie Mae' before her demise. The captain was an experienced seaman of approximately fifty-five years of age. His men loved him and responded to his orders like a well-oiled machine.

This day, he knew he was on a mission to the small island of 'Crandle's Keep' to rescue the Americans and some people there from a sea beast or something. His orders weren't very specific, and his superiors felt that his warship was more than enough to deal with this, more than likely, giant squid or oversized killer whale! The captain chuckled as he thought of the claims of a 'sea monster'... or some such thing... received by the young radioman before losing contact with the boat.

His reverie was interrupted by a report from his sonar operator. "Mi Captain! We have sonar contact!"

The older captain responded calmly, "Yes, Miguel! What do you have?" He left the command chair on the bridge and stood by the speaker.

"It appears to be two large masses, close together, moving toward us from the port bow, Sir! I cannot make a more accurate assessment because the signal is probably somewhat distorted by a thermal layer between!"

The captain thought the sonar had picked up a large school of fish or maybe even whales, but he was too experienced a mariner to take anything for granted. "Sound general quarters, Number One!"

The command was relayed, and the klaxon chimed. Like so many ants, disturbed in their mound, the men of the 'Hijo' scurried from whatever they were doing to their assigned combat location, and unlike the smaller patrol boat earlier, the much more heavily armed destroyer escort was prepared for any eventuality... except, perhaps, coincidence and fate!

The executive officer reported that all hands were at their battle stations and awaiting further orders.

"Good... very good, Number One!" The grizzled commander said with the pride of a father. "Okay, steady on! We'll continue, dead slow, until sonar clears the thermal layer and explicitly describes what he has down there!"

Our Big Boy had been carefully tracking a tightly clustered pod of gray whales that had the horrible misfortune of entering the deserted waters around the island... *his* waters! The whales, especially the adults, had sensed the danger stalking them and had maneuvered the pod into a very tight formation for security. The pod had also gradually sped up their trek around the island and rapidly left the 'dead' waters behind. Yet, their ingrained sense shouted danger!

He had patiently fallen in behind the pod, slowly closing in on them, when *he* felt the familiar vibrations coming from the surface in the distance ahead.

Still, *he* could feel the nearness of the trailing members of the pod, and *his* hunger was becoming overpowering. *He* dived down below the whales, increasing speed so that *he* narrowed the gap to only a few hundred yards, and was about to begin spiraling up to attack when the surface sound became much louder, and *he* now picked up a pulsing clanging, emanating from this large thing! Also, the surface 'creature' was moving very slowly, while the whales seemed to move off much more rapidly than before.

Therefore, *he* naturally chose to leave the whales for later and concentrate on the slow-moving 'thing' that made such a disturbance above!

While *he* began *his* dive to attack position below the 'Hijo,' the whales had unwittingly helped *his* cause! They had risen to the surface, giving the sonar operator on the 'Hijo' a clear 'ping,' confirmed by the lookouts a few moments later...whales!

Upon this notification, the old captain breathed a sigh of relief and perhaps issued his most tragic and misinformed command... "Alright, Number One! They're whales! He leaned to the intercom and quickly checked his sonar operator, just to make sure. "What does it look like, sonar?"

"One part of the pod has cleared us, Captain, well off the port bow and is moving away! The other part seems to be milling around below us... probably looking for garbage or something! I'll let you know when they clear, too!"

"That's fine, Sonar; let me know!" The captain smiled at his executive officer and ordered, "Secure from general quarters, Number One! This time, ensure Zuardi remembers to remove the fuses from the depth charges and lock the racks. We don't want one of his screw-ups setting a 'can' off under us." He chuckled, "It could ruin our whole day!"

The XO, short for an executive officer, laughed and had the boatswain's mate signal to secure, and all the men locked down their weapons and were leaving their combat stations... When the rest of the vessel erupted almost six feet out of the water, throwing many of the crew, already on deck, into the sea!

This strike had also caused one of the fully armed depth charges to fly off the ship's fantail and settle into the water directly below the propeller shafts and engine room! Since the heavy explosive pack's triggering device had not been set, the charge would begin at the shallowest point... a mere fifty feet below the vessel!

Meg had gone deep below the ship, and like many times before, *he'd* turned upward and increased *his* speed to such a point that his powerful momentum would likely kill or disable *his* prey, making it an easy feed for 'Meg's cave-like jaws.

This time, however, the massive impact failed to buckle the thick steel plating of the ship's keel, and the shock on the cartilage of *his* snout sent numbing feelings throughout *his* nervous system and caused *him* to swim quickly away from this 'thing' to regroup for another attack.

As *he* retreated into the dark inkiness below, a small drum fell into the water behind him and settled into the water under the ship.

On board, the captain was thrown into the bulkhead, face first, causing him to almost lose consciousness, but he had the presence of mind to turn the intercom switch to the radio room's setting. "Radio room!... this is Captain Romo!... Transmit 'S-O-S' and do not stop until I tell you!... Understand?"

"Si, Mi Captain!" came the trembling, high-pitched response.

The XO had also been shaken, but he came up the stairs where he'd fallen and reported the terrible news to his captain. "Sir! We have collided with something unbelievably large under the surface! The screws are entirely destroyed, and we are dead in the... He couldn't finish his report because, at this moment, the errant depth charge detonated under the rear section of the keel, again lifting the ship out of the water. This time, however, the explosive concussion ripped open the engine room hull like a tin can, and the sea poured into the compartment.

The deluge surged into the ship with an urgency that defied containment. The crew's attempts to secure the watertight doors were futile as the water rushed in, inundating the vessel's aft two-thirds. Trapped below deck, many crew members succumbed to the rapid drowning. Above, on the deck, the massive warship began to list, its stern sinking deeper into the unforgiving ocean.

As he bellowed into the wall-mounted microphone, the captain's voice cracked with desperation. "Radio! Have we received any response to the S-O-S? No answer!" Panic edged his words. "Radio! Answer me!" Still, the silence persisted. Unknown to the captain, the most recent explosion had thrown the transmitter cabinet onto the operator, killing him instantly. His distress signal, the 'S-O-S,' had indeed been picked up by an Argentine trawler, which had inadvertently strayed off course in pursuit of a bountiful catch. However, the trawler's skipper had grasped the essence of the emergency but not the location. Armed with this incomplete information, he broadcasted the relayed distress call on a general frequency, hoping other ears would catch it and continue relaying until it reached those who could aid the beleaguered vessel.

Amidst the chaos on the 'Hijo,' lifeboats were lowered, crammed with crew members fighting for survival. The captain stood on the bridge's railing, a somber witness to the scramble. Satisfied that most of his crew who weren't trapped below had found refuge on the lifeboats, he turned his attention to his escape. Beside him, the severely injured XO clung to his shoulder. As they surveyed the tumultuous waters, what they saw defied belief—the colossal fin approaching the lifeboats appeared to dwarf them.

The XO rubbed his eyes, questioning his senses, yet the looming fin remained real. And then, horror incarnate, the massive, tooth-lined maw rose from the water, enveloping one whole boat and a significant portion of another. The anguished cries of the dying or the dead resonated even at their distance.

Frozen in disbelief, the captain and the XO watched the grim spectacle unfold. Only the ship's sudden jolt shattered their trance, jerking the captain back to reality. The crewmen in the awaiting lifeboat gestured urgently for them to hurry, and the captain snapped into motion. They hurriedly descended the stairs, their eyes locked on the encroaching sea that devoured the ship's deck.

As they reached the landing, the captain instructed his crew to row the boat about thirty yards away and wait. Though the men seemed on the verge of protest, the captain's authoritative presence stifled any objections. With the XO in the care of his men, Captain Romo turned and stumbled toward the ship's forward armory. Frenziedly, he rummaged through crates until his hands found what he sought. With a duffel bag over his shoulder, he collected six items, his mind calculating the precise balance between the weight and his weakened state. He wished he could carry more, but he was acutely aware that any additional burden might pull him under in his current state of exhaustion.

With a heart racing in sync with the ship's impending descent, Captain Romo tied the bag's mouth shut. As he fled the exterior, his eyes met a nightmarish sight—a relentless deluge had conquered more than half the ship, and the bow was tilting sharply upwards, defying nature's balance.

Driven by instinct and desperation, he clambered over the railing, his heart hammering in his chest. A swan dive, hasty but calculated, propelled him into the depths of the azure ocean, the water swallowing him with a chilling embrace. Breaking the surface, gasping for air, he found salvation by the boat closing in on him. Hands reached out, yanking him from the water's clutches as the crew strained at the oars, propelling the vessel away from the impending whirlpool that the sinking ship would inevitably birth.

Wrapped in a blanket, the executive officer, who had endured the blast alongside the captain, inquired in hushed tones, "Mi Jefe,

390 SIDNEY ST. JAMES AND JEREMIAH SHERMAN

please, enlighten us. Why did you risk your life? Why did you return?" The captain's gaze encompassed all the faces on the small boat, all eyes but the XOs scanning the waters for the monstrous presence that had already claimed their comrades.

Though terror gripped him like a vice, the captain's warrior spirit refused to waver. He believed that any creature, no matter how colossal, could be injured or slain if it inhabited the ocean. Grasping the crumpled bag beneath him, he retrieved its contents, unveiling a revelation that could mean salvation or demise.

"My children..." The captain's voice was weary, yet resolute, as he spoke in his unique blend of Spanish dialect. He brought forth the object from the bag, his hands trembling slightly with a mixture of trepidation and resolve. With a slow, deliberate movement, he raised the softball-shaped thing, offering it for their collective scrutiny, each set of eyes gravitating toward it.

A chorus of gasps escaped from a couple of seamen, their voices laced with disbelief. "Bombas! The capitan has brought grenades with him to fight the thing!" Their words hung heavy with both hope and uncertainty. In contrast, the XO, a more educated soul among them, raised a voice of reason tinted with concern. "Mi capitan, permiso! But considering the colossal size of the creature, do you genuinely believe these will prove effective in ending its life?"

The captain's response carried an air of wisdom and quiet determination, his eyes reflecting the fear and determination that had spurred him on. "I cannot say for certain, Milio. Perhaps. But by the grace of God, they will, at the very least, deter it from making a meal of us. It's our sole chance." The rhythmic paddling ceased, oars lifted from the water and poised for action, the crew's eyes locked on their captain's face, expressions a blend of hope and fear.

Glancing around, they assessed the situation. Only three boats remained afloat, including theirs. The other two rode side by side, heavily laden and perilously close to the water's edge. Panic-stricken men on those boats pushed against the waves with desperate strokes as though racing to outpace an impending doom. The captain's heart tightened in realization; the same nightmarish fate that had befallen their crewmates now awaited these beleaguered souls.

The passing minutes seemed interminable, the gap between their boat and the others growing until the distant vessels appeared as mere specks on the horizon. An illusion of fortune's favor seemed to embrace them, or so the captain dared to hope. Yet, in the chaos of survival, such respite was fleeting.

Abruptly, as all eyes strained toward the two stricken boats, the waters convulsed in a display of raw power. The sea surged and churned, a towering column of foam and fury engulfing the vessels. The creature emerged from within this watery maelstrom, its immense form rending through the air with terrifying force. One boat met its doom as the creature's bulk crushed it beneath its weight, while another was lifted skyward, its crew flung into the void, an image of horror etched forever in the minds of those who bore witness.

The harrowing echoes of screams carried across the expanse of water, a horrifying testament to the monstrous fury that had descended upon them. Those gut-wrenching cries persisted, a haunting symphony of death until the insatiable creature claimed all that had survived its initial onslaught. Desperation and terror lingered in the air, suffusing the atmosphere with a palpable dread that seemed to hang like a heavy shroud.

In the ensuing half hour, the beleaguered group in the final boat clung to one another, their minds a maelstrom of prayer, anticipation, and anguished watchfulness. The captain's ears caught one man's plea, a personal entreaty that cut through the chaos. "Madre de Dios! Hear our prayer! Please deliver us from this spawn of Hell!" It was a cry born of desperation, a soul teetering on the precipice of hopelessness. Yet, amid their hearts pounding, there was only silence – no divine intervention, no respite from the looming doom.

Eyes wide with dread, they scanned the expanse around them, anxiously awaiting the telltale signs of the monster's approach. The tension was a living entity, a malevolent force that squeezed their hearts and clouded their thoughts. Each wave that lapped against the boat's hull seemed to whisper of impending doom, a chilling reminder of their vulnerability in the face of an unstoppable predator.

Amid their fear, the captain's gaze fell upon a young, muscular seaman named Ramos, his fingers trembling on the edge of his sanity. The captain's voice edged with authority and compassion, piercing the ominous air. "Ramos! You possess the strength that I lack in my twilight years. When I give the word, pull the pin and hurl the grenade so that it lands directly in the beast's path – near enough for the full force of the explosion to reach it. Do you comprehend?" Ramos nodded, his gaze fixed on the small explosive device that held the fate of their lives.

The creature advanced, an embodiment of terror propelled by unseen forces. Their collective breaths hitched as its immense form drew nearer – one hundred and fifty yards, then one hundred, then seventy-five. The moment of reckoning was at hand. "Now, Ramos! Pull the pin and throw it!" The captain's command shattered the suffocating silence.

With clenched determination, Ramos acted. He pulled the pin, releasing the tension that bound the fate of all on board. The explosive left his hand, arcing toward the creature that had unleashed a torrent of anguish upon them. The world seemed to hold its breath, time suspended in the wake of this life-altering decision.

The explosion reverberated through the water, a shockwave of raw force that reached the creature's senses. In the realm of the monstrous beast, chaos erupted anew. The grenade's shrapnel tore through its flesh, inflicting pain that radiated like fire. The creature twisted away in agony, a frenetic whirlwind of wrath, unleashing geysers and churning waves that threatened to engulf the boat.

Yet, despite their meager victory, their fate remained uncertain. The captain's eyes never left the retreating beast, an unspoken understanding passing between him and his men. He knew their respite was short-lived, that the creature's descent into the abyss was but a temporary retreat.

Seizing the moment, the captain tore open the bag of grenades, distributing them among his crew. Urgency fueled their actions, a desperate attempt to inflict further harm upon the creature that had become the embodiment of their terror. "Quickly! Throw them where you think it will dive! We must wound it further, force it to avoid us!" His voice trembled with a mixture of fear and resolve.

With determination etched on their faces, the crew followed their captain's lead. The grenades were armed, pins pulled, and the small explosives hurled with a mix of hope and desperation. The sea absorbed their efforts, the explosions punctuating the waters. Their collective hearts raced, the vibrations of terror mingling with the fading echoes of detonations.

Amid their turmoil, the creature's response was a symphony of agony and rage. Though not lethal, the explosions left their mark, inflicting pain upon an already wounded adversary. And so, with its tormentors still in pursuit, the creature retreated, driven by a visceral need to escape the searing pain that now plagued its every movement. Its destination was clear: the island, which had once been its domain, was now its refuge from the relentless onslaught of destruction.

The battle between man and monster had only just begun, and as the creature sought solace on the shores of "Crandle's Keep," a small boat of determined souls clung to a glimmer of hope, their journey far from over.

JAKE AND TESORO HAD finished their preparations, and Amy had managed to scrounge up the fixings for a Spartan breakfast of bad-tasting coffee and thick cream of wheat from the pile of rescued items.

They had just finished forcing down the concoction, and Jake was tying a length of rope around the long length of pipe that would be lowered into the water along the edge of the remaining pier for Amy to use as an alarm if necessary.

Tesoro was adjusting the air tank's support straps and double-checking the underwater flashlight when he looked up and said, "Jake, I suppose we should go and get this done, no?... I mean, it gets no earlier, and each minute we wait is a minute we don't see that big son-of-a- bitch, right?":

Jake saw that Johno was really strung out, and even he felt the mounting stress and apprehension. So, he agreed. "Yeah, you're right, Johno!... Amy! Whaddaya Say? Ready to watch over us while we go down there?"

Amy's gaze locked onto Jake's, and in that fleeting moment, she caught a glimpse of something more profound than the words they exchanged. Resignation seemed to emanate from his features, like a shadow cast by the weight of their impending task. And what was that? A hint of farewell? A silent understanding that words couldn't capture?

With a voice steadied by her determination, Amy replied, "Of course I am! If he comes anywhere near this lagoon, you'll know about it!" She gripped the hammer in her hand, her knuckles white, as if channeling her conviction through the steel tool.

A feeble smile graced Jake's lips, an attempt to convey confidence in their plan, yet his eyes betrayed a different story. Within their depths swirled an undercurrent of sorrow and regret, emotions too complex to put into words. It was a look that Amy knew all too well, a mixture of acceptance and yearning, a recognition that their time together might be measured in moments.

"Good! That's great, Amy!" Jake's voice held a veneer of reassurance, masking the depths of emotion beneath. His facade of resolve couldn't conceal the tenderness in his gaze or the unspoken sentiments that hung heavily in the air.

In that fleeting exchange, their unspoken connection spoke volumes. It was a conversation of glances and shared understanding that transcended words. The world around them faded as they stood suspended in time, their hearts murmuring what their lips dared not utter. As the weight of their mission pressed upon them, Amy and Jake found solace in the unspoken bond that tied them together, which seemed to grow stronger as they faced the unknown future that awaited them.

Johno had observed the interchange between Amy and Jake and felt that he had to intercede to diffuse the harsh feelings generated by the two. "Hey! Jake! How 'bout we do this thing? No time like the present, right?" His speech was sharp and forceful, and it had the desired effect.

Jake snapped to the younger man, who acceded to Tesoro's suggestion. "I guess you're right!" Jake gave one last glance to Amy and stood up, slinging the tank pack over one shoulder and grasping the spear gun, flippers, and spears in the other. "Okay, Johno! Let's go!" He strode toward the harbor.

The trio stood together, an unlikely alliance forged in dire circumstances. Two appeared to be the most unlikely candidates for this perilous mission. Yet, upon closer scrutiny, Jake defied any preconceived notions. With a demeanor that belied his rugged exterior, he emanated the aura of a seasoned SEAL, every inch the warrior he had been in his previous life. To those who dared to delve into his eyes, a chilling transformation would have been unveiled—a steely resolve, a frigid focus that could send shivers down the spine of even the most stalwart of observers.

Once filled with warmth and laughter, these eyes now bore the mark of a lethal predator. They mirrored the internal battle raging within him—an internal reckoning with the reality of what lay ahead. He was not merely a defender of lives but a harbinger of death, poised to execute his mission with unwavering purpose.

As their journey led them to the terminus of the remaining pier, Jake's gaze remained fixed on the horizon, a calculated intensity gleaming in his eyes. Amid the desolation of their surroundings, his unwavering focus illuminated a path forward. He gestured for Johno to indicate where Tesoro believed his boat's stern had descended beneath the water's surface.

In this pivotal moment, their collective fate hung in the balance, teetering between survival and annihilation. As the two warriors prepared to dive into the depths, their resolve and determination were etched upon their faces, each embodying the spirit of a survivor, each step an affirmation of their will to overcome the impossible.

Being savvy to the ways of the sea, even at such a young age, Johno felt that his reckoning was very accurate, and he pointed to a spot about 150 yards out, on a line, directly heading for the mouth of the harbor.

While they were in the final stages of rigging up for the dive, Jake mentally noted their intended underwater destination. When they both had checked each other's tanks, harness, and regulator, Jake went over and helped Amy, who was struggling with the installation of the long pipe, and with the big man's help, the job was finished rapidly.

Jake shifted his focus to Amy, a sense of urgency underlying his periodic glances toward the harbor's entrance. With a tenderness that contrasted the gravity of the situation, he placed both hands on her shoulders and spoke in a voice that carried the weight of imminent danger. "Amy... Listen carefully. Look at the opening to the sea, right there, and then at the spot we're headed to. If you spot anything, even the slightest anomaly, I need you to pound on this pipe with everything you've got. Keep pounding until we resurface or until you feel the slightest inkling of danger yourself. And if that happens..." He paused, his grip on her shoulders unconsciously tightening, eliciting a wince from Amy. Realizing his inadvertent intensity, Jake quickly released his hold.

"Jake!" It was Amy's turn to show her courage, and she placed a small, cold hand on the side of Jake's face as she answered him. "I can see what you mean! If 'Meg' does show up, you won't have much time to react and try to escape...even if I see *him* on the other side of the portal! So, my big darling!..." She stroked his cheek gently. "You can rest assured that I will do my part because I want to see where we go from here!" With this, she leaned up and kissed Jake quickly on the lips.

Tesoro had been watching, and he was experiencing feelings of respect and admiration for Jake that he'd never let himself admit existed in the past. Then, he cleared his throat, breaking Jake's invisible bond with Amy.

"Yeah! I know, Johno! Let's get wet!" He walked over to the smaller diver and sat next to him, where both of them donned their flippers and, after spitting in their masks to break any condensation, they put these on, too.

Finally, they stood facing Amy, waved at her, and then jumped backward in unison into the blue water behind them!

The water was murky and cold, and after switching on their lanterns, Jake motioned for Johno to follow him. After referring to his compass, Jake swam with slow, measured strokes on the line that Johno had pointed out and downward at the bottom.

On the pier, Amy felt a chill along her spine, and it wasn't from the winds, which were beginning to pick up from the south. She was having her doubts about this mission. *"Maybe,"* she thought, *"we should have tried to tough it out and wait for help to arrive. Surely, Lamar had gotten the message out, and their salvation was only days... perhaps hours... away!"* She shook her head to clear away these thoughts, though, and, instead, watched the opening to the ocean, unflinching, with the binoculars she wore around her neck.

Meg had swum entirely around the island upon *his* arrival from the encounter with the rescue ship, but *he'd* found none of the plentiful food that *he'd* frequently discovered in recent days. Therefore, he was beginning another tour when *he* saw two gray objects hurrying across *his* path, from the ocean and toward the island.

The two dolphins had sensed *his* presence several minutes earlier, and the terror this had caused in their advanced brains and nervous systems had driven them to make a dash for the relative safety of the harbor lagoon, where they had felt a sense of security in the past.

Of course, their agility and speed would have protected them from the mountainous creature that threatened them, but their instincts only served notice of the present danger and not their natural ability to avoid it. Thus, the sprint for the protected inner waters...where Jake and Tesoro swam!

Jake had been swimming along the bottom of the harbor in a slow, back-and-forth, 'grid-like' pattern, looking carefully for the recently wrecked section of the boat. Tesoro was swimming around an area adjacent to Jake's in an expanding spiral, also flashing his lantern back and forth.

Suddenly, Johno's light caught a flash of white from a patch of Sargasso-like vines to his right, and he scurried to investigate. To his relief, it was. Indeed, the aft part of the boat they'd been searching for, he took the hilt of his knife and banged it against his own tank to attract Jake's attention.

Jake heard the clanging from about twenty yards away and saw the flash of Tesoro's light, dimly, through the murky water. He knew the clanging noise and bolted through the water to Johno's location.

Upon reaching the wreck, Jake found Johno peering down into the black opening of the hatchway, the key ring for the locker in his hand, but the smaller man was delaying entrance for some reason.

Jake went up to Johno, close enough to see his face through the mask's lens, and pointed adamantly at the opening, following with a shrug.

Jake saw the look of fright on Johno's face behind the mask and realized that the other man was afraid of entering the darkened interior of the wooden craft below them.

Jake understood the situation's urgency and knew he couldn't spend time soothing Johno's apprehensions. Without words, he extended his large hand, pointing at the key ring in Johno's grasp with his other hand. Johno's nod conveyed his understanding, and he placed the key in Jake's open palm, which Jake closed firmly to prevent the shifting currents from taking the precious key away.

Before diving into the dark recesses of the boat, Jake ensured that Johno was looking at him. He used two fingers to gesture at his faceplate and then made a circular motion with his arm, conveying that Johno was to keep a vigilant lookout while Jake retrieved the desired items. Before Jake's descent, Tesoro tapped him and signaled toward the hatchway, indicating the locker's location.

Jake responded with a reassuring index finger-thumb circle, indicating that he understood, before disappearing beneath the deck.

Alone in the water, Johno felt a chilling sensation crawl up his spine, unrelated to the cold temperature. Turning in a continuous circle, his imagination conjured up looming, monstrous shapes in the water around him. Though it was just his imagination at play, these moments would shape the next half-hour into the most pivotal and ominous in Johno's turbulent life.

Meanwhile, Jake navigated through debris and obstacles, his flashlight casting erratic shadows. He finally spotted the doors of the gray steel cabinet in the corner. He carefully worked the key into the lock, his breath held as he turned the key. After a resistant start, the tumblers surrendered, and the latch clicked open.

Inside the cabinet, an array of switches, wires, and illegal fishing paraphernalia greeted his searching gaze. Amid the items, Jake discovered an ammo box marked 'blasting caps.' Opening it, he found a collection of copper-cased underwater blasting caps with wire pigtails. Securing them in his belt pouch, he continued his search. At last, his fingers brushed against six large wax-paper-wrapped cubes emblazoned with the ominous label "U.S. GOVT., C-4, High Explosives, HANDLE WITH EXTREME CARE!" Safely stowing them in a mesh sack tied to his belt, Jake prepared to gather Johno and return to shore to prepare the explosive package.

As he adjusted his course to follow the two fleeing dolphins, Jake navigated the narrow passage again, slowing his pace. This allowed the agile dolphins to dash toward the far end of the lagoon, maneuvering through the pier's maze of poles and cross members. They sought refuge from the impending threat they sensed.

Above, on the wooden planks, Amy focused on the harbor entrance, her eyes scanning for the distinctive fin that signaled 'Meg's' arrival. Beside her lay the heavy hammer, and she peered through binoculars. Suddenly, the first dolphin leaped into the air, mere feet from her. The surprise elicited a scream and sent her stumbling backward, arms flailing like an injured bird trying to escape. In the chaos, her hand struck the hammer, sending it tumbling into the water below.

"Shit!" She exclaimed at the loss of the hammer. "Damn dolphins!" She watched the two mammals dashing to and fro and exclaimed. "Now's not the time for a show, guys!" Then, she looked up and saw the tall fin disappearing beneath the surface...inside the harbor itself!

"Oh, Christ, no!" She realized that letting the dolphins momentarily capture her attention could prove catastrophic for the two men below.

She then noticed that she'd lost the hammer and began to panic. Her eyes snapped to every inch of her surroundings, searching for something... anything... that could send a 'clanging' sound to the men in the water...now with the giant fish in close proximity!

After a few seconds, she saw a broken piece of the destroyed pipe system, which fed the CAT engines, and she ran gingerly over and tried to work the four-foot length of pipe free. She kicked it, worked it with her hands, and, after a few seconds, it gave and broke off in her hands.

With determination, Amy clutched the piece of metal like a makeshift baseball bat, its cold weight a strange comfort in her trembling grip. Returning to her original spot, she swung the metal with desperate fervor against the tied pipe, creating an urgent metallic rhythm, a frantic *clang-clang-clang* reverberating through the air.

Every resounding strike echoed with her hope and desperation, a beacon calling out in the eerie silence of the night. *"God! I hope I'm not too late!"* she whispered to herself between breathless beats, the tension in her voice betraying the intensity of her fear.

Meanwhile, Tesoro remained vigilant, his eyes darting in all directions, his heart racing as the anticipation of an impending threat hung heavy in the air. Unbeknownst to him, a mere arm's length away, Jake was preparing to emerge from the submerged wreck, his flashlight piercing the darkness as he made his way toward the hatchway.

Yet, in this critical moment, the beam of light became a fateful beacon, attracting Johno's attention. His focus, drawn to the glimmer in the darkness, robbed him of awareness, leaving him vulnerable and oblivious. In this vulnerable instant, an unimaginable terror loomed closer, creeping up on him at a chilling pace, waiting to strike.

Jake's head emerged from the hatch, and he saw Tesoro watching him. Jake also saw, behind Johno and coming on rapidly, the mountainous shape that... "Oh, God, No!" He thought as he expelled large air bubbles in a muffled scream and pointed, panic-stricken, over Tesoro's shoulder before diving back into the dark hallway he'd just come from.

Johno saw Jake's panic and stiffened in shock and fear. He forced himself to turn slowly, his eyes trying to see around the sidewall of his mask! When he had almost finished the one-hundred eighty-degree turn, he felt the water begin to carry him on some new current, and he snapped the rest of the way to see the tremendous cave-like jaws opening and closing the last thirty-foot gap. Johno only had time to whisper one final thought to himself, and his bladder voided in total fear... *"Oh, God, forgive me!"*

Then, he was swept, uncontrollably, into the depths of 'Meg's' throat, where the pressure of the surrounding muscles crushed the life out of his frail body!

Jake had withdrawn far enough into the darkened corridor that the bubbles from his tank were contained within the enclosed spaces around him and, thus, not in the surrounding waters, where they would inevitably attract the deadly denizen swimming there! As it passed outside the opening, he saw the seemingly endless gray mass, and Jake knew that Tesoro had faced the ultimate justice for his past guilt!

Jake allowed himself a few seconds to grieve? ...he was surprised that he actually felt pains of regret for his former arch nemesis' passing, but this feeling passed as quickly as it had come to be replaced by an instinctually sharp survival mode that caused him to ready himself for combat...a sensation that came flooding into his conscious thought from his SEAL experiences in times long past!

He readied the spear gun with an explosive-tipped projectile that he would instead not use because he knew that, if he did so and missed, the resulting concussion underwater could incapacitate him, at best, and seriously injure him at worst.

Still, the spear did represent a formidable weapon of discouragement as a last resort.

Jake inched his way forward, cautiously pushing his head through the hatchway, his heart pounding like a distant drum. The darkness engulfed him, rendering his initial survey futile. Panic hovered on the edge of his consciousness as his mind struggled to decipher the shadows. He blinked, willing his eyes to adjust, and then, with a surge of dread, he shifted his gaze upwards.

The monstrous silhouette was there, a dark shape cutting through the water above. Time seemed to slow as he realized that the nightmare was real—Meg was there, just as fearsome and colossal as he remembered. The realization was punctuated by the frantic, rhythmic banging of the pipe—a signal of terror orchestrated by Amy.

Amy, perched on the pier, had her breath snatched away as the towering dorsal fin materialized only two hundred yards from her position. Frozen for an instant, she sprang into action with an instinctive urgency. The heavy piece of metal felt alien in her grip as she swung it against the pipe, each resounding clang a desperate cry for help, a heartbeat syncopating with the chilling presence of Meg moving ever closer.

As she had expected, 'Meg' changed direction and moved in a sweeping circle, bringing *him* onto a course directly toward her spot on the wharf! She banged a little longer until she was confident that the guys had heard her, then threw down the pipe and sprinted for the safety of the island's higher ground.

Below, Jake saw the gargantuan's response to the banging and *its* predictable path toward the source. He also heard the 'clang-clang-clang' stop and knew that Amy would be running for safety.

Now, Jake saw his chance and, drawing on all the strength he could muster, he swam like a madman along the bottom, in the direction of the previously wrecked pier pilings, where he felt he could hide until an opening presented itself for him to climb up and sprint to the security of the land above.

When he'd almost reached his target, he saw the monster veer slightly in his direction, causing the creature to only brush the pier, leaving it intact!

Jake made a quick mental calculation and knew that 'Meg' would reach him before he could reach the pilings. Therefore, he took the spear gun from his shoulder while still swimming with his flippers at top speed and readied to fire. He was sure he would be critically hurt at this distance, but he had no choice! His finger squeezed the trigger. But, before the gun ejected the destructive missile, a much smaller gray shape zipped past his shoulder, directly toward the approaching leviathan!

Jake was knocked head-over-heels by the near miss, and he lost his grip on the spear gun, sending it into the silt and vegetation below.

When Jake regained his orientation, he saw that the two dolphins had engaged 'Meg' in a crazy game of 'chicken,' challenging their enormous opponent and causing *him* to turn away from Jake, at least for the moment, to pursue these two daring and agile 'pests!'

Jake took an instant to see if he could recover the spear gun, but failing to do so, he continued his race to the docks.

Upon reaching the forest of pilings, he took off his flippers and scrambled up to the top and onto the jagged edge of the remaining decking.

After catching his breath, he looked at the water's surface and saw 'Meg's' fin moving erratically over near the entrance rocks. He jumped to his feet, slung his tanks, belt, bag, and flippers over his shoulder, and dashed for the little knoll above the pier, where Amy waved breathlessly!

As Jake cleared the pier and began ascending the dockside hill, Amy rushed into his arms, relief flooding her voice. "Thank heaven, Jake! I thought I'd lost you! The dolphins distracted me, and 'Meg' entered the harbor before I spotted him!"

Her gaze shifted between Jake and the sea before returning to him. "Oh! Where's John...?" The words caught in her throat as Jake silenced her with a somber shake and whispered response. "Didn't make it!"

Together, they fixed their eyes on the colossal tail, its movement gradually veiling behind the cliffs that framed the harbor's tranquil waters. Jake's voice carried a note of certainty. "He'll be back when he gets hungry. And we'll need to get this ready for him." He held up the wet mesh bag, its contents—six cubed packages—glistening ominously.

"The C-4?" Amy confirmed with a mixture of concern and determination.

"Yeah, and it looks like enough to level a good-sized building," Jake replied, his gaze fixed on the explosive potential in his hands. Suddenly, a transformation swept across his face, unsettling Amy. His eyes locked onto hers with an intense coldness that pierced through her. "It's certainly enough to blow that big bastard all the way to Hell and beyond."

However, Amy's practicality intervened. "Well, I'm sure it is, but how do we get 'Meg' into the right position to get the most out of the explosives...without blowing ourselves up with it?"

The determination in Jake's expression gave way to consternation as he stared out at the sea. "Damn!" The bag of explosives met the ground with a rough thud, causing Amy to wince involuntarily.

"Don't worry, sweetheart!" Jake reassured as he drew Amy into a tight embrace. "This is really stable stuff!" He retrieved a small bag from his waist pouch and displayed its contents. "Look! These are what's needed to set off the explosive. They're blasting caps—smaller explosive sticks that trigger the larger reaction." Amy nodded, her worries somewhat eased by her trust in Jake.

Jake wrestled with the pack of caps, his frustration evident. After a few minutes, he turned to Amy, his eyebrows furrowed. He exhaled sharply and admitted, "Everything is too rough right now. I just can't think straight!" He met Amy's eyes, his desperation palpable. "Let's go over to the cabin and try to relax. Maybe I can come up with something there. What do you say?"

Amy gripped Jake's arms, her voice tender but determined. "Try to regain your composure, Jake. I know it's easier said than done, considering all we've been through." She locked her gaze onto his, her sincerity unwavering. "But we're the only two left, and we can't be certain if the Navy has received the message. We might be stranded here for weeks. And I don't believe we could endure that long without food and water. Could we?" Her words carried a weight that echoed their dire circumstances.

Jake's expression softened somewhat, and he pulled Amy to his chest and hugged her tightly for a long time. Neither of them said anything, both lost in worried thoughts.

After a bit, Jake had calmed, and they walked, in close tandem, to the temporary stockpile of salvaged material and equipment in front of Amy's cabin.

Jake made a fire from some dried brush and a busted old wooden swing that he'd retrieved from the side of the cabin, where it had deteriorated for a long time. At the same time, Amy rummaged through the provisions and ran across the cheese cloth-wrapped chunk of sea lion meat that had been salt & air curing since the fire. She cut half of the roast and trimmed and washed some roots, similar to turnips, and when Jake had the fire going, he put the roots in a pot of tolerable water and stuck the roast on a long stick that he supported over the fire, with an 'X' of two sticks tied together.

Soon, they had a well-cooked dinner, and Jake could boil a pot of horrible coffee from an old tin he found in one of the boxes. When the meat was cooked and had a charcoal-blackened appearance, Jake removed it from the fire and stuck the spit into the ground so the roast could cool.

Amy had located some old tin plates, pitted worn utensils and placed them in two settings on the two-chair makeshift table on her cabin's porch.

The sun was sinking in the west when they sat down to eat, and neither cared much for their meal, less than appetizing, smell, and taste. They knew, however, that they had to keep up their strength if they expected to have any hope of facing the coming challenges.

Sitting across from each other, the silence between Amy and Jake was filled only by the sound of their tentative nibbling on the meager meal before them. After a while, Amy emitted a humorless chuckle, her eyes fixed on a piece of meat skewered by her fork. "Don't you find it a little humorous?"

Looking up, Jake's expression became inquisitive. "What?" he queried.

"Well, here we are, trapped on this island... probably the only people within a thousand miles... by some prehistoric beast that wants to make us his next meal..." Jake tried to interject, but Amy continued. "And!" She brandished the chunk of meat to emphasize her point. "We are eating the same food that he's probably eating tonight! I just find it a little curious, that's all!" With that, she popped the meat into her mouth and returned her focus to her plate.

Jake saw her point and gave a nonchalant nod before returning to his food. However, only a few seconds passed before he snapped his fingers and exclaimed, "Wait a minute! What did you say?"

Taken aback by his sudden outburst, Amy replied cautiously, "Well, I... uh... I said I found it curious that we're probably eating the same thing that 'Meg' is eating!" Her own confusion was apparent.

"Exactly!" Jake's eyes widened with excitement. "That's how we're going to kill the bastard!" His excitement seemed almost giddy, and Amy regarded him as though she thought he'd lost his mind.

"Okay! So, you want to share this wondrous revelation with me... or what?" Amy's words conveyed frustration, her patience wearing thin with Jake's disjointed thoughts.

"Oh, sorry!" Jake realized Amy hadn't entirely caught onto his train of thought. "Look! You're absolutely correct! 'Meg' loves sea lions! They're probably his favorite dish!" His enthusiasm was palpable as he continued. "Okay! We need a way to get the explosive in a place near 'him' where it will do the most damage, right?"

Amy's expression brightened with understanding, albeit hesitantly. "Right...so..."

Jake wasn't about to let the opportunity slip away to explain his plan. "So-o-o... we kill a sea lion bull, stuff his carcass with the explosive, and hang him off the pier, where his blood gets in the water! 'Meg' catches the scent, comes to claim his dinner, and, when he's swallowed the bait...BOOM! We set off the C-4, and no more 'Meg!' What do you think?"

"Brilliant!" Amy responded sincerely, though a shadow of concern lingered in her eyes. "The only thing is, how do we hang the body of a large enough bull from the lagoon to the pier down there?" Her gaze shifted to Jake, a mix of skepticism and support.

In an instant, Jake's demeanor shifted from elation to doubt. "There is that," he conceded. "I guess we could drag it."

Amy eyed him skeptically, unsure if he was serious. "You aren't serious, are you? It's just you and me, Jake! One of those big bulls could weigh what..." She trailed off, not needing to finish her thought.

"Alright! Alright! You're right!" Jake's enthusiasm was tempered. "I was grasping at straws! Let me think about it! But I still think it's the way to go!" He pressed on, determination in his voice.

Amy shared Jake's belief that the idea held promise but struggled with the logistics. "I agree, Jake! We just have to figure out how to get a big lion from the other end of the island to the pier."

Jake was bobbing his head, slowly and absent-mindedly, in agreement with her remarks while thinking about a solution to this very problem.

They spent the next hour or so discussing all sorts of potential procedures...and then systematically shooting each of them down!

After brainstorming to the point of mental exhaustion, they agreed to sleep on the issue and were preparing to turn in when Amy doubled over and screamed in pain.

"Oh, God, Jake! I think something doesn't agree with me!" Jake grabbed her arm and helped ease her onto the porch swing. She was sweating now and obviously in severe agony.

Grimacing, she asked Jake for tissue... quickly... and pushed him away as she ran like a drunken sailor around the cabin to some bushes beyond.

Jake knew food poisoning when he saw it; in this case, it seemed severe!

Amy returned in a half-hour and appeared pale and weakened. She, too, realized what her problem was. "Jake! This isn't good...not good at all! If I keep this up, I will become severely dehydrated..." She panted and wheezed. "...and I won't even be able to walk much by tomorrow. Is there anything in the boxes that might serve as a cathartic?" Jake was becoming deeply concerned about Amy! Under normal conditions, a quick trip to the emergency room would cure everything!... However, there wasn't an emergency room...or medical facility for a thousand miles.

"Tell me, Amy! Are your muscles beginning to cramp yet?" Jake knew the symptoms.

"Some, but not bad!... Why? What are you thinking?" She inquired.

Jake was rummaging through the boxes. "I'm not sure, but I found an old bag of rack salt, and we have a little passable water left. If I boil the water well and dissolve a good portion of the salt, it should serve as your paregoric and a replacement for some of the electrolytes you're losing to dehydration! What do you think?"

He watched her features contort briefly before she responded. "Should work! I'm game for anything now! I'm not sure I can straighten up at all!" She was frail by this time.

Jake poured a half-coffee pot full of water and re-stoked the dying fire. The water was boiling within ten minutes, and Jake let it do so for another five minutes before adding two palms full of salt crystals to the pot.

The mixture returned to a boil, and Jake, again, waited a few minutes for all the salt to dissolve. After being sure that no salt was left in the bottom, Jake used a rag to pour a steaming cup of the liquid for Amy, and after it had cooled sufficiently, she held her nose and drank as much of the brew as she could.

It hadn't even been down for a minute when Amy rolled to her feet and bolted to the far railing. Here, she bent over the wooden bar and heaved uncontrollably for what seemed a long time to Jake. In reality, it took only a couple of minutes.

Finally, Amy turned and leaned back against the railing, her face turned, eyes closed, to the heavens. "Oh, man!" She exclaimed. "This is a bad bout, Jake! It really is!"... But I think this did the trick!"

Jake stroked her cheek, which felt cold and clammy, and asked gently. "Do you think you can lie down for a while, or do you believe you're going to have more...ur...episodes?"

She smiled despite her discomfort. "I think I can lie down...at least for a while if you'll give me a hand inside."

Gently, Jake wrapped an arm around her, his touch comforting as he guided her toward the bed. With careful consideration, he fluffed her pillow and gently helped her slip off her shoes. Amy settled onto her side, her body still bearing the residual tension that prevented her from fully stretching out. Leaning in, Jake planted a soft kiss on her cheek, his warmth evident as he whispered that he'd be outside on the porch if she required anything. Retrieving two cushions from the well-worn sofa, he fashioned a makeshift bed on the porch and stretched out. The moment's tranquility embraced him, and before he could even realize it, sleep's embrace took him under.

CHAPTER 22
A Cold Chill in the Air

The following day broke with a colder chill in the air, and Jake woke with a start when a chilly gust swirled across the porch.

He looked at his watch and saw that it was almost eight in the morning, and when he tried to stand, rubbing the sleep from his eyes, he found that his muscles ached terribly. *"No doubt..."* He muttered to himself. *"...from the luxurious bed I slept on!"* He chuckled at his own humor and then thought of Amy.

He rushed into the cabin and found her, limbs askew, sleeping soundly; she was probably in the position she had been in all night. He was worried by how pale she still looked, so he sat beside her and gently stroked the hair off her forehead, causing her to stir and, eventually, to wake.

She looked up at Jake through still-tired eyes, and after adjusting to her weakened state, she placed her own hand on Jake's cheek and frowned slightly.

"I think I'm pretty much over the main bout, Jake... but I don't believe I will be strong enough to help you today!"

Jake smiled softly and said. "Don't worry about me! I think I've got the answer to our little dilemma." Amy raised her eyebrows as if to say..."Oh! And what is that?"

I'll shoot a large enough bull over by the lagoon, stuff the explosive in him... there! Then, I'll drag him over and hoist him under the rock bridge, where the blood can drip into the inlet beneath."

Amy began to see the logic, and she nodded slowly in agreement while Jake completed the description of his plan.

"When I get the thing secured, I can stand off, and, when "our big friend" comes for *his* prize, I'll wait until *he's* swallowed the carcass... then, I'll push the button, and, bang! No more 'Meg!'"

Amy lay there, staring down at a spot in the vicinity of her toes, thinking about the plan, and after several minutes, she voiced her only genuine concern. "Well, it sounds like it should work... but when you are getting the carcass into position, won't you be terribly exposed should *he* show up earlier than expected?" Her voice carried her deep feelings for Jake, and he, in turn, displayed his feelings for her by leaning over to kiss her briefly before answering.

"Of course, there's always a risk, Amy! But I'll try to get that done as quickly as possible to minimize any exposure, okay?" Amy hesitantly indicated that she concurred, but then, what real choice did either of them have... they both knew it!

With deft hands, Jake coaxed the flickering embers of the fire back to life, coaxing out tendrils of warmth from the remaining logs. A kettle of leftover coffee was suspended above the flames, sending the familiar, comforting aroma wafting through the air. It was a small gesture, but he knew the brew's warmth would offer Amy some solace.

After ensuring Amy was settled as comfortably as the circumstances allowed, Jake turned his attention to her well-being. He laid out a small flare gun kit within her reach, a signal of safety in case of unforeseen trouble. Jake then meticulously assembled a duffle bag, selecting and packing the essentials he'd need for the task ahead. Satisfied with his preparations, he slung his trusty rifle across his back, fingers brushing against the cold metal reassuringly.

Shouldering the duffle bag, he ventured towards the trail that snaked its way through the island's foliage. Each step carried a sense of determination, his mind resolute in its purpose. The rustle of leaves beneath his boots provided a rhythmic cadence as he made his way to the distant lagoon.

Challenging combat assignments had not been unfamiliar to Jake in years past, and he regressed to that heightened state of awareness and focused intensity inherent in most warriors about to face death in one form or another!

When he had traversed the trail to a point just short of the spring at the end, he slowed and crept cautiously through the final leafy barrier that separated him from the broad expanse of still, clear blue water of the lagoon in front of him.

Crouching, he brought his rifle to his shoulder and scanned the pool's perimeter from right to left. He did, in fact, spot two mid-sized sea lions on the far opposite bank, scurrying themselves, but he knew that either of them would present a significant logistics challenge, getting them all the way to the lake. No, there had to be an animal closer!

He had finished his initial scan of the surrounding area and was starting back in the opposite direction when a bush near the water's edge waved at the edge of his scope's view field.

Jake took a breath and steadied his attention on that spot. After a few moments of watching the bushes move, a large male burst from the vegetation and slid, noisily, into the water.

"Damn!" Jake thought. "That would have been a perfect candidate!" But Jake watched helplessly as the large animal swam out from the shore, and he knew that, as long as the sea lion was in the lagoon, it would be practically impossible for one person to retrieve the body!"

Suddenly, as if in answer to Jake's silent prayer, the bull wheeled erratically, made a bee-line back to the shore, lumbered up onto the bank about twenty yards nearer Jake than its previous spot, and disappeared into some tall reeds and sparse shrubs.

Jake squatted low and began a silent stalk, moving in absolute silence toward where he felt the beast would be.

He checked the rifle one final time to ensure it was loaded and ready to fire and readied the weapon before him.

As Jake moved with purpose through the undergrowth, his senses were on high alert, attuned to the primal rhythm of the island. The silence was punctuated only by the distant sounds of the lagoon's gentle waves and the rustle of leaves underfoot. His focus was unwavering as he navigated the terrain, a predator on a mission.

A flicker of movement caught his attention, a dark shape materializing from the corner of his eye. He brought the rifle to his shoulder with practiced precision, the barrel aligning with the target. The sea lion, sensing danger, bellowed in panic, but before it could escape, a shot rang out, a deafening echo in the stillness. The bullet found its mark, striking the animal in the shoulder, instantly ending its life. Its massive form slid towards the water's edge, a force of momentum that threatened to drag it into the lagoon.

Without hesitation, Jake abandoned his rifle and sprinted towards the carcass, heart racing as he fought against the relentless pull of gravity. He dove forward, arms outstretched, his fingers finding purchase on the sea lion's hind flipper. Rocks and brush scraped against his body as he clung to his prize, his determination battling against the powerful force of nature.

Gasping for breath, he managed to halt the sea lion's descent just inches from the water's edge. He lay there, chest heaving, a mixture of relief and exhilaration coursing through him. The realization of the close call hung heavy in the air, and for a brief moment, the adrenaline coursing through his veins overpowered the exhaustion.

With measured determination, Jake rigged a rope around a nearby tree, using its leverage to drag the massive sea lion inland. The struggle was arduous, a battle of strength and willpower against the formidable weight of the animal. But every inch gained was a testament to his resolve, a step towards the ultimate goal.

Jake's gaze shifted from the inert form to the glistening waves in the distance as the sea lion's body rested on the ground. His hands worked methodically as he cut and gutted the animal, his movements deft and precise. A bed of palm leaves became a makeshift tray for the viscera, preserving them for later use.

Time seemed to bend as he meticulously prepared the carcass, ensuring the innards remained intact and hidden. He linked the six explosive blocks to a common terminal on a remote detonator box with painstaking attention. The small, black device became a nexus of power, connecting the volatile potential of destruction to his purpose.

A curved sacking needle and nylon twine emerged from his duffle, tools for the delicate task ahead. Holding the cavity closed with his knees, Jake's hands moved deftly, sewing the flesh together. His heart raced with every stitch, the weight of his plan heavy on his shoulders. As he sewed, he flipped the "standby" switch on the detonator, setting the wheels in motion. The device was armed, primed to unleash its destructive potential at a moment's notice.

Throughout the process, his gaze often drifted to the distant ocean, wondering where the elusive predator lurked. A shiver of anticipation ran down his spine, mingling with a surge of anger that fueled his resolve. His muttered words carried both menace and determination, an ominous promise that fate was closing in on the very creature that had terrorized them.

The island bore witness to the convergence of emotions: Jake's vengeance, nature's cycles, and the rhythmic lapping of the waves against the shore. It was a precarious dance, a symphony of anticipation and dread, as the stage was set for a confrontation of titanic proportions.

Amy was immersed in a fragile recovery in the quiet of her cabin, her body slowly reclaiming its strength. The air was heavy with uncertainty, each breath a reminder of the dangers that loomed. Then, a sudden cacophony erupted from the harbor, and a symphony of splintering timbers and crashing debris reverberated through the air.

Her heart raced, and adrenaline surged as she forced herself to her feet, determined to investigate the source of the commotion. Weak steps carried her outside, where the chaos of the scene below assaulted her senses. The sight that met her eyes was one of destruction and terror.

'Meg,' the colossal predator, dominated the scene, a living nightmare unleashed upon the remnants of the pier. Like a force of nature, he tore into the remaining supports, his fury and violence leaving nothing but splintered remnants in his wake. The once-sturdy structure was reduced to a mere memory, swallowed by the churning water.

Fear tightened its grip around Amy's heart as she struggled to comprehend the sheer power and brutality on display. Something had driven 'Meg' to this point of uncontrolled aggression, a fury that defied reason. She strained her eyes to make sense of the chaotic scene, seeking any hint of what had pushed the monster to such extremes.

Then, a lone figure emerged from the turmoil, a small gray dolphin leaping gracefully from the water. It repeated the breathtaking spectacle repeatedly, drawing Amy's attention with its persistence. But it wasn't just the spectacle that held her gaze but the intention behind the dolphin's actions.

As the seconds ticked by, Amy realized this dolphin was deliberately taunting 'Meg.' The idea seemed almost preposterous, a desperate challenge from a creature that was dwarfed in comparison. Yet, it was an act of defiance that carried a purpose.

The dolphin's intelligent eyes seemed to lock onto Amy's, a shared understanding of the tactics.

In the depths of 'Meg's' primal consciousness, an equally powerful force was at play. The dolphin's relentless assault had a purpose beyond mere provocation. The night prior, 'Meg' had succeeded in capturing and devouring the dolphin's mate—a brutal act that ignited a firestorm of emotions within the surviving male. Driven by grief and fury, the dolphin was enacting its own revenge, seeking to strike at 'Meg,' where he was most vulnerable.

Each time the dolphin leaped from the water, its sharp snout targeted the sensitive tissue around 'Meg's' eyes. It was a calculated attack aimed at blinding the monster, robbing him of his sight, and turning the tables to his advantage. Amy's gaze shifted between the fierce dolphin and the enraged 'Meg,' a realization dawning upon her that the struggle between these two creatures was far more intricate and strategic than she could have imagined.

The scene below painted a chilling tableau of defiance, revenge, and survival. The echoing clash of titans, driven by complex emotions and an unyielding will to endure, set the stage for a battle of wits and physical prowess. As the drama unfolded before her, Amy's heart raced with terror and awe, a witness to the ancient dance between predator and prey, intensified by the bonds of intelligence and a thirst for vengeance.

However, during this 'cat-and-mouse' exchange, the smaller creature was, unknowingly, being herded by 'Meg' back in the direction of the harbor channel, and, about sunup, when the rays of the new morning were piercing the surrounding gloom, the dolphin found itself in a restrictive space, with but one escape... into the broad, bottomless expanse of the quiet, dark harbor.

The sleek mammal zipped to and fro, seeking refuge from the colossal predator that also had found its way into the same enclosed area.

As the vicious animal slowly emerged from the harbor depths, the dolphin swept in from the side and nailed 'Meg' behind the eye.

This latest assault infuriated the giant beast to where his fury was all-consuming. His entire nervous system drove the massive muscles into a frenzy, and he accelerated rapidly in pursuit of his pesky nemesis.

Sensing an increasing danger, the dolphin sprinted across the open waters to swim among the large beams and poles of the remaining pier at the water's edge.

'Meg' was driven by a blind rage, and with the momentum of a runaway freight train, he went through several layers of supports, like so many toothpicks, in pursuit of his prey.

On the surface, planking flew through the air, and pieces of telephone poles and cross-beams. It was the results of this massive destructive force that drew Amy from her cabin.

As Amy watched the demolition below, she couldn't help but think. "If he is here, doing this, he isn't threatening Jake!"

Of course, this was a given fact, and one, if known by Jake, would have provided him with the relaxation to focus all his attention on completing his preparations.

However, he frequently paused to scan the surrounding ocean, thus causing his work to drag out much longer than necessary.

After two hours, though, Jake had dragged the gruesome package along the shallow edge water of the lagoon to a spot underneath the cover of the rock bridge against the shore, and he was ready to haul it up into position for 'Meg's' hopeful attack.

Jake deftly unraveled the coil of rope as he climbed up the back of the bridge. Every step was calculated, every move purposeful, as he carried the rope to the middle of the weathered deck. At this moment, he knew the importance of precision—every action could mean the difference between life and death. Sweat glistened on his forehead, his heart pounding as he worked with desperation and determination.

His eyes scanned the bridge, seeking out the smoothest notches on each side of the deck. He secured the rope with practiced ease, allowing the remaining length to dangle into the water on the opposite side of the stuffed sea lion carcass. Time was a luxury he didn't have, but there was no room for error. The intricacies of his makeshift pulley system had to be just right to execute his audacious plan.

Across the harbor, 'Meg's' reign of destruction had culminated in the ravaged remains of the pier. Amy watched, her apprehension growing as the menacing silhouette of the monster moved with an eerie grace. The giant fin meandered, a malevolent force seemingly directed by its whims.

Her heart raced, fear knotting in her stomach, as a realization struck her with brutal force. 'Meg' was heading toward the lagoon, toward Jake. Panic surged through her veins, the moment's urgency cutting through the remnants of her illness. She knew that Jake would be alert, but her intuition screamed at her to warn him—to ensure he had every chance to defend himself.

Struggling against her still-lingering weakness, Amy hurriedly slipped on her sneakers and set off to the lagoon. Every step was a battle against her own body, but the adrenaline of fear lent her strength. She staggered and steadied herself, pressing forward despite the resistance of her own frailty.

With each footfall, the distance to the lagoon shortened. Nausea retreated, replaced by a fierce determination as she neared the spring. Her eyes darted around, scanning for any sign of Jake. And then she saw him—a sight that chilled her to her core.

Jake, her protector, dangled from a rope over the water, suspended in a dangerous limbo. Horror surged within her, a gut-wrenching realization of his vulnerability. Her pace quickened, breathless urgency spurring her forward as she stumbled toward the rocky overpass where he hung.

But then, an unexpected motion caught her eye, diverting her attention. Her gaze shifted beyond Jake toward the ocean's expanse. There, she saw the distinctive dorsal fin, unmistakable and foreboding. 'Meg' was on the move, closing in on the lagoon and on Jake.

Tears of frustration welled in Amy's eyes as she halted her charge. She watched the fin, her heart pounding in her chest, praying that Jake would sense the impending danger. She watched as the fin moved, quartering toward the end of the island, yet somehow missing Jake's position for the moment.

Jake struggled with the rope, focusing on the task at hand, oblivious to the approaching peril. He tied off the rope, his face a mixture of determination and concentration. The horror of his situation, though, wasn't lost on him. He could sense Amy's frantic warning, and he turned, fear gripping his heart as he realized his lapse in vigilance.

The monster wasn't far away, its presence an impending doom lurking in the water. A sense of urgency surged through him, fueling his movements as he waved at Amy. A brief gesture to let her know he understood, to reassure her even as adrenaline coursed through his veins.

Jake moved, determined to extricate himself from the water's grasp. He backed away, the putrid, bloody mess he'd created trailing behind him. Every step carried the weight of fear, each movement a battle against time. He knew that 'Meg' was drawing closer, that every second counted.

The water swirled around him, the trail of blood mingling with the frothy current. In his wake, a dark red trail stretched out—an offering, a lure, a calculated risk. He knew he was running out of time, and the reckoning was inevitable. Yet, he pushed forward, focusing on his task, driven by purpose and survival.

Fear, determination, and a pulsating sense of urgency merged in a symphony of emotions as the final act of this dangerous dance played out. The hunter became the hunted, the roles shifting with the tides. Each decision, each move, carried the weight of life and death, and as the tension mounted, it was clear that the outcome hung in the balance between the monster's insatiable hunger and the ingenuity of a desperate man.

His sensory perceptions failed to alert him to the rapidly ascending seabed below him. With a forceful thrust, his snout plunged deep into the shifting sands and shale, triggering an overcompensation that sent his massive body angling upward at an acute tilt.

Jake, almost within reach of the carcass he was pushing, forced the remainder of the bloody mass into the swirling currents around him and began his journey toward the safety of the shore, where Amy stood watching with bated breath. But his progress was halted suddenly, just ten yards from the land, by an explosive eruption of water and froth, a violent display originating around fifty feet across the inlet.

Amy's face transformed into a portrait of fear as she remained captivated by the unfolding spectacle. Time seems to stretch in extreme trauma, and the following seconds pass in agonizing slowness. Her scream of terror, coinciding with Jake's desperate fight for the shoreline, appeared to stretch infinitely.

The emergence of the colossal gray head from the gushing spray created the illusion of a gradual ascent as if the mountainous body would follow at a leisurely pace. Yet, this perception was shattered as reality crashed down within seconds. Jake's limbs propelled him in a desperate dive, his body landing on the dry ground with arms outstretched, fingers digging into the terrain for traction.

Meanwhile, Amy recoiled, throwing her arms up as she scrambled away from the bridge of rocks.

In that fleeting moment, Jake's gaze shifted to the behemoth's massive bulk, hurtling through the air at an acute angle, directly toward the bridge. An expletive escaped his lips, his hands bloodied as they clawed into the pebbles and earth while his legs churned beneath him in a burst of speed.

Finally, on his feet and running, the resonating cacophony of 'Meg's' collision with the stone bridge reached Jake's ears—a deafening crash and rocks snapping. Newly created boulders were launched in every direction as the colossal creature rammed the bridge, expelling the explosive-laden carcass into the lagoon beyond its reach.

Thankfully, unscathed by the flying debris, Jake reached Amy, breathless, and turned to join her in witnessing the harrowing spectacle unfolding in the lagoon before them. 'Meg's' momentum had been halted by the unforgiving granite, and with a resounding impact, he plummeted into the inlet's gap. A perilous position for the massive predator—the water here was shallow, rife with jagged rocks on the seabed. Before their disbelieving eyes, 'Meg' thrashed side to side, his cavernous jaws agape as he struggled to escape the rocky trap.

The enormous shark's movements were a desperate dance of survival, a frantic attempt to free himself from the clutches of the lagoon's grip. His powerful tail thrashed against the water's surface, each motion a forceful push against the seabed. The open maw, once an emblem of terror, now seemed almost pitiful as it opened and closed involuntarily.

With agonizing slowness, 'Meg' began to slide back into the deeper waters from whence he'd come. But the escape came at a cost; weakened by his encounter, his movements slowed, and the water that flowed over his gills was insufficient to sustain his massive frame. As he inched his way to freedom, the once-terrifying predator was reduced to a creature struggling for survival, a stark reversal that had Jake and Amy spellbound in awe and dread.

Fear gripped Jake as he clung to Amy's arm with a vice-like grip. "Look! I think he may suffocate! He's not getting any water over his gills!"

Amy covered his hand with her own, a mixture of desperation and longing in her eyes. "Oh, Jake, if only...!" Her realization dawned: the creature was mustering the strength to reverse its predicament. "Oh, NO! Jake..." Her voice quivered as she pointed at the colossal gray mass, inching its way back to the depths.

Jake's desperation fueled his search, his focus darting from point to point around the lagoon. "There!" he pointed and dashed toward the shoreline to his right.

Amy followed, a bewildered expression clouding her features, as she watched in terror as Jake plunged into the water, just twenty yards ahead of 'Meg's' gaping maw. Suddenly, she understood the madness behind Jake's actions—the explosive-laden sea lion's body had floated to the weed-lined bank, and Jake was pushing it toward the struggling leviathan.

"Jake! This is nuts! He won't take it now!" Amy's voice wavered, her arms flailing in a futile attempt to dissuade Jake, who was dangerously close to 'Meg's' crushing teeth.

Jake pressed on, heedless of Amy's warnings, driven by a surge of adrenaline as he faced the monstrous threat head-on. The stench and spray from 'Meg's' mouth assailed him, its foulness almost halting his progress. The waves generated by the creature's thrashing threatened to knock him off his feet.

"Jake! Have you lost your mind?" Amy's screech of desperation went unheard as Jake stood firm at the threshold of the predator's gaping jaws.

Digging his feet into the silty seabed, Jake gripped the C-4-filled package with a resolute grasp. His muscles coiled, poised for the final shove, propelling the explosives into 'Meg's' oscillating jaws. But before he could act, 'Meg's' colossal head emerged from the water, and with a violent lurch, it slid back into the depths beyond the fractured rock bridge.

Jake stumbled backward, narrowly avoiding the thrashing beast's violent gyrations. He watched in frustration as 'Meg' regained footing and swiftly retreated into the encompassing deep.

Sprawled on the shore, soaked and cursing, Jake scowled at Amy. "Well, son-of-a-bitch! That's just fine! So, how will we get this 'sausage' down our friend's gullet?" He observed the fearsome fin fading into the distance, vanishing behind the jutting promontory at the mouth of the inlet.

Amy remained transfixed by the fading presence of 'Meg,' her gaze unbroken until the behemoth disappeared entirely. Only then did she shift her attention to the predicament Jake had presented. With a deep furrow in her brow, she studied the weighty 'parcel' bobbing before Jake. "Well... I doubt he'll return here, not even for this... uh... feast!" A scoff punctuated her words. "His aversion to this area is deeply ingrained now that he's experienced the danger of being stranded. He'll likely avoid it altogether... at least for a while. You buy that?" She paused for Jake's agreement, which came without hesitation.

"Okay, our only option is to find a spot with a gentle incline and heave this thing onto the shore."

"But then what?" Jake interjected, already having a hunch about the answer.

"We both grab that rope and drag it to the harbor!" Amy's determination was evident, though her expression revealed her distaste for the task.

"All the way up that long hill?" Jake motioned toward the winding trail leading back to their compound.

"Listen, Jake!" Amy's frustration was palpable. "I can't think of a better way to give us any shot at taking him on. Can you?"

Amy's stress was evident, her stance challenging Jake to provide an alternate strategy to face 'Meg'—a challenge he couldn't meet.

As the day advanced, Amy and Jake wrestled the heavy burden inch by inch up the rocky hill. By mid-afternoon, they had covered only three-quarters of the distance, their energy-sapping to exhaustion.

Jake could see that Amy was struggling from the day's exertion and the lingering effects of her previous night's sickness. But he admired her tenacity; she had given her all to help him. Yet, as the harbor came into view, Amy's condition deteriorated, her strength all but spent.

"Amy, your cabin's just beyond that outcrop there..." he steadied her, pointing ahead. "You need to lie down for a while."

Amy panted and swayed unsteadily as she protested, "No! I can help you..."

Jake cut her off. "Look, one more pull on that rope, and you'll pass out. Then you'll be no help to me or yourself, Sweetheart." He released the rope and gently guided a weakened Amy to her hut. Once inside, he laid her on the bed and removed her shoes.

Examining her closely, he realized her color was off, and she was nearly semiconscious. Her mumbling suggested she might even be hallucinating. "Amy, listen to me. I'm going to make you a drink. It won't taste good, but it'll help you rest and regain energy, so you'll be better tomorrow." A feeble smile and a soft squeeze of his hand were her response.

Outside, he rekindled the fire they'd abandoned early that morning. While the wood caught, he rummaged through their supplies until he found the special root tea Bolo had introduced him to. Using a piece of fabric as a makeshift filter, he strained the remaining fresh water into a pot and set it on the fire. Once it boiled, he mixed a large mug of the bitter concoction and brought it to Amy, who had drifted into a fitful sleep. Gently, he woke her and coaxed her into consuming the liquid. After overcoming the taste, she managed to finish the mug, and within fifteen minutes, she sank into a much-needed and calmer slumber than she'd had in days.

Once confident Amy was resting peacefully, Jake ventured out to rig a harness from the tow rope and began dragging the massive load toward the docks. However, when he emerged from the bushes, his progress stopped at the sight of the decimated piers. "Son-of-a-bitch," he muttered. "Can't we catch one damn break?" But then a realization struck him, and he patted the pocket of his vest jacket, relief washing over him as he felt the remote trigger still secure.

"Wow," he thought. "Now I just need to figure out how to get that big 'motherfucker' to swallow this package... without swallowing me with it."

He resumed his march, reaching the former shoreline where the pier met the land. He dropped the rope and climbed up to a small knoll, where he sat down and, before long, succumbed to exhaustion and slipped into slumber.

CHAPTER 23
Transmissions Were Received from the Island

U nknown to the two sole survivors on the island, the merchant ship that had picked up the S-O-S from the doomed naval vessel earlier had finally reached the home port authorities of the stricken craft, and operations were underway to get their flagship, a well-maintained, full-sized WWII vintage destroyer, underway to the vicinity of the incident, and, if necessary, on to Crandle's keep! But, the naval commander had contacted the old Commandant of the militia, and he had informed them that, as of a few days earlier, Jake Crandle, himself, had reported that all was okay on the island.

The Commandant harbored a fondness for Jake, and his furrowed brows and stroking chin testified to his growing unease. The notes before him held his attention for the better part of an hour. Eventually, he reached for his phone and dialed the Naval base, his fingers tapping the familiar digits. Determinedly, he recounted his discoveries, urging the highest-ranking officer he could reach to deploy a destroyer to Jake's island.

"I believe, Sir, that you'll uncover a colossal surprise on that island," he spoke deliberately, his Spanish laced with an Indian-inflected accent. "Instruct your Captain not to second-guess his instruments or his eyes, nor those of his crew. Tell him to engage and obliterate any potential threats to his ship without hesitation. Do you grasp the urgency, Sir?" The voice on the other end probed for specifics, but all he could offer were conjectures.

"I assure you, Sir; we've lost three vessels we know of, all with their crews. We're clueless about the cause, except for one frantic communication mentioning some monstrous assailant attacking our frigate!" Silence hung briefly before the military voice responded, colored by disbelief. "What?! A monster? That was a steel-hulled, heavily armed warship! What sort of creature could sink it with its entire crew without a trace, and we have no reliable information?"

The seasoned mariner recognized that reasoning would get him nowhere with this individual. He simply requested that the senior naval officer issue orders to respond with maximum force to any dubious sonar or radar readings. The older man's passion was palpable, and despite his skepticism, the naval authority agreed to issue the directive.

After hanging up the phone, the old Commandant sighed, burying his face in his hands as he muttered to himself. *"Oh, my boy, Jake! What have you gotten yourself into? No, what have you gotten all of us into?"* He gazed out the window, contemplating the vast expanse of the ocean, his silver hair catching the light as he shook his head, wondering what mysteries lay beyond the distant horizon.

Back on the island, Jake wrestled with the challenge of rigging a crosspiece between two of the tallest remaining poles, furthest from the shore. The task confounded him as he sought to reach the poles and affix the crosspiece, a perch for the now-decaying carcass.

Jake's vigilant eyes scanned the harbor's entrance despite his efforts, watching for any signs of 'Meg's' emergence. At least, for now, the formidable creature remained absent from view.

Using a small hammer and rusty nails salvaged from a box of supplies, he took two twelve-foot timbers from a short section of the pier that had escaped 'Meg's' onslaught. Jake built a temporary bridge, maneuvering them onto a solid vertical riser with a surviving cross-section, firmly attaching the near end. Carefully, he crawled across the improvised scaffolding, securing the other end in place.

Over the next few hours, Jake methodically constructed a narrow platform connecting the broken pier section to one of the two adjacent support pilings on the outer edge of the former main cross wharf, about thirty yards from the shore.

After installing the crosspiece between the two vertical poles, Jake dragged the bloating explosive package to the water's edge. Tying the end of the rope to another length of older rope set aside earlier, he was confident their combined length would reach the crosspiece. Floating the fleshy package on the water's surface, he tied the rope around his waist, then cautiously crawled along the elevated trestle, reaching the crosspiece. Untying the rope from his waist, he lay flat and secured it to a heavy piece of wood. Looping the rope over the crossbar, he allowed it to dangle into the water.

The trickiest part came next. Dangling from the bridge's timber nearest the rope, Jake plunged into the cold water. As his head resurfaced, he couldn't ignore the vulnerability of his position. Should 'Meg' choose that moment to make an appearance, Jake would be over thirty yards from safety, defenseless.

Nonetheless, he pulled the rope, slowly guiding the massive torso toward him. Gradually, the essential cargo floated beneath the crosspiece. Holding his breath, Jake tugged on the rope with increasing force until the body was hoisted nearly halfway out of the water. Securing the rope to a broken crossbeam, he performed a final check of his surroundings before swimming back to shore.

Abruptly, with the morning sun cresting over the cliffs on the island's eastern side, the tranquility was shattered by a deafening explosion along the rocky seaward wall. Jake instinctively knew what it was. "Holy shit! Incoming!" he exclaimed, wincing at the sound. The second detonation followed immediately, impacting the cliff wall that had once been the harbor entrance's eastern side. The explosion sent boulders cascading into the already shallow channel. As Jake scrambled from the water, he turned to see the unfolding chaos, a familiar sense of dread washing over him as he spotted the towering fin swiftly entering the protective waters of the lagoon.

A third-round erupted, this time striking closer to the harbor's center, mere yards from Jake. His frantic arm-waving escalated as he darted along the bank, attempting to grab the attention of someone aboard the ship. On his second turn, he spotted Amy, who had been roused from her cabin by the booming detonations. She waved a blanket and jumped in desperation.

In the harbor's depths, 'Meg' circled like a captive beast in its cage, allowing Jake and Amy to focus on the ship's perplexing and irrational actions.

Fortune smiled on the two beleaguered souls on the island, though. For abruptly, one of the lookouts, who had been watching 'Meg's' progress, happened to catch the flailing shirt and blanket in the corner of his binoculars' field of vision! He immediately rang the bridge and yelled for the Captain to order a cease-fire, as survivors were on the island!

The Captain's command resonated, and the barrage ceased. The abrupt end of the gunfire starkly contrasted with the turmoil that had unfolded just moments before.

The young Captain of the destroyer had experienced an intense rollercoaster over the past two days. The tumultuous journey had begun over forty-eight hours prior when he was rudely awakened from his slumber by two militiamen. They informed the young officer that the senior and more experienced commander of their fleet's prized vessel was on leave and untraceable. Consequently, the top brass assigned this eager, fast-rising officer to lead the mission. None of the higher echelons of military leadership anticipated anything beyond a routine search and rescue operation. The inexperience of the young officer in a leadership role went unnoticed, as the mission was perceived as straightforward.

The newly promoted commander had arrived at the ship brimming with confidence and polish. The more the crew saluted and snapped to attention in his presence, the more his ego fueled his decisions and behavior. The ship's departure and its swift journey to the waters surrounding Jake's island were marked by an air of uneventfulness.

However, the veneer of smooth sailing shattered with a single 'ping' from the sonar. It was important to note that the young commander had received his mission orders directly from the Admiral in a face-to-face conversation. Information tends to morph as passed from one person to another, so the Admiral's originally concise orders had grown somewhat vague when they reached the Captain. "Take the ship to Crandle's Keep at the best speed and watch for survivors from two missing vessels en route. Once you reach the island, assess the inhabitants' situation and provide assistance if needed. Report back to headquarters accordingly. Clear?" The gruff presence of the senior officer was both imposing and intimidating, and the junior officer hesitated to seek clarification that might portray him as ignorant. Consequently, his response was simple and deferential, "Yes, Sir! No problem, Sir!"

The older man remembered his early days when he, too, was wet behind the ears and desperate for his first command, and he smiled and patted the young man on the upper arm. "Yes...well, that's fine, Castro! You'll do well, I'm sure!

They exchanged salutes, but as the old man started to walk away, he stopped, remembering his discussion with the former militia commandant, and yelled after the other man.

"Oh! Castro!" The younger man trotted back and snapped to attention.

"Sir!" He barked

"At ease, Castro! Listen, there probably won't be any problems on your mission, but... ah... if you encounter anything... uh... unusual or out of the ordinary..." He paused, unsure how to put this, and Castro interjected.

"Yes, sir? If I run into any problems? ... What kind of problems, sir?" A skeptical look crossed his face, and he waited for the other shoe to drop.

"Never mind, Castro! Just use whatever means you find necessary to overcome whatever problems you encounter! Understand?"

The realization struck the commander like a bolt of confidence. The 'Old Man' had extended the ultimate note of trust and authority to him. "Yes, Sir! Thank you very much, Sir!"

Had young Castro seen beyond his ego, he might have probed the Admiral for more specifics on "unusual or out of the ordinary" situations. However, this was not the case, so the two men parted ways, marching toward their fates. Captain Castro's destiny was about to take a sharp turn.

Returning to the present, the sonar operator's voice broke the ship's silence. He reported a substantial signature on the sonar scope, about thirteen hundred yards off the bow. The depth was confirmed at five hundred feet, and the object appeared to be moving somewhat perpendicularly to the ship's course.

Castro's curiosity was piqued by the reported size of the target—a whopping 100 feet long. With a mix of arrogance and assumption, the young Captain suspected they were tracking a submarine. But from whose navy?

Capitalizing on this event to assert his newfound authority, Castro instructed the boatswain to sound general quarters. Across the ship, crew members scurried to their assigned battle stations like ants reacting to a sudden disturbance. Once all station chiefs confirmed readiness, the Captain's voice boomed across the ship-wide public address system, conveying a seriousness that matched the situation. "Men! We are tracking an unknown submerged craft of some kind. We must remain at our combat stations until we determine its intentions, whether peaceful or aggressive. I will keep you updated as the situation unfolds. That is all!"

He replaced the microphone in its rack and descended into the dimly lit combat information center, where the sonar operator kept a vigilant eye on the large signature dominating his scope's screen. Standing over the operator's shoulder, Castro demanded information. "Report, Mister! What's the target doing?"

As he responded, the bearded sonar chief locked his gaze on the screen. "It appears to be moving in random courses, Mi Captain, staying at the forward edge of our scanning range."

"Any signs of aggression?" Castro's voice held a note of hope, which grated on the nerves of the seasoned sonar technician.

"No, mi Captain. No... Wait a moment! Capitan! The target is turning directly toward us! It's descending and should pass beneath us in... approximately ten minutes at its current heading and speed!" Sliding a rule-like device to calculate the target's projected position, the sonar technician turned to Castro, awaiting his orders.

Recalling the Admiral's counsel to use whatever means necessary to overcome unusual or out-of-the-ordinary problems, Castro felt that this situation definitely qualified as an unusual problem. He grabbed the intercom mic and contacted the depth charge stations. After determining the target's depth, a staggering eight hundred feet, he set the charges to detonate at seven hundred feet. The gunnery officer, observing from the fire direction tower, breathed a sigh of relief, knowing the Captain had taken charge of the potentially disastrous depth charge engagement.

"The target is almost upon us, mi Captain. Your orders?" The sonar petty officer removed the hydrophones from his ears, awaiting the imminent order to release the charges. And indeed, it came.

"Drop charges, side, and aft!" Castro's orders signaled a change in his approach to the giant creature stalking them. He decided to track and study the beast, searching for an opportunity to defeat this new and formidable foe.

This time, 'Meg' was the one to experience shock and impact. The depth charges detonated about a hundred feet above, tossing the massive fish around like a ragdoll in a tempest. It took a few minutes for him to regain his bearings, and he swam away from the area, avoiding another explosion. He nearly breached the surface during his disoriented recovery, exposing his huge fin. The sharp-eyed lookout on the ship spotted it and alerted the Captain with frantic screams. At first, Castro dismissed their behavior as drunkenness on duty, but their continued insistence drew him to the railing outside the bridge. He brought his binoculars to his eyes, wiped the lenses for good measure, and gazed in disbelief. The sight before him was unchanged. Fueled by determination, he ordered the large deck guns to target the fin.

Now more willing than ever, the gunnery officer sighted the fin on his fire direction plotter and relayed the firing plot to the gun commanders. "Fire!" Castro's order prompted two loud blasts from the forward mounts. In eight seconds, at a range of fifteen hundred yards, two towering fountains of water erupted, one twenty-five yards to each side of the zigzagging fin.

"Adjust and fire again, 'Guns'!" The Captain's orders flowed effortlessly to the gunnery officer. Within a minute, the second pair of cannon shells soared toward the creature. This time, the projectiles split between the retreating creature's sides, exploding about ten yards away. The impact drove 'Meg' forward in an effort to escape the unfamiliar onslaught.

On the ship, the crew and Castro both spotted the distant island. They also acknowledged that the creature was putting more distance between itself and the destroyer. In addition, the unmistakable reality was that the massive 'shark' was headed straight for the landmass. "Keep adjusting and fire at will! Helm, make flank speed for that island. I believe that's our destination!" The Captain's binoculars lowered, and he observed the continued cannon fire, noting the increasing misses due to the widening distance.

The ship surged forward as the 'flank' command spurred the boilers and the three massive propellers into action. Gradually, the range of their quarry began to decrease. However, the Captain recognized that they were closing in on the island, risking the loss of their target. "Guns! Commence zigzag and bring all main batteries to bear on the target. We must stop it before it reaches unnavigable waters!"

"Aye, mi Captain! Understood!" The gunnery officer sprang into action, plotting firing solutions for the ship's quartering track as it veered diagonally across the creature's path. As he finalized his calculations, he heard the Captain's orders to initiate the first turn. As the ship adjusted its course, the gunnery officer commanded the three main turrets and the two secondary batteries amidships. Consulting his stopwatch, he gave the order: "Fire!"

Five guns discharged their deadly shells at once, and within a few seconds, the rounds all impacted near 'Meg,' the closest falling within twenty feet and driving the creature to dive in response.

Even though they were coming up on the island, the water was still deep enough to allow the intimidating fin to disappear, for the moment, under the surface, depriving the ship's gun crews of their target!

Castro was shaken by this development and felt he'd better make the best speed directly to the island! Therefore, he ordered that the ship resume a direct course and discontinue 'zigging!

This resulted in the destroyer closing within a mile of the island in no time!

Suddenly, As the Captain lined the ship up to attempt entry into the harbor, the horrifying fin reappeared, only a few hundred yards ahead, also moving very quickly in the port!

Castro yelled for the front turret to fire at will, but it took a few minutes for the battery to reload from its stand-by status. When it was ready to fire, the monstrous dorsal was entering the portal channel ahead, so the turret chief snapped off a round too quickly, and it struck the cliff adjacent to the entrance, showering the water behind the fish with rocks and dirt!

The fire control officer saw that the target was nearly disappearing into the harbor lagoon; thus, the gun crew was driven to force off another shot in near-record time. This one landed beyond the entrance to the main port itself, missing the fish again by some distance!

The gunnery chief was about to order another shot when the Captain yelled in the intercom for a cease-fire! Two people had been spotted on the charred bluffs on the far side of the harbor, and further firing was too dangerous, the 'skipper' had informed them.

As all the bridge contingent watched through their own binoculars, one of the people on the island, a man it seemed, waved frantically from the middle of his body to his right, the ship's left. Young Castro observed this for a few minutes, wondering what the dark-haired fellow wanted, especially since the vessel had ceased firing.

Then, it struck him! "Full left rudder! Emergency stop!" He shrieked into the intercom.

The helmsman and engineering people responded immediately, but the overwhelming mass of the large ship was sluggish in its response! It had just begun to slow, and its pointed bow had started to veer to the left when everyone on the bridge was jarred violently into the rail!

"Captain!" Came the expected report. "We have struck an underwater obstruction and are taking water just aft of the bow!"

"How badly are we damaged? A badly shaken Castro screamed into the microphone.

"Not too bad, Captain! However, I feel that we need to leave to effect repairs!" The Chief Engineer suggested.

Castro scanned his surroundings and took stock of their situation before deciding. "Very well!" All Stop! He barked! "Engineer! Be advised! I want to know when you feel secure that we can safely continue the mission!"

He turned to his executive officer and whispered, his voice laden with concern, "I suppose it's in the hands of those poor souls on the island to hold on until we're back in operational shape."

At that moment, the intense atmosphere on the bridge was shattered by a lookout's urgent voice, "Bridge! Someone on the island is signaling with Morse code! There's a flashing light!"

Every head on the bridge turned toward the source of the commotion. Sure enough, a flickering light pierced the darkness, emanating from the same dark-haired man waving them away earlier. An aura of curiosity mixed with suspense enveloped the bridge crew.

Castro's analytical mind kicked into gear. "Does anyone here know Morse code besides me?" he questioned the room, his gaze fixed on the blinking light. Simultaneously, he began jotting down his interpretation of the signals.

"Si, mi Captain!" one of the signal yeomen responded.

"Excellent! Please transcribe what you believe they're conveying," Castro directed, his focus never wavering from the flashing light. "We'll compare our notes when the message concludes." The yeoman swiftly began to transcribe the signals alongside the Captain.

After a few tense minutes of deciphering, the Captain and the yeoman independently read "end of message." They exchanged their interpretations, and Castro nodded to himself, satisfied.

With the written notes laid out in front of him, Castro issued his following command into the wall microphone with determination, "Sonar, Guns! Maintain a vigilant watch for any sign of that monster emerging from the harbor. If it surfaces, use your discretion: stop it, eliminate it if possible, or force it back into the harbor. It seems the people on the island believe they have a method to kill the creature. If they do, we'll grant them the opportunity."

The yeoman swiftly flashed back in response, "Understood! Will comply!" The petty officer acknowledged the order and activated the ship's shuttered searchlight, sending a reply in Morse code to the island.

Castro continued to watch the figure on the shore, his eyes narrowed with curiosity and uncertainty. As the man on the island waved in acknowledgment, Castro whispered to himself, his gaze unwavering, *"Alright, my friend. The stage is yours. I can only hope you know precisely what you're doing."* The tense atmosphere held as the ship's crew turned their attention back to the ongoing repairs and waited in suspenseful anticipation.

CHAPTER 24

Cannon Shells Fall Uncomfortably Close

With a steely determination etching his features, Jake absorbed the ship's message and crossed over to Amy, who stood among the bushes, clutching Jake's rifle. His voice was resolute as he addressed her, "Alright, Amy, we've got him cornered." Taking the gun, he ensured its loaded status and swung it over his shoulder. "Lead me to that wounded dolphin."

Amidst the chaos of the destroyer's attack, Amy had noticed a commotion in the near corner of the otherwise tranquil harbor. Though the tumultuous cannon fire had temporarily obscured her view, the flapping of a dying dolphin's fin had caught her attention. Her initial thought was to end the animal's suffering with a well-placed shot from Jake's rifle, but when she informed him about the dolphin's plight, his reaction surprised her. He was animated and eager to help, asking her to fetch his rifle and guide him to the injured creature.

As they approached the scene, Jake's gaze was met by the sight of a dolphin with a substantial chunk of flesh missing from its side. The gruesome wound had driven the animal into shock, causing it to flounder helplessly in the water. It had drifted perilously close to the rocky shallows, a tantalizing target for any extended pole or pike.

Jake deftly tied a slipknot at the end of the remaining rope and, with the skill of a makeshift engineer, crafted a snare-like noose at the tip of a lengthy two-inch-wide tent pole. He extended the rope from one end, attaching it loosely to the pole's other extremity.

"Alright, Amy, I plan to loop this rope around the dolphin's tail. I want to bring it closer to the explosive before I put it out of its misery," Jake explained, his voice tinged with urgency. He scanned Amy's expression, seeking understanding.

Amy hesitated, aghast at the strategy. "Oh, Jake, that seems so cruel. There must be a better way—" Her words were cut short by Jake's interruption.

"Listen, Amy," Jake interjected, his tone firm yet pleading, "that ship out there is in bad shape. I saw it when I signaled them off. If we don't act before nightfall, 'our friend' might slip past them in the dark. They can't track 'Meg' accurately amidst the rocks and channels. If that happens and their damage slows them down, they won't be able to catch up and end 'Meg's' rampage. We have to do this, and yes, the dolphin will die. But its blood on the rocks will attract 'Meg' faster. I didn't know how to do it until you mentioned this method. Please, Amy, understand the necessity."

Amy hesitated momentarily, grappling with her aversion to animal cruelty. Finally, she nodded, albeit hesitantly. "Alright, I suppose I see the logic in it. It's just... hard."

"I know, Amy. It's not easy for me either," Jake admitted. "But we need to act. Let's get this done."

Jake navigated the treacherous terrain with the bulky snare pole, almost stumbling several times. Amy held Jake's rifle and waited on the rocky slope nearby.

Jake managed to approach the ailing dolphin cautiously, avoiding its panicked movements. Carefully, he positioned the pole and loop behind the dolphin's tail, lowering the loop into the water. His movements were deliberate and slow, the tense atmosphere palpable.

"Amy, put the rifle down quietly and come grab the end of the rope," Jake instructed urgently. He was ready to tighten the noose but wanted to be cautious.

Amy gently placed the rifle on a patch of grass and hurried to the rope's end, her grip firm. "I'm ready," she affirmed.

With a deep breath, Jake pulled the pole, cinching the rope around the dolphin's body. The creature twitched violently before succumbing to injuries, lying still in the water near the rocky jetty lined the shoreline.

Taking five minutes to ensure the dolphin was no longer struggling, Jake guided the lifeless creature along the jagged rocks. His efforts navigated the dolphin around obstacles until he reached a point where he had to wade into the water to bring it closer to the explosive bait dangling above the water.

As Jake ventured into the dark water with his chest submerged, he moved slowly to avoid creating disturbances that could alert 'Meg' prematurely. He reached another piling, its crosspiece miraculously intact, mere feet away from the hanging carcass. He secured the rope and started returning to the shore, his movements cautious and purposeful.

While Jake performed this crucial task, he couldn't shake the memory of the depth charges and shells that had hammered him just hours earlier. Despite the confined space of the harbor, his nerves still smoldered from that brutal assault. A growing restlessness gnawed at him, a reminder of his confinement in this watery prison devoid of substantial sustenance.

As 'Meg' lurked in the depths, a churning blend of frustration, anticipation, and hunger gnawed at him. The confined space weighed heavily, and the ceaseless torment of starvation and captivity threatened to overshadow his fear of the surface enemy waiting beyond the harbor's edge.

In fact, so much was *his* hunger growing that *he* swam, to and fro, across the width of the harbor like a caged lion at feeding time! The cold blackness around *him* yielded no scent of food nor any vibration out of the ordinary, which would show a promise of prey.

He had been traveling *his* watery 'prison' for over three hours and was on the verge of returning to the open water beyond, regardless of *his*... what?... fear? When *he* picked up the unmistakable smell of blood, along with a very short fluttering, on the surface, near the far shore to *his* rear! *His* hunger lust grew more potent by the minute, and this new excitement was too much for *him* to ignore. *He* dived down in a spiraling turn, bringing *him* onto a direct line for this unmistakable food sign. *He* had also gone to the bottom of the harbor and hugged it as *he* began to close in, faster and faster, on this promising target!

When Jake had gotten to the shore, he quickly grabbed his rifle from Amy, and, without hesitation, he pumped two rapid shots into the mortally wounded porpoise, causing a considerable amount of blood to spread out into the surrounding water! Then, he and Amy waited and prayed because the afternoon daylight would only last for another hour or two, and if 'Meg' didn't rise to the bait...!

They needn't have worried because, as they watched, the water in front of the bait began to boil, and the broad gray snout, jaws opened wide, broke from the surface and was almost in position to scoop up the demolition-filled carcass when the great fish executed a typical shark-like action and rolled onto its side to attack!

In a synchrony of realization, Jake and Amy understood that the carefully orchestrated plan might veer off course. Their hearts pounded as they watched in helpless horror. 'Meg,' with the dead porpoise and its tethered poles, narrowly missed the intended target. The moment was agonizingly slow. Their breaths held as the massive creature glided by, taking the bait with it. Then, with a swift yet eerie grace, 'Meg' retreated, sliding back into the murky embrace of the harbor's dark, rippling waters.

As the immense fin vanished momentarily, replaced by the calm surface of the harbor, a renewed wave of fear gripped Jake and Amy. Their gazes locked, and in that shared look, they exchanged a cascade of emotions—fear, desperation, and an unspoken understanding of what must be done. Jake's eyes conveyed intensity and resignation that shook Amy to her core.

A tender touch of Jake's roughened hand on her cheek was her only comfort before he abruptly retrieved his knife and raced toward the water. A crescendo of screams erupted from Amy's lips, her voice echoing across the harrowing scene as Jake halted at the water's edge. With a swift, determined motion, he dragged the blade across his forearm, a deep gash opening up, blood flowing freely into the sand at his feet. Jake bore the pain, his eyes fixed on the task, driven by an unwavering purpose.

Diving into the water, his movements frantic and unbridled, Jake swam with all his strength toward the baited explosive. His disarrayed splashing and noise were deliberate, meant to lure 'Meg.' Amy's heart clenched at the sight, her anguish palpable as she watched the man she cared for risk everything to save them both.

As Jake reached the hanging carcass, he worked swiftly to untie it. Moving back until his feet touched the harbor's bottom, he pulled and released the rope in a calculated frenzy, inducing tumultuous movements in the water around him. Meanwhile, the gash on his arm spilled blood into the surrounding liquid, a grisly beacon meant to draw 'Meg' in.

Meanwhile, 'Meg,' driven by an insatiable hunger, had detected the scent of blood. Though meager, the smell was irresistible, overpowering any rational thoughts. The lingering traces of his last meal had faded, and a primal need gripped him, urging him to feed. The small source of blood in front of him became his focus as he set his course. Ignoring other stimuli, 'Meg' embarked on his relentless journey across the harbor toward the scent, his pace accelerating with a chilling urgency.

Near the harbor's entrance, the scene had not gone unnoticed. Jake observed the ominous dorsal fin veer from its exit trajectory, disappearing beneath the water's surface. His heart raced with a mix of excitement and trepidation. His gaze shifted back to Amy, who stood perched atop the bluff, a silent guardian of their fate, her heart entwined with his in this desperate struggle.

Jake yelled. "Amy, I can't see anything! You should have the first glimpse when *he* decides to surface. So, watch carefully and scream at the first sign because I'm pretty vulnerable out here!" Jake's voice denoted a slight sign of fear, which Amy found incredibly out of character for him.

"Don't worry!" She yelled back, her eyes never leaving the water that spread out before Jake. "I feel like screaming right now!.... But I'll definitely cry to high heaven when I see that monster!"

Jake nodded his understanding and continued to splash the carcass in and out of the water. He had gradually back-paddled toward the shore until he came to the rope's end to gain as much distance as possible from the explosive-filled body. He now enjoyed only about fifty feet and knew that the harbor dropped off steeply to the outside of the posts that held the deadly package. If "Meg" decided to attack from below, Jake also realized that he would have to pull extra hard to get the explosives high enough for the creature's great open jaws to scoop it up as *it* passed.

Further, Jake knew, with a numbing feeling in his stomach, that he probably wouldn't be able to hold the carcass up long enough and still be able to escape the great body's momentum at the same time... But he knew he had to try.!

The minutes dragged on, stretching into eternity as the water's surface remained undisturbed. For Amy, a sinister blend of dread and hope brewed within her. She held her breath in a precarious balance of anticipation, fearing that the monstrous predator might resist their devised lethal temptation. A desperate wish lingered that 'Meg' might retreat into the open ocean, where the vengeful warship awaited its final reckoning.

In stark contrast, Jake's mounting unease tightened its grip. Doubt gnawed at the edges of his resolve, threatening to erode their painstaking efforts. With each passing moment, he feared that the elaborate plan might crumble into futility. The energy that had fueled his ceaseless exertion was dwindling, his muscles straining and aching under prolonged strain.

But then, at long last, a ripple of movement marred the harbor's calm façade. A shadow, at first faint, swiftly grew and expanded, a harbinger of impending doom. Amy's heart surged as she recognized the ominous sign. Her voice erupted in an urgent yell, piercing the silence, "Jake, he's coming! Right in front of you!"

Jake, attuned to the water's subtleties, had already perceived the turmoil beneath. He scrambled backward, muscles straining, his fingers tightening on the rope holding the baited package. With adrenaline surging through his veins, he fought to raise the explosive above the water's surface, desperate to keep it out of 'Meg's' lethal reach.

Below the waterline, 'Meg' was locked onto his target, his predatory instincts overriding any caution. His powerful body surged, propelled by an insatiable hunger. Yet the underwater terrain altered unexpectedly, forcing him to adjust his attack trajectory. He turned, a creature of muscle and instinct, his course changing, his jaws yawning open, ready to seize his quarry.

Suddenly, his immense form broke through the surface with a thunderous crash. Water erupted in a torrent of white foam as

'Meg' breached at a violent angle. His gaping maw swept up the dangling bait, the explosive-laden carcass disappearing into the depths of his cavernous mouth. Inches separated Jake from the monstrous creature as it surged past, a nightmarish brush with death that left him trembling.

With terror gripping his heart, Jake fought to escape the nightmare. He powered through the water, desperately reaching the shore, a relentless will to survive, propelling him forward. But fate would not be swayed so easily. As 'Meg' propelled himself upwards, his colossal body created a wave that surged towards Jake with an unforgiving force. Helpless against nature's fury, Jake was lifted and thrown, his body colliding with the unforgiving bluff.

Impact and pain merged into a nauseating haze. Jake's ribs screamed as they broke under the weight of the impact. The wind was knocked out of him, leaving him gasping for breath, a crushing weight pressing down. Dazed, he struggled for awareness. His vision blurred as he clung to consciousness.

Amid the chaos, Amy's voice reached him, her frantic shouts cutting through the fog of pain. She held the trigger in her hands, her eyes wide with terror. Jake's heart raced, the moment's weight crashing down upon him. He took the trigger, his trembling fingers gripping the device, an instrument of salvation or despair.

As 'Meg' gradually faded into the distance, the harbinger of doom receding into the horizon, Jake's fingers trembled over the trigger. His resolve hardened, fueled by the sacrifices and the lives at stake. Amy's tear-filled eyes bore into him as he whispered words of hope, his voice carrying his determination and love. He turned away, his gaze fixed on the departing fin, and pushed the button.

Yet the stark silence that followed was deafening. The explosion of soundless anticipation filled the air, a cruel suspense that paralyzed them both. Seconds stretched into an eternity of dread as they waited for the verdict of their desperate gamble.

"NOTHING!" A shattering realization pierced through Jake's being. Horror gripped him, an icy hand clutching his heart. The button that was meant to usher an end to their torment had failed them. His instincts guided him to disarm and rearm the trigger, hoping beyond hope that some malfunction had occurred.

Far away, aboard the crippled warship, a similar determination was in play. The gun crews had sighted the dorsal fin emerging from the lagoon, a towering silhouette against the waning light. The frenzied orders to fire resounded, the ship trembling as the artillery unleashed its deadly payload, an act of vengeance aimed at a relentless killer.

Jake's fervent search for salvation bore fruit as Amy's cry pierced through the haze of desperation. Her eyes locked onto Jake as he once again rewired and was soon to pull the trigger again. His breath hitched as he descended the slope, the pain from his injuries warring with his determination. The trigger and his finger met in his trembling hand, a small object that held the power to determine their fate.

A heavy breath filled his lungs as he stared at the instrument of salvation. His fingers clutched it, his resolve unyielding. An unspoken pact passed between them, a shared understanding of the stakes they faced. Jake's voice, steady yet heavy with emotion, filled the air as he held the trigger, his words a whisper of finality and courage. A tear mirrored in Amy's eyes, a testament to the love and sacrifice that bound them.

Then, as the dark figure of 'Meg' retreated, vanishing into the horizon, Jake's finger pressed the button once more. And in that breathless moment, as time seemed to suspend, as hope and despair intertwined, they awaited their destiny.

When the smoke cleared, nothing was left of "Meg" but a frothy red spot on the water, surrounded by unrecognizable floating bits of assumed body pieces from the beast.

Jake's cheeks puffed out as he looked at Amy and expelled a sigh of relief! Amy entered Jake's arms and sought security and comfort as their long, painful ordeal ended!

While they stood there in silence, both recalled the losses they had endured...Bolo, Toombs, Jenny, Darwin, Amos...yes, and even Johnno and Jojo, Jake thought! Jake also wondered how many more had suffered similar fates in those recent tumultuous times, forever changing his life!

He caught the subtle sound of a sniffle, turning his gaze toward Amy. Tears traced a glistening path down her face, her countenance a mixture of beauty and pain, as though the tumultuous events had etched themselves upon her soul. With a gentle but resolute gesture, he drew her closer to his side, the warmth of his embrace offering a semblance of solace amidst the chaos.

Their eyes met in a shared exchange of emotions, a silent understanding passing between them that words could never fully capture. The world seemed to fade away, leaving only the two of them standing amidst the aftermath of their epic struggle. Amy's gaze shifted, her attention drawn to the waters that had witnessed the cataclysmic clash.

Her voice trembled with relief and lingering sorrow, her words reflecting the weight lifted from their shoulders, yet also a poignant reminder of the lives lost. "Oh, Jake... all those lives lost... is it truly over?" Her eyes remained fixed on the waters, where traces of red mingled with the ebbing waves, a somber testament to the battles fought and the price paid to quell the destructive force that had haunted their lives.

The destroyer's klaxon blared several flourishes, and Jake could make out many individuals around the bridge waving their arms. Jake and Amy returned the wave in unison and moved over to the small knoll, which had played a significant part in this whole drama, and sat down to wait for the people from the ship to come and get them.

They stared deeply into one another's eyes, and, with the daylight fading, both knew that they had become bound together by forces beyond their imaginations, and they realized, jointly, that they would remain so for the rest of their lives!

Then, they shared a long, tender kiss...not so much with passion as a demonstration of the mutual acknowledgment of their deep feelings for each other and the confirmation that the terror, which had been this gargantuan... THROWBACK....of nature was, in fact, finished!

At least, as far as they knew!

CHAPTER 25
Jake Confesses to the Commandant

The long boats from the warship had begun arriving before dark, and they pitched a base camp with food, water, medical personnel and supplies, and a RADIO!

With Amy standing over his shoulder, Jake had confessed with the old commandant on the mainland and found out what they already knew, deep down, was the case: that the "Maggie Mae" had been destroyed, as well as the supply ship and one other smaller frigate.

Jake had asked about survivors, just to be told that they had, only the day before, been in a position to send out two large "Sea Horse" helicopters to scour the suspected area where the vessels had, most likely, been attacked. Nothing had been found, though, as of yet!

Captain Castro had come ashore by this time, and he, Jake, and Amy had shared a bittersweet moment of reflection before they all sat down to a hot meal prepared by the ship's personnel... the first decent meal that Amy and Jake had enjoyed since the fire days earlier.

Following this, they related their whole experience, minus the part about the sailor who'd died at first, to the Captain and some of his senior officers! To a man, they had been greatly sympathetic and offered Jake and Amy sincere condolences for losing their friends.

Around midnight, Captain Castro, who had been monitoring radio reports, informed them that the repairs to his ship should be completed by around noon the following day, and they could depart for home.

Jake and Amy thanked him for everything and adjourned to a private tent with a field shower and two field beds installed. After each took long, refreshing showers and dawned fresh clothes from the ship's stores, they laid down and slept through the night.

They both awoke shortly before the sun came up to find the camp already alive with activity. Sailors were eating breakfast at a long, portable table at one place while others were striking the tents in another.

An unfamiliar officer came up to them and saluted smartly. "Senor Y Senorita, my Captain sends his apologies, but he was called back to the ship only two hours ago. We must load up and await the arrival of the two search helicopters to refuel them for their return trip. The Captain is upset about the delay and is talking to his superiors about this now.

He has asked that I see to your comfort. I am Lieutenant Vega, the ship's quartermaster." Again, he saluted. "At your service!"

The well-dressed young officer escorted Jake and Amy to a private table set for two, and the seamen showed up with a tasty breakfast, which they wolfed down quickly.

The young lieutenant waited to the side until Jake and Amy had finished and escorted them to a waiting boat for the short trip to the ship.

During the boat's passage through the harbor entrance, Amy grabbed Jake's arm and squeezed it. Jake patted her hands gently while he scanned the waters around the boat for any sign of the creature that had exploded so spectacularly in front of their eyes the previous day. Jake almost felt that, at any moment, a massive circle of teeth would rise around them from the murky depths, but this didn't happen, and they completed the rest of the journey to the large naval vessel ahead.

Upon their arrival, Jake and Amy were shown to their staterooms and told that the Captain requested their presence on the bridge, and they followed their escort up several flights of stairs to the ship's command center.

"Ah, welcome, my friends!" Captain Castro had changed into a fresh uniform and greeted them each with a firm handshake. He guided them to a railing, which overlooked the island, and, for the first time, Jake could see the big picture of destruction that had been visited upon his house.

Castro saw Jake's expression of sorrow and expressed his condolences. "I am very sorry, Senor Crandle, for your terrible loss here. Please... tell me... do you plan to rebuild your facilities?"

Jake jerked a quick look at the Captain. He hadn't thought about it until the young officer had brought it up. Then, Jake glanced over at Amy, who was staring intently at Jake.

After a few seconds, Jake took Amy's hands and slowly shook his head from side to side.

"No, Captain! I have experienced enough tragedy for a lifetime here!" His eyes were steadily locked with Amy's as he continued. "I think I will move back to the United States and try to recover the life I left many years ago! The past should remain in the past..." He didn't finish his thought because Amy prophetically finished it for him.

"And so it shall!" She squeezed his hands tightly as she spoke her words with deep emotion.

The rest of the day passed uneventfully. While the ship was made ready for sea, they awaited the arrival of the rescue helicopters that had been crisscrossing the areas where survivors, if any, were expected to be.

From time to time, the Captain would send word on the progress of the search to Jake and Amy, wherever they were at the time, and once, shortly after lunch, while Jake stood looking resignedly at what had been his whole world, a young petty officer approached him and informed him that one of the helo's had, in fact, found three rafts with survivors from the lost frigate.

Jake expressed his thanks and suitable joy over the news, but still, deeply inside, Jake harbored a glimmer of hope that they would find some sign of the "Maggie Mae" and his three friends who manned her.

Amy had gone back to her cabin with a headache, so Jake decided to stay on deck and take this last opportunity to take in his island because he had decided to try and sell this tiny speck in the ocean for whatever he could get and move back to the island in the Caribbean, where this fateful intersection with destiny had begun for all of them seemingly so long ago.

The minutes became hours, and Jake stood motionless, his hands gripping the rail and his eyes staring blankly at the remains of his compound. Blankly, his tortured mind replayed the whole chain of events that had befallen Amy, him...and all the others.

"Excuse me, Senor!" Jake snapped out of his nightmarish recollections to find another seaman wanting to inform him of something.

"Yes, seaman?" He spoke with the ingrained bearing of an officer.

"Senor, mi Capitan wishes me to tell you that the second group of people has been located by our aircraft. The Captain believes they are from the merchant ship that was to deliver provisions to your island! However, only a few people were in the rafts, and the rest are feared lost!"

The young man was proud of his English and waited for Jake's response.

"That is good news! Please, thank the Captain for me!" Jake replied politely, but as the 'white hat' turned to return to his duties, Jake asked, "Oh! Please! Did any search craft report spot any wreckage from a pleasure craft? It would have been white-in-color, I imagine."

The other man thought for a moment and then shook his head. "No, Senor! I am sorry. Do you know of such a vessel operating in those waters?" The question was innocently presented, and due to this fact, Jake avoided answering sarcastically.

"Yes, my young friend... yes, I did!"

The other turned, embarrassed and uncomfortable at this revelation, and quickly moved up the ladder to the next deck.

Jake took a breath, let out a sigh, and made his way to the stateroom to check on Amy.

He found her lying awake on her bunk, staring at the ceiling, but the intercom blared to life before they could say anything. "Senor! Senorita! One of the helicopters is coming in, and I thought, perhaps, you would like to be there when its occupants board!"

Jake flipped the switch on the gray speaker box. "Thank you, Captain! We will be right up!"

Jake offered Amy his hand, and she took it. Jake pulled gently and helped her to her feet. He could see that she was totally beaten from the long, continuous, stressed conditions she had lived with for many days, but she gamely joined Jake for the short trip to the main deck, where the survivors from the helicopter would arrive. They reached the front and emerged as the big craft settled on the helipad.

Both of them were hoping for some news about their friends. Even if the worst was reported, at least it would bring closure to their worries and concerns.

The rhythmic thumping of rotor blades grew softer, eventually fading to silence. Several figures cloaked in orange blankets were carefully assisted from the helicopter on the ship's deck. Among them, one man stood out, an older figure commanding respect from the group. Jake's intuition told him this was likely the rescued crew's senior officer, perhaps the captain. With determined steps, he approached the bearded man, a mix of concern and urgency etched on his face.

"Excuse me, sir," Jake addressed the elder man, his voice carrying a genuine tone of consideration. "Do you speak English?" The officer's gaze shifted to meet Jake's, surprise flickering briefly in his eyes as he processed the abrupt interaction.

"Si, Senor!" The tattered officer replied, his grasp of English evident in his response. "Not well, but I speak." As he spoke, his eyes swept over Jake, assessing him, sizing him up.

Jake's tone was sympathetic and earnest as he continued, "I'm truly sorry to approach you like this, sir, but my friend..." He gestured toward Amy, standing at a slight distance. "...and I desperately seek information about three of our friends. They took our boat out a few days ago to send a warning about the creature that I presume sank your ship." A surge of hatred flashed in the senior officer's eyes at the mention of the creature, a testament to the horrors they had endured.

"Have you heard anything about them?" Jake's voice held a note of urgency, his gaze fixed on the older man, awaiting his response.

"Si, Senor," the officer's response was confused as he recalled the events. "Your friends managed to transmit their message to another ship closer to the coast. We, on the other hand, were already dispatched to these waters to investigate the missing vessels before the attack by that 'Hijo del Diablo!'" His tone dripped with venom as he referred to the creature.

His gaze bore into Jake's, his following words laden with emotion. "My young friend, we have all witnessed this beast and the terror it brings. Your friends and many of my men are resting with angels now." The officer's eyes glistened with unshed tears, a mix of sorrow and camaraderie bridging the gap between them. "I wish it could have been different, but they are at peace in paradise."

As the officer turned to tend to his crew's medical needs, Amy walked over to Jake, her eyes reflecting both sorrow and hope. Jake's touch offered comfort as he squeezed her arm, standing united in their shared grief.

"It's not entirely certain, Jake," Amy whispered, her voice tinged with a glimmer of hope. "Perhaps one of them..."

But Jake's gentle interruption cut through her fragile optimism. "Amy, sweetheart," he interjected, his tone soothing, "I'm afraid the truth is that they're gone. If there was anything more to know, we would have heard by now."

Amy met his gaze, her eyes filled with understanding and lingering disbelief. "Maybe the radio malfunctioned, and they're still out there, facing engine trouble or something," she offered, her voice wavering with a hint of desperation.

Jake's firm but gentle grip on her arms brought her back to reality, grounding her in his unwavering presence. She sought solace in his embrace, tears threatening to spill over. His reassuring touch and murmured words helped soothe her frayed emotions until she pulled away, wiping the damp trails from her cheeks.

"I'm okay now," she declared, her voice steadier. "Let's go to the dining room and see if survivors have more information." Jake hesitated, unsure what they might find, but Amy's resolve spurred him to follow her lead. Together, they went to the officers' wardroom, seeking answers from the survivors.

Their conversations yielded little new information, yet the exchange brought a sense of closure to the uncertainties that had plagued them. Around 45 minutes passed in these discussions when the ship's intercom announced the return of the second helicopter, running dangerously low on fuel after an extended search.

Rushing to the catwalk overlooking the helideck, Jake and Amy scanned the skies. Their eyes fixed on the horizon, spotting the helicopter's swift approach. Amy first caught sight of the aircraft, descending in a straight, unsteady line rather than the usual methodical circling and controlled landing.

As the helicopter touched down, its pilot slammed the brakes, the aircraft's momentum causing one wheel to veer off the landing area and onto the safety netting. An emergency team surrounded the plane, securing it and assisting the disoriented survivors.

Amidst the commotion, the familiar faces of the final survivors emerged from the helicopter. Struggling to identify anyone from their group, Amy and Jake strained to make out familiar features. Hope and fear intertwined as their hearts raced while they waited.

No recognizable figures appeared at first, and Amy's heart sank as she turned to walk away. But something made Jake look back again, his peripheral vision catching a glimpse of golden hair from the crowd surrounding the helicopter. Suddenly, as if by fate's benevolence, two young officers gently guided a distraught blonde woman out of the aircraft.

"Mother of God! Jenny!" Jake's exclamation rang across the deck, his voice accented with disbelief and sheer joy. His frantic waves caught the attention of the small blonde figure, who turned her head, her eyes locking onto Jake's.

In a moment of exhilaration, Jenny's arms flailed over her head as she called out incoherently, her blanket slipping from her shoulders. Jake's eyes welled with tears of relief as he shouted back, his voice catching in his throat.

Amy, too, had registered the figure's identity, her joyous cries mingling with Jake's. The emotions they had bottled up amidst the chaos now flowed freely, unburdening their souls of fear and sorrow. As the three friends reunited, their arms encircled one another in a tight embrace, tears of happiness mingling with the pain and loss that had become all too familiar. In a world marred by tragedy, this small moment of redemption provided a glimmer of light and hope to sustain them through the years to come.

EPILOGUE

TWO MONTHS LATER... Amy and Jake had escorted Jenny to the States, where she entered a program of psychological therapy, and, for a time, both Jake and Amy stayed in Miami and visited the young blonde frequently.

Jake had been fortunate that, with the notoriety of the incident with 'Meg,' he had found an anxious buyer for his island...the Brazilian University where Lamar Toombs had been pursuing his research. The institution's governors had jumped at the chance to acquire the island and construct a research facility over the burned remains of Jake's former home.

As for Jake and Amy... they had tightened their romantic bonds, which began during their recent adventure. However, as part of the purchase of 'Crandle's Keep,' the University had offered Amy a senior fellowship position there, with the funding and staff necessary to follow through with the research of the warming current that had brought her to the recent fateful events, which had changed her life. Also, she could finish the Ph.D., which had been her life's goal.

Still, during one of their many private evenings in Miami, where they had discussed their deepening mutual feelings for one another, Amy had sincerely offered to give up this momentous opportunity to be with Jake and build a life with him.

But, to her surprise, Jake seemed to know Amy better than she knew herself. He had taken her right hand in both of his and spoken to her in a low voice that cracked with emotion.

"I love you, Amy... a great deal! That much I am sure of! ... But, I also realize that you followed a dream, half a world away, that brought you to me and the tragedies we both will live with for a long time to come."

He paused for a moment, obviously struggling with deep inner thoughts.

"No, Sweetheart! As much as I want to keep you, now that I have found you... I want you to complete your dream... get your doctorate! Then, if you still have a spot for me in your heart, I will be back where it all started for me, too!

I called the people on the island who had bought the fishing and canning company from me after the old couple's death, and they are anxious to have me return. So, I will be buying back a piece of the company and trying to settle into a life of complete routine for the first time in my life."

"Oh, Jake!" She had piped in. "I want to be with you... Now!... forever!" Then, she kissed him... hard and passionately... for a long time.

Jake responded in kind, and when the kiss ended, he continued, his lips only inches from hers and quivering slightly.

"I feel the same, Honey, but if it's meant to be, it will be... when you finish your work! Agreed?"

She thought momentarily while analyzing her feelings, then nodded slowly... Yes!

A few days later, after the last visit to a rapidly improving Jenny, Jake put Amy on a plane destined for South America and, after he'd watched it disappear from sight, he walked sadly to another gate and, his mind scrolling through all the unforgettable things that he'd experienced, especially the monstrous fish... 'Meg!'... that had been the center of all that transpired... Jake boarded his own flight... to oblivion!

THE END (MAYBE)

Did you love *Throwback - Terror Beneath the Waves*? Then you should read *Nevaeh & Crux Ansata Part I & 2 Anthology in the Omega Chronicles*[1] by Sidney St. James!

NEVAEH - THE LOST CITY OF NEMEA
CRUX ANSATA - THE LOST CITY OF ANKARA
PARTS ONE & TWO IN THIS FANTASY ROMANTIC THRILLER
SIDNEY ST. JAMES
Omega Chronicles
Books 2 & 3
[2]

Books 2-3

Omega Chronicles

Nevaeh & Crux Ansata Part I and II

Book 2 of the Omega Chronicles, Part I

"If you were to destroy the belief in immortality in mankind, not only love but every living force on which the continuation of all life in the world depends, would dry up at once." – Fyodor Dostoevsky

Many people believe that being immortal is a bliss, something that is priceless... something that one would do next to anything

1. https://books2read.com/u/bQRXYD

2. https://books2read.com/u/bQRXYD

for. Would it be a bliss to live long enough to see all your loved ones perish? To wander around the world in loneliness, for every friend you ever made have run out of time to spend with you? Personally, I think not! It's not a bliss. If anything, it's a downright curse.

This story about the lost city of Nemea is a subgenre of the fantasy or science fiction genres that involves the discovery of an unknown world out of time and place. The second novel in the Omega Chronicles series is also a subgenre of the late Victorian adventure romance. This story has a similar theme to other mythical kingdoms, The Lost City of Altinova in Book 1 and others, such as Atlantis and El Dorado.

Lucas Petersen, a professor at the University of Texas, is resting quietly in his apartment on Guadalupe Street near the main campus. There's a knock at his door that surprised him. He is visited by Tommy Hansen, a good friend. With him, he brought a steel box, set it down at his friend's table, and explained his unusual request, including the fact that he was soon to die. Part of the request was that the contents of the box couldn't be disclosed for twenty years.

*****

Book 3 of Omega Chronicles: Part II, a Sequel to Nevaeh, Part I

"True love is not necessary the number of kisses, or how frequently one gets them, TRUE LOVE is the feeling that still remains long after the kiss is over."

Crux Ansata – The Lost City of Ankara is a gothic-fantasy novel that follows as a sequel to Nevaeh – The Lost City of Nemea from the Caves of Chivateros in Peru. It is Book Three in the Omega Chronicles.

Freja Jensen, contemplating retiring from BeeBop Publishing Group in Austin, Texas, received a brown paper parcel in the mail. She opened the package and saw that it was from Lucas Hansen, or his pen name, Lucas Pedersen. With the letter was a manuscript.

Another letter received was from a doctor who asked to remain anonymous. Included in a small teakwood box was an ancient sistrum, an Egyptian musical instrument with magical powers, and had the etching of an ankh on top.

In this sequel to Nevaeh – The Lost City of Nemea, a twenty-year search begins by Lucas and Oliver Hansen to try and find Oliver's lost True Love. You might ask, "What is true love? No one can really define what it is. Thousands upon thousands of people will have an answer. Many answers will point to a feeling they experience, but never has the Truth been more known until one reads the dramatic conclusion in this sequel, CRUX ANSATA.

In the case of Oliver Hansen, also known as the Golden One, his love, unlike feelings, doesn't come and go. It stays with him for over twenty years as he searches for that one true love, the Goddess Nevaeh. He explores through the good and the bad... and when we say bad, we mean really bad!

Read more at https://www.facebook.com/sidneystjamesshow.

Also by Sidney St. James

Beneath the Waves Series
Throwback - Terror Beneath the Waves

Bridget Flynn Detective Series
Bridget Flynn - A Female Detective
Bridget Flynn - A Female Detective
A Prince of Their Own

Demon Gorge Trilogy
Room of Death - Here Today and Gone Tomorrow
Fate - Eventually Everything Connects
Standing in the Shadow of Death - The Sword of Damascus
Demon Gorge Trilogy Box Set

Gideon Detective Series
Rosenthall - Bete Malefique des Bois
Gideon Returns - A Damsel in Distress
The Dusty Adler Murder Mystery

Phantom of Black Rock Cove
The Transformist
El Transformista
Ace of Spades - Volume 1
Gideon - The Final Chapter (Volume 2)
Lady in Red
Ace of Spades (Vol. 1) & Gideon - The Final Chapter (Vol. 2)
Gideon Detective Murder Mysteries Box Set: Books 7-9

James' Recipe Series
Wild Game Recipes - Squirrels, Bullfrogs, Alligators, Rabbits,
Armadillos and More
Recipes that Won Chili Cookoffs in Texas
Duck and Goose Recipes from the Wilds of Eagle Lake, Texas and
the Rock Island Prairies
Grandma's Homestyle Cooking Recipes

Lincoln Assassination Series
The Lost Cause - Lincoln Assassination
Lincoln Assassination Series Box Set: Books 1 - 5
Lincoln - Pursuit and Capture of John Wilkes Booth
Lewis Thornton Powell - The Conspiracy to Kill Abraham
Lincoln
The Knights of the Golden Circle
Mary Elizabeth Surratt - "Please Don't Let Me Fall!"

Love Lost Series
It Takes Two to Tango (Volume 1)

It Takes Two to Tango (Volume 2)
Tears Are Words from the Heart
Let Me Drive
Belem Towers - Only Two Will Ever Know
The Curse of Knight's Island
Norderney Island
The Winds of Destiny

Omega Chronicles
Omega - The Lost City of Altinova
Nevaeh - The Lost City of Nemea
Bonaventure - Three Years on the Island
Crux Ansata - The Lost City of Ankara
Nevaeh & Crux Ansata Part I & 2 Anthology in the Omega
Chronicles
Omega Chronicles Books 1 - 3 - An Anthology

Self-Guided Creative Writing Series
Taglines Unveiled - Crafting Memorable Dialogue Hooks

Texas Outlaw Series
Sam Bass - A Dead Man's Hand, Aces and Eights

The Faith Chronicles
The Rose of Brays Bayou - The Runaway Scrape
Adversity - Keeping the Faith

Faith - Seventy Times Seven
Genesis - Stepping Onto the Shore and Finding It is Heaven
Hallelujah - He is not Here; He Has Risen (Luke 24: 6)
Seeing the Power of God
Living in God's Word
The Faith Chronicles: Books 1 - 3: An Anthology
The Faith Chronicles Box Set: Books 4-6

The Storm Lord Trilogy Series
The Flaming Blue Sword
Nine Months Will Tell
The Three Keys to Armageddon
The Storm Lord Trilogy Box Set: Books 1 - 3 An Anthology

The Whodunnit Series
Murder in Horseshoe Bay - Death Comes Quietly
Jaded Lover - Things Are Getting Heavy
Under Cover Queen - Sequel to Jaded Lover
The Amaryllis Murder Mystery
Murder at Morgan Park
Checker Cab Murder Mystery
Destiny Waits - Murder at the Lakeside Museum
Lollapalooza - The Case of the Woman in Black

Victorian Mystery Series
This Old House - A Lily Blooms in the Jaws of Hell
I Am Woman - I Am Invincible

Victorian Romance Series
I Am Woman - Hear Me Roar

Standalone
True Love Ways
I Go to Pieces - Part 2: Sequel to True Love Ways
Guitar - Truth is Strange - Stranger Than Fiction
Refuge of Death - A Kiss for a Kiss
The Runaway Scrape
Das Ausser Kontrolle Geratene Kratzen
La Raspado Fuera de Control

Watch for more at https://www.facebook.com/
sidneystjamesshow.

Also by Jeremiah Sherman

Beneath the Waves Series
Throwback - Terror Beneath the Waves

Printed in the USA
CPSIA information can be obtained
at www.ICGtesting.com
CBHW050150061123
1667CB00007BA/4